Imaginary Dragons

Book Three

Of the American Nomads

N.L. Mclaughlin

Printed by: Twisted Sky, LLC

ISBN: 978-1-7367059-7-1

Proofreading provided by the Hyper-Speller at

https://wordrefiner.com

Cover art provided by: Meagan McLaughlin

EMcLaughlin@gmail.com

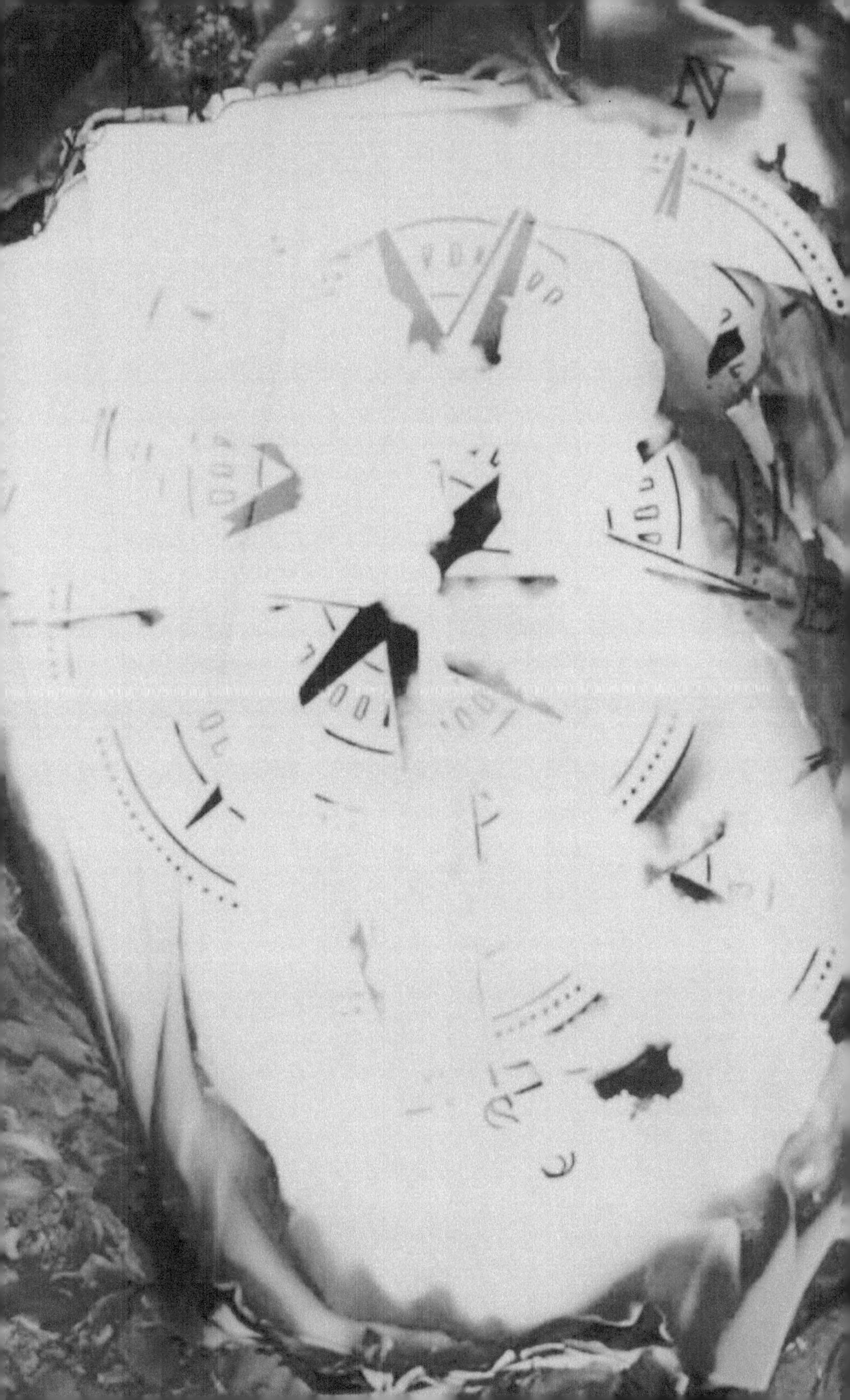

To Vic,
I hope you realize how awesome you are.

"Men who fear demons see demons everywhere."
— Brom, The Child Thief

"My whole life has been spent walking by the side of a bottomless chasm, jumping from stone to stone. Sometimes I try to leave my narrow path and join the swirling mainstream of life, but I always find myself drawn inexorably back towards the chasm's edge, and there I shall walk until the day I finally fall into the abyss."

— Edvard Munch

Chapter One

*F*INN! *WHAT DID YOU DO?*

The gentle sway of the iron beast provided little comfort. Huddled in a corner, rocking back and forth, arms wrapped around his knees, Finn tried to block out the voices.

Please Stop! He pulled at his hair and banged his head against the steel wall of the gondola, hoping to shake loose the words that shouted repeatedly in his head.

What did you do?

His right hand, covered in blood that was not entirely his own, throbbed with the pain of multiple bruises and slashes. He screamed and scrubbed his palms on his pants. The stains remained. A crimson reminder of his violent actions.

Tears covered his face. *What did you do?* The voices in his head echoed loudly as he closed his eyes. River's shouts, the pathetic sound of Beth's whimpers. And worst of all, the broken-hearted sound of Teague pleading with him.

Why didn't he stop? Why did he keep punching? How could he have done this? Why did he just blow up everything he ever loved?

What did you do?

"I don't know!" he screamed to the void.

Finn stared at his trembling hands. The voices raged, blending into one, constant ear-piercing scream. He cried until he was numb. Tiny particles of rock and dust swirled around his body. He exhaled, unable to purge the metallic scent of dried blood from his nostrils. Empty, tired, and alone, he allowed the motion of the train to lull him into a deep, exhausted sleep.

A violent jolt awakened him from his uneasy slumber. Disoriented and sore, he glanced around. The train slowed, the sound of grinding metal rung in his ears. He climbed to his feet and peered over the lip. Though still too far to see, he imagined the yard wasn't far up the tracks. A second jolt nearly knocked him off his feet. He was in no condition to have a run-in with a member of the train crew, so he climbed out of the car and jumped to the ground.

Standing on the gravel, he stared down the tracks as the train faded away, wondering when another would roll through. The sky overhead was black with no sign of daylight—there would be no train for several hours. He took in the area. A small field of brown grass and rocky soil, followed by a thick line of trees, stood behind him. Across the tracks stood an open field. He was no longer in the desert. So where was he?

A crisp breeze carried a faint scent of burning wood. There was no sign of people in his immediate area. Feeling worn out, Finn crossed the tracks and sat down under a tree. He didn't know where he was, nor did he have any supplies other than the clothes on his back and the Bowie knife attached to his belt.

"You okay, mister?" said a small voice behind him.

Finn spun around to find a young girl kneeling on the ground on the other side of the tree. He scanned the area, wondering where she came from. Was she there when he walked up? How did he not see her?

The little girl stared up at him with big, brown eyes. Her black hair was neatly pulled back into two long braids.

"I-I'm sorry," stammered Finn. "I didn't see you."

She flashed an innocent smile. "It's okay. I'm used to people not noticing me."

It was the middle of the night. Even in his current state of mind, Finn understood that a child so young had no business being outside alone this late.

The little girl fiddled with a grimy tennis ball.

He followed her gaze, noticing for the first time, the small mound of dirt, topped off with a wood cross fashioned out of two twigs. A blue dog collar with a set of tags dangled from one of the cross arms.

He looked around nervously and asked, "What are you doin' out here?"

The little girl adjusted the cross. "I come by every night. I sneak out when my auntie's asleep because she doesn't like me coming out here alone." She touched the collar. "This is where Una is buried." She peered up at Finn. "I miss him. There isn't anyone to play with at home. Everyone's always so busy." She shrugged. "So, I come out here and tell him about my day just like I always did when he was alive." She held up the tennis ball. "This was his favorite ball. I leave it here, to remind him." She sighed. "So, he doesn't forget about me."

"You shouldn't be out here alone," said Finn.

A bright smile swept across the little girl's face. "My name's Mika," she said, ignoring his admonition. "What's yours?"

"Finn," he replied. "You need to go home. It ain't safe out here alone."

"Is that where you're going?" asked Mika.

He shook his head.

"I'm not alone," said the little girl, flashing the sweetest smile. "I'm talking to you."

"That's just it," replied Finn. "You shouldn't be talkin' to someone like me, especially alone at night like this."

"Ain't that the truth," said a gruff, older woman's voice.

The distinct sound of a shotgun shell being chambered rang out in the night. Finn looked up to find the barrel of a shotgun pointed directly at his head. A stocky, gray-haired woman held the weapon firm as she stared down the sight.

"Get up," she commanded.

Finn stood up with his hands out. "I—"

"Shut up," she spat. "Get away from the child."

"Auntie, no!" shouted the little girl. "He's my friend. He jumped from the train."

"You be quiet," barked the old woman.

Finn realized how this must have looked to the old woman, a stranger, covered in blood, sitting under a tree talking to her granddaughter. "Look, it's not what—"

A shot rang out, causing a plume of dirt to erupt at his feet. He jumped back as the old woman racked another round.

"Get off my property," she hissed.

Finn took two steps backward. There was no way he was going to turn his back on the old woman. When another shot rang out, he darted his eyes left and right, trying to figure out the best way to escape. A warm gush of air flew past his shoulder.

"The next one ain't gonna be a warning," stated the old woman.

Fully aware that she meant every word, Finn turned and ran off into the brush. The skeletal limbs of trees and shrubs slashed his skin as he crashed through the dark. He ran until he reached a paved road. Heart pounding, lungs on fire, he bent over, hands clasping his knees, waiting for his heart rate to normalize.

He stood up, put his hands on his head and paced back and forth. The weight of the evening crashed down on him. *Finn! What did you do?!* The voices shouted. Desperate to leave the world behind, he took off running.

Stars sparkled overhead in the black night sky as cold air wrapped around his body conspiring with his own sweat to chill him to the bone. Finn ran until he could run no more. Every time he slowed his pace, the voices resurfaced. *What did you do? Please stop!* The buzzing in his head intensified. Small flashes of light popped into the corner of his vision. His head ached.

He searched the area. As far as he could see, there was open land, the black sky, and the road. A giant bridge was the only thing in sight. Finn stumbled toward the structure.

A vast crevasse opened beneath him. The wind whipping along the rocky corridor made for an eerie background to the sound of the blood pumping in his skull.

He stopped in the center of the bridge, reading the random messages scrawled on the metal rail. "Don't give up." "You are loved." He ran his finger across a message that read, "It gets better." A mournful smile spread across his face. *No, it won't.* Finn stared over the metal rail at the flowing river below. The cool, rushing water beckoned him, whispering a promise to carry him away from the pain —from the voices.

He stepped upon the middle rung, pressing his calves against the top rail. The wind billowed around him, whipping his hair into his face and drying his tears. *Let go.* The pounding of his heart drowned out the voices. A sense of peace fell over him. He leaned forward.

"Scooter! Stop!" shouted a strange voice.

Finn startled, nearly losing his balance.

A dog barked and, once again, the voice called out, "Scooter! No! Help! Please stop the dog!"

Finn opened his eyes to see a yellow dog barreling along the bridge, dragging a red leash behind him. Several yards away, an old woman limped pathetically, unable to catch up with the animal.

Not my problem.

The dog barked and ran toward the edge of the bridge. Finn watched in horror as the animal was about to plunge into the gorge. On instinct alone, he jumped off the rail and dove for the dog's leash, catching it in just enough time to yank the mutt back from the edge. The dog turned and ran to him, licking his face and wagging his tail.

"Stupid dog," muttered Finn, scratching him behind the ears.

"Thank God!" said the old woman, struggling to catch her breath as she hobbled close.

"Scooter, you dumb dog."

The dog whimpered and leaned so close to Finn, he was practically on his lap.

"You saved his life," said the woman. "I thought for sure he was gonna jump."

Finn nodded. "He's safe now." He pushed Scooter away and rose to his feet. "You should wrap this around your wrist or something," he said, handing over the leash.

Scooter barked and lunged for Finn, yanking the leash from the old woman's hand.

"These old hands ain't what they used to be," said the woman. "He's far too rambunctious for me to hold on to tonight." She smiled pathetically. "Would you mind helping me get the dumb dog home?"

Finn wrapped the leash around his wrist. He looked left and right along the road and saw no light, no sign of civilization. "Where's home?" he asked, warily.

"About a half mile or so that way," replied the woman, pointing into the darkness.

"I don't see nothin' out there but dark," replied Finn. He eyed the old woman suspiciously.

"Oh honey," she chuckled. "You don't have to worry about me. I ain't no threat to you." A friendly grin spread across her face. "I prefer my men to have a couple dozen more years on them." She eyed him up and down. "And a lot more meat on their bones. Someone as young and thin as you—" She winked. "I might break you in half."

Finn couldn't help but grin at that.

Scooter barked.

"My name's Violet," said the woman.

"Finn."

"Okay, Finn," said Violet, "You gonna help an old woman get her rambunctious dog home safe?" She rubbed her hip. "Or are you gonna let me struggle on my own?"

Finn studied the old woman in the moonlight. Her eyes were as bright as the long, white hair she pulled back in a loose ponytail. The smile on her face was genuine. He saw no sign that she was being anything but truthful. He sighed and agreed to escort the woman and her dog back to their home.

The walk along the side of the highway was peaceful, peppered here and there with little snippets of information from Violet about the plants in the area. Finn nodded along respectfully, pretending ignorance about each plant's healing or herbal properties, even though he already knew most of it.

They turned off the highway, onto a gravel road. Small hills rose all around. Perfectly shaped, and spaced just right, they were obviously man-made. Finn wondered what sort of neighborhood this was.

"Just a few more yards up ahead," said Violet.

They turned down a narrow driveway and came to a stop in a small, ornate yard. Metal sculptures adorned the area, rocking and twirling in the soft desert breeze. The musical sound of wind chimes rang out.

The home itself was buried inside the mound, with only one wall facing out toward the yard. Off to the side stood two large cisterns, while a tall windmill spun lazily nearby.

Inside, the home had an earthy feel, with its curved walls and vaulted ceiling. A wood stove sat in the center of the open, circular floor plan.

"Come on into the kitchen," ordered Violet. "I'll put on some tea and make you something to eat. Are you hungry?"

"Always," replied Finn. Suddenly aware of the coating of dirt and blood all over his body, he glanced down at his hands.

"Tell you what," said Violet, her tone soft. She moved closer to Finn. "Why don't you get yourself cleaned up first?" She laid a gentle hand on his shoulder and guided him toward a narrow hall. "The bathroom is down here. I have some clothes on hand, left here from my son, that might fit you. Though you're gonna need a belt." They entered a bedroom.

The scent of stale air assaulted Finn's senses, as though the room hadn't had visitors for a while. For the most part, the room was decorated as though a man about his age lived there, but it had the distinct vibe of abandonment.

Violet opened a closet, and after rummaging around for a moment, turned back to Finn, holding a set of clothes.

Without skipping a beat, the old woman dropped the clothes upon the bed, then steered him toward the bathroom, where she clicked on the light, bathing the room in bright, white light.

"Nothing like a hot shower to set things right," she said. "You go on and get cleaned up. I'll get some food set up for you. It'll be ready when you get out."

Without another word, Violet stepped out of the room, closing the door behind her.

Finn stood in place for a moment, taking in his surroundings, trying to adjust to all that had just taken place. He stepped into the bright bathroom and closed the door. The room smelled like lavender and chamomile. A stark contrast to the scent of blood that emanated from him. He reached in and turned on the shower, letting the water cascade over his filthy hand. A warm cloud of steam rose into the air.

He stood before the mirror, taking in his full measure. The figure staring back at him was shocking. His eyes were swollen and bloodshot. Grime and filth had settled deep into every pore. His hair was a wild mass of tangled locks all over his head. Dried blood crusted all over his face and neck, blending in with the mottled yellow and purple bruises. It was nearly impossible to tell the difference between dirt and blood on his clothes.

A pathetic moan crept up from deep inside his chest. He clasped a filthy, blood-stained hand against his mouth to stifle the cry he could feel creeping up from his lungs.

The blood. He had to purge his senses of the metallic scent of blood. Finn tore the filthy clothes from his body and stepped under the stream of hot water, letting it pour down on him. Emotions exploded in a violent torrent of pain, anger, heartache, and self-loathing. Sobbing, he collapsed against the cold tile.

Finn! What did you do?!

The voices were there, yelling and berating. Confusion and sorrow swirled in his mind. Was he dreaming? If so, this was the worst nightmare he'd ever had. He stared down at his hands, at the blood melting away in the warm water. This wasn't a dream—this was real. He grabbed a washcloth and scrubbed.

When he emerged from the bathroom, the sound of rock music greeted him. The tantalizing aroma of bacon wafted in the air, causing Finn's mouth to water. Upon entering the kitchen, a tail-wagging Scooter and Violet's warm smile greeted him.

"Well, ain't that an improvement? You look much better now." She shoved a plate of bacon and eggs across the counter. "Go on, dive in. It ain't getting any warmer."

Unable to move, Finn stood still, staring blankly at the plate filled with warm food, at the old woman standing nearby with her sweet, caring smile and the friendly dog wagging his tail. It was all surreal. Once again, he found himself questioning whether this was a dream or not. It sure felt like one. How did he get from a nightmare by the river to this calm, inviting scene?

Violet walked out from behind the counter and placed a soft hand on Finn's shoulder, causing him to wince from the immediate pain as her hand touched one of the many bruises on his body. He pulled back.

"I'm sorry," said Violet. "Come on over and have a seat." Barely touching his elbow, she gently guided him to the chair, then placed the plate down before him.

Overcome by the promise of a warm meal, Finn's mouth watered. His stomach grumbled. Violet let out a soft laugh. "I got plenty more if you want it."

Without another thought, he dove in. Setting his focus on the food in front of him, he forced his mind away from the dark thoughts by tapping the rim of the plate with his finger and counting each tap. Thirty-five, thirty-six, thirty-seven.

By the time he was done, he had devoured half a dozen eggs, a ridiculous amount of bacon, and nearly half a loaf of bread. Violet didn't mind. She stood by dutifully, filling his plate each time he emptied it.

When he finished, Finn leaned back against the chair.

"Thank you," he croaked. The vulnerable sound of his voice was foreign to his ears.

Violet smiled. "You're very welcome," she replied. "It's the least I could do after you saved old Gus over there."

The dog yapped and wagged his tail.

"Gus?" asked Finn, confused. "I thought his name was Scooter?" His body tensed.

The old woman exhaled. "You caught me," she confessed. "His real name is Gus. Dumb Gus to be exact."

"Why did you say it was Scooter?"

She smiled. "Because I'm an old woman and in the heat of the moment, the only name that came to mind was Scooter. Besides, how many people would come running to help a dog named Dumb Gus?"

Feeling uneasy, Finn pushed the chair back and rose to his feet. If this old woman had lied to him about something as simple as the name of her dog—what else was she lying about? He should have known better than to let his guard down. There was no such thing as a selfless person.

"Calm down, calm down," said Violet. "There's no need to get nervous. If you just wait for a second, I'll explain it all to you."

"I'm waiting," replied Finn, angrily.

Violet cleared her throat. "That bridge is a place of sadness. You weren't the first person to consider doing what you were gonna do out there."

When Finn didn't respond, the old woman continued, "Lots of people have come before you, and lots more will come after. Some'll succeed and some won't. Some of them might even find a reason to step back away at the last moment." She nodded at him. "Much like you did."

"Is that what this was?"

Violet nodded. "More or less." She strolled over to the couch and plopped herself down.

"Forgive me, but I'm gonna sit down." She removed her shoe and rubbed her foot. "My feet are killing me. It's been a long day."

Finn didn't move. Anger swelled in his belly. Every second that passed, his distrust for this woman grew.

"I had a son." Violet pointed to a series of photographs along the wall. A dozen pictures displayed the life of a young man, from smiling infant to toddler, to school age and into young adulthood. As the pictures progressed through the years, the smile faded. The face of the young man became more serious until, finally, it appeared sad.

"Tyler," said Violet. "He was such a beautiful little baby. His smile could light up a room. He had a heart as big as the sun." The old woman sighed and wiped away a tear. "Thing is, he wasn't meant to be in this world for very long."

Finn walked closer to the wall and studied the images.

"One night, he tried to take his life on that bridge," said Violet.

The old woman's words hung heavy in the air. Unable to think of anything to say in reply, Finn stood in silence, waiting for her to continue.

"I lived in town back then. I remember the night he tried it. How solemn he was." She glanced up at Finn. "He was so resolute. It was an eerie calm—so unlike him." Violet moved her head from side to side. "I should've known."

"He didn't do it." Her voice perked up. "According to him, he was ready to go, but something made him stop. He sat down on the sidewalk and took in the calm night air." Violet stretched her back. "That was when he saw a man a few yards away. He didn't notice Tyler sitting there in the dark. The man climbed up on the rail and was ready to let himself go. According to Tyler, something took over him. He ran as fast as he could to the man and pulled him back onto the road."

She sighed and locked eyes with Finn. "They sat on the side of the road talking about nothing but everything at the same time.

When the sun came up, the man thanked Tyler for saving his life, then the two parted ways."

"From that day on, my son dedicated himself to saving people from the bridge. I sold the house in town, and we bought this place. That way, we could be closer to the bridge."

"Where's he at now?" asked Finn.

"Fate is a fickle bitch." Violet sighed. "Six months after that night, he was diagnosed with stage four cancer."

Finn gasped.

The old woman nodded her head. "Life ain't ever easy. A young man finds his purpose—a reason to live and fate comes along and snatches it away." She snapped her finger.

"He hung on for another year," continued Violet. "Slowly deteriorating day by day." She stared at Finn. "Every night he was up there on that bridge. He saved many lives during that time. All the while, knowing his was coming to an end."

Violet stood up and rubbed her hip. She walked over to a liquor cabinet and poured two glasses of whiskey. On her way back to her chair, she handed one to Finn.

"I promised him I would continue his work till the day I pass and can be with him again."

The whiskey calmed Finn's nerves. He took a seat on the couch. "So, what, you go out there every night?"

Violet nodded. "I ain't always successful." She shook her head.

Gus hopped up beside Finn and rolled into him, demanding attention. Finn chuckled and rubbed the old dog behind his ears.

"I enlisted Dumb Gus here. He's old, but he's a hell of a lot faster than I am. If nothing else, he can get up to the person way before I can. He gets their attention."

"You sent him up to me," said Finn.

Violet shrugged. "Actually, he went up to you on his own. I just made it look like it was more than it was."

"Why?"

"To make you step off that rail," replied Violet. "To give you a chance to change your mind."

"So, why fake his name?"

Violet flashed an impish grin. "Like I said, I'm an old woman. It's what came out of my mouth in the heat of the moment, so I went with it."

Finn smiled down at the cheerful dog and scratched him behind his ears.

"You feel a little better now?" asked Violet.

Finn shrugged. He didn't know how he felt other than numb.

"There's no need to talk about it. But if you want to, I've been known to be a good listener," offered Violet.

"There's nothing to talk about," replied Finn.

Violet scoffed. "There's always something to talk about." She contemplated him. "Where's your family?"

"I don't have one."

"Everyone's got a family," scoffed Violet. "I'm gonna bet that somewhere out there, your mama is worried sick about you."

Finn shook his head. "Wherever she is, my mother isn't worried about me."

"I find that hard to believe," replied Violet. "Mothers have a special bond with their children. They may not always show it, but in their heart of hearts—they would surrender their soul for their child."

"Not mine," replied Finn, wincing at the fierce tone of his words. "Neither she nor my father have any sort of love for me." He stared down at the floor. "The feeling's mutual."

Violet nodded and let the topic rest.

They spent the next couple of hours making small talk, sipping whiskey, and giving Dumb Gus all the attention he desired. Finn was thankful for the reprieve.

Violet invited him to get some rest in Tyler's old room. Exhausted and sore, he accepted the invitation. In the morning, he would decide what to do. He wrapped the comforter around his tired body as he lay on top of the soft mattress. He yawned and surrendered himself to the quiet of sleep.

Finn! What did you do?

He startled awake, covered in sweat, a scream trapped in his throat. Finn stared up at the ceiling. Once again, tears flowed from the corners of his eyes. The pain in his body was nothing compared to the misery in his soul. His mouth dry, he made his way into the bathroom for a drink of water.

Finn winced as he glanced at the hollow man in the mirror. He opened the medicine cabinet and found a prescription bottle of painkillers, the kind they gave to cancer patients. He swallowed two immediately, then made his way back to the bedroom where he shoved the bottle in his freshly washed pants pocket, then lay down and waited for the pills to make the world go numb.

Chapter Two

TEAGUE FIDGETED IN THE HARD PLASTIC CHAIR. This was taking too long. Overhead, fluorescent lights buzzed, casting a sickly glow upon everyone around him. Somewhere down the corridor, Cash was being taken care of by the doctor and his assistant. He hadn't seen River in a while, so he assumed things were okay.

Zac sat beside him, shifting in the chair, occasionally glancing at Teague with that worried parent look of his. Stoney was nearby, crouching on the floor, head back against the wall, eyes closed. At least someone could relax.

Over by the counter, Beth hovered near a water cooler, filling a paper cup. She downed the liquid in one gulp and then refilled the cup, only to down it just as quickly. She said nothing and didn't even look over to make eye contact. If one were to walk in and see the group at that moment, one would assume that Beth was a stranger to Zac and Teague.

Porter's arrival was a welcome diversion. A way to pass the time waiting for news about Cash. He was everything Teague had imagined. His smooth, deep voice had a calming effect on everyone. His mannerisms emitted a confidence that was rarely seen, garnering him an instant level of respect. With his ready smile, bright eyes and air of calm, Teague couldn't help but feel relaxed and thankful that the older man had arrived.

For over an hour, Teague, Zac and even Beth, at times, sat enthralled as they listened to Stoney and Porter recount the days they served together in the Marine Corps. They talked about how they didn't want to go back to life as it used to be. So, they hopped a train and kept riding for a couple of years. Porter had to stop when his mom took ill. He caught a ride back home to Dallas, where he took care of his mom until she passed.

It was during that time that he met the love of his life. After having their first child, it was time for Porter to take life seriously. Unable to get the Nomad's lifestyle out of his system, he took a job working for the railroad.

It was this job that allowed him access to all the information he shared with the Nomads.

From time to time, Stoney passed through the Dallas area and paid a visit. Over the years, the two remained steady as close friends. When Stoney had his near-death experience, Porter offered his services. From that point forward, Porter was the Nomads go-to for info.

A flurry of activity erupted down the hall as a set of large doors whooshed open. Doc walked toward their group, pulling the surgical mask down under his chin.

"Your friend is going to be all right," he said. "He lost a lot of blood, but the bullet didn't hit an artery." The doctor made eye contact with everyone in the group. "He's damn lucky."

"How soon can we move him?" asked Stoney.

Doc sighed and ran his fingers through his hair. "We'll know as soon as he wakes up. River's back there with him." He smiled. "She'll let us know as soon as he opens his eyes." Doc turned his gaze to Teague. "It's your turn, young man. Let's have a look at you."

As though summoned by will, Doc's assistant materialized, pushing a wheelchair. "Let's bring you to the back."

Teague's muscles screamed in pain as they guided him into the wheelchair. Until that moment, he had forgotten about his injuries. That was no longer the case as nerve endings he didn't know existed cried out, slamming him back to the reality of all that had happened.

They carted him to a sterile area in the back where they removed his bloody clothes, took x-rays, and determined a course of treatment. The pain meds were a welcome addition, numbing his senses and his mind, as well as his aching soul. Like an angel, River appeared, hovering over like a mother hen.

"Shouldn't you be watching Cash?" asked Teague.

River flashed a gentle smile. "I can see him from here." She pulled open the curtain, exposing the bed where Cash lay. "He woke up a few minutes ago." She set a chair in between both beds and sat down. "He passed out again not long after. He'll be fine." River placed a soft hand on Teague's arm. "It's time to focus on you."

Doc returned. "Good news. Nothing's broken." He studied the bruises on Teague's face. "Though, to be honest, that's a damn miracle."

The severe woman was back, quietly setting up a suture table.

"You're gonna need some stitches, but aside from that, you'll be fine." The doctor pulled a clean set of gloves from a box. "I'll do my best to keep the stitches small and clean to limit scarring." He removed the gauze covering the cut under Teague's left eye. "Just stay still and we'll get this done."

Teague lost track of time, vaguely aware that Cash awoke again; this time, staying awake long enough to tease him over the fresh scars. The doctor bantered back and forth with him, defending his stitching technique.

When it was done, Teague had six stitches below his left eye, four above his right and two at the corner of his mouth. Doc was certain those would disappear once they healed.

"How much longer are we here for, Doc?" asked Stoney, as he entered the room, Zac, Porter, and Beth in tow.

"You should be good in a couple of hours," replied Doc. He set about examining Cash's leg.

"This one's gonna need bed rest for a bit, then physical therapy to strengthen the leg muscle."

"How long is that gonna be?" asked Teague. Panic welled up inside. He glanced around at the others. "We need to get back out there."

Doc shook his head. "Cash here won't be able to do much of anything besides recuperate." He stared at Teague. "You also need at least twenty-four hours, minimum, to rest."

Teague shook his head and struggled to raise himself from the bed. "Thanks for everything, Doc."

Zac placed a firm hand against Teague's chest, pushing him back down against the soft mattress.

"Zac," protested Teague. "You know we gotta get back out there while the trail's warm." His eyes darted around the room, anger seething inside at the piteous expressions on all their faces.

"Max, D.B. and Bells are at the trailer," replied Zac. "Gunner and Nate are almost there."

"I've already given them the info on the train he hopped," interjected Porter.

Zac quickly followed that up with, "Gunner and Nate will follow the trail. The others'll stay in the trailer as long as possible."

"What happens when Gunner gets there and Finn's already gone?" demanded Teague.

"I'll be tracking the train's progress," replied Porter. "We'll figure it all out from there."

"Mais la!" shouted Teague. "That's a stupid way to go about it!"

"Baby," said River.

"Don't patronize me!" shouted Teague.

"Look Teague," said Zac.

"Piqué-toi!" shouted Teague, glaring at Zac. Tears filled up his eyes. "By the time anyone gets to these places, he's gonna be gone." He hated the desperate sound of his voice breaking with each word.

Stoney stepped close to the bed. "Look, son, everyone knows what we're up against. There's a whole Nomad army out there, rushing around the countryside to lend a hand. Let us do the heavy lifting for a while. As soon as you're fit, you can dive right in."

Teague felt a sharp pinch in his left arm. He glanced over just in time to see the severe woman step away, an empty syringe in her hand. The drugs were already taking hold. Numbness spread throughout his body, dulling and relaxing both his muscles and his mind. He tried to feel angry, but the need to close his eyes over-whelmed his emotions. He was floating, the people who surrounded him dissipated into wispy clouds of smoke.

Chapter Three

"HE'S GONNA WANNA BEAT SOMEONE'S ASS WHEN HE WAKES UP," stated Zac, as he stood beside the now unconscious Teague.

"He'll be out for a few hours," said the nurse. "Depending on how far you have to go, you should be able to get him there long before he wakes."

Zac nodded. "Thank you, ma'am." He pointed at Cash. "Is he ready to be moved?"

The doctor finished applying a fresh bandage on Cash's leg. He peered up over the rim of his glasses. "He's fine. Just take it slow." He looked down at Cash. "And remember to finish the antibiotics."

Cash nodded.

River immediately set about gathering his things.

"If you need anything else, call me," said the doctor.

Stoney held a wad of money out to the doctor. "Thanks so much, Sir. I honestly don't know where we'd be without your help."

The doctor smiled and accepted the money. "I do what I can." He and the nurse stepped out of the room.

Stoney rode with Porter in his truck while Zac drove the van with the others. The five-hour drive from the clinic to Terlingua was done mostly in silence, punctuated here and there with the occasional, off-color joke. Dark humor was the only way they knew how to deal with stressful times.

The updates from the others out there searching for Finn rolled in at a steady pace. River was back to herself now that Cash was fine. No longer stressed and single-focused, she was a welcome partner for Zac. It was good to have someone else he could count on.

He peered into the rear-view mirror. Cash was sitting up, alert. Still ashen, the color was gradually returning to his skin. He even had enough energy to pop off with an occasional joke. Doc was right, he would be fine.

Next to Cash, arms folded, a sullen frown across her face, sat Beth. She had said little since they arrived at the clinic. Whatever was going on in that head of hers, Zac hoped she would snap out of it soon. He didn't have time to hold her hand.

Stretched out across the far back seat lay Teague. The nurse was right. Whatever drug she gave the boy, he was out for the duration. It was for the best. If he was awake, he'd be fighting and arguing about wanting to join the search for Finn. It was better he rest, there would be plenty of time to worry later.

It was nearly dawn when they rolled into Stoney's compound. Zac's body was running on empty. Exhaustion settled deep inside his bones, his movements were sluggish as he pushed himself further, first getting Cash settled, then Teague.

Stoney cooked up a breakfast fit for kings with eggs, bacon, and pancakes. Zac devoured the food with the zeal of a starving man.

The sun cast its warm glow across the desert landscape when he finally made his way back to the room. A quick check confirmed that Teague was still sleeping. Zac laid out his sleeping bag on the floor in front of the door and blocking the window. This was to make sure Teague couldn't sneak out while he slept. He knew it wouldn't be long before the drugs wore off and Teague would be ready to hit the road, but Zac needed some rest. In a few hours, they would make their way back to Arizona or wherever the hell Porter said the train had gone. It was going to be an arduous task, trying to find someone who didn't want to be found. Especially someone like Finn.

Zac yawned and stretched his arms. His muscles cried out for rest. He popped his back and neck, then settled in against the hard surface of the carpeted floor.

He awoke to the soft sound of a camera's click. Warm sunlight peeped through the slit in the curtains above his head. He blinked to clear the fog of sleep from his eyes and wiped his face. Another round of clicks. Teague came into focus, crouching close by, holding his phone out in front of him. Click, click, this one accompanied by a bright flash of light.

"Fucking creeper," said Zac, wiping the crusted drool from his cheek while sitting up.

Teague smirked. "I can't help it. I'm bored." He made a gesture with his hand. "I would've left but, you blocked the exit."

"Oh yeah," replied Zac, "I did, didn't I." He smirked.

"Couillon."

"I love you too, dumbass," replied Zac. He reached for a bottle of water sitting on the floor.

"I wouldn't do that," warned Teague. "I couldn't leave the room, which means the bathroom wasn't an option." His lips curled up into a wild smirk. "A man's gotta do what a man's gotta do."

Zac placed the bottle back on the floor. "Thanks for the warning. I'm guessing your kindness means you don't wanna beat my ass."

Teague's face went serious. "Oh, I still wanna beat your ass."

"Fair enough," agreed Zac. He nodded toward the phone in Teague's hand. "Dare I ask what's with the pictures you're taking of me while I sleep?"

An impish grin swept across Teague's face. "You're one ugly couillon when you sleep. Drooling all over yourself. Snoring like a buzz saw."

"Fuck you," retorted Zac. "I am a sexy man." He flashed a smile as he raked his hand through his hair.

"Well, what you lack in true beauty, you make up for in unwarranted confidence," chuckled Teague.

"Hur, der, hur," snickered Zac, quietly reveling in the fact his brother was being his normal self, at least partially.

Teague wiggled the phone in front of him. "I'm gonna share this with every woman you hit on. Let her be the judge." He grinned. "Or give her fair warning." He clicked on the phone, opened a photo, and faced the gadget toward Zac, revealing an image of him sleeping, mouth open, drool leaking from the corner of his mouth into a puddle of saliva on the pillow.

Zac studied the photo. "I don't know what you're talking about. That is one sexy bastard right there."

The chuckles that erupted from Teague made Zac's heart sing.

When the laughter died down, Teague became serious again. "We gotta leave today. Or, at least, I do." He shook his head. "I can't wait till Cash is ready."

Zac nodded. "We will. We'll find him. Promise."

"Anyone ever tell you not to make promises you can't keep?" Teague's face was a mask of seriousness.

"Who says I can't?"

Teague snickered and lifted the bottle of water to take a drink.

"Hold it," warned Zac. He nodded toward the bottle in Teague's hand. "Didn't you—"

An impish grin appeared on Teague's face. He unscrewed the cap. "Not only are you ugly as hell, but you're also a gullible fool." He took a swig from the bottle. "I lied." He gulped down the rest of the water. "And I was thirsty."

"That's just plain wrong," replied Zac, shaking his head.

There was a gentle tap on the door, followed by River's soft voice, "Y'all awake in there? Come on out and get some food."

Zac stood up and pulled open the door. The bright sun assaulted his eyes. River stood before him, a silhouette, with hands on her hips, a halo of sunlight highlighting the outline of her body.

"You been listening against the door?" asked Teague.

River shook her head half-heartedly. "Well, maybe. But how else was I supposed to know if y'all were awake or not?" She smiled. "I'm gonna need to see those pictures, Teague."

Zac shook his head and sighed. "Go ahead, but be careful. Ain't no tellin' how your hormones'll react when you see all the pure manliness."

"I'll do my best to contain myself," chuckled River.

It was already well past noon when the trio left the room. Porter had left hours ago, deciding he could be of more use back home on his computer. After a quick check on Cash, the others gathered on the back porch and devoured a feast of steak and fresh vegetables. They spent the rest of the afternoon visiting with Cash, organizing their plan of action, and catching up with the progress of the others who were already participating in the search for Finn.

As the sun set in the distance, River and Beth drove Zac and Teague to the nearest train yard in Presidio. After a teary goodbye, the boys promised to post updates on their progress. That way, when Cash was up for travel again, it would be easy to reunite.

From his perch on the back porch of a grain car, Zac watched River and Beth recede in the distance. An uneasy sense of foreboding sunk deep within his bones. While he talked a good game in front of Teague, he wasn't sure they could find Finn.

Chapter Four

Hollow sadness overwhelmed River as she watched the train carrying Zac and Teague recede into the distance. For the first time in a long time, she found herself truly torn. She knew Teague needed her—he needed everyone right now. But Cash needed her as well. The best solution was to split up and allow Zac to handle Teague while she took care of Cash. Still, her heart ached to be there with them; to join in the search for Finn. Wherever he was, he had to be in an awful state. River didn't want to consider what Finn could do in his current condition.

Fortunately, the ride back to Stoney's turned out to be a pleasant distraction. Beth was in a good mood, playing with the radio and happily singing along with the music. It was an enjoyable reprieve from all the stress and sadness.

They arrived at the compound to find Spinner and Bella, waiting with open arms. A welcome sight indeed. Warm hugs and soft words of encouragement were just what River needed.

"Have you seen Cash?" asked River. "Is he up?"

"Yes, we saw him," replied Bella. She smiled gently. "We took good care of him for you while you were gone. He ate some food and then fell asleep." She spun River around and guided her toward the porch. "Now it's your turn, dear. You need to keep your own strength up."

Once again, Stoney had outdone himself. River's stomach rumbled. She wondered if Zac and Teague had stopped to eat anything yet. The thought of them alone made her sad. She forced herself not to think of Finn, that would surely throw her into a pit of despair.

While River gobbled down as much food as her stomach could hold, Stoney, Spinner and Bella recapped the events of the day.

According to updates, Gunner and Nate made it to the trailer where Bells, D. B., and Max were still waiting, hoping that Finn would return. He hadn't yet.

Back home, Porter had figured out the train that Finn hopped. It was heading east into New Mexico. Gunner and Nate wasted no time as they hopped a ride heading that way. Meanwhile, Tripp and Sam were heading west toward Santa Fe; when everything went down, they were in Memphis. They planned to hit up all the known stops and camps along the way until they met up with Gunner and Nate.

Ben, Mara, and Tanner were roughly two hours out of Terlingua. Once they arrived at the center of town, Stoney planned on driving out to pick them up and bring them to the compound.

River couldn't help but feel overwhelmed with joy at how suddenly everyone in their unusual family jumped into action when needed. The love this group had for one another was more than she had ever imagined possible. This was a real family. She was sure they would find Finn soon, and the family would be whole again.

"I'm gonna go peek in on Cash," she said, hopping to her feet. Inside the cabin, she did her best to be quiet, but the creak of the door gave her entry away.

"How'd it go?" asked Cash, sitting up against the headboard of the bed.

"Our boys are off," replied River, doing her best to sound upbeat. She sat on the edge of the bed and gave him a peck on the lips.

He smiled and pulled her in closer for a longer kiss.

"Did you miss me?" She smiled at him.

Cash responded with another kiss, then he leaned back. "From the sound of it, everyone's got all the bases covered."

River nodded. "It feels kinda weird staying behind though," she said. "It makes it easier knowing that the others are already out there, searching."

"We'll be out there soon enough." Cash tapped his leg. "As soon as I can walk."

"There's a good chance he'll be found long before then," offered River, her tone hopeful.

Cash sighed. "I hope so—"

"But you don't think so."

He shrugged. "There isn't anything anyone could do to stop Finn from disappearing."

"Once he calms down, he'll change his mind," replied River.

"There's a chance he won't."

Irritation bubbled up inside of her. "He will," she stated. "Whether he wants to admit it or not, he needs us." Tears pooled in her eyes.

Cash didn't reply. He merely looked on as she continued.

"He and Teague are together forever. Nothin's gonna break their bond."

"I want to believe that every bit as much as you do," replied Cash. He wiped a tear from her cheek. "Sometimes things don't go the way we want them to."

"Work out what way?" demanded River. "Look, we're not having this conversation. We're gonna get you all healed up, then we're heading out to find Finn. Everything will be normal once we find him. Period." She stared deep into Cash's eyes, daring him to argue.

He didn't.

The door to the room burst open. In a flurry of activity, Ben, Mara, and Tanner spilled in.

"How's it going, my brother?" asked Ben, as he walked to the bed and embraced Cash.

Tanner poked Cash's thigh. "Feel anything?"

"Quit poking it," replied Cash. "I don't want to feel it."

"Ah, don't enjoy the painkillers too much," warned Tanner, with a grin. "Take it from me, that hole might look shallow, but as soon as you fall in, you realize it's a bottomless pit."

"How are you doing?" Mara asked River. Her eyes swept down to River's hand that was entwined with Cash. "Oh, my gosh!" she exclaimed. "Get out! That is so awesome!" She placed her hands on her hips. "It's about time! Don't you think it's about time?" Mara asked Ben, who nodded in response.

Ben cleared his throat. "Moving on to other news," he said. "How's our boy Teague?"

"I dropped him and Zac off in Presidio earlier," replied River. "He seemed fine. As fine as can be, at least."

"He's in good hands with Zac," said Tanner. "They'll be okay."

"No sign of Finn," said Ben.

Silence hung heavy in the room as they processed their emotions over the entire ordeal.

"With everyone out searching for him," said River, "we should have no problem finding him soon."

Ben shot Tanner a look of disbelief.

Mara wrapped a soft arm around River's shoulder. "We're gonna find him."

"Can I beat his ass when we do?" asked Ben.

"Line starts behind Zac," quipped Tanner.

Cash chuckled. "I think Teague's got dibs on what's left."

Ben scoffed. "That's assuming anything's left after Gunner finds his ass."

"I don't care what shape he's in," said River. "As long as he's found, we can sort everything else out."

Chapter Five

"WHAT TIME IS IT?" ASKED SHANE.

"Literally five minutes since the last time you asked that question," replied Catalina, her dark, brown eyes never leaving the computer monitor.

Shane shuffled papers on his desk. A meaningless task to help pass the time while he waited for what could very well be the most important meeting of his life. He looked at his watch; the damned device must be broken. He tapped the face and lifted his wrist to his ear, hearing the gentle tick-tock. This was taking forever. He never knew time could creep along so slowly. It was maddening. He scanned the security monitors along the wall. Manny and Pillar were shooting pool, while Odie watched, drinking a beer. A lone patron sat at the bar, nursing a glass of whiskey, watching Marisol behind the bar, unloading bottles into the cooler.

"Mari's stocking the beer in the wrong cooler again," said Shane.

Catalina sighed and peered up at the monitors. "I see, we've gone from shuffling papers and asking for the time every few minutes to nitpicking the way our daughter is restocking the beer cooler."

Shane stared at the monitor. The young man at the bar fiddled nervously with his lighter, hardly taking his eyes off of Mari. Each time she came close, he diverted his gaze, then as soon as she turned away, his eyes would be right back on her. Shane couldn't help but smile. The young man had every right to be nervous, Mari was very much her mother's daughter. Strong-willed and beautiful, she had little patience for games and scheming. Whatever she couldn't handle on her own, which wasn't much, her extended family of outlaws could. Not to mention her stepfather, who was known as a no-nonsense badass, due his inclination to handle things outside of the law.

Catalina removed her glasses and pushed back her chair. She sauntered across the room, swaying her hips, smiling seductively as she removed her hair tie. Her long, dark locks cascaded down around her shoulders. "What you need is a distraction." She climbed on Shane's lap and kissed his neck.

As much as he enjoyed her attention, he wasn't in the mood for distractions. His body stiffened as he continued watching the monitors. He hated waiting, let alone waiting for information as important as this.

Catalina pulled away and sighed. "I see you're intent on stressing every second until Derrick shows up." She kissed his cheek and tousled his dark, brown hair, peppered here and there with shocking strands of white.

Shane loved Catalina, more than he thought he could love another woman. After Melody died, a part of his soul died with her. It took several years for him to even consider falling in love again, even longer to act on it. Luckily for him, Catalina was a patient woman.

He remembered the first time he met the Sanchez family. After getting out of the Marine Corps, Manny convinced him to come home with him. He insisted it would be good for his pops to have another son around. Not having anything else to look forward to, Shane agreed. The family welcomed him with open hearts. Mami became the mother he never had, with her loving smile and warm heart, it took her all of ten minutes before she began stuffing him with food. Papi was another story. He welcomed the newcomer with open arms and a watchful eye. A wise businessman who had ties to the cartel, he was slow to jump at new people. In time, Shane proved himself and the old man took him under his wing. Before he died, he passed along all his influence, contacts and knowledge to his two sons, Manny and Shane.

Over the years, Shane's shattered heart fused back together, though the pieces didn't quite assemble the same as before. For as long as he could remember, the world seemed to draw him into a particular way of life; one without limits or rules. One that existed outside the margins of law and order. For a brief time, with Melody, he believed he could be something different, her father didn't share the same mindset. The old man saw Shane as nothing more than a common ne'er-do-well. It took the loss of Melody and years of coping with drugs, alcohol and violence before Shane realized the old man was right, he was born to be an outlaw.

Shane leaned hard into his true calling and parlayed Papi's connections with the underworld into solid business assets. As each of his former Marine buddies got out and joined him and Manny in El Paso, Shane's gang grew with both manpower and a particular expertise. In almost no time, they were known throughout the underground as ruthless men.

The antics and excitement of outlaw life kept Shane busy for years, allowing him to ignore his broken heart. The life he lived before ceased to exist; his time with Melody and the dreams of his son, all faded into the haze of daydreams and fantasies. His was a world with little gray area. Kill or be killed, act or react.

During that entire time, Catalina was there. From the first day, he met the family, she was there with her beautiful smile, her dark eyes and her fierce attitude. They slept together occasionally, but Shane allowed no more than that. He kept an emotional distance that would push away any other woman—not Catalina. Whatever the reason, she saw something in him he couldn't see. Come to think of it, the entire Sanchez family saw something special in him. Even little Marisol adopted him right away. She told her friends in school he was her dad; he didn't mind; he adored her and it made him feel good to think that he would have made a good father. Marisol held a special place in his heart, nestled between the empty tomb he stored the love for the son he never met and Gabriela, his seven-year-old daughter with Catalina.

Shane stared at the monitors. No sign of Derrick, he was running late. "Where the hell is he?" he said aloud. He hated it when people ran late. Especially on his dime. A retired cop, Derrick was a resource that Shane and his men relied on for well over a decade. Not the most crooked, but also not very upright and respectable. The man had a knack for finding people; especially people who didn't want to be found. If anyone could locate his son, it would be Derrick.

"It is odd," replied Catalina, as she climbed off Shane's lap. "Derrick's not one for being late. Especially since he knows how important this is to you."

As soon as Catalina finished her sentence, the door to the bar opened and Derrick strolled in. A sense of relief washed over Shane, only to be replaced with a deep sense of dread. What if he found nothing? What if the boy is dead, after all? He didn't think he could get through another bout of grieving for his son. He stared at the screen, frozen in place. His mouth dry, palms sweating, his heart raced in his chest.

Catalina placed a soft hand on his shoulder. "Come on, Babe. This is it. Let's go find out about our boy."

Shane swallowed against the lump in his throat. Ever since learning his son was alive; this was the moment he waited for. He poured himself a shot of whiskey and tossed it down, feeling the warm liquid rush throughout his body, calming his nerves.

When he and Catalina wandered up to the bar, Manny and the others were already waiting. Mari poured several shots and passed them out. A sense of nervousness pervaded the air.

"You're late," growled Shane.

Derrick ignored the barb. He pulled a laptop and file from his briefcase, then put his glasses on. "You should be nicer to me," he stated. "After what I went through at the hands of your spawn and his friends, you owe me." He slid an invoice across the bar top. "I expect every cent of that to be paid. A little extra won't hurt either."

He's alive! That's a good sign. Shane tamped down a sense of cautious optimism. "Let's see what you have for me."

Derrick tapped the bar, waiting for another shot. Mari glanced over at Shane, who nodded. She filled the glass and Derrick tossed it down without pause. He cleared his throat and opened the folder. "Okay, first let me say there's good news and bad news. If it's alright with you, I'll start from the beginning."

"Jesus!" exclaimed Manny. "Good, bad, middle, beginning, however you wanna start, just get on with it, asshole."

Shane smiled, as usual, he and Manny were on the same page. "Start wherever you want," he said. "Just get on with it."

Derrick flipped through the documents in the folder. "As you know, Tricia Caldwell adopted him. She took the baby down to Austin. A couple of weeks later, she married a man named Daniel McCann. The official birth certificate says the baby's name is Finnegan Shane McCann. She had this planned out well. She knew the poor bastard would buy whatever lie she told him." He handed over the birth certificate.

"What kind of man is this, Daniel?" asked Shane.

"Not good," replied Derrick. "At first, he was, I suppose. Daniel was a firefighter for AFD for quite a few years. All the way until he went to prison."

"Prison?" asked Catalina, stunned. "For what?"

"We'll get to that, hold on," replied Derrick. He pulled out several papers. "I got these from a nurse who worked in the local emergency room. Apparently, there were more than a few incidents where Daniel brought the boy in with a broken bone or unexplained lacerations requiring stitches."

Shane's blood boiled. He stared down at the slip of paper, his eyes falling on one entry by the ER doc stating, "Injury caused by mother. Father found the patient in this condition upon returning home from his shift. Possible maternal abuse situation. Discussed potential counseling."

A firestorm of anger ignited in Shane's gut. The bitch not only stole his son, but she also abused him. She hurt him enough that he ended up in the emergency room often. Pushing his anger aside briefly, Shane made a solemn promise to find Tricia and put an end to her.

Derrick slid a small stack of papers across the bar top. "Everything seemed to come to a head on this night."

The top sheet was a copy of an arrest record for Daniel. The words "attempted murder of thirteen-year-old son" were circled in red. Mug shots were attached to the back. Shane stared at the images, imagining what it will be like when he gets hold of this animal and wrings the life out of him with his bare hands.

An audible gasp erupted from Catalina; a trembling hand pressed against her mouth. Tears welled up in her eyes as she handed a stack of photographs to Shane.

After seeing his wife's reaction, Shane wasn't sure he wanted to look at the images. It had to be bad. He glanced down, an image of a child's face—his son's face, purple and bloated, covered in blood, stared up at him through swollen eyelids. Shane thumbed through the images, each one worse than the last. Blood spattered walls, the child's face disfigured with welts and ugly purple bruises. The only place Shane had ever seen a child injured this badly was in a foreign land, after a bomb went off in a small village.

This bastard's gonna die in the worst way possible.

Next came the hospital records, detailing all the injuries and surgeries to piece the child back together. So much damage to his son's body. Shane read the description of seizures and permanent damage. His vision red, he forced himself to read it all, to commit every bit of it to memory as he made a promise that this animal was going to pay.

"Daniel pleaded out. The judge sentenced him to ten years with the possibility of parole," said Derrick.

"Good," stated Pillar. "It'll be easy to take care of the son of a bitch."

Manny shook his head. "Nah, man. This bastard deserves to suffer." He looked over at Shane. "I'm thinking of burying him in the desert up to his neck and letting the ants eat him alive."

Catalina nodded. "It's a start."

Derrick cleared his throat. "He was released eight months ago." He handed over the release form. "Apparently, he was a model citizen inside."

Shane scoffed. Of course, he was. "Where is he now?"

"I'll get to that," replied Derrick.

"Tricia?" asked Shane.

Derrick shook his head. "She has disappeared. I have to admit, I spent little time searching for her, as your son was the priority. But all of my cursory searches turned up nothing. I'll keep looking and see if I can find anything."

"What about Finn?" asked Catalina.

A sneer swept across Derrick's face. "Suffice it to say, the apple didn't fall far from the tree," he stated as he stared at Shane.

"You gonna elaborate, or am I supposed to beat it out of you?" asked Shane.

Derrick opened his laptop and began typing. "He disappeared shortly after his fourteenth birthday. Tricia reported him as a runaway, but no search was ever done, at least, none that I could find. My best guess was that he lived on the streets for a few years. Just another homeless teenager."

He opened a social media site. "The kid was a ghost. No trail to follow. I was about ready to give up, but then a friend sent me a video." He looked up from the screen. "I recently got into survivalism, so my buddy thought it was something I'd be interested in."

"This better be going somewhere," warned Shane, his patience wearing thin. "I don't care about your hobbies."

"It is, it is," replied Derrick. He clicked play on a video. "The video was a short clip of a group of teens camping. My guess, based on the landscape, is they're somewhere in the hill country. Anyway, it wasn't so much what they were doing, as it was who was doing it." He paused the video and spun the laptop around, facing Shane.

Shane's heart swelled as he stared down at a young man with one blue eye and one amber brown. His son was alive. Healthy, strong, and grinning from ear to ear. A sense of relief swept over him.

"He looks like you," said Manny.

"With his momma's hair," added Catalina.

"My baby brother's not bad looking," interjected Mari.

The group stood in silence as the video played. An occasional chuckle would come out as they watched the young man and his friends collect crawdads from a shallow riverbed. The video zoomed in on a tall, muscular redhead.

Mari paused the video. "Hello, handsome!" she exclaimed. "Who is this hottie?"

Shane grunted and hit play again, ignoring her outburst.

Derrick spun the laptop around and typed. "Obviously, those eyes are a dead giveaway."

He gestured to both his eyes, then toward Shane. He cleared his throat and went back to typing. "I looked up the original video and the account that posted it and found this." He slid the laptop over to Shane.

Another video played. This time, Finn and his friends were standing atop a train car. Arms outstretched, leaning into the wind, the looks on their faces were pure ecstasy.

A smile stretched across Shane's face. Seeing his son happy and surrounded by friends made his heart sing. He clicked on the profile of the person who posted the video.

The face of a smiling young woman beamed up at him. She was very young—a teenager. An innocent, naive-looking girl. Shane scrolled down the page, like so many teens, she sure loved posting selfies. Image after image of herself smiling or making silly faces with captions. Shane wondered when something relevant would pop up.

"There is one thing," said Derrick. He pulled the laptop back and once again, set to typing. "It may or may not be a big deal, but it's something you're gonna have to be okay with if you intend to go forward." He clicked on another video, then passed the laptop to Shane.

This one was in a dimly lit house. A cake sat atop the table, covered in various-sized candles. A blond young man stood smiling as the others, Finn included, sang happy birthday. Shane watched, transfixed and overjoyed. He's alive.

As he watched the blond open presents, he couldn't help but smile at the sweetness of the whole affair. It came time for Finn's present. He disappeared and returned with a wadded-up brown paper bag.

"He has his daddy's wrapping skills," teased Catalina.

Shane chuckled.

The video went silent and everyone froze. Shane reached down to touch the trackpad, but Derrick stopped him.

"It's not frozen, just wait a sec," said Derrick.

The blond stared at the wristband while Finn described the details. Shane already knew where this was going, he could tell from the body language. Catalina placed a soft hand on his arm. Then Finn and the blond—Teague was his name—kissed.

Derrick paused the video.

"Why'd you pause it?" asked Shane.

"Are you okay with this?" asked the detective.

"Okay, with what?" Shane was genuinely confused.

"With his relationship," replied Derrick, glancing around nervously.

"What kind of assholes you take us for?" blurted Manny. Odie and Pillar nodding their heads beside him.

"Don't get your panties in a bunch," defended Derrick. "Some people have a real issue."

"We aren't some people," insisted Catalina.

Shane looked up from the screen. "Until several months ago, I thought my son was dead. Seeing him alive, healthy and happy goes beyond any of my wildest dreams. I don't care who he loves, the fact he's alive is all that matters."

Catalina smiled. "I always wanted a son. Now I have two."

Shane nodded in agreement.

"More than that," interjected Derrick. "He's got a whole posse." He scrolled through the video, pausing at one point. "Her name is River." He played the video forward, then stopped. "This one's Cash."

"This is Nomad Girl." He focused on Beth. "As far as I can tell, she joined them a few months ago. The others seem to have been together for years."

Shane looked over the faces one by one, happy to hear Finn had a tight group of friends. The knowledge that his son wasn't out there alone in the world eased some of his worries.

Derrick moved the video forward and paused one more time. "And this asshole is Zac." He rubbed his chin.

"Hello Zac!" exclaimed Mari, as she pulled the laptop closer.

"Hey Pillar," said Manny, slapping the bigger man's arm. "That one looks like he could give you a run for your money."

Pillar grinned proudly.

"I feel like I've seen him before," said Manny. "He looks really familiar."

Derrick scoffed and sneered, shaking his head.

"You seem to have a real problem with the redhead," said Shane. "Care to explain?"

"He's a sneaky bastard," stated Derrick, rubbing his chin. "They all are."

"I'd like to give him a run for his money," interjected Mari.

Shane glared at the girl. He turned his focus back to the detective. "You gonna back that statement up with some details?" he asked.

"I caught up with them in Flagstaff," explained Derrick.

"So, you saw Finn?" asked Catalina, her face lit up.

Derrick nodded. "For a moment." He rubbed his chin one more time. "Then the redheaded barbarian cold-cocked me."

Manny, Pillar and Odie broke out laughing.

"These kids are growing on me," said Manny.

Barely able to contain his smirk, Shane asked, "Now, why would he do that?"

Derrick looked down at the floor. "They called me a pervert."

"Well, I see no lies there," taunted Manny.

The detective glared. "I found this camp of drifters. Finn and his group showed up not long after."

"So, you saw him," said Catalina. "How did he look?"

"I didn't exactly see him," replied Derrick. "He and the red-haired goon hung back in the trees. All I could see was his silhouette."

"Smart boy," said Shane under his breath. "So, what triggered the confrontation?"

Derrick cleared his throat. "I wasn't the only person hunting them." He stared hard at Shane. "Daniel was there."

The very mention of the man's name made Shane's blood boil.

"He showed up an hour or so before they did," continued Derrick. "He must know about Nomad Girl, because as soon as River, Beth, and Cash showed up, he disappeared into the trees. I kept an eye on him, as best as I could."

"Anyway, River wandered off alone into the woods. Daniel was right on her heels." He glanced around at the group. "I didn't know what he had planned, but I couldn't let him hurt the girl—any of them. So, I followed."

"I wasn't really following her, I was tracking Daniel. She ducked behind a tree, I caught a glimpse of him nearby. Next thing I know, your son and his friends surrounded me. I tried to explain, but the Viking knocked me unconscious."

"Yo, I just gotta say I love this boy," said Manny, through fits of laughter.

"So," prodded Shane. "What happened next?"

"I woke up, zip tied to the ass end of a train heading north," replied Derrick.

Laughter erupted all around, even Shane could no longer hold back.

"These kids have my wildest respect," said Manny.

"Yeah, yeah, laugh it up assholes," said Derrick. "Just remember the chuckles when you're paying the bill." He nodded toward the invoice he handed Shane earlier. "I was stuck on that goddamn train for almost two days before it stopped in a train yard where a security guard was actually doing his job." He paused. "You know, it's no wonder these kids can get away with hopping trains, no one does their goddamn jobs anymore."

The laughter didn't subside, with every word uttered from Derrick's mouth, it intensified.

"Yuck it up. Yuck it up, assholes," scoffed Derrick. "Do you know how freaking cold it gets in the mountains this time of year? No coat, no food, no water; I could have died."

"Yeah, but you didn't," replied Manny, still doubled over from laughing.

Derrick glared at Manny, which only sent the other man further into a laughing fit.

Shane waited until everyone calmed. "So, am I safe to assume, if we follow this Nomad Girl's account, we'll be able to find my son?"

"Not anymore," replied Derrick. "By the time I could get free and thaw out, everything changed. She closed her account, and the group disappeared."

"Don't worry, I archived all her videos and posts way before that," said Derrick. "You can watch those." He handed a thumb drive to Shane. "But there isn't any new content. They're ghosts again."

Shane cursed under his breath, "Dammit! So close!" He turned to Derrick. "Any idea what happened? Is Daniel behind this?"

Derrick shook his head. "Your guess is as good as mine. The trail is cold. I spent a couple of weeks trying to rekindle a lead." He shrugged. "But, there's nothing." He slid the rest of the folder across the table to Shane. "This is the end of what I can do on that front, for now."

Catalina got to her feet. "Come with me Derrick, I'll get you paid out."

As they disappeared into the office, Manny flipped open the folder and spread out the photos of Finn and his friends. He tapped the image of Zac. "I knew he looked familiar," he said. "Doc!"

Shane cocked an eyebrow. "What about him?"

"Pillar!" said Manny. "Ain't this the same kid we saw at Doc's?"

Pillar leaned over and studied the pictures. "Yeah, that's him for sure." He tapped the side of his head. "I remember the Texas star."

"You gonna explain?" asked Shane.

Manny nodded. "The last time we made a drop of meds to Doc, a group of kids came into the clinic." He nodded toward Pillar. "He saw them come in."

Pillar nodded. "They were pretty messed up. Someone did a number on them. One had a gunshot wound."

Anxiety coursed through Shane's body. "Which one? Who was shot? Was it Finn?" he demanded.

Pillar stared down at the photos. "No." He shook his head. "It was this one." He tapped the photo of Cash. "The blonde girl stayed by his side the whole time." He pointed to Zac and Teague. "These two stuck close to one another, and this one—" He tapped the photo of Beth. "She wandered off to the side, away from the others. Like she didn't wanna be there."

"Where was Finn?" asked Shane.

"He wasn't there," replied Pillar.

"That blond one was fucked up," said Manny. "He looked like he went a round against a pack of angry apes and lost. Pillar's right, our boy wasn't there. It was just his friends."

Icy fear gripped Shane's insides like a vise. He tried to speak, but the words got stuck in his throat.

Manny jumped to his feet. "I'm gonna call Doc. He'll be able to fill in the blanks; might even have a way to find them." He pulled out his phone and stepped outside.

Frozen in place, Shane studied the photographs. He picked up the one of Finn and stared. His son was alive. Where the hell are you now? He wondered.

Chapter Six

A BLAST OF CHILLY AIR HIT TEAGUE IN THE FACE, carrying with it the earthy scent of oil and metal mixed with rock and desert life. He scanned the area in search of Gunner and Nate.

Ever since the night of Finn's breakdown, Gunner, Nate, and the others were out searching for him. Following the path that Porter laid out, they rode from one stop to another, taking care to search for any sign of their missing friend. According to the message board updates, so far there was nothing of any merit to share.

A blanket of silence hung between Teague and Zac, like a shroud separating them into two different worlds. While Teague lived mostly in his own mind, lost among his memories and worst fears, Zac kept up with the group in the chat, occasionally breaking the silence with an update or two. Now and then, a pang of guilt would interrupt Teague's catastrophic thoughts, making him feel guilty for being so silent and distant. A tiny part of him wanted nothing more than to feel at ease again. To converse with Zac, at least take part in the conversation with the others. But the larger part of him insisted on receding deep into his mind, to a place where he wallowed in every dark thought and every cruel thing he ever did. As much as he tried to escape the spiral, he couldn't shake free. His only respite was the few moments when he focused on Finn.

As the train slowed, Teague wished a silent prayer. Please let this be it. Barely able to contain his anxiety, he jumped from the train, hitting the ground close to Zac. Following the coordinates that Gunner sent, they made their way to the small campsite.

As they entered the clearing, little Gypsy gave out several ferocious barks, only to devolve into a wiggling mass of fluffy dog fur as soon as she recognized the newcomers. Four silhouettes sat around the fire. Teague immediately identified them as Gunner, Nate, Tripp and Sam.

"Glad you made it," said Gunner, wrapping his giant arms around Teague, nearly crushing him. A beefy hand lifted his chin into the light as Gunner surveyed the damage. "Looks like Stoney's doc did a good job stitching you up." His face softened. "This whole mess breaks my heart. How are you holding up, son?"

Tears welled up in Teague's eyes, his lips trembled as he struggled to string together a sentence. Unable to hold up the facade any longer, he broke down and sobbed, all the while, hating himself for being so weak.

Gunner stood silent, arms wrapped around him, waiting for the younger man to let it all out.

A pathetic whimper followed by a gentle scratch on Teague's leg snapped him out of it. Wiping his face, he glanced down at Gypsy. The moment their eyes locked, her tail sprang into action, wagging back and forth feverishly. Thankful for the diversion, Teague reached down and scooped the pup in his arms. She promptly went about licking his entire face.

Gunner slapped a heavy hand on his shoulder. "We have food ready." He gestured to the small fire. "We figured you'd be hungry."

"Sweet!" exclaimed Zac, as he stalked over and took a seat.

The savory aroma of meat over a fire wafted through the air.

Teague inhaled. "That smells like steak," he said, glancing over at Gunner.

The older man flashed a wide grin. "It is. We decided on something special for dinner since you guys were joining us."

"We stopped at the local market when we got here," chimed Nate. He poked at the slabs of meat sizzling on the metal grill above the fire.

Teague's mouth watered. His stomach grumbled.

"I think it's ready," said Zac, plate in hand.

Nate shook his head. "Nah, it's still too raw."

"Raw my ass. A good steak is always half alive."

"This is what I've been trying to get across to him," said Tripp.

"It needs to be cooked till the center is barely pink," said Nate.

"You cook mine like that, and we're gonna have a problem," replied Zac. He stabbed his knife into a steak and plopped it down on his plate. "Cook yours till it's charcoal, if you want. This one's mine."

Teague pulled out his knife and stabbed another steak. "I like mine the same way he does." He was followed up by Tripp and finally Sam, who flashed a sheepish grin and shrugged.

Nate shook his head. "Go on, when you get sick, don't say I didn't warn you."

There wasn't much chatter to be had around the fire as everyone devoured their meal. The steak was everything Teague imagined it would be. The flavor of the wood fire mingled with the savory meat melting in his mouth. From the first bite to the last, he relished each mouthful. When he finished, he wiped the blade of his knife on his pants and placed it back in its sheath. A shiny, metal flask made its way to him. He took a small swig, basking in the warm sensation of the liquor as it poured down his throat and into his belly.

Gunner pulled out a map and spread it out so that everyone could see. "We're here." He placed his finger down just north of Santa Fe. "Now, according to Porter, the train Finn hopped came through this area right here." He swept his finger across the map. "There's two yards and a couple of side outs along this track. Any of which our boy could have jumped off at. Which is why we all split up and spent the last few days checking them out."

"Any sign?" asked Teague.

Gunner shook his head.

"We went as far up as Taos. Nothing," said Tripp.

A sharp pang stabbed in Teague's gut as he recalled the gorge outside of Taos. He tried to push aside the image in his mind of the bridge. A flash of Finn standing at the rail, ready to leap to his end, sent shivers down his spine.

"Nothing," stated Tripp, one more time for emphasis, as though he knew what Teague was thinking. "Porter checked the local police reports. There's no report about anyone jumping for the past month."

Relief washed over Teague. He nodded.

Gunner sighed. "From this point, we're flying blind. It's anyone's guess as to where he went, so I'm asking you." He locked eyes with Teague. "Do you have any idea where he might have headed?"

Teague studied the map. So much wide-open space in every direction. His heart sank, this was going to be like finding a needle in a haystack.

"I think he would have gone west," said Nate.

"Tripp and I are of the mind that he'd head to the mountains," added Sam.

"Where do you think he went?" Gunner asked Teague.

Everyone sat silent, staring.

Zac swallowed a sip of whiskey from the flask. "Finn would wanna stay away from major cities and stuff like that. All those people make his skin crawl."

Teague nodded in agreement. "Oui, he would definitely stay away from major cities."

"That's a start," replied Gunner. "So, what do you recommend? West? East? North?"

A sense of hopelessness washed over Teague whenever he looked at the map. What if they chose the wrong direction? Just peering down at the sheer expanse of land they needed to cover made it all seem like a lost cause.

"Any word from Bells, D.B. and Max?" asked Zac.

"They're itching to get out and help with the search," replied Gunner. "This whole time, they've been camped out near the rundown trailer. Waiting." He shook his head. "Finn hasn't returned."

"According to Max," said Tripp, "They're gonna give it another full day, then they plan to head out wherever we tell them to go. Another set of eyes can only be a good thing."

A gentle nudge from Zac pulled Teague from his swirling thoughts. "So, what do you think?"

Teague breathed in deeply. The feeling of despair was overwhelming, robbing him of any ability to think clearly. He fiddled with the bracelet wrapped around his wrist. The flask made its way back to him, he took a long pull, wincing at the whiskey burn as he forced himself to swallow.

Gunner cleared his throat. "Here's what I recommend." He placed a finger on the map. "Nate and I will head west. Tripp and Sam can go northwest and you two can go straight north into Colorado." He glanced around at everyone. "Sound good?"

Tripp and Sam exchanged a glance, then looked back at Gunner and nodded.

"Sounds good," replied Zac. "Looks like we got Colorado."

Teague wanted to say something, but the words were trapped behind the giant lump in his throat.

"I'll tell Max and his crew to head north from Arizona," said Gunner. "Teague, you got anything you want to add?"

Teague swallowed and cleared his throat. "Nothing." He stared down at the map. So many miles. For the first time since leaving Terlingua, he wondered if they were even going to find Finn. The realization that he may never see him again hit Teague like an anvil against his chest. His heart pounded against his ribs; it was difficult to breathe. He was having a panic attack. The world swirled around him; blackness encroached around the edges of his vision. His stomach turned, threatening to expel the steak he just consumed. He placed his palm on his forehead and focused on breathing to calm his racing heart.

Gunner folded the map and put it away. "It's gonna be okay, son," he said. "We're gonna find our boy."

Lips trembling, holding back tears, Teague nodded and rubbed his eyes.

Across the fire, Tripp lighted a joint and passed it over. "Here," he said, exhaling a cloud of smoke. "This'll help."

Over the next couple of hours, the others kept the chatter light. They did their best to avoid the very mention of Finn. This helped considerably, as Teague could relax and breathe again. He was thankful for his friends, even though he was wallowing in misery.

The next morning, they said their goodbyes, then each group set out on their own paths.

Chapter Seven

"Come on," pleaded Manny. "You must have kept some sort of info about them."

Doc sighed and shook his head. "Do you see me keep records on any of your guys?"

Anger grew deep in Shane's belly. Not so much at Doc, because he understood the nature of the man's business. The anonymity was something he and his guys took advantage of often. He wasn't angry with the doctor. He was angry with himself for having hoped it would be that easy.

"Let's go over it one more time," said Shane. "From the beginning."

Doc cleared his throat. "Got a call from Stoney." He held up a hand. "Before you ask, no, I don't know his real name."

A few feet away, Manny scoffed.

"How did he know you?" asked Shane.

"He used to hop trains. Had a real nasty accident one time and, luckily for him, one of the people he happened to be with brought him to me."

Shane nodded. "How long ago was this?"

"Years," replied Doc. "Way before I met you, fellas."

"So, you stayed in contact with him?"

"Look, I've said it before." Doc shook his head. "I don't stay in contact with anyone. Sure, I have some repeat clients." He glanced at Manny and Shane. "Much like the agreement I have with you."

"Come on Doc," interjected Manny. "You don't have an address book or something?"

Doc raised an eyebrow.

"I certainly hope not," stated Shane. He understood Doc's policy on privacy. However, right now, it was very much in the way of his goal to find his son.

"Let's go back to this, Stoney," said Shane. "Anything noteworthy about him? Anything that we could use to find him?"

"He's ex-military." He tapped his left forearm. "Has a Marine tattoo."

Shane nodded. "That's a good start. Any idea of his age?"

"He's probably a few years younger than you."

"Any other tattoos? Has he ever said anything that could give you an idea where he comes from?"

Doc shook his head.

"He must be local," said Manny. "At least, not too far away from here."

"He could be anywhere within a four-hour radius," replied Shane. "That means he could be in Texas, New Mexico or Arizona."

Manny sighed and shook his head.

Shane turned his attention back to Doc. "How about the kids? Tell me about them."

"All I can tell you is the names they went by," replied Doc. "Stoney was the man who contacted me. The other, older man with dark skin wasn't someone I knew. Not too sure of his name. The one who had the bullet wound was Cash. The girl who stayed by his side was River. There was a blond who needed some stitches on his face. His name was T or Teague. He had a funny way of talking. Definitely a southern boy. Then there was the big redhead, Zac. He was distinctly Texan." He paused as though he were scanning his memory. "There was another girl, I don't know her name because she kept quiet and stayed a distance away from everyone. But she was a part of their group."

Shane held out the photo of Finn.

Doc shook his head. "Sorry. That one was not with the group. The one named Teague mentioned the name Finn. He was adamant about getting out and finding him. We put him under so he could get some rest. The last I saw them, they loaded up into an old van and a newer model truck." He glanced up at Shane. "I'm sorry. I have no more information for you. It's the nature of my business to not maintain records. You know this."

Shane sighed. The irony of it all was not lost on him, the very reason he trusted Doc was also the reason the trail to his son had vanished.

"What do you wanna do now?" asked Manny.

Shane raked his fingers through his beard. He didn't know what to do next. Helplessness was not a feeling he was well acquainted with—it was not something he intended to hang on to. He held his hand out to Doc. "Thanks for everything, man."

"Sorry I couldn't be more help," replied Doc.

In the parking lot, Shane stopped beside his truck and looked around. This would not be easy. He turned to Manny. "Get Derrick on board to find anything he can about Tricia and Daniel."

Shane climbed into the cab of his truck. "When you have Derrick set up, start calling everyone we know."

Manny nodded.

"Make sure it's perfectly clear that if they find Daniel, they're to keep him alive. He's mine." The mere mention of that man's name sent fire through Shane's veins. He climbed into his truck and fired up the engine. Lost in contemplation, he drove home, listening to Manny organize people over the phone. If Shane was going to find his son, he was going to need all the help he could rally.

Chapter Eight

P OP, CRACKLE, POP.

The sound of their small fire echoed around the clearing that Teague and Zac had chosen as their campsite. A mere twenty yards away, through the gnarled woods, the train yard sat quiet for the evening. They would have to wait till the early morning for their next ride.

Almost two weeks had passed since they saw any of the others. Teague wasn't keeping up with the group's communications, he left that task in Zac's hands. Time seemed to move much faster now. He began each day with a deep sense of loathing and closed his eyes each night, feeling hopeless and lost. No matter what he did, he couldn't shake the feeling that he was running a losing race. The distinct feeling that no matter how fast he ran, how little sleep he got, he would always be several miles behind.

He spent most of his waking hours deep inside his own head, picking through his memories, holding up the good ones, pushing back against the overwhelming sorrow that hovered ever so close, waiting for the opportunity to settle in and take over. At night, his dreams were full of horrific scenes, all revolving around himself being hopelessly incapable of protecting himself or anyone he loved.

Through all of this, Zac stood by. Patient, calm and silent. Never too jovial, never too down, seemingly aware of Teague's need for solitude, Zac kept conversation to a bare minimum. The space that had once been full of laughter and easy chatter was now filled with uncomfortable silence. Teague couldn't help but think perhaps it was time to split off from Zac. To separate from everything he had known—everyone he cared about.

Pop, crackle, pop.

"You've hardly touched your food," said Zac.

Teague stared down at the plate on his lap. The smell of canned stew wafted up to his nostrils, making his stomach turn. He poked an overcooked potato; nothing would make him put this into his mouth. "Any word from the others?"

"Max, D.B. and Bells are in Utah," replied Zac. "They haven't picked up a trail." He poked at the embers in the fire. "Tripp and Sam are in northern Nevada, nothing there either."

"Gunner and Nate?"

Zac sighed. "They're in southern Oregon. They haven't come up with anything either."

Pop! An ember exploded and bright, red sparks floated into the air, climbing higher and higher until the cool night air dampened their glow, leaving them to float to the ground.

"Cash is doing a lot better," said Zac. "He's up and moving around some."

Silence.

"He's dying to get back out here. To help with the search."

Teague continued to poke at the sad, overcooked potato.

Zac continued, "Ben, Mara and Tanner have set out. They're gonna cover Cali."

"We should split up," blurted Teague.

"Come again?" Zac leaned closer.

"We can cover more ground if we split up."

Zac shook his head and leaned back. "Ain't gonna happen."

Teague put the bowl on the ground at his feet. "It makes the most sense."

"No, it doesn't."

"Hear me out—"

"No!" Boomed Zac. "I ain't hearing any of this out. Splitting up is not an option." His face, a mask of firm resolve. "And if you even think about takin' off during the night, I will track you down and beat your ass. Don't make me tie us together, 'cause I will, if that's what it'll take."

A small chuckle escaped Teague's lips. He knew Zac meant every word he said—that made it all funnier. Suddenly, they were laughing out loud. It felt good. Teague couldn't recall the last time he laughed so heartily.

"Thank you," he said.

"For what?"

"For just being you. You're a great friend."

Zac scoffed. "Damn right I am." He flashed an impish grin.

Pop, crackle, pop.

Teague stared into the flames. "I'm sorry I'm such a shit friend."

"You're not."

"I can't get out of my own head," said Teague. He looked up at Zac, tears gathering in his eyes. "I don't wanna live in here." He tapped the side of his head as he spoke. "But I don't know how to crawl out."

Zac sat silent, watching and listening.

A tear escaped the corner of Teague's eye, running down his cheek only to get caught in the weeks' worth of stubble that had grown. He wiped the wetness away. The floodgate had opened, and there was nothing he could do to stop the torrent of emotions.

"Things keep playing in my head." Teague wiped his hands on his thighs. "It's like a bad horror movie."

"Things? Like what happened that night?" asked Zac.

Teague nodded, then shook his head. "Not just that night. Everything." A sharp pang stabbed in his gut. Tears streamed from his eyes. "Why do you stay with me?"

"You're my brother," replied Zac. "I love you." He paused. "I ain't gonna leave you, and I ain't gonna let you leave."

"I don't deserve that kind of loyalty." Teague rubbed his eyes.

"You let me be the judge of that."

Teague shook his head. "There's shit about me you don't know."

"And I don't care."

"Mais la!" blurted Teague. "Would you just listen for once? You should care."

"If you're tryin' to convince me to desert you, it ain't gonna work."

"I've done things—"

"We all have," replied Zac.

Teague shook his head. "Not like this."

"I'm all ears."

"Way before I met up with Finn—" Saying his name out loud cause a stabbing pain deep in Teague's heart. He wondered if it would ever become easier. He swallowed. "I hooked up with a group in Houston. We did the usual shit; petty theft, pan handling, selling drugs." He paused. "Selling sex."

Zac nodded.

More tears. Teague's heart raced in his chest. He was about to confess his darkest deeds. He was sure this information would be the end of Zac's devotion. Some things cannot be forgiven or excused. Perhaps this was for the best. Resolute in his determination to lay it all bare, he continued.

"There was this group who ran the streets. They controlled all the drugs and just about everything else. They wanted runaways. The younger, the better." Teague glanced over at Zac.

No expression.

"It was my job to befriend the new runaways. To lead them to the handlers, who would then get them hooked and turn them out."

Zac stared, unblinking.

"You heard me, right?" prodded Teague. "I conned lost kids into trusting me, then handed them over to monsters who used them up and spit them out."

Still no response from Zac.

This was killing Teague. "Don't you have anything to say?"

"You were a kid yourself," replied Zac. "You didn't know much better."

"Mais la! Taton? I knew exactly what I was doing! Those kids trusted me. I knew I was ruining their lives." Teague stared down at the fire. "And I didn't care. I even believed some of them deserved it."

Silence.

Crack, pop, hiss.

"I was good at it too," continued Teague. "The handlers rewarded me with just about anything I wanted. They called me 'T'." His palms were sweaty and his muscles trembled. "There was this girl. She couldn't have been more than fifteen." He stared Zac in the eyes. "Her name was Zoe. She came from a cozy suburban life. When I first met her, she was full of angry teen angst against her parents, prattling on and on about how uncool they were." He stared into the fire. "She was a lot like Beth when we first met her." Teague shook his head. "I hated her so much."

Zac's face was stone.

"I flirted with her, got her to trust me and then, like all the others, I turned her over to the handlers." Teague's mouth went dry. He wiped his sweaty palms on his thighs. "Over the next few weeks, I watched the light disappear from her eyes. She became hollow, broken, and empty." He glanced at Zac. "She died inside. Became just like the rest of us. And I enjoyed every minute of it."

"One night she came to me, begging to help her leave. She pleaded with me to help her contact her parents. She swore they would take us both in, no questions asked."

"Do you know what I told her?" He peered up at Zac.

"I told her she was worthless. That there was no way her family would ever want her back. That she could never go back to the person she was before." Anguish settled deep in Teague's heart as he recalled that night. How Zoe's face sank and grew dark. The despair in her hollow eyes. He recalled his lack of empathy for the girl. "She ran away sobbing. I didn't care."

Teague placed his hand against his chest. "I didn't care." He raked his fingers through his greasy hair. "A few hours later, sirens erupted a couple of blocks from my usual hangout. I followed the lights and sound. A crowd had gathered, so I worked my way through to see what all the noise was about." He paused and inhaled, attempting to calm his nerves. "It was Zoe. She had climbed to the roof of this seedy motel and jumped." Images of that night flashed through his mind. The squawk of police radios, the flashing red and blue lights, the hum of the whispering crowd. The vivid imagery of Zoe's lifeless eyes staring up at the evening sky as the coroner pulled the sheet over her body.

"As I watched them take her away, I realized the role that I played in her decision. She came to me for help and all I gave her was more of a reason to do what she did. I could have helped, but I didn't care enough about her to even consider it."

Silence.

"Something changed after that. I grew to hate everyone I knew. I hated myself. I wanted to die." Teague sighed; The weight of the story was off his chest, but it was still hard to breathe. "Not long after, I left the city. Hitched a ride out and landed in Austin." Once again, Teague looked Zac in the eyes. "I seriously contemplated whether it was worth it to keep going. I had nothing but a bunch of bad memories. Life was pointless." He looked away. "I made a plan."

"That's when you met Finn," said Zac. His voice was soft.

Teague nodded.

Zac sat up straight. "Seems as though he saved your life."

Once again, tears exploded from Teague's eyes. "He did."

Silence fell upon them.

Pop, crackle, pop.

Teague could take it no longer. "Are you gonna say anything? Tell me what a piece of shit I am? Anything?"

"It's not my place," sighed Zac. "You did what you did. All of us have done things we're not proud of to make it from one day to the next."

"Not like that!"

Zac stared at Teague. "Look. I ain't gonna make excuses for the things you've done. I don't even care to rationalize or judge them. Only you can judge yourself. Only you can forgive yourself. Were the things you did wrong? Yeah, they were. Does that make you a shitty human being?" he shrugged. "I will tell you that the Teague I know has a heart as big as Texas. He would die for his family. He's exactly the kind of man I want by my side, watching my back." A sad smile swept across his face. "The past is just that—the past. It makes no sense mulling it over again and again. You've got to forgive yourself, no one's gonna do that for you."

Teague wiped his face and rubbed his hands on his legs. "You wouldn't have been the type of person I was."

"Now, come on," replied Zac. "You know you can't compare yourself to this." He made a sweeping gesture with his hands down his body. "Because I'm fucking awesome," he quipped. "This level of awesomeness can only exist in very rare circumstances."

A burst of laughter lightened the mood. Teague quietly promised to do his best to be the man Zac believed him to be.

Chapter Nine

A HEAVY BLANKET OF CLOUDS BLOCKED THE STARS, leaving the sky black as pitch. Finn walked along the tracks, the sound of his footsteps crunching in the gravel echoed all around him. After leaving the old woman and her well-trained dog a while back, he lost track of time and direction. The pills not only numbed his pain, they silenced his thoughts and dulled his concentration. This was the desired effect.

He stopped by a railroad crossing and sat heavily on the ground. His only possessions were a water bottle and the items in his pockets. The pills were wearing off. Once again, the voices were seeping through.

Finn, stop, please. What did you do?

He shook his head in a feeble attempt to shake the voices away.

You're a fuckup.

He pulled out the bottle, popped the top off and, using the last gulp of water, he swallowed the last pill.

"Stop it!" Finn shouted aloud to his own mind. His words bounced off the surrounding emptiness.

You suck! You're a loser! You deserve to be alone.

Tears burst forth from his eyes, a cascade of grief overwhelmed his emotions and his mind. *You're gonna die alone.*

"Shut up!" He cried out, banging his fist against his forehead.

Time to hit the eject button.

His thoughts roiled in his head, conspiring against his very existence. The screams of his friends mingled with his catastrophic thoughts, creating a cacophony of noise that gave way to a high-pitched ring.

Eject.

The pill wasn't working—not yet, anyway. Even if it did kick in, what was he going to do next time? He had no more.

Clock out.

Sorrow crashed down on his soul like a tsunami. A never-ending flow of tears coursed down his face.

Cash in your chips.

In the distance, a train whistle blew. Still far away, it was heading toward him. Finn climbed to his feet. The whistle called out one more time. Beckoning him toward the tracks.

He stepped over the rail, planting his feet firmly on a wooden tie. The train whistle bellowed—closer this time. He could hear the wheels rolling on the metal tracks. A faint scent of grease and diesel wafted on the light evening breeze. Finn tilted his head to the sky, rather fitting that he would go out alone in the darkness.

You deserve no better.

The train rolled closer. Just a little longer and the voices will be silenced—the pain will be gone. Forever.

The vibrations of the train rumbled through his feet. The whistle blasted—the sound was deafening. Eyes closed, chin pointing toward the stars, arms held open, Finn welcomed the end.

The train whistle blasted, the air was thick with the smell of grease, iron and gravel. He inhaled and stood firm.

A flurry of activity erupted, something soft and heavy slammed against him, knocking him off his feet. Rolling on the ground, coarse gravel dug deep into his exposed skin. The train whooshed by in a cloud of dust. A moment later, it was gone.

"What the hell are you doing?" A strange voice demanded.

Finn glanced up at the dark-skinned stranger standing before him. His eyes grew blurry and the world around him dimmed. It was a hell of a time for the drugs to kick in. The noise in his head subsided, his body floated on air. He welcomed the coming sense of detachment.

"What is wrong with you?" the man asked with a heavy accent.

Finn couldn't place the accent; he didn't care that much about it either.

"Stupid child." The man hooked Finn's arm around his neck and wrapped a strong arm around his waist. He began walking, carrying Finn along with him. "High as a goddamn kite," he stated, with a disgusted sigh and a disapproving shake of his head.

Where they were going was a mystery to Finn, one that he simply couldn't muster enough emotion to care about. His body was floating, held aloft by the arms of the strange man with the heavy, foreign accent. He didn't have it in him to fight or argue, all he wanted to do was revel in the quiet in his mind and the numbness of his emotions. The world dropped away.

A sudden jolt awakened Finn as he was slammed against a hard surface. He tried to open his eyes, but they refused.

"Alright, here we are," said the man. Holding him in place with one hand, he unlocked a door with his other. "Okay, young man, just a little farther." The stranger led Finn over to a worn-out sofa and unceremoniously let him drop.

The cushions enveloped his body. He relaxed and closed his eyes, feeling as though he were floating on a soft, fluffy cloud. Oblivion. That was the goal—that was where he wanted to be. Once again, the world dropped away.

Finn awoke to the warm glow of morning light and the aroma of fresh coffee. His mouth was dry, he licked his parched lips and instantly regretted it.

"Good morning," boomed a deep voice.

Finn didn't recall the man's voice being so deep and masculine. He opened his eyes and peered up. The man hovered above him, his eyes bright and friendly.

The strange man smiled one of the most authentic, radiant smiles Finn had ever seen while he held out a glass containing water.

"Go on." He prodded as he handed the drink to Finn, who swallowed the entire contents without pause. "My name is Tayo," he stated. The warm, genuine smile was still on his face.

"Finn."

Tayo chuckled. "Nice to meet you, Finn." He strolled into the kitchen and returned with two mugs containing steaming, hot coffee. He handed one over and took a seat in the worn-out chair beside the couch.

Finn didn't know what to say. Was he supposed to thank the man for knocking him off the tracks, even though he wasn't thankful for that? He wanted to yell at the man but was unable to bring himself to do it, mostly because of the honest and friendly expression on his face.

"Are you feeling better now?" asked Tayo.

Finn nodded and took a sip from his warm mug. The coffee filled his mouth with flavor.

"Nothing better than fresh coffee in the morning," said Tayo. He took a sip. A moment later, a solemn expression spread across his face. "There is no need to talk about what you were doing out there last night, if you don't want to." He flashed a gentle, knowing smile. "But if you do, I can assure you, I am a good listener, at least that is what I have heard my entire life."

Truth be told, Finn recalled very little about whatever happened the previous night. He preferred it that way. "Where are we?" he asked.

"Needles," replied Tayo.

"Where's that?"

Tayo took another sip of coffee and swallowed. "California, my young friend."

California. Aside from the fact that he didn't know where the hell Needles was, Finn was satisfied that he was at least heading in the right direction. "How far are we from LA?"

"A few hours directly west from here." Tayo sipped from his mug. "You have friends or family there?"

Finn didn't respond and instantly felt bad about it. To change the topic and the overall mood of the moment, he asked, "What's your story, Tayo? You always go around, bringing strangers home to sleep on your couch?"

Tayo slapped his knee and chuckled. "I assure you; you are the first ever such person. Though I do like to help others. The world has given me so much, I feel it is my obligation to give some back."

Finn glanced around the shabby, little apartment. Between the cracked and stained walls, the worn-out carpet and the obviously secondhand furniture, it was hard to see what Tayo meant. From his point of view, the man didn't seem to have an abundance of anything.

"Each of us has the power to make the world a little better for the people we come across," continued Tayo. "Wouldn't you agree?"

"I suppose," replied Finn, not really agreeing with his own words.

Tayo gave out a hearty chuckle. "Each day on this earth is a gift, my friend. A new opportunity. A new chance to make things right or better."

"Or fuck things up in unimaginable ways," blurted Finn.

"Yes," nodded Tayo. "That too. And once we do that, we have the next day to fix the things we broke."

"Some things can't be fixed."

"This is also true," replied Tayo. "Then we can get to work on rebuilding. Making things better than they were before."

Finn stared. This man was probably one of the most positive

people he had ever come across. "Sometimes there's nothing left to rebuild."

Tayo smiled. "Then we move on. We learn from our mistakes, and work toward forgiveness while working hard to never make the same mistakes."

"You sure have a lot of positive opinions for someone who lives alone in a shabby apartment," snapped Finn. As soon as the words passed his lips, he regretted saying them. He shook his head. "I'm sorry. I shouldn't have said that."

"Apology accepted," said Tayo. "For the record, I do not plan on being alone forever. My future wife is out there." He waved his arms. "I will meet her when it is the right time."

Finn couldn't help but chuckle.

"Now, I am starving," said Tayo. "You must be as well. I will make us some breakfast. We can talk more when our bellies are full." He stood up. "The bathroom is right there." Tayo pointed."I put a fresh towel on the sink if you wish to clean up." He turned and strolled into the kitchen.

Finn sipped from his mug, taking in the room, processing the exchange with Tayo. As much as he tried to dislike the man, he couldn't. Tayo's confidence and positivity were infectious. So much so, even Finn felt a little more upbeat than he had in days. He downed the rest of his coffee and went into the bathroom to clean up.

The delectable aroma of fried eggs and sausage permeated the air of the tiny apartment.

As soon as he laid eyes on Finn entering the kitchen, Tayo smiled and gestured. "Come take a seat."

Finn stared down at the plate before him. Fried eggs, sausage, fresh tomato slices and toast tantalized him. He was ready to make short work of this meal. Fork in hand, he moved to dive in.

Tayo raised a hand. "Hold on," he said. "We must say grace before we eat." He folded his hands and bowed his head.

Not wishing to offend, Finn bowed his head and waited patiently as Tayo said his thanks to whatever god he believed in.

When he finished his prayer, Tayo looked up and said, "Okay, let's dig in."

Bite after bite, the food was every bit as tasty as it promised to be. The eggs were cooked to perfection, with just the right amount of runniness in their golden yellow center to be swabbed up with a piece of perfectly buttered wheat toast. The sausage exploded with flavor in Finn's mouth. Each bite, uncovered yet another hidden herb or flavor. From the moment he scooped his first mouthful to the last piece of fresh tomato, Finn savored every bite.

"You were hungry," observed Tayo. "Glad to see my cooking skills are appreciated." He pushed his chair back and climbed to his feet. "Help me clean up, then we will get you on your way to wherever you are headed."

Finn had to admit, he liked Tayo. He had an openness that Finn had never seen before. It made you want to help; to be better, for no other reason than to win the man's approval. The need to impress someone was such an odd sensation for Finn, he couldn't recall a time when he felt this way about anyone, let alone a stranger. Tayo emanated a deep sense of well-being, of contentment. Finn was torn between a desire to get on with his journey and the urge to remain for a little while longer. But the voices had other ideas.

A waste of space like you would only drag this cheerful man down. They whispered in his mind.

It was nearly noon when they headed out for the truck stop at the edge of town, where Tayo worked as a cook.

"Looks like this is it, my young friend." He grabbed hold of Finn and gave him a firm hug. "Remember, today is a new day." He smiled warmly.

Finn stepped back and returned the smile. "Thank you," he said. "For everything."

"Next time you come through town, be sure to stop by for a visit," said Tayo. He took a step away, then paused and turned to face Finn one more time. "Fate caused our paths to cross last night. She has something in store for you." He winked. "Good things await you."

Finn stood and watched as Tayo entered the truck stop. It didn't take long for the darkness to return. The voices were back, gaining strength. He needed to get to LA where he could find what he needed to silence the noise in his mind.

Chapter Ten

"WHAT TIME YOU GOT?" asked Teague, pacing in circles while gnawing on his nails.

Zac glanced up at the sky. "I suppose it's around noon."

Teague pulled his phone from his pocket.

Zac didn't have to guess what Teague was looking at, he knew he was scanning the group message board, yet again, for any sign that the others were held up. Of course, they weren't, Zac knew this, but Teague was running a little low in the trust department lately, faith in anything was hard for him to maintain.

It was hard to believe, four weeks had passed since they left the others down in Terlingua. A whole month. Zac rubbed the scruffy beard along his chin as he pondered. He couldn't recall a time since becoming a Nomad, when he had gone so long without the entire group. He missed Cash's humor and River's lighthearted sense of calm. She had a way of making things feel like it was all gonna be okay.

For the past few weeks, Zac felt as though a huge chunk of his heart had been ripped out and left in the sun to dry, leaving behind a giant black hole that, if allowed, would consume the entirety of what remained. He had to admit, he missed Finn something awful. Not nearly as bad as Teague—no one could miss Finn as bad as Teague. He wondered how the others were holding up. Did Finn's absence affect them the same way?

He stared at Teague. The lack of eating regularly, coupled with very little sleep and the physical strain of hopping one train after another in a hopeless attempt to catch up with a ghost, had taken a serious toll on him. Gone was the bronzed, healthy, happy-go-lucky soul, leaving in its place a gaunt, haggard and drained man who hardly resembled Teague at all. Even his hair had changed from the golden, beach blond to something of a colder, platinum tone. His sunken face was covered in a patchy, overgrown, light-brown beard.

Probably the oddest and most disheartening of changes that had overtaken Teague was in his eyes. They used to be a bright and friendly pale blue, but now they were icy, narrow, and calculating. It was as though a darker person had snuck inside Teague's body and was now wearing it like a skin suit. The thin, easily agitated figure pacing around, gnawing his nails, was nothing like the Teague, Zac had always known. He didn't like it.

A train whistle called out from the forest.

"It's about time!" exclaimed Teague.

Zac's anxiety gave way to relief. In a few minutes, their family would be reunited. After a full month long separation, they would finally be back together. Whole again—well, almost whole.

The sound of the train rolling along the tracks echoed across the valley, bouncing off the mountains. Zac and Teague stepped back into the tree line. The whistle called out; the train slowed.

First, the engine rolled past, followed by a second and third, finally the cars came rolling by.

Zac's heart soared when he glimpsed blonde dreads peeking out between the last two grainers. He didn't want to admit it, not even to himself, but he feared the others missed the ride and that he would be stuck alone with Teague for a little longer. Even acknowledging he felt that way hurt him to his core. It wasn't so much that Teague was a burden, or that Zac was tired of babysitting him. It was because deep inside, Zac knew Teague was suffering. That his pain was so deep and so thorough, it was out of reach for Zac to do anything about it. He was helpless. All he could do was watch his brother waste away in the dark hole of despair he had been wallowing in. The hope of being reunited with the others brought on a sense of relief. Surely River could get through to Teague. She had that nurturing way about her. If anyone could get through to him, it would be River.

The train rolled past, leaving a cloud of debris and dust in its wake. Across the tracks, Cash, River and Beth were brushing themselves off and gathering their packs.

Zac whistled as he and Teague burst from the thicket to greet their friends.

"Woo-hoo!" exclaimed River, arms out, ready for an embrace.

She wrapped her arms around Zac's neck and hugged him tightly. A sense of happy calm washed over him. For the first time in weeks, he felt as though things were going to be okay.

River kissed him on the cheek and pulled back, inspecting him. "Looks like you need a razor," she said playfully, as she ran a soft hand across his chin. She stepped in front of Teague; her facial expression instantly changed to one of concern. "Hey, baby," she cooed, as she wrapped her arms around him.

Beth came up and hugged Zac. "Smells like y'all could use a shower too." She chuckled as she wrinkled her nose and pulled away.

"I suppose we do," admitted Zac.

Cash greeted him with a hug. "My brother," he said.

Zac took a good look at Cash. The last time he saw his friend, he was hanging on to consciousness by a thread. Seeing him stand before him, healthy, fit and well-rested, was a relief.

"You look great."

Cash nodded and pulled Zac close, and nodded toward Teague. "How come my brother looks like death?" he whispered.

A wave of emotions crashed over Zac. "I did my best." He shook his head. "He won't eat—hardly sleeps." Zac fought back tears. "He ain't himself."

"I see that," agreed Cash, with a nod. "We're here now," he said. "River'll snap him out of it."

"That's what I'm hopin'," admitted Zac, with a sigh.

Cash clapped him on the shoulder. "Come on, let's get things right again."

Chapter Eleven

IVER STUDIED TEAGUE IN THE MIRROR. "You know," she said. "I think you look good with longer hair." She moved her fingers through his freshly washed hair. He smelled like soap, a big improvement from the man who greeted her.

Thanks to Stoney, they had enough money to get a hotel room, a decent meal and still have money left over. River was thankful for his foresight; she didn't think it was necessary until she laid eyes on her boys.

The healthy, robust Teague she knew was replaced by a gaunt, sorrowful creature. His face was hollow and angry. At first sight, River knew she would do everything in her power to bring back the old Teague—the real Teague.

"What do you think?" she asked.

"If you think so," he replied, with a shrug. "I honestly don't care."

"I think it looks good longer too," added Beth, trying to help in her own way.

River winked at Beth. "That's two expert opinions. We're letting it grow."

Beth was distant from most of the group after the blowup. Sullen, and always wandering away, she hardly spoke much, especially after Zac and Teague left. River was certain that she was going to leave as soon as an opportunity presented itself. But that wasn't how it played out. As time passed, Beth came around. As Cash grew stronger, so did Beth in her own way.

When it was time to catch up with Teague and Zac, Beth took part in the planning with enthusiasm. For all intents and purposes, she was a different person. It was refreshing to see. River liked the new Beth, she enjoyed seeing the confidence flow from the younger woman.

"I'm glad the facial hair is gone though," said Beth. "It didn't look like you at all."

River had to agree with that assessment. She didn't much care for the look of facial hair on him.

"Yeah, well, when you're busy, shaving isn't a thing you can do often," defended Teague.

"Well," interjected River. "We're here now and we're taking a long-needed break."

Teague stared at his reflection in the mirror. A distant look in his eyes. "Finn's probably got a full beard by now." A melancholy look spread across his face. "If he goes a week without shaving, he starts lookin' like a mountain man."

The look in his eyes broke River's heart. She wanted to say something to make him feel better, but no words came to mind.

"We should get back out there," he said.

"No," replied River. "Showers, full bellies, and a good night's rest." She looked him directly in the eyes, fighting back the urge to wrap her arms around him and weep. "We got the first two out of the way, that leaves a good night's rest."

Teague shook his head. "One night could mean we miss him."

"Miss him where?" asked Beth. "Do you have any idea where he is?"

"We've been following the path he would've taken based on the train he hopped." seethed Teague.

Cash sauntered up to the mirror. "Let's stick a pin in this conversation." He placed a hand on Beth's shoulder, warning her to stop pushing. "We're all together again, let's enjoy it."

Teague softened. "I haven't told you yet, but you look great." He grinned. "Seems as though the couple's life agrees with you."

River kissed Cash on the cheek as she wrapped her arm around his waist.

He responded by running his hand along the small of her back and kissing her on the forehead.

She leaned close, enjoying the warmth and comfort that emanated from him. She finally understood what she had always read about. The bond, the closeness, it all made sense now. She never wanted to lose this feeling. Her heart ached for Teague just thinking about the pain and loneliness he must be feeling.

The bathroom door burst open with a gush of steam and the chemical scent of cheap hotel soap. Wearing only his boxers, Zac sauntered into the room, a towel draped around his shoulders as he rubbed his hair dry. He leaned into the mirror and ran his fingers through his unruly beard. "Mhm," he sighed. "Even with all this hair, I'm still one hot man."

River chuckled as she shoved him playfully. "You're about to lose most of that hair, brother. I need to see your face again."

"I hate to interrupt this modest conversation," interjected Teague. He pushed the chair over to Zac. "But we should work up a plan for tomorrow." He stepped away. "I got some ideas on where Finn would be heading. With any luck, we might catch up to him."

Through the mirror, Zac and River locked eyes, sharing a silent moment of concern.

"There's plenty of time for that," responded Cash. He placed his hand on Teague's shoulder and gently guided him across the room to the pizza. "You need to eat." He placed a large slice in Teague's hand, then guided him to the closest chair. "Like River said, first food, then sleep, and tomorrow we search."

River turned her focus to Zac. Upon closer inspection, she could see the worried look in his eyes. They all had that same look. They were all concerned that they might never see Finn again. The thought created a stabbing pain in her heart. She wondered if Finn was doing okay. Did he have people around him? Was he cold, alone, and hungry? Or worse, did he do something awful? Was their search futile?

These were questions that kept her awake at night.

"Don't take too much off the top," warned Zac, disrupting River's thoughts.

She smiled. "Okay Bubba," she quipped. "I'll keep you real pretty." She winked.

"Well, that ain't gonna be too hard to do," responded Zac. "Considering what you're working with."

River gave him a brief hug, his natural ability to put people at ease was one of his most endearing qualities. You couldn't help but feel like everything would be okay when he was around. They had a long road ahead, but as long as they were together, they would weather it all just fine. With a happy heart, she quickly went to work on the unruly mass of auburn curls.

Chapter Twelve

"Yo, Finn, tell this fool, I ain't no bank. I don't do credit."

Finn sat perched on the curb, watching as Tigre argued with a customer.

"Come on, I'm good for it," argued the wiry teen. He ran his fingers through his greasy hair, then wiped them on his dirty jeans.

"Yeah, you and everyone else," scoffed Tigre. "This fool thinks he's gonna get over on me." He shoved Finn. "Yo, Homie, am I a bank?"

The banter was interfering with Finn's buzz. He didn't want to be dragged into the stupid conversation. He wanted to be left alone.

It had been a few weeks since landing in LA, honestly, Finn could hardly recall how long it was, the entire time being an endless blur of pills and sleep. Tigre was the first person he made friends with—if you could call their relationship a friendship. Were people ever truly friends with their dealers?

Upon arrival, Finn didn't know where to go or who to hook up with, so he did what came naturally—he walked.

Cities were such awful places, he hated everything about them.

The stench, the overcrowding, the ever-watchful eye of the police or nosy gawkers. Finn couldn't understand why anyone would choose to stay in such a place. Especially if they had other options. His hatred of the urban lifestyle was exactly why he went there. He was sure the others would search for him, so it was best to go someplace they would never consider he would go. Plus, he was guaranteed to have access to plenty of drugs to silence the voices and dull the pain of his shattered soul.

On the first day, he spent the afternoon wandering among the denizens of the city, poaching the odd wallet whenever the chance arose. By the time sunset came along, he had amassed fifty dollars in cold, hard cash. More than enough to cover his needs for a few days. After purchasing a sandwich from a small deli, he set out in search of the one thing that was plentiful in these places. The magic pills that would make one more day above ground tolerable.

With that singular mission in mind, he made his way toward the beach and the boardwalk, where he knew instinctively that the people he needed to find would be gathered.

The area was teeming with people of all ages, sizes, and variations. More than once, he had to swerve out of the way to avoid colliding with someone who wasn't paying attention to their surroundings. This was exactly what he loathed, about people in large settings. The endless parade of faces with the corresponding smell of laundry soap, perfume, cologne, and body odor. It was nauseating.

The mixture of noxious scents made his stomach turn. A headache was brewing; at first a dull throb but slowly it grew into a steady, skull-pounding beat. His nerves were on end, causing his entire body to twitch and tremble. He needed a quiet, out-of-the-way spot to sit and rest. Under the boardwalk, he found just the right space. Hidden away from the throng of humanity, he stepped into the shade and leaned against one of the giant wood pillars, allowing himself to slide down to the soft, warm sand. Arms resting atop his knees, he inhaled, filling his lungs with salty air. To one side, the ocean waves rushed to shore; to the other, a multitude of voices created an endless drone of white noise. Finn glanced up to the clear, blue sky. A memory floated around the edges of his mind, coming closer into view. His mind played a scene, it was the first time he and Teague, accompanied by Cash, had visited the ocean—this very ocean. He could feel the soft, warm sand between his toes. Beside him stood Teague, eyes closed, chin tilted up to the warm, afternoon sun. He turned to face Finn and flashed a warm smile.

Tears stung his eyes; he pinched them shut.

What did you do? The voices berated. *Are you really surprised? You're a loser.*

"Yo, homie," came a weak, raspy voice.

At first, Finn thought it was yet another one of the many voices in his mind, but then he realized he hadn't heard this one before. He peered around the post to find a young Latino laying in the sand. Hand against his side, crimson blood oozed out between his fingers. Sweat soaked his dark hair and streamed down his face, mixing with sand.

"Wanna help me out?" he asked through labored breaths.

Finn glanced around; they were alone. If he got involved, the odds were that things could go horribly wrong. By far, the best decision would be to get up and leave. He turned his focus back to the young man. He didn't appear to be a threat. Finn sighed, knowing he would regret this. "What's your name?" He moved closer.

"El Tigre," replied the man. He held out a bloody hand, then scoffed and let it drop onto the sand.

Finn gestured to the wound Tigre was clutching. "Mind if I get a look?"

"You some sort of medical person?"

"Nah," replied Finn, shaking his head. "But I've personally been the victim of more than a few nasty injuries." He flashed a wry grin.

Tigre chuckled, then coughed. "What's your name?"

"Finn." He lifted Tigre's hand, uncovering a slender stab wound. Blood pumped out to the beat of the young man's pulse. He placed the young man's hand back down atop the gash. "You need a doctor." He scanned the area again in search of any sign that the perpetrator was still around.

"No shit," replied Tigre. "That's why I asked you for help."

"Did you know the guys who did this?" asked Finn.

Tigre shrugged. "It's a hazard of the job. Crazy Bastards always wantin' to take what's not theirs."

"You got someone to call?" asked Finn.

"I thought you were never gonna ask," replied Tigre. "My phone fell out of my pocket. I think it's out there somewhere." He gestured toward the beach.

"Well, then we got a problem," said Finn. "'Cause I don't have a phone."

Tigre scoffed. "Who the hell doesn't have a phone in this day and age?"

Finn shrugged. He climbed to his feet and brushed off his hands. "Where were you out there? Maybe I can find it."

"In the sandy area."

Finn rolled his eyes. "Oh well, that narrows it down considerably." He peered down at the young man's hand, the blood steadily oozing through his fingers. "Keep pressure on that."

He stepped out into the bright sunlight, blinking to adjust his eyes. Scouring the area below his feet, Finn followed what appeared to be footprints that lead away from Tigre. Sure enough, not more than ten yards away, he came upon the phone, half buried in sand, the glass front shattered. Small bags containing pills and powder were scattered nearby. Finn scooped up the bags, stuffed them in his pocket, then brought the device back to Tigre.

"You found it?" asked the young man, his breathing strained.

Finn handed over the device, then knelt aside Tigre, listening. Whoever was on the other end was angry. Finn could hear him shouting curses in Spanish. The entire conversation was in Spanish, all of which Finn understood clearly. However, he pretended to have no idea what was being said. Tigre was a dealer. The man on the phone was his boss, a man who was higher on the food chain. This was a highly organized, very large operation.

Tigre finished the call, then clutched the phone to his chest. "My man is on his way."

"Good to hear," replied Finn. He moved to climb to his feet, but the young man grabbed hold of his arm.

"Stay," he said, nervously. "I'd like some company." A heavy smile spread across his face.

Finn understood. He settled down cross-legged in the sand.

"Can I tell you something?" asked Tigre.

Finn stared and waited.

"Your eyes are freaking me out, vato."

The two shared a welcome chuckle, then once again, the somber mood was back. If Tigre's friends didn't get there soon, he might not make it.

The wait seemed to be hours, the reality, however, was more like twenty minutes.

A sharp whistle called out. "Yo! I found him," a deep male voice bellowed.

A large, muscular man, followed by another, equally large man, made their way under the pier, heading straight for them.

"Hermano," said the first big man. "What the hell happened?"

While the second man inspected Tigre's wound, a conversation about the entire event ensued. Finn did his best to look confused, or at least as though he understood none of it, but he understood all too well what had happened. An attempted robbery gone wrong. Tigre thought he got away, only to be ambushed on the beach where one man stabbed him with a long hunting knife.

The conversation turned to Finn. Tigre explained how he had helped him. This part was tricky because Finn was pretty sure he gave himself away when he perked up at the mention of his name.

The big man turned to him. "I've never seen you before. You just get into town?"

Finn's heart pounded in his chest. These men were not people you wanted to come up against. It took everything he had to restrain his fight-or-flight response. He nodded. "Today."

The big man stared at him for an uncomfortably long time, then suddenly smiled. "My name's Javi." He extended his hand. "Thank you for taking care of my brother."

Finn took the giant paw in his hand.

"This here is Nando." Javi gestured toward the other man. "It's safe to say, our man Tigre owes you his life." He flashed a mischievous grin, then finished in Spanish, "I'm sure we can come up with a way he can pay you back."

Adrenaline shot through Finn's body. The big man knew he understood everything. Electricity coursed through his limbs as his brain screamed at him to run. He swallowed hard.

Javi shook his head, still grinning. "You're a smart one. Don't worry. It's all good. We owe you one. Most people around here would have kept on walking, but you—" A kind expression overcame Javi's face. "You stayed and helped him. That makes you solid in my book."

Finn's pulse calmed, but his mind still told him to leave as fast as possible.

Without another word, Javi and Nando carried Tigre away. Finn collapsed against the pillar and sighed in relief. He pulled a bag from his pocket, inspected the contents, then popped a pill in his mouth. Leaning back, he listened to the soothing sound of the waves crashing against the shore as he waited for his nerves to calm.

A few days later, he ran into Tigre again, standing behind a small trinket shop. As soon as he caught sight of Finn, the young man's face lit up. "Hey, Finn!" he shouted, as he ran up alongside. "You're still around."

Finn nodded.

"I'm glad to see it," said Tigre. "I never had time to thank you." He held out a small bag and shrugged. "It's the least I can do."

Finn took the bag.

"How long are you planning on sticking around?"

"Not sure," shrugged Finn.

Tigre's tone turned conspiratorial. "I got a business proposition for you, if you're willing."

"I'm listening."

Tigre smiled. "How about you stick close and keep an eye out for me? Those other guys snuck up on me. I'd like to avoid that again, you know?"

Finn nodded.

"I'll make it worth your while." Tigre pulled out a roll of bills.

"I'm not sure I'm gonna stick around here much longer."

"Then our agreement will hold as long as you are," replied Tigre.

Finn mulled over the offer. If he was going to stick around for a while, it made sense to have access to a supplier. He agreed, and a deal was struck. From that point on, whenever Tigre was working, Finn was nearby. The steady flow of cash kept him out of potential trouble while the pills and powder kept the voices at bay.

"Yo, get the fuck out of here!" shouted Tigre. He shoved the scrawny teen away. "Don't come back unless you got some cash."

The kid sneered, then skulked away.

Tigre shook his head. "I cannot believe these kids today, man."

Finn snickered. "And you wonder why you got stabbed."

A young man with coal-stained clothes sauntered up. His hair was an unruly mass of dreads, his face covered in piercings with a red line tattooed across the bridge of his nose. Finn tucked his head low; this man was a traveler. He wasn't anyone Finn knew personally, but the community was small. If the others were searching for him, word would be out. Finn didn't want anyone from the community to see him—he didn't want to be found.

The traveler made his purchase, then wandered off to rejoin his friends who were standing close by.

"Correct me if I'm wrong," said Tigre. "But it looks like that dude made you nervous. Someone you know?"

Finn shook his head, eyes still locked on the ragtag group walking away.

"I'll take that as a maybe," said Tigre.

Finn considered his predicament. He had forgotten that riders like to travel through SoCal, especially the beach area. The warm air, free camping and abundant substances made this a prime stop for wandering types. The longer he remained stationary in this particular place, the more likely he would be spotted. Perhaps it was time for him to move on. But where?

He thought his best bet was to head further into a city. One that didn't have a heavy population of travelers this time of year. One where he could disappear, yet still be able to get the drugs he needed to tame his mind. San Francisco.

Finn climbed to his feet and turned to Tigre. "I think it's time for me to move on."

"What? I thought we had a deal, homie," said Tigre genuinely confused.

Finn nodded. "Yeah, but I need to head out."

Tigre cast a glance in the direction where the travelers had wandered. "So, you did know them?" He nodded.

"No," replied Finn, shaking his head. "But I know others who could run into them. It's time for me to leave."

"I get it," replied Tigre. "It sucks, but I get it." He handed Finn some cash with three pill packets tucked inside. "If you come back this way, look me up."

Finn smiled. "If anyone ever comes around looking for me—"

"Do I look like a rat?" interjected Tigre. He grinned. "Finn who?"

"Good man," said Finn.

After a brief handshake, Finn wandered off toward the highway where he thumbed a ride from a trucker heading north to San Francisco.

Chapter Thirteen

"GIVE ME SOME GOOD NEWS," said Shane, dropping heavily into his chair. Derrick's folder with all the information about Finn sat atop the desk blotter, dog-eared and worn. Over the past few weeks, Shane had devoured all the info in the folder. He read and reread the documents, studied the pictures, and memorized every detail. His son was alive, but he might as well not be. In many ways, knowing the boy was alive but out of reach was far more heartbreaking than when Shane believed he was dead. There were few things in this world Shane loathed, more than being powerless.

Manny lit a cigarette, took a drag, and exhaled. "I wish I had some for you, brother." He sighed. "Unfortunately, I got none."

"Any word from Derrick?"

Manny shook his head. "At least nothing more than we heard the other day." He took a drag and exhaled. "The woman disappeared." He snapped his fingers. "One day she just up and left."

Shane scoffed. "I'll bet Daniel got to her." He stared down at the folder. "He lived with her long enough to have a list of reasons a mile wide to off her. Lord knows, there's probably an army of people who want her dead."

"She sounds like a real winner," replied Manny.

"Don't even get me started."

Manny chuckled. "Don't hate me for this, but I'm not too sad she did some things she did." He paused and grinned mischievously. "If she hadn't done you the way she did, we'd have never met."

Shane scoffed. "Don't take this the wrong way, but I'm not too sure that was a worthwhile tradeoff."

"You mock," defended Manny. "But I believe things happen for a reason."

"And what was the reason behind this fucked up mess?"

Manny shrugged. "The Lord's gonna do what the Lord's gonna do. We can't know his mind. Someday, all this is gonna make sense."

"Now you sound like Father Killoran," scoffed Shane.

"Father Killoran." Manny exhaled loudly and leaned back in his chair. "Now that is a name I haven't heard in a long time." He chuckled. "We did him dirty more than a few times."

"Poor, naive bastard," replied Shane. "He was hell-bent on saving me from myself." He shook his head and sighed. "Let's hope wherever he is now, he ain't dealing with people like us anymore."

"Last I heard of him," said Manny. "He set up shop in San Fran. He said his role in life was to save as many lost souls as possible."

Shane chuckled. "Well, let's hope he's gotten better at it. He sure as hell didn't do much for us."

A gentle tap at the door interrupted their banter.

"Yeah!" shouted Shane.

The door creaked open and Mari stepped forward. "The delivery guy is here. He needs a signature."

"I got it, boss," said Manny. He stood up and stretched, cracking his back. "You know, I used to have Father K's number. I might just call him and see what he's up to."

"You do that, Manny," replied Shane.

The door closed, sealing out all the noise from the bar, leaving

Shane alone at his desk, just him, the worn-out folder, and the buzzing sound of the overhead lights. His eyes scanned the wall of monitors. It was early, so the bar was empty. Aside from a couple of regulars, Mari and Manny, things were calm. He let his eyes wander to the collage of photographs hanging on the other wall, pinned there as a reminder that Finn was alive.

Shane leaned back in his chair and stared up at the ceiling. A deep sense of unease grew stronger each day that passed without news. He knew something awful had to happen that resulted in the Cash kid being shot. But what happened to Finn? What happened to the other one, Teague? Who beat him so badly? All these unanswered questions grated on Shane's nerves. Loose strings and unanswered questions made his eye twitch.

He slid open the bottom drawer of his desk and pulled out a metal box. Inside were the only reminders of the life he left behind so many years ago. The items collected from the old man's house, his marriage certificate to Melody, a single dog tag, and the ultrasound print out of his son. He ran his finger over the image, remembering the last time he saw Melody.

⚜ ⚜ ⚜ ⚜ ⚜

On leave for one week between boot camp and infantry school, Shane sat with Melody on the big front porch, swaying gently in the warm summer breeze.

"How about Shane Michael Ryan the second?" asked Melody. Her hand unconsciously rubbed her belly.

Shane chuckled. "Does that mean our daughter would be named Melody Ann Ryan." He held up his hand and made an air quote gesture. "The second."

"That's silly," replied Melody. "No." She stared down at her belly. "Come to think of it, our other sons might feel left out."

85

"Other sons?" Shane cocked an eyebrow. "You say that like you're expecting to have more."

Melody giggled. "Oh, we're having more. Lots more." She held out her hands. "A whole army of our own. Boys and girls." She placed a soft hand on his chin and kissed his cheek. "All of them with eyes just like their Papa."

Shane sighed. "Let's just get through this one first, then we can talk about our army."

"I got it!" Melody snapped her fingers. "How about Finnegan Shane Ryan? We can give all the boys your first name as their middle name."

"Only if we do the same for all the girls, with your name."

"Deal," agreed Melody, flashing the sweetest smile. Her eyes went wide. "Oh!" she shouted. She grabbed Shane's hand and placed it on her belly. "Feel that? It seems as though our baby boy approves of his name."

A small body glided beneath his hand. It was a shocking yet beautiful feeling. He imagined a tiny hand, or foot, pressed against his. His baby boy was in there. Healthy and strong, he was already with them, sitting on that sunny porch. A gentle kick from inside the womb startled Shane. He pulled his hand away and stared down at his palm, the sensation of his son's movement forever imprinted on his soul. For the first time, the reality settled in. He was a father.

⋇—⋇—⋇—⋇—⋇

The door to the office swung open.

"Dad, look what I made!" Gabriella ran into the office, her wavy, brown hair pulled back into a tight ponytail.

She peered up at him with eyes that mirrored his own and smiled. "I made this in school today." The little girl held a picture out for him.

"Alright, let me see this masterpiece of yours," said Shane. The painting was of five figures holding hands, two large, one man and a woman, two slightly smaller, male and female and one small girl in the center, her hair tied back in a ponytail. All holding hands, smiling. "This is beautiful, Gabby," said Shane.

"I added Finn," she replied proudly.

Shane smiled. "I see that, I also see you made sure everyone's eyes are accurate."

Gabby smiled and stood tall. She strolled over to the wall of photos and pulled one down. "Is he gonna come home soon?"

"We're working on it, sweetie," said Cat, as she took the photo from the little girl's hand and put it back on the wall.

Gabby spun on her heels and climbed up on Shane's lap. "I hope he's here before Christmas. I have a great idea for a present for him."

Shane swallowed. "Me too, princess. Me too. I'll tell you what." He lifted the little girl in his arms and walked over to the wall. "Let's hang this right here with all the other photos. That way I can look up and see all y'all in one place."

Gabby beamed, as together, they placed her artwork on the wall.

"Okay, Mija, let's leave your father to his work." Catalina leaned close and planted a peck on Shane's cheek. "Don't stay too late," she whispered.

He hugged the little girl and kissed Catalina goodbye. A moment later, he sat alone, once again, just him, his memories, and a bunch of photographs.

Chapter Fourteen

T HE COOL MOUNTAIN BREEZE CARRIED THE SOFT SCENT OF DECAYING LEAVES AND PINE NEEDLES. River always loved the smell of mountain air in late autumn. It was the best time of year to travel. The days were comfortable, and nights were the perfect temperature to snuggle up in front of a warm fire. She breathed in, relishing the cool, fragrant air pouring into her lungs.

The door to the motel room creaked open, Cash stepped outside carrying two, red plastic cups. He flashed an adorable, crooked smile, then strolled over to join her by the pool.

"What's everybody doing inside?" she asked.

Cash handed her a cup. "The usual." He shrugged. "Zac convinced Beth to play a round of poker with him." He chuckled. "She sucks as bad as he does."

"How's Teague doing?"

"Same." Cash removed his shoes and strolled over to the pool.

"I wouldn't do that if I were you," warned River.

He sat on the edge of the pool and dipped his feet into the cool water. "It's not that cold."

River giggled. "I wasn't talking about the water temp." She pointed. "I was talking about the dead squirrel floating over there."

Cash jumped to his feet and took a seat in the chair beside her. "Lounge chair, it is then," he said, with a visible tremble to his body.

They sat quietly, listening to the gurgle of the water, basking in one another's company. It was the quiet times like these when River felt her love for Cash the most. The fact they could spend hours just sitting alongside one another, doing absolutely nothing, was one of her favorite things. Of course, their lovemaking was unmatched, and she loved his jokes and playfulness. She wondered why it took her so long to acknowledge her feelings for him. A pang of guilt overcame her as she thought about Finn and Teague. They once had this same sort of relationship. Their ease with one another was something River could only dream of having. Her dreams had been answered, and theirs seem to have been dashed.

She didn't say it out loud, but with each passing day, her hope of ever finding Finn had died. The feeling that all their efforts were futile, that they would never know what became of him, had settled deep in her bones. She tried not to think too much on it, for fear it would prompt her to voice it aloud. That would kill Teague, she understood that well. He needed to keep looking, or at least feel as though they were looking. He needed to cling to the hope that they would find Finn.

River looked over at Cash, she knew how she would feel if he suddenly disappeared one day, and she never wanted to know that sort of pain.

Cash smiled at her. "Whatcha thinkin'?"

"Teague," she replied, fighting back tears.

"Yeah, I hear ya." He took her hand in his, then leaned over and kissed her on the forehead. "I wish I could say it's gonna be alright." He shook his head. "But I don't know."

"I know. I think I've known for a while now."

"When we got off that train and saw Teague that first time after weeks out here." He paused and swallowed. "I think I knew then."

River nodded. "I didn't want to consider it, so I did my best to ignore it." She glanced over at the door to the motel room, then back at Cash. "We're wasting our time. Aren't we?"

Cash sighed and nodded. "I don't think we're gonna find Finn." He stared down at his feet. "Of all the people I've ever known, Finn is the one person I know, without a doubt, could disappear forever and no one would be able to find him."

"It's eating Teague up inside," said River.

"I know." He placed a gentle hand against her cheek. "If anything ever happened to you, I'd feel the same way."

She kissed his hand, then pulled away. "I'm worried about Teague."

"Same."

"He doesn't eat or drink unless I force him. He doesn't sleep until he's so exhausted, he's gonna collapse. He's lost so much weight—"

"I know," replied Cash. "He's in hell right now."

"We need to get him out of his own head."

Cash shook his head. "We can't. There's nothing we can do that'll pull him out of this. He has to do it on his own."

"And what if he can't? What if he keeps falling and we lose him, too?" River stopped abruptly; she could hardly believe she allowed those words to escape her mouth.

"Look," said Cash. He sat up and took her hand. "I don't know how this is gonna play out. I'm hoping for a happy ending where Finn is found, he and Teague make up and things get back to the way they used to be." He kissed her hand. "I'm not so sure that's possible anymore. All we can do is stay strong for Teague and be there for him when he needs us."

"This is so wrong."

"I know," he replied.

Saying the words out lout, hearing Cash say in his own way that he agreed with her, that it was hopeless, was too much. The levee had broken. River no longer had the strength to pretend things were going to be okay. Grief, anger and heartache roiled inside, churning and churning out of control. She leaned into Cash's chest and let loose a torrent of tears.

Chapter Fifteen

"We should head west," Beth suggested. "To LA or San Francisco."

"That's stupid," scoffed Teague. "Finn hates big cities, especially those two. He says they're too busy and filthy."

"He's got a point," said Zac, rubbing his chin.

The door opened with a gush of crisp night air. River strolled into the room, followed by Cash. Her face was pink and blotchy, as though she had been crying.

"Got a point about what?" asked River, plopping herself down on a bed.

"I say we head west," replied Beth. "We should go to a city like San Francisco." She pointed to Teague. "He says there's no way Finn would go there."

River looked around the room. "I'm inclined to agree with Teague. I don't think Finn would go near a big city. For sure, not San Francisco."

Teague stood up. "He wouldn't," he stated. "He's hidin' in the woods somewhere. That's the only place he'd go."

Beth was tired of this whole charade. For weeks they played

along with Teague's imaginings. She stood by and followed along like a good, little friend as they rode from one desolate forest to another, always in search of someone who didn't even want them to find him. She was done playing along. Life was too short for this. If the others wouldn't put a stop to this ridiculous charade, she would. She climbed to her feet.

"I say we head to Los Angeles or San Francisco," she stated, with much more force.

"I already told you," replied Teague. "He ain't in either of those places."

Beth placed her hands on her hips. "How are you so sure?"

Teague spun around to face her. "Because I know him. He hates cities, he would never go there."

"Maybe you don't know him as well as you think you do," snapped Beth.

"What the fuck does that mean?"

"I mean," she stated, holding her ground. "That maybe you have no clue where he'd go. Maybe the person you thought you knew wasn't the real Finn after all." Beth glanced around at the others. "Maybe you're all wrong about him."

A round of protests erupted.

Beth stood firm. One way or another, this wild goose chase was ending.

"Okay Beth," said Zac, calmly. "Let's hear why you think he'd be out west."

Teague scoffed and stomped toward the vanity. His back to the room, he watched through the mirror.

"If I wanted to hide from everyone I know," replied Beth slowly. "I'd make it a point to go to the one place they would think I'd never go. Y'all just said he'd never go to LA or San Francisco."

Cash and River nodded.

"Then that's exactly where I would go," said Beth. She folded her arms. "Because it would be the last place anyone would search for me."

"That's stupid," scoffed Teague.

At this point, Teague was useless. He was the last person any of them should listen to. Beth noted the facial expressions of everyone else. Zac leaned against the wall, rubbing his chin, contemplating her point while River and Cash shot glances back and forth in that annoying way that couples do, using their own private language. Oh, how the two of them grated on Beth's nerves. There was a time when she hoped they would finally admit their feelings for one another, that they would be the couple they both wanted to be. Who would have guessed they'd become the same annoying couple like everyone else.

"How is it stupid?" demanded Beth.

Teague spun around and flailed his arms wide. "Because it is! You don't know shit about Finn."

That was it. Beth was done being insulted and berated. She was done chasing after a person who didn't want to be found. If she were being honest about it, she didn't really want to find Finn. After all, the last time she saw him, he tried to kill her.

"I know plenty about him," replied Beth. The sharpness of her tone surprised herself. "I know he's the son of a monster. A maniac who tried to kill us all." She stepped forward. "I know he's exactly like the man who raised him. He's violent, untrustworthy and sick." She tapped the side of her head with her index finger. "He's selfish and a narcissist. He left his friends in the dust without a second thought when we needed him most."

Teague moved close. "Shut the fuck up, Beth!" he seethed.

"No! I'm not gonna shut up!" shouted Beth. "I'm done being quiet. I'm done following your insane ass all over the countryside from one freezing cold, hillbilly place to another. I'm done playing along with you!" She jabbed a finger in the center of Teague's chest. "You need to face reality. And it starts with you admitting that you couldn't control your feral pet. He lost his shit and attacked not only you but me, too." Beth nodded toward River. "He went after River too."

"I don't want him back," she continued. "I'm sick of wasting my life searching for someone that I couldn't care less about. He's not worth my time." She locked eyes with Teague. "He doesn't want to be with you. The sooner you accept that—"

"Fatras!" shouted Teague's as his hand crashed down on the side of her head, sending Beth careening to the floor. He glared at her with cold, rage-filled eyes.

Zac stepped up and pulled him away.

Beth's face stung; she rubbed her cheek. She could hardly believe it, but here she was again. This time, instead of Finn, it was Teague. Hot, seething rage erupted in her gut, burning through her entire body. She jumped to her feet, grabbed hold of the ceramic lamp on the table, lifted it high and brought it down hard over Teague's head. He collapsed to his knees; blood trickled down the side of his face.

Cash kneeled beside Teague, trying to get a look at the injury.

"Beth! What the fuck?!" demanded River. She charged forward, balled her hand into a fist and swung, hitting Beth directly on the side of her mouth.

Beth stumbled back and wiped the blood away with the back of her hand. "Poor River," she seethed. "You think you're so special. That the whole world revolves around you." Beth paused, holding back hot tears of rage. "All you want is for all the guys to want you." She stepped close, her face mere inches from River's. "You aren't special. You're just another ho."

River moved to punch her again, but this time Beth was ready. She blocked the blow and grabbed a handful of blonde dreads, then yanked as hard as she could. To her surprise, River responded with a full-body blow, slamming Beth against the wall with a loud oof, knocking the air from her lungs. Followed immediately by several solid punches to the side of her head. Unable to fend off the assault, Beth closed her eyes and covered her head with her arms.

"Let go of me!" shouted River.

Beth opened her eyes to see Cash, his arms wrapped tightly around River, pinning her arms to her sides. He stepped back across the room, River flailing and bucking. A string of curses flew from her mouth, one after another.

Zac moved toward Beth.

She backed up. "Don't touch me!"

He held his hands up and paused.

Beth wiped a trickle of blood from her nose. Her head aching from a dozen tiny spots all over. "I'm done with this shit!" she shouted. "Fuck this!" She turned to Zac. "And fuck you!"

Zac reached a hand toward her, but Beth was having none of it. She lurched her arm away, out of his reach.

"I said, don't touch me!"

"You need to calm down," warned Zac.

"What?!" demanded Beth. "Calm down?" She glared at Zac. "You fucking calm down!" She gestured toward River, who was still struggling against Cash. "Why don't you fucking tell that to the rabid bitch."

River broke free and sprinted for Beth.

Zac stepped between the two, using his body to block River's momentum.

"Get out of my way!" shouted River blind rage in her eyes.

Cash grabbed her from behind again, only to have her rear back and slam her head against his face. Blood erupted from his nose. "Zac! Get her out of here!" He clung to River, trying desperately to maintain his hold.

Zac lunged down and lifted Beth over his shoulder. He carried her outside, kicking and flailing. As soon as the door closed behind him, he put her down.

Beth shoved him with all her body weight. He barely moved. Hands balled up in fists, she pounded against his chest. Hot tears ran down her cheeks. "Fuck you! Fuck all of you!"

Zac didn't respond. He stood silent, calm in that maddening way he had. This only served to further enrage Beth. "Why are you taking her side on this?! You know damn well that I'm right." She sniffled and wiped her face, hating the fact she was crying. With a long sigh, Beth stepped away, plopping herself on the curb.

Zac sat down beside her, still silent.

The air felt cool against her sweat-soaked clothes, sending a chill up her spine. "You know I'm right," she insisted. "You're never going to find Finn."

Zac nodded. "Least not until he wants to be found."

His matter-of-fact response surprised her. "Then why? Why encourage Teague?" asked Beth. "Why let him drag us all over the place for something even you admit ain't happening?"

"Because he's my brother. He's hurting, and he's lost." Zac breathed heavily. "He needs us right now."

"How is encouraging his delusions helping him?" asked Beth.

Zac stared out into the distance. "It's what he needs right now." He shrugged. "I'm not sure if it's the right thing to do or not. But it's all we can do for him."

"You should tell him the truth."

"People don't hear things they don't wanna hear, no matter who's telling them." He sighed. "When he's ready, he'll listen. Not a moment before."

"It's all so stupid," said Beth. "Why wait around for that? Why waste your time? Don't you want to move on?"

"From what?"

"From this." Beth waved her arms. "From all of this. It's depressing." She shifted her body to face Zac. "Don't you just want to have fun again?"

"Life ain't much fun without the people you love—without your family."

"So, find a new family," suggested Beth. "Head out with me. We'll create our own family. A new one. A better one."

He shook his head. "Family ain't something you can crumple up, toss away and remake whenever you want. The people you love aren't disposable." He stood up. "They're not replaceable." He turned around and stared down at Beth. "I'm not leaving my family." He paused. "Are they messed up right now? Yeah." He nodded. "Are things ever gonna get back to the way they used to be?" He shook his head. "I don't know. Either way, I'm not going anywhere."

"I can't stay," blurted Beth. Fresh tears sprung forth, running down her cheeks. "I'm leaving."

Zac nodded, a solemn look on his face. "You gotta do what's best for you." He turned and walked back inside the motel room, leaving Beth alone outside.

She sat on the curb and sobbed uncontrollably. The truth about it all finally set in, she was the outsider—she always would be. No matter what she did or how much time she spent with the group, she would never be family. Even now, they worried more about Finn than they did about her. They cared more about the person who attacked them and ran away than they ever would for her. With calm resolve, she wiped the tears from her face and told herself that come morning, she was heading out on her own.

Chapter Sixteen

"Ah!" shouted Teague through gritted teeth. He couldn't decide which was worse, the pinch of the needle or the feeling of thread being pulled through his flesh. River was doing her best to be gentle, but from time to time, her emotions would get the best of her and she would pull a little too fast, or tie the stitch a little too tight.

"Shh, shh," she whispered. "I'm sorry this is taking so long. I'm not as good at it as you are."

"I'm okay," replied Teague, wincing as the needle punched through the skin one more time. "Just take your time."

"Stupid, selfish bitch," mumbled River. "I should've never fought so hard for her to come along."

"She's just speaking her mind," interjected Zac, as he entered the room. "She has every right to say her piece."

As he closed the door behind him, Teague took note that Beth didn't return with Zac. He agreed with River about Beth. Perhaps things would have been better if she never joined their group. Daniel would've never found them without her stupid videos. On top of that, it was her big mouth that pushed Finn over the edge.

If she wasn't there, poking and prodding, he would've never gone off. He would be there with them all right now, where he belonged. Beth was the outsider. She was the one who didn't belong in their family. Finn was right all along. Beth would never be one of them.

"No one cares what's on her mind," replied River. "That girl needs to learn to keep her mouth shut sometimes."

A sharp pain erupted in Teague's head as another stitch was pulled a little too hard. "Ouch!" he shouted. "You know, I can do this myself." He went to stand, only to have a firm hand placed on his shoulder, forcing him to remain in the seat.

"I've got this," stated River. "Stay put. We're almost done."

Zac pulled up a chair. He grabbed a bottle of beer, popped the cap, then straddled the seat, resting his arms atop the chair back. He took a long drink from the bottle, then peered at Teague. His face was a mask of concern. "How bad is it?"

"Bad enough," replied River.

"Just a few stitches," responded Cash, holding a blood-stained hand towel against his face.

"Five. Five stitches," stated River. She cut the thread and stepped back. "That's five unnecessary stitches. Five things that shouldn't have happened." She crossed her arms.

"How're you feeling?" Zac asked Teague.

"Now that she's done fixin' me up, I feel fine." Teague smiled at River.

"How's Beth?" asked Cash.

Zac sighed. "She wants to leave."

"Good!" exclaimed River.

Teague studied Zac's expression. Deep inside, he agreed with River, good riddance to Beth and all the drama she brought with her. He held back speaking or showing any emotion because he wasn't sure how Zac was feeling about it all.

Truth be told, he didn't want Beth to stay. If she left on her own, that made things easier on him and everyone else. He was pretty sure that Finn wouldn't want to be around her, so for that sake alone, it was best she leave.

"What are your feelings on it all, Zac?" asked Cash.

Zac stared down at the bottle in his hand. "I told her it's her choice." He glanced around the room. "It's probably best for everyone." He emptied the bottle in one gulp. "Honestly, I'm up for whatever has less drama."

Cash chuckled. "I'm up for anything that doesn't end with my nose bleeding."

River scoffed and hit him playfully. "Next time, don't get in the middle of things." She kissed him on the cheek. "You're lucky it wasn't worse."

"Oh, I'm sure of that," replied Cash, wrapping his arm around her waist.

"It'll be a relief for Finn when he gets back and sees she's gone," said Teague.

The room fell silent, the others passing glances back and forth. They didn't have to say it out loud, Teague knew exactly what they were thinking. Every time he brought up Finn, they would pass that same look around. It annoyed him.

Zac stood up abruptly and walked over to the small fridge. He pulled out another beer and gestured to Teague. "Want one?"

Teague shook his head. He wanted something much stronger—something to take the sting of his fresh stitches away. He reached into his pack and pulled out a small envelope of pills.

"How many more of those you got?" asked River.

Teague shrugged. He dumped the contents in the palm of his hand and counted. "Four." Then he swallowed one dry as River watched with a concerned look on her face. "What?" he asked.

"You've been taking those pretty regularly lately," she replied. "I'm just wondering if it might be time to stop taking them."

"Are you implying I have a problem?" asked Teague, irritated.

Silence.

Anger bubbled up inside him. "Well, I don't." Teague locked eyes with them all, one by one. He tapped the side of his head. "In case y'all forgot, I just had a lamp smashed against my skull."

"And earlier today?" pressed River. "What was the reason, then?"

"Mais la!" blurted Teague. "How is me taking a pill now and then an issue? How is it any different from the amount of flower Cash has been smoking lately?"

"Hey now," interjected Cash. "Don't drag me into this."

"Look, baby," said River, her voice suddenly soft. She walked over to Teague and wrapped her arms around him. "I love you. I'm just a little concerned about you." She stared him in the eyes. "You can get mad at me for questioning you, but know this—" She smiled. "I worry about you because I love you."

Teague's anger melted staring into River's eyes. He buried his head against her neck and hugged her. A torrent of emotions churned their way to the surface. Confusion, doubt, anger, and sorrow bubbled and frothed. Something inside snapped, opening the flood-gates. He hugged River tightly and sobbed.

The room was silent. Cash and Zac stood locked in place as River held him close.

"Shh, shh, shh, it's okay," she whispered.

Teague pulled away and wiped his face. He hadn't cried like that in weeks, he wasn't even sure where it came from, he was pretty sure he cried himself out long ago. "I'm sorry I got angry with you," he said to River.

A loving smile spread across her face. River reached up and gently wiped a tear from his cheek. "It's okay, baby. I understand." She gestured to Zac and Cash. "We all understand."

"Yeah, brother," said Zac. "We get it."

Teague sunk heavily onto the edge of the bed. He leaned forward and raked his fingers through his hair. Tears continued to well up in his eyes. He couldn't stop himself. No matter how hard he fought to hold them back, more tears came—an endless flow of them, it seemed.

"Sometimes I can't breathe," he said aloud. "It's like my throat closes up on me, so tight I can't get any air through." He hung his head low and stared down at the floor. "And then there're other times I get so angry." He balled his hand into a fist. "I wanna strike out." He shook his head. "Or run away." Teague glanced around the room. "I feel like I'm losing my mind."

River kneeled on the floor in front of him, her big green eyes staring up at him with nothing but pure love. "Baby." She took his hand in hers. "You're not losing your mind." She touched his cheek with her soft hand. "What you're feeling is your broken heart. And what you're going through is natural reaction to that."

Teague stared at River, her expression full of love and understanding. He looked over at Zac, who responded with a curt nod. Then to Cash, who smiled and nodded. "Why do y'all put up with me?"

"It's a family thing," replied Zac.

"We're not going anywhere," added Cash.

The tears subsided, followed by a deep sense of hopelessness. "What if we never find him?" The words poured out of his mouth. For the first time since the whole nightmare began, he uttered the words he was most terrified of speaking aloud.

The others looked on in silence. No one moved.

"It's been way too long," continued Teague. "We haven't seen a sign of him. No one has." His soul ached. "What if he's dead?"

"That's not—" attempted Zac.

"You know damn well it's possible!" shouted Teague. He stared at Zac, then turned to River, pleading.

River said nothing, instead, she wrapped her arms around him and held him close.

Their silence told Teague they all secretly agreed with his darkest thoughts. This only heightened his anguish. His heart raced, it was difficult to breathe. He pinched his eyes to hold back more tears. "Sometimes I think it would be easier if he was just dead." He sighed. "Because the alternative is that he's gone because he doesn't want to be with us anymore." Tears streamed down his cheeks. "He doesn't want to be with me." His voice broke with each word.

Zac sat alongside him, wrapping a muscular arm around Teague's shoulder. "That ain't it," he whispered. "Brother, if there is one thing I know without any doubt, it's that Finn loves you with all his heart. You two are connected." He smiled. "I promise you that wherever he is, he's feeling your absence. He's in pain."

"That doesn't make me feel better," said Teague.

Zac chuckled. "I suppose not. But you needed to hear it."

Teague looked around. "So, what do we do now? Do we keep lookin'? Do we get on with our lives?"

Cash stepped forward. "We keep going. But maybe we stop now and then and have some fun." He shrugged. "You know, to remind ourselves that life is more than struggles."

River nodded. "I agree," she said. "We keep our eyes open, but we take time to live."

Teague nodded.

"I want you to know that I absolutely believe we're gonna find him," said Zac.

Teague smiled pathetically. "How else are you gonna beat his ass?"

"Exactly!" stated Zac, with a grin.

Chapter Seventeen

A COOL BREEZE RUSTLED THE LEAVES, moving the tree limbs just enough to glimpse the full moon hanging overhead. Beth and Zac hunched low, hidden among the brush as they waited for the next train.

The others were determined to continue searching for Finn. Beth simply couldn't bring herself to care what happened to him, let alone burn another day of her life searching for the person who tried to kill her. She had no other choice than to head out on her own. She knew the ropes—how to catch on, hop off and everything in between. She didn't need the group. It was time for her to move on.

River, Cash and Teague chose to stay behind at the hotel rather than come see her off. Though not a surprise, their decision still stung a little. Sure, she expected a cold shoulder from Teague, truth be told, she didn't care what he thought or did. He was just like Finn. As far as Beth was concerned, both could disappear, and she wouldn't miss them.

As for Cash, he was much closer to the others than he was to Beth. Sure, he got along with her, and she had no complaints about him. In the end, he would do whatever River wanted him to do. It was almost sad how completely he had given himself over to her.

It was River's snub that hurt the most. After all, they had been to one another. River was the older sister that Beth never had. There was an unspoken bond between them—or so Beth thought. Apparently, she was wrong, and the bond only went one way. Well, as far as Beth was concerned, it was better to find out now than later. As much as the truth hurt, it was best she knew and could get on with her life.

A world of traveling adventures awaited.

The plan was to catch a ride on a train heading south. Her goal was to get to Houston, then hop east through New Orleans and on to Florida. Once there, she would hop a quick ride down to Tampa, where she planned on spending the winter. Several months ago, during happier times, she met a couple of riders at a camp. They swapped contact info and stayed in touch. When she decided to leave the Nomads, Beth reached out and found that the duo was in Tampa and intended to stay there through winter. They invited her to join them, and of course, she jumped at the opportunity. She always loved the beach; it was going to be wonderful to spend a couple of months there. When she closed her eyes, she could almost smell the salty air and feel the warm breeze against her skin.

"You got everything?" asked Zac, his deep voice cutting through the darkness.

Beth nodded. "Yeah, I do."

"Who're these guys you're meeting up with again?"

"We met them a long time ago, way before everything. You remember, we were at a camp outside of Salem."

Zac shook his head. "I don't—"

Beth sighed. "That's right, you were too busy making out with tattoo girl." She rolled her eyes.

A sly smile spread across his face. "Now her, I remember." He looked at Beth. "I don't recall your two friends."

"Oh well," shrugged Beth. "Why do you care so much, anyway?"

A sad expression crossed his face, making Beth regret her words.

"Because I care about you," he replied.

Beth stood silent, trying to think of words to say.

Zac continued, "I just want to make sure you'll be okay. And that you're not hitching up with some losers."

It made Beth sad to hear him say those words. She decided to leave because she assumed none of them cared about her. Of course, she knew Zac was not like that, but it was easier to leave if she kept him in the same group with the others. Hearing him say he cared, complicated things. It made her want to stay. She brushed those feelings aside. The others didn't want her as much as she didn't want them. She stared at Zac, the moonlight cast its glow over his face. She was going to miss him. An inkling of regret settled in her heart.

"I meant what I said earlier," she said.

"Meant what?"

"That you should come with me. That we can travel and have fun and make another family. A better one." Beth studied his reaction. "No more pretending to care about Finn or worrying about his crazy father—"

"I don't pretend to care about Finn," interrupted Zac, a slight tone of anger in his voice. "And Daniel's dead. I killed him with my own two hands." He looked down at his hands, then back up at Beth. "And he ain't Finn's real father. Teague—"

"Whatever," blurted Beth. Anger rose inside her. Hearing him make excuses only solidified her resolve that leaving was the right choice.

The train whistle blew, calling out in the night. It was time to go. Beth donned her pack.

"Okay, so you know the rules about riding," said Zac.

Beth nodded, adrenaline pumping through her veins. This would be her first solo hop. Her first ride without the Nomads. Excited and a little scared, she readied herself.

"And Beth," Zac grabbed hold of her arm. "This isn't goodbye."

A sudden flush of sadness washed over her. In that instant, she realized she would miss this giant, redheaded fool more than anything. Oh, why couldn't he have left things where they were? Unable to hold back her tears, she reached up and touched his face. "Come with me," she said.

He pulled her hand away, slowly shaking his head.

The train rolled past. First the engines, then came the grainers. Five cars, seven—it was time. Beth leaped forward and wrapped her arms around Zac, hugging him tightly. "Okay, this is not goodbye," she whispered.

"You got my number," he said. "Stay in touch."

Beth stepped back and adjusted her pack. She gave a curt salute, then turned and ran alongside the train. She grabbed hold of the handrail at the back of a grainer and effortlessly pulled herself aboard. Once on, she put her pack down and peered out, back to where Zac was standing. He gave one last wave, then ducked back into the trees.

Alone, with her thoughts, the cool night air and the sound of the train rolling along the tracks, Beth reveled in her success. Her first solo hop went off without a hitch. She was born for this. She didn't need anyone. She pulled out her phone, opened her social media app and relaunched Nomad Girl. Her first post, was a selfie of her making a silly face, holding two fingers in the air. "Your girl's back y'all. Houston, here I come."

Chapter Eighteen

"THIS WAY! HE'S DOWN HERE."

After almost two decades working with homeless kids in San Francisco, Father Killoran had so many run-ins with the denizens of the street, he adopted the hard rule to not follow anyone down dark, secluded alleys. When Aidan ran up to him, desperate for help, the priest brushed aside his suspicions and followed without a second thought. After all, Aidan was a unique case.

Small of frame, timid and sad, that was the best way to describe the teen. He showed up one day while Father Killoran was out doing his rounds. Two of the more seasoned members of the streets had trapped the skinny kid between them and were shoving him back and forth like a couple of cats toying with their prey. As soon as the larger duo saw the priest, they stopped what they were doing and took off running.

Aidan tried to put up a strong facade, but Father Killoran knew better. Without help, this kid wouldn't make it very long in the harsh world he had found himself. From that moment on, the priest vowed he would keep this child safe and maybe one day, Aidan would find his way back home.

Over the years, Father K, as the kids called him, had seen his fair share of desperate teens randomly appear on the streets. Alone, cold and angry, helping these kids was the old priest's mission in life. It was his calling to take care of them, to keep them safe and try to shepherd them back home or back into the world, away from whatever demons forced them to run.

The farther they walked down the narrow passage, the darker the alley grew. Father K's nerves were on high alert. "Aidan, this had better not be a wild goose chase."

"It isn't," assured Aidan. "Come on."

A rat scurried out from behind a dumpster. The fetid stench of a week's worth of garbage permeated the air.

Aidan stopped abruptly and spun around. "Right here!" he blurted.

A young man, or at least it appeared to be a young man, it was hard to tell in the dim light, sat huddled on the ground. Back against the wall, his arms wrapped tightly around his legs. He didn't look up when Father Killoran came near.

"What happened?" asked the priest.

"Some rich lady bought me a sandwich," explained Aidan. "I went to the park to eat it, but ran into a couple of guys." The teen shook his head. "I've never seen them before. Anyway, they jumped me." Aidan glanced down at the pathetic being on the ground. "He came out of nowhere and stepped in to help me." Aidan raked his fingers through his hair. "They stabbed him."

Father Killoran made the sign of the cross, muttered a silent prayer and kneeled before the young man. "Can you hear me?"

No reply.

"My name is Father Killoran."

Nothing.

"I'd like to help you, if you'll allow it."

Silence.

The priest cleared his throat and moved closer. He had more than his fair share of run-ins with scared, injured young men. Much like feral animals, one had to approach with extreme caution because at any moment, they could, and most likely would, attack out of a sense of self-preservation.

He reached out a tentative hand. "May I have a look at your wound?"

The young man flinched.

"Come on, Finn," pleaded Aidan. He turned to the priest. "That's his name."

Father Killoran nodded, never turning his focus away from the young man. Never turn your back on a feral animal, especially one who is injured. "Hello Finn," he said with a little more force. "You helped my young friend here, so I'd like to repay the kindness."

Finn glared at the priest through greasy locks and stretched his legs out before him, exposing a large, dark, crimson stain from his waist to his knee.

The priest held his hands in plain sight as he dragged a small flashlight from his pocket. "I need some light to survey the damage. Is that okay?"

Finn nodded, never taking his eyes off him.

"Alright, let's see what we have here," said Father Killoran.

A bright burst of light erupted in the alley, illuminating everything for the first time. Used needles, fast food trash, and general filth littered the ground. A dead rat decomposed nearby. At least the source of the mystery smell was exposed. With the beam of light, he followed the blood stain up to Finn's side, where thick, red blood oozed from a tear in his filthy, gray T-shirt.

"May I?" asked the priest, as he moved to lift the soiled garment.

Finn didn't respond verbally; he merely lifted his arm.

Father Killoran took that as a good sign. He lifted the shirt, exposing a two-inch-wide gash on the young man's side. The lighting wasn't good enough for the priest to get a good handle on the seriousness of the injury. He needed to convince Finn to come back to the rectory so he could properly assess the matter. He shined the light on the young man's pale face.

Two differently colored eyes peered back at him. One blue, one amber brown—Father Killoran had seen eyes like these before. His mind scrolled back into his past, digging up an ancient memory of a hopelessly optimistic, young priest trying to help a deeply pained, young Marine.

He shook his head, bringing his thoughts back to the here and now. "I'd like to bring you back to my rectory and have a better look."

Finn stared at him, emotionless. "Ain't I a little too old for you?"

Father Killoran was confused. "Excuse me?"

The young man's lips curled into a wicked grin. "I thought your type preferred young boys."

Ah yes, the old, pedophile-priest jab. Father K had his fair share of those barbs over the years. Sometimes, people said it in jest, while others meant every word. He stared at Finn, unable to discern whether he was joking or serious. After a moment's reflection, he decided that a little sarcastic humor was the proper reaction. "Ah," he said, with a nod. "I see we have ourselves a real smartass."

"Wow," scoffed Finn. "A priest who cusses."

At this point, the old priest would take any interaction he could get. Finn's posture had relaxed. The fact he was bantering was a good sign. Father Killoran decided to roll with it and see if he could use this to his advantage so he could help this young man. He cleared a space beside Finn and took a seat. "We're all imperfect." He pulled out a cigarette and leaned forward to light it.

"Wow! You smoke too," quipped Finn. "Ain't you supposed to keep your body pure, and all that stuff?"

Father Killoran exhaled a cloud of smoke. "Wrong religion. I belong to the one that acknowledges that we, as humans, make mistakes and don't always take care of ourselves." He took a long drag, then exhaled. "Besides, it's far better I smoke these, as opposed to going around yelling at everyone who pisses me off."

Finn cocked an eyebrow. "I thought you were all supposed to be calm and full of light and love." He smirked, then winced in pain.

A glance at Finn's side told the old priest that the wound was still bleeding. He locked eyes with the young man. "Like all God's children, we're a mixed bag of flaws and emotions."

"Didn't y'all take a vow to not be that way?"

Father Killoran shook his head and exhaled. "We just promised we would do our best to not give in to our darker sides. Sometimes we succeed." He shrugged. "Sometimes we fail."

"And sometimes you diddle, little kids," snapped Finn.

The words had a biting tone to them. The priest refused to be goaded into a confrontation. Finn was testing him, and he was not about to fail. He thought back to the time he had to banter with another young man with similar eyes. He didn't do so well back then, he would do better this time. "Everyone will face final judgment one day," he replied.

"Is that what you believe?"

"I do." Father K nodded.

Finn scoffed. "Then you're stupid."

A sense of urgency overcame the priest. The young man was reconstructing the wall around himself before his very eyes. "Tell you what," he said. "You let me take care of that wound, and then you and I can banter back and forth about what's right and wrong with the world."

Finn stared. Cold. Calculating. "Got anything for pain?"

"Depends on what kind of pain we're talking about," replied Father Killoran, knowing full well Finn wasn't talking about ibuprofen. A small twinge of regret washed over him. It never got easier to see these young people waste away moving from one high to another.

"We can start with physical," responded Finn. A cunning glint in his eyes.

"Sounds like a good plan," replied Father Killoran. "Aidan, help me get our friend Finn back to the rectory so I can patch him up."

Chapter Nineteen

T HE RECTORY WAS A SMALL, plain building set behind the giant, stone-faced church. In every way that the church was impressive, the rectory was the exact opposite.

Finn wasn't typically inclined to go anywhere with strangers—especially those offering help, but the circumstances as they were, he didn't have any other choice. The priest seemed legit enough. As for the kid, he was too small and pathetic to be a threat to anyone. How the hell did someone so weak and scrawny ever think they could survive on the streets?

The walk back to the rectory was roughly five, grueling blocks. The wound on his side weeping the entire way, spilling droplets of blood on the filthy pavement, co-mingling with all the used syringes scattered about. The taste of metal was strong in his mouth. Those two goons got him pretty good. Finn made a mental note to never get involved with another man's beef again. Truth was, he knew better; he learned this lesson years ago and never had an issue following his own advice. He couldn't quite put his finger on his reasoning to break his own rule.

"Turn on the main light," the priest said, to Aidan. The room filled with the cold light of fluorescents.

"Alright Finn, I'm just going to have you sit in this chair right here."

A sharp pain erupted in his side as Finn lowered himself onto the wooden seat. A gush of warm blood flowed down his side, seeping into his already-soaked pants. The scent of old coffee and burnt toast hung heavy the air.

"While you remove your shirt, I'll gather the supplies we need," said the priest. Without another word, he disappeared down a narrow hallway, only to return a moment later carrying a red first aid kit. He placed it atop the table. "Okay Finn, let's see what we have here." The older man placed a pair of wire-rimmed glasses on his face and leaned forward, causing the glasses to slide down the bridge of his nose. He glanced up at Finn. "Lucky for you, I have plenty of experience with wounds such as these."

Finn watched Father Killoran warily as he cleaned and inspected the wound. Aidan paced about the kitchen nervously. The kid had so much pent-up energy, it was wearing on Finn's nerves. Something about the kid was off. He was small, almost freakishly so. He behaved as though he were much more formidable than he was. The kid reminded Finn of a chihuahua—insecure and terrified on the inside. Why would someone like that even try to be on the streets? Aidan belonged back home in his comfy, suburban home, not on the streets where he was guaranteed to be attacked and beaten up.

"Luckily, the wound isn't too deep," said Father Killoran. "This will be an easy repair."

A moment later, a sharp pinch signaled to Finn that the stitching had begun. "You got something to take the edge off?" he asked.

The priest peered up, a perplexed look on his face. He regarded Finn for a few moments, then hopped to his feet. "I have some of these." He tossed a pill bottle to Finn.

Just your run-of-the-mill bottle of pain meds. While it would probably do the trick, this was hardly what he meant. Without opening the bottle, Finn placed it down atop the table and pushed it aside.

Father Killoran scoffed. "Well, I have nothing stronger." He sat down in the chair again. "And if I did, I wouldn't be in the habit of passing it out." He pushed his glasses up to the bridge of his nose. "Looks like we're raw doggin' it, then."

Finn burst out laughing. He had to admit, this priest was a surprise in every way. Though, he never had interactions with a priest before, so he had nothing to base this on. "Are all priests like you?"

"Some are," replied Father Killoran. "Many are not." He finished tying a stitch, then pushed the needle through again. "I spent some time as a chaplain in the Marines. I guess you could say that's where I honed my sarcasm skills." He smiled.

A crash erupted across the room. Aidan had knocked a coffee mug to the floor, where it shattered.

"The broom is in that closet." Father K pointed. He never looked up, he simply stated where it was and expected Aidan to pick up his mess.

Finn had to admit, he respected the old priest. He moved like a man who knew the world well. He knew how dangerous men could be, yet he had no fear. "How long have you been here?"

"In San Francisco?" asked the priest.

Finn nodded.

"Almost two decades." He tied off another stitch, leaned back, and inspected his work. "Looks like we need one more."

Another stab of the needle.

"So, you been doin' this the whole time?" asked Finn.

Father Killoran tied off the final stitch. "Yes, I have." He applied a bandage. "You're going to want to keep that dry and clean. You don't want it getting infected."

"I can take care of it," replied Finn.

"I'm sure you can," replied the priest. He stood up and cleared away the refuse. "I'm feeling hungry. How about you?"

Finn's stomach grumbled; he couldn't recall the last time he had a warm meal. Food sounded like a great idea. "I could use a bite," he replied.

The priest smiled. "Dinner it is then." He spun around on his heels, barking orders to Aidan, who promptly followed each command. In short order, they had whipped up a tasty meal of chicken parmesan.

"So, I have to say, I don't recall seeing you around before," said Father Killoran, leaning back in his chair.

"Maybe you're not as alert as you think you are," replied Finn.

The priest grinned. "One thing you'll discover about me is that I know my people." He took a sip from his wine. "You stick around here long enough, you'll find out, everyone knows who I am." He nodded toward Aidan. "Ain't that right, son?"

Aidan swallowed and nodded. "Everyone around here knows Father K." He flashed an uneasy smile.

Finn couldn't get over how awkward Aidan was in his own skin. It was as though he were always acting, forever terrified he would fall out of character. The more he watched the young man, the more his initial pity gave way to a slight and slowly growing feeling of revulsion. He turned his focus to the priest.

"So, you're the go-to man around here?"

Father Killoran stared with smiling eyes. "It all depends on what one wants. I'm here if anyone needs help or food or just someone to listen." He tapped his right ear. "I'm a great listener." The smile faded from his eyes. "What I am not is someone you can bullshit. I'm also not a good source of drugs or money."

Finn gave a curt nod.

"Father K saved my life," said Aidan. "If he hadn't intervened, I would've been killed."

"Seems like you have a habit of pissing people off," replied Finn, his tone harsh. After all, he almost died sticking up for this weakling who belonged at home, snuggled under his space-themed comforter, not on the streets. "Seriously, what the hell are you doing out here?"

Aidan flinched and looked away.

"That's a little harsh," stated Father Killoran. "Everyone who is out here has their reasons. Sometimes they're running from something—usually themselves." He stared directly at Finn. "And other times they're here because they're still fighting imaginary dragons."

Finn scoffed. "Imaginary who?"

The old priest's eyes lit up. "You mean to tell me you never heard the tale of Saint George's retirement?"

Finn shook his head.

"Do you know who Saint George is?"

"He's the one who fought dragons, right?" replied Finn.

Father Killoran nodded and smiled. "Well, what do you think happened after he conquered the dragon?"

Finn shrugged.

"He went into retirement, of course," said Father K. "I mean, there's no need for a dragon slayer when there are no dragons. Wouldn't you agree?"

The priest took another sip of his wine. "Here's the thing about fighting dragons. If you do it long enough, it becomes a major part of who you are. Your identity." He stared unblinkingly. "When it's over, it's almost impossible to stop fighting. You're sure the dragon is around every corner. Waiting for an opportunity to attack."

Father Killoran lit a cigarette. He offered the pack to Finn, who passed.

"Now, Saint George was not spared this." He took a long drag and exhaled. "He was sure dragons were everywhere. So, he did what you would expect him to do."

Finn twitched his nose. "He kept fighting his imaginary dragons," he replied.

Father Killoran nodded. "That he did. What do you think the outcome was?"

Finn shook his head, he had a feeling he knew where this was going. "Why don't you fill me in."

The priest flashed a wry grin. "Unable to control his desire to fight, he turned his ire on everyone around him. Innocent people, guilty people, those who loved him, everything he built up, you name it, nothing was safe in his presence. His rage and need to fight led him to destroy everything in his path. Everything that was important to him. Everything he loved."

The story went exactly how Finn thought it would. He sat still, staring at the priest. "It's a fairy tale."

"It is," replied the priest. "And, like all fairy tales, it has a very important lesson to impart."

"Argh! There be dragons about," blurted Aidan, followed by an uneasy chuckle.

The kid was getting on Finn's last nerve. Everything about him screamed, "kick my ass."

"That's not quite the point, Aidan," said Father Killoran, his tone paternal and condescending. He turned to Finn. "The moral of the story is that there are indeed times when dragons need slaying. However, once the dragons are gone, one needs to put down the sword and learn how to live peacefully again, lest you destroy everything you care about."

Finn stared, clenching his jaw, struggling to formulate a response.

Father Killoran flashed a gentle smile. "My entire career, beginning with the military, has been helping people overcome their need to fight imaginary dragons. To move on and live their lives full of love and hope."

"A life filled with love and hope ain't in the cards for everyone," argued Finn.

"There's no such thing as a cursed man," scoffed the priest. "There's no such thing as fate. Good or bad, we alone are in control of the lives we lead."

"Sick people don't choose to be sick," argued Finn. "Kids born to abusive parents didn't choose that either."

The priest nodded. "Ah, I can see you and I are in for a lot of great conversations." He pushed his chair back and rose to his feet. "I'd love to continue our conversation. Why don't you stay the night in the shelter? You and I can pick up our chat during breakfast in the morning."

Finn smirked. He expected more push back from the priest. He was almost disappointed. There was no way he was going to spend the night in some homeless shelter, surrounded by the stench of piss, listening to old men talk in their sleep. "I'm gonna pass on that one, Father." He climbed to his feet.

"I understand," replied Father K. "But please, promise me you will be here bright and early for breakfast." He followed Finn to the door. "I can't promise the food will be great, but I can promise excellent conversation."

Finn nodded, but he didn't intend to be back in the morning. He left the little building behind and strolled down the street. Much to his dismay, like a stray puppy, Aidan followed along, a little too closely.

"So where are we going now?" asked the younger man.

"I'm going this way," stated Finn, pointing down the street. "You're going anywhere else."

Aidan stared back with pathetic, doe-like eyes.

"You hear me," said Finn. "Get lost."

The younger man looked as though he were about to cry, this only made Finn angrier. He had to get away from this kid. He turned and stalked away, leaving Aidan, sad faced and all, behind. Finn had a mission in mind, and it didn't involve babysitting. The night was young, what he needed most was something to take the edge off. Something to prevent the turmoil from surfacing in his head.

Chapter Twenty

Father Killoran watched as Finn disappeared around the corner, his heart broke every time he ran into lost souls. Based on the condition of his inner arms, the priest knew where the young man was heading.

Such a waste. The old priest dedicated his entire life to save those who were lost. The pain and heartache written on their faces. One could read their souls through their hollow, darkened eyes. So much misery, Father Killoran wondered sometimes whether it was worth it. After all, what could be the purpose of such suffering?

He pulled a bottle of whiskey from the cupboard and poured himself a glass. The vision of Finn's eyes haunted him. How odd to see those eyes again. His mind wandered back to a memory from years ago. A time when a young priest, fresh from seminary, was tasked with informing a young Marine that he had lost both his wife and child. The anguish in the young man's eyes—his incredibly unique eyes, was almost too much for everyone in the room. Father Killoran watched as the heartache gave way to rage, then hopelessness, and finally an eerily cold darkness.

He took a sip of the whiskey, recalling the first time he tasted the amber liquid. Intent on saving the soul of the young Marine, Father Killoran made himself available twenty-four hours a day. He hung around the barracks, tolerating jibes and taunts from all the men. For the most part, the one person he was there for wasn't much of a conversationalist. The young man barely had two words to say to the priest after that first meeting. His best friend, however, was the avenue that the priest used to gain access.

What was his name? Nearly two decades had passed and the priest sifted through his memories. First, he found the face—a young Latino with black hair and deep, dark brown eyes. Manny! That was his name. Always wisecracking, but also respectful of the priest. Now, who were the others in the group? Father K remembered one was a giant of a man with a thick northeast accent, either New York or Philly, the priest couldn't recall which. Pillar was his name. And there was one more. Father K scoured his memory. This one was a little more difficult, as there were no real distinct details about the young man—other than he had a thing for blowing things up. Odie! Yes, that was it.

Father Killoran smiled and knocked back the rest of his whiskey. Yes, those boys gave him a run for his money. They tested his faith in God, humanity, and redemption.

How odd, after all these years, to see another damaged, young man with those same eyes. Father K didn't believe in coincidences. He firmly believed there was a purpose for everything and a sign such as this should not go unheeded. He poured another glass, then made his way to his tiny bedroom. It was nothing spectacular, a simple bed with a small table at its side and a lamp that never seemed to cast enough light for his aging eyes. In the corner stood an old, worn-out desk. He placed the glass on the stained wood surface and opened a side drawer, pulling out an old address book.

He thumbed through the pages until he came to S for Sanchez. There it was, the phone number for Manny's mom and dad. Manny was raised a devout Catholic. It was his upbringing that gave the priest access to the group. When they all got out of the military, it was

Manny who gave the priest his parent's phone number—in case he ever needed them.

Father Killoran smiled, reveling in the memories that played through his mind. The smile faded as Finn's face came to mind. The hollow, hateful, forlorn look in his eyes.

He downed the rest of his drink. There was a reason this young man was brought into his path; it was time to figure out what that was. So many years had passed and he wasn't even sure if Manny's parents even had the same number, let alone if they were alive. He dialed anyway.

The phone rang three times.

"Hola," came the sleepy voice of an older woman.

Suddenly aware of the time, Father Killoran glanced down at his watch, realizing it was ten p.m., his time. She was in Texas, which meant it was midnight for her. Too late to turn back now, he cleared his throat. "Hello, I'm so sorry for calling at such a late hour," he apologized. "My name is Father Killoran of the San Francisco Diocese."

"Oh!" gasped the old woman on the other end, her tone instantly more alert. "There's no reason to apologize. What can I do for you, Father?"

That's a good question. What was the purpose of his call? He cleared his throat. "I used to know your son, Manny." He paused. "I was his chaplain in the Marines."

"Oh yes, Father! I remember. Is there something wrong?"

"No, no!" replied the priest. "He and his buddy Shane came to my mind. I was only looking to reach out and see how they're doing."

"Manny could use more god in his life," scoffed the old woman. "There's no reason he's not married by now."

Father Killoran chuckled. It seemed as though Manny had changed little over the years. "How about Shane?" he asked. "Are they still in touch?"

"Shane is happily married to my daughter Catalina," replied the old woman, her voice resonating with pride.

"That's wonderful news!" replied the priest. He sighed in relief.

It was good to hear Shane had found some peace and happiness in the world.

"Would you like me to have Manny call you back?"

Father Killoran shook his head. "No, no," he replied. "No need for that."

"I'm sure he would love to catch up," said the old woman. "Maybe you can nudge my son a little about the importance of marriage." She sighed. "Or maybe remind Shane that I'm not getting any younger and I would like more grandbabies."

He smiled, realizing where Manny got his tenacity from. "I'll tell you what," he replied. "Feel free to give them my number and let them know I'd love to catch up sometime."

"Wonderful!" exclaimed the old woman.

"Be sure to let them know there's no rush or urgency. That it's only to catch up."

"I'll remember," replied the old woman.

After a brief conversation about the importance of grandchildren, they said goodbye and hung up. Alone in his room, listening to the hum of electricity, the scent of whiskey lingered around his empty glass. Unable to shake the sense that something important had been placed in his path, Father Killoran's mind focused once again on Finn. There was a reason the Lord brought this young man into his life. He had to figure out what that reason might be.

Chapter Twenty-One

T HE SALTY SCENT OF SEA MIST WAFTED THROUGH THE AIR, temporarily pushing out the stench of feces, urine, vomit, and decay. Ben took advantage of the momentary rush of fresh air and inhaled deeply. San Francisco was the top city on his list of least favorite places to go, the second being New York, not just the city, but the entire state. Having grown up in and around New York City, the entire state was tainted for him. There was no place he could go that didn't remind him of the life he left behind. It wasn't as though he had a bad childhood, it was the complete opposite. Private schools, expensive family vacations, road trips through Connecticut, ski trips around the world; you name it, Ben's earlier life was one of privilege and comfort, which is precisely why he could hardly stand remembering it. The phoniness, the fake prestige. It was stomach turning; enough to make one want to run away from it all. Was it any wonder why he ran as far and fast as possible?

"Watch out!" boomed Tanner's deep voice.

Ben looked down to find a steaming pile of feces on the sidewalk, right in front of him. He shook his head and stepped over, keeping a wary eye open for anything else.

The city of San Francisco had undergone a dramatic slide into the abyss over the past few years. When Ben first hit the rails, San Fran was a city with a fifty-fifty split of the dark side and the bright. Over the years, the dark side won out, absorbing anything light, hollowing it out and taking it over. Gone were the street artists; in their place, drug-addled human beings barreling down the road to their own demise. It was depressing to see.

After so much time searching, with no luck at all, Ben was ready to get on with his life. After all, it had been a long time since anyone had seen Finn. For weeks everyone they knew had been running around the country, looking for someone who either didn't want to be found or, the less favorable possibility; opted out of life. The daily updates had gone from hopeful, to sad, to downright depressing. When Ben first tried to broach the subject of ending the search, Mara would hear none of it. This effectively ended any chance of an open discussion with Tanner, who, Ben was sure, felt the same as he.

Mara was determined to find Finn. Unwavering in her resolve, Ben went along with the charade, but he didn't believe there was any hope that a happy ending would be had. He glanced over at Mara, her face a mask of determination as she scanned the area, searching inside tents when they passed by.

Ben would do anything for her. The fact he was in this hellhole of a city hopping over piles of shit and used needles was proof enough. She was his world. And their world was about to increase by one more. His eyes slid down to her slightly protruding belly. In less than five months, he would be a father, for better or worse, he was now responsible for the life Mara carried within her belly. He sure hoped he was up to the task. The only example he had of raising a family was the one way he vowed he wouldn't. He didn't want this little person to grow up surrounded by fake, soulless, unhappy people. He didn't want him or her to feel the pressure to conform to that lifestyle. No, Ben was going to do things differently. Their child, or children, if you listened to Mara, would live a life of freedom, a life of adventure and wonder.

"I need to stop for a second," said Mara, her hand unconsciously rubbing her belly.

Ben smiled. She was so beautiful.

"What?" she asked, as she nudged him.

He shook his head. "Nothing, Babe. Just admiring the love of my life."

Mara sighed and leaned in to kiss him.

"This is all cute and all," interjected Tanner. "Think you two can contain it long enough to be clear of this area?"

Ben looked around. The scent of urine assaulted his nostrils. He wrinkled his nose. "Yeah, I think we've searched this place enough." He turned to Mara. "He's not here."

"He's here," she stated flatly. "I can feel it."

"Feelings aside," quipped Ben. "He'd never come here."

"I have to agree," said Tanner. "Finn would never come to a place like this."

"Everyone's been saying that," blurted Mara. "But I think he's smart enough to go someplace where he knows no one would look for him."

"I'm not disagreeing with you—"

"Yes! You are!" She glared at Ben, then at Tanner. "Both of you are!" She stepped back and folded her arms. "I'm not leaving this city until we've searched everywhere."

"That's a lot to search," said Tanner in protest.

Mara stared angrily.

Ben knew when Mara set her mind to something this hard, there was no talking her out of it. He sighed. "Okay, tell you what." He placed a gentle hand on her shoulders. "We'll stay for a couple of days and search. But—"

"Here we go," interrupted Mara.

Ben shook his head. "Shh," he said. "Let me finish."

Mara stared. "Go on."

"We're gonna get a hotel room." He glanced around. "In a somewhat cleaner area of town. Tanner and I can go out and search." As soon as the words escaped his lips, Ben knew it was a mistake.

"Are you seriously telling me to stay home and wait?"

Ben shot a look at Tanner, who merely shrugged and stepped back. "No, no, no," argued Ben. "It's just that—"

"Just that what?"

Mara leaned closer, giving Ben the sense he was skating on thin ice. He had to choose his next words carefully.

"You're in no condition to be wandering around in this drug-and-germ-infested jungle." There, he said it. Come what may, he said his piece out loud. Ben stood firm, steeling himself for the coming barrage.

As if he were thinking the same thing, Tanner stepped back another yard.

"In no condition?" asked Mara, fury in her eyes. "What exactly does that mean?"

"Well, um—" attempted Ben.

"Shut it!" commanded Mara. "You listen to me." She pointed a delicate finger at Ben. "I am perfectly capable of determining what I can and cannot do. You got that?"

Knowing better than to say anything, Ben nodded.

Mara spun to face Tanner. "Do you?"

Tanner raised his hands in surrender and smiled. "Yes ma'am," he replied.

She set her attention back to Ben. "We'll get a motel room, because we're staying in this city until we know for sure Finn isn't here."

Ben nodded again.

"And we're gonna go out and look for him. All three of us. Together."

"How long?" asked Ben.

"How long what?"

"How long are we gonna be here until you accept he ain't here?"

"He's here." She stepped back. "I can feel it in my bones."

Ben smirked. "Is that anything like the feeling you had that you absolutely needed peanut butter and marshmallow sandwiches?"

Mara glared at him. "Completely different, smartass."

Behind her, Tanner giggled.

The conversation was over. A decision was made, much to the dismay of Ben, they were staying in this god-awful city for a few days. He sincerely hoped it wouldn't be too long, he wasn't so sure how long he could take the overwhelming stench.

The motel was nothing special. It was the cleanest they could find close to the areas they would be searching. Ben tried to convince Mara that they could get a cleaner room a little further out of the city, but she insisted they stay close. So, this seedy, nicotine-stained hovel it was.

Lacking confidence in the room's security, they hid their gear out of sight and headed back out in search of dinner.

"We want a greasy burger," stated Mara, rubbing her belly.

"I was thinking Thai," replied Tanner.

"We could hit both," suggested Ben. "I'm pretty sure we could find them here. That is, unless the city has fallen too far off the cliff."

A slight-bodied young man moved toward Ben. Aware they were about to collide, Ben moved to the side a little, only to have the young man move the same. They bumped shoulders. As the stranger passed, Ben felt a tug from his belt. He grabbed hold of the chain that was attached to his wallet. "Hold up." He yanked the chain, pulling the wallet free of the stranger's hands. "Yo, asshole!"

The kid spun around, mouth agape, eyes wide in fear, he couldn't be over sixteen years old, with the narrowest features Ben had ever seen on a man. His features aside, what struck Ben most were the young stranger's eyes. One blue, one brown.

"Well shit!" exclaimed Ben.

Mara gasped while Tanner snuck up behind the kid, effectively blocking any escape.

Ben smirked. "You suck at this," he stated.

The kid stepped back only to bump into Tanner, who towered over him. It was almost comical how small this kid was.

"Is that your natural eye color?" blurted Mara, moving closer.

Ben stepped between her and the stranger, otherwise, he was sure she would walk right up to the kid.

"It's okay," prodded Mara, her tone soothing and soft. "We're not gonna hurt you." She glared at Ben and then at Tanner, who didn't budge.

The kid seemed to relax.

"Your eyes," continued Mara, "remind us of a friend of ours. We've been looking for him." She moved closer. "His name is Finn." She pulled out her phone and scrolled through the photos, stopping on an image of Ben, Mara and Finn, standing together, smiling.

A slight twinge of sorrow rushed forward as Ben stared down at the photo.

Mara held up the phone. "Have you seen him?"

The kid's body language told Ben everything he needed to know, as if the colored contacts weren't enough. This kid knew Finn. Mara was right, Finn was here. Whether he was still around remained to be seen.

"I-I don't think—" stammered the kid.

"Y-You don't think what?" insisted Ben. His patience was wearing thin. On top of it all, it didn't help that something about the kid made his skin crawl. He couldn't quite put his finger on why, exactly.

Tanner stepped up and placed a giant hand on the scrawny shoulder. "We just want to see him," he stated.

"What's your name?" asked Mara.

"Aidan."

Mara smiled. She stepped closer. "My name's Mara. This is Ben and that's Tanner."

The young man's eyes darted from one to the other, clearly uneasy.

"Aidan," said Mara. "Is Finn still around?"

The kid glanced up at Ben, then quickly over to Mara. He nodded slowly.

A bright smile exploded on Mara's face, Ben had to admit, he also felt elated.

"I knew it!" Mara shouted triumphantly. She leaned close to Aidan. "Where is he?" she prodded. "Is he nearby?"

"He never mentioned any friends," stated Aidan.

"Did you ever ask him?" asked Ben.

Aidan shook his head.

Ben scoffed. "Then why would you think he would ever mention us?"

A confused look washed over Aidan's pathetic face.

"Tell you what, buddy." Ben cupped a hand on Aidan's shoulder. He could feel the kid's collar bone through the fabric of his shirt and jacket. "Why don't you bring us to wherever Finn is. I'm sure he'll thank you for it."

Aidan shook his head and opened his mouth, but no words came out.

"Let me word it this way." Ben stepped close, so close he could almost touch noses with the kid. He stared directly into his eyes. "You bring us to our friend, or this'll be the last conversation you'll have for a long time." Ben flexed his grip on Aidan's shoulder for emphasis. "You gettin' me?"

Aidan swallowed hard. Once again, his eyes darted from one to the other. Unable to lock onto a sympathetic face, his shoulders sank. He sighed and nodded. "He's a couple of blocks from here." He shrugged. "At least that's where I saw him an hour ago."

Ben sighed. An hour ago was a lifetime. Odds were slim that Finn was still there. "Where does he stay?"

"He's usually down in that area," replied Aidan. "Getting high."

Ben shot a glance at Tanner just in time to see his body sink. In a moment, they went from elation over the prospect of finding Finn to despair over what condition their friend would be in.

"Can you please take us to where you saw him last?" asked Mara.

Reluctantly, Aidan agreed, mostly because Ben made sure he understood, there was no alternative.

They passed a tent encampment that reeked of vomit and stale alcohol, the stench was enough to make Ben question whether he wanted to drink ever again. The entire walk, Aidan chattered away with Mara, Ben had a difficult time discerning whether she was truly interested in Aidan's stories or if she was merely humoring the small teen to keep him moving. On Carmel, they walked past a series of tents, a few oblivious, high people and one strangely sober, yet serious-looking man. Ben assumed he was the dealer.

Aiden stopped in front of an alley. "He was down here," he said, gesturing for the others to follow.

Every nerve ending in Ben's body was on high alert. He motioned for Aidan to go first with him close behind, followed by Mara and Tanner, bringing up the rear. As they picked their way down the alley, Ben quietly cursed himself for allowing Mara to come along, if things went south, he had so much more to lose with her around.

The farther they walked into the alley, the darker it grew. Trash lay strewn about, rodents and insects scurried around in the corners. The air was dank and stale, with a heavy under current of feces and urine. Ben couldn't help but wonder if the foul odor would be permanently burned into his sense of smell.

Aidan stopped suddenly, falling to his knees. At first, Ben thought the kid tripped, until he saw a pair of legs wearing camo pants and black boots. He grabbed hold of the teen and shoved him away, vaguely aware of the fact he nearly tossed the kid across the alley.

Finn lay at his feet, unconscious, drug paraphernalia scattered all around him. Covered in filth, his friend was unidentifiable.

Over his shoulder, Mara gasped and fell to her knees. Hands outstretched, she whispered, "Finn! Baby, we're here." Her voice trembling. She lifted his head and brushed away the filthy hair from his face.

Tanner squatted alongside Finn and poked at the used needle

and debris. He lifted Finn's arm, exposing the scabbed track marks. A deep, saddened sigh escaped his lips.

This was not the Finn Ben knew. In his wildest imagination, he could never guess this was how he would end up. He fully expected to find his friend in the mountains, living off the land like some sort of hermit. This was too much to take in. A very large part of Ben secretly wished they hadn't found him.

"Let's get him out of here," said Tanner. He leaned forward and lifted Finn's limp body onto his broad shoulders.

Ben stood back, staring in awe of his friend's strength. He wasn't sure he could lift Finn, even though he appeared to have lost a considerable amount of weight.

With little conversation, they made their way back through the streets to the seedy, little motel room. The entire time, Finn hardly moved at all. Tanner placed him gently upon a bed and Mara immediately took to cleaning him up.

In the better light, Ben could see just how bad things were. It was horrific. Gone was the Finn who was robust and powerful, the creature that lay before him was thin, decrepit, and sickly. His dark unruly hair lay in greasy, knotted locks across a sunken face covered in a grizzly, full beard and filth. He reeked of B.O. and vomit. Ben wanted to look away, but he simply couldn't.

No one said a word. Ben and Tanner stood nearby while Mara went about cleaning Finn.

"There baby," she cooed. "That's as good as I can get it right now." She brushed his hair away from his face, then looked up at Ben. "We need to get some food."

Ben blinked. He could hardly believe she was hungry after all this.

"He needs to eat when he wakes up," she stated. Mara peered up at Tanner and repeated, "We need to get some food so he can eat when he wakes up." She turned to Ben. "You two can go, I'll stay with him."

"Hell no!" blurted Ben. "You're not staying here alone with him!"

"It's Finn," protested Mara.

Ben shook his head. "I'll stay with him." He gestured toward Tanner. "You two go get the food and bring it back. I got him if he wakes up."

Tanner nodded and, with hardly another word, he ushered Mara out of the room, closing the door behind them.

Ben walked across the room and slid open the window. He needed some fresh air. He flopped into a chair and sat silently staring at the unconscious body of one of his dearest friends. Mara was right, Finn was here. They found him, or what was left of him. The question remained whether that was a good thing or not. He pulled out his phone and posted to the group.

Finn stirred and moaned.

Ben sat up straight, waiting.

Finn's arm lifted, he rubbed his eyes and moaned, then looking around the room, he locked eyes with Ben and sat up slowly.

"Good evening," said Ben. "Or good morning." He shrugged. "Whatever."

Silence.

"I see you don't have much to say at the moment," continued Ben unabashed. "That's okay, because I need you to listen right now, anyway."

Ben leaned forward, elbows resting on his knees. He stared directly into Finn's eyes. "I'll make this simple. I see you've gone completely feral. Now, we've all seen what you're capable of when you're raging." He paused and studied Finn's reaction. "We're not gonna have any of that. Not now, not ever."

"In a few minutes, Mara and Tanner are gonna come through that door with some food," continued Ben. "Mara's gonna want to take care of you. You're gonna let her." He sat back in the chair and stared at Finn for a long while.

Silence.

Ben stood up and walked over to the side of the bed, leaning ominously over Finn. "If you even so much as lift a finger against her, or make her cry—" He moved close, still maintaining a safe distance. "I will personally make sure it's the last thing you ever do in this life." He paused and stared for emphasis. "Now, nod once if you understand my point."

Never blinking, Finn gave a curt nod.

"Good boy," said Ben.

The door burst open. Mara and Tanner entered the room, their arms were laden with bags of food.

"You're awake!" exclaimed Mara happily. She opened a container of take out, grabbed a spoon, and plunked down on the bed beside Finn. "It's cream of asparagus. It smells delicious. Open up," she said, as she shoved a spoonful into Finn's mouth.

Chapter Twenty-Two

WALKING THROUGH THE DESERTED REMAINS of what was once an impressive amusement park outside of New Orleans, Teague couldn't help but feel as though he was strolling through a living, breathing metaphor for his entire life. Once grand and full of the promise of a great future, the mother of all storms came raging through, destroying everything in its wake. All that remained of the dream was the decaying bones of what used to be. He couldn't help but feel a certain kinship to the devastated park. After all, he too had suffered his own version of Katrina. There were days he felt as though all that was left of him was nothing more than an empty vessel.

While the others went about establishing their campsite for the night, Teague took a moment and stepped away. Since Finn left, Teague's sleeping accommodations had been simple. No longer in need of, or desiring, the solitude of a tent, he opted instead to sleep by the fire. Zac was good company and a solid listener, which was what he needed for a time.

But now, talked out, cried out and drained, what Teague yearned for most was solitude. A few moments alone, away from the banter of the others. He had no plans to leave the group; at least, not at the moment. The thought of being alone all the time gave him more anxiety than the constant banter of others.

He picked up a stone and tossed it at a small, pale blue building. All the glass had been broken long ago, but a few shards remained. His first toss went wide, so he scoured the ground for another rock. The second one struck the target, a large splinter of glass dropped to the ground, shattering into smaller pieces among the rest.

Teague sauntered past the Pontchartrain Flyer, the only two remaining gondolas dangling precariously from the frame. Past the Zydeco Scream roller coaster, once impressive with its triple loops, now covered in vines and Spanish moss, it was still quite impressive. In many ways, the old roller coaster was far more terrifying in its current form than it was when brand new and operational. Gravel and debris crunched beneath his boots, the sound echoing off the skeletal structures, only to die among the forest overgrowth. Nature was taking back her territory. Teague wondered what the park would look like a hundred years from now. Would it be a tropical forest, or will someone come along one day, bulldoze the entire area, and build apartments or quaint suburban homes?

Who knew what the future held for anything? For anyone?

He passed the once-grand Festival Mall building and turned onto the path that led to the Goodtime Gardens. In its heyday, jazz musicians would be scattered about, playing music, and chatting with patrons. Teague sat down under the last remaining gazebo, glancing up through the gaping holes in the canopy at the cloudless sky overhead. He listened to the sound of the gentle breeze blowing through rusted skeletons. This time of year, there were scarcely any critters around to make noise. The silence allowed one to sit quietly and listen to the whisper of decay.

Teague wondered what lay ahead. He knew no matter what, he would do his best to remain with his friends. Truth be told, the thought of being alone again was far too painful. He simply didn't trust himself. So, what did that leave? Was he doomed to live the rest of his days in limbo? Was he supposed to move on? How was he going to do that?

His mind wandered into the past, to a time when things were much simpler, when two young runaways fell in love. He pulled a photo strip from his pocket, the kind that's taken in one of those photo booths in places where tourists go. He found it among Finn's belongings, buried in an old book. A wistful smile spread across his face. Finn always had a knack for saving the strangest of things. He fingered the leather wrapped around his wrist.

Teague stared down at the photo strip, recalling the day it was taken with such clarity it stung. The scent of spring flowers mingled with river water. The chorus of birds fluttering about. The feeling of hope and excitement for what the future would hold. How nervous he felt before he landed that first kiss. He closed his eyes and conjured the moment.

⸙

"Who would've guessed that dude would have so much cash on him," said Finn, exuberantly.

He rifled through the wallet to make sure there was nothing he missed. Once confirmed, he tossed it into a nearby trash can.

"Eighty-five, ninety-five," counted Teague. "One hundred—" He peered up at Finn.

"Looks like we got one hundred and twenty dollars."

"Yes!" Finn laughed and slapped Teague on the shoulder. "So, where we eatin' tonight?"

Teague smiled. "Anywhere we damn well want to."

Finn's face lit up. "Well, you know what I'm gonna say."

"Let me guess," teased Teague. "It's probably not soup and sandwiches."

"Hell no!" exclaimed Finn.

"Prime rib it is, then!" replied Teague.

"Now you're readin' my mind."

The duo made their way down the narrow sidewalk, toward Jesse's restaurant, cutting through the throng of tourists, taking care to avoid falling into the river.

"What are you two doing here?" asked Jesse. She studied Finn and Teague in that older-sister way she had. "What did I tell you two about picking off my customers."

"We ain't here to mark any of your customers," replied Teague.

"We're here to eat," interjected Finn, jutting out his chin proudly.

"Uh, huh," replied Jesse. She stared for a long moment, then leaned close. "You got some poor fool's money, didn't you?"

Finn flashed an impish grin. "Let's just say we found it."

"Uh, huh? You mean you found it in some poor fool's wallet." Jesse shook her head. "That could've been someone who was coming here to eat. You two could've just robbed me of a patron."

"So what if it was?" asked Teague. "We're here with the cash now. Think of it this way." He grinned. "Same money, but a much better-looking clientele."

Jesse laughed. "I can hardly argue with that. But I still think you two won't tip as much as he would've." She spun around. "Come on then," she said, over her shoulder. "I don't have all night. Let's get you seated."

The meal was a vast improvement over anything they had eaten in a long time. Savoring every bite, Teague took his time. Finn, on the other hand, devoured his like a starving wolf. The sight of Finn eating made most people queasy, for Teague, it was just another endearing quality that he loved about him. Finn was raw. He was nothing if not painfully honest. If he didn't like you, he put no effort into pretending.

Four months had passed since the fateful Christmas eve when, in a fit of drunkenness, Finn confessed his feelings for Teague. That was the first time their lips ever touched. Until that moment, Teague hadn't allowed himself to consider Finn in that way. After all, they were best friends. They needed one another to survive. Their bond was stronger than any bond Teague had ever shared with another person. He couldn't imagine life without Finn.

This was exactly why, when Finn awoke, on Christmas Day with no recollection of the kiss, Teague went along with it, pretending as though nothing unusual happened. He vowed he would never bring it up, that he would push aside his true feelings for the sake of maintaining their friendship.

But deep inside, Teague yearned to tell Finn. At first, terrified that allowing a relationship to grow would bring their brotherhood to a devastating end, he found himself wondering whether things could be different. When he closed his eyes, he could feel Finn's lips against his. He could imagine an entire lifetime together.

The problem remained, even though Finn confessed his love for Teague that night, he was blackout drunk. Immediately following the kiss, the moment was abruptly interrupted by Finn running to the edge of the porch to vomit. Thus, the questions forever hovered on the edge of Teague's mind. Did he mean it? Was it just the rantings of a drunken teen? Who initiated the kiss? Teague could hardly remember. The only thing he did recall vividly was how he felt when their lips touched. The only thing that existed at that moment was the two of them standing on the rickety, old back porch of the blue house.

"Earth to Teague." Finn snapped his fingers inches from Teague's nose.

"Wh-what?" he asked, startled.

"Just wonderin' what you're thinking about."

Teague shook his head and shoved another piece of steak in his mouth. "Nothing," he mumbled.

"You know," continued Finn. "You've been doing that a lot lately. What gives?"

"Doing a lot of what?"

Finn shrugged. "Staring at me and fading out like that. It's like there's something wrong with me."

"No," protested Teague. "I'm just spacing." He tapped the side of his head. "My mind wanders sometimes."

"How come it only happens when you're starin' at me?"

Teague grinned. "Maybe I'm just tryin' to block out that face of yours, I see it a lot."

"Maybe you just can't look away from my awesomeness."

Teague nearly spit out his drink. "If that's what you wanna go with," he replied, chuckling. And then his heart sank a little.

Dinner was fantastic. They were having so much fun, even Jesse got in on the jokes from time to time. Dessert had to be at the local gelato stand, so they paid the bill, left Jesse a nice tip, which she staunchly refused, then headed back out onto the Riverwalk.

Passing under Navarro Street, the throng of people was almost too thick.

Finn brushed his hand along Teague's arm, then jumped up onto the edge of a concrete planter. Arms out for balance, they made their way free of the moving mass of people. Halfway through, they came across Bo, one of the older denizens of the streets. An old army vet, Bo spent his days and nights on the streets alone. He spoke of a family that no longer existed. Of sons and daughters who no longer cared for the old man. The thought that one could have a loving family one day and the next be destitute and homeless—left behind by all those who used to love you, was far too heartbreaking.

"Hey Bo," said Finn. He scurried up the incline and sat beside the old man.

"How's your night going?" asked Teague, as he took a seat beside Finn.

"Oh, you know," replied the old man. "Same old, same old." He pulled a small package wrapped in wax paper and unwrapped it, exposing half a sandwich. "Jesse gave this to me earlier." He held it out in front of him. "You boys hungry?" he asked. "You can have some of this with me."

Finn shook his head. "Nah man, we already ate," he replied. He glanced at Teague; a silent conversation took place between them.

Teague pulled the money from his pocket. He locked eyes with Finn, who merely nodded.

"Hey Bo," said Teague. "Here's twenty dollars." He held out the cash. "Go get a hot meal or something."

The old man peered up at Teague, then Finn, then back to Teague. "You boys shouldn't be giving away your money." He shook his head. "Certainly not to an old man like me."

"We want you to have it," said Finn.

"Oui," added Teague.

Bo stared at the money. "I am feeling kinda hungry." He patted his belly. "You sure?"

Teague nodded and held the money out further.

"You boys are somethin' else," said the old man. Tears welled up in his eyes. "The world is a better place because of you two."

"Psh," scoffed Finn. "I'm gonna bet the old man we took that money from earlier would have a different opinion."

Bo laughed. "You two boys are one of the few bright spots in this old man's life. Thank you."

Finn stood up. "Don't say that too loud." He winked at Teague. "I don't wanna ruin my reputation." He flashed a smile, then slid down the incline to the planter's edge. At the bottom, he turned around and asked, "You comin'?"

Teague slid down and followed, a few steps later, they emerged from the underpass. Here the sidewalk was much wider, allowing them some space to spread out.

They sat by the water's edge, eating their gelato and watching the tourists move past. Teague could hardly think of a time he felt more at ease around someone. Finn just brought it out of him—his presence made Teague calm. His mind wandered back to the kiss.

"Hey." Finn nudged him. "Wanna do something fun?"

"Like what?"

Finn pointed to a photo booth on the other side of the river walk. "Let's go take our picture."

"Lead the way."

Finn laughed and leaped to his feet. He signaled for Teague to follow, which he did. They weaved their way in and out of small groups of tourists, up the stone staircase to the street above. Cars and trucks whizzed along the road, the traffic lights beeped and signaled for pedestrians to cross. A sharp left down another flight of stone steps and they were back on the Riverwalk. Once again, Finn took the lead, coaxing Teague with a gentle sweep of his hand along his arm, sending a shiver down Teague's spine.

At the photo booth, Finn drew back the curtain and gave a low bow. "After you," he said, with a flourish.

The booth stank of stale alcohol and urine. Teague wrinkled his nose and scooted over to make room for Finn. The tiny compartment left little space for the two of them, it was intended for couples.

Finn squeezed in and drew the curtain closed. "Gimme some money," he said, with a hand gesture.

It was a struggle to get his wallet out of his rear pocket in that tiny space, Teague wrestled a couple of dollars free and inserted them into the machine.

"Okay, now what," he asked Finn.

"When the light goes off, make a stupid face."

Teague stared, waiting for the light. Nothing happened. "Is it broken?"

Nah," replied Finn. "Probably just needs a little coaxing." He flashed a toothy grin, then slammed his hand against the screen.

Nothing.

Finn hit the machine again, this time, the walls all around them rattled.

"Maybe not so hard," warned Teague.

"It can handle it," replied Finn.

A timer appeared on the screen and began the countdown from ten.

"Hah! I told you," proclaimed Finn proudly. "Now, just get ready to make a stupid face." That impish grin appeared again. "The stupid part should come easy for you."

Teague responded with a shove, which triggered a wrestling match where Finn held on to Teague's hands and shoved playfully. When the machine beeped, they paused long enough to make silly faces for the first picture.

The countdown triggered again.

Teague no longer heard the machine. The room no longer felt too tight. The only thing he could focus on was the feeling of Finn's hand holding onto his. His pulse quickened. Something changed in both of them, a silent permission. Teague leaned forward and gave Finn a quick peck on the lips. Fear rose inside. What did he just do?

With a serious face, Finn placed his hand against Teague's cheek and pulled him close. Their lips met and at that moment, all of Teague's fears fell away. This was right. This was how it should be. He couldn't live with it any other way.

A loud beep erupted from the screen. "Please collect your photograph."

They kissed one more time, then slid out of the booth. A swarm of people passed by. Finn touched Teague's arm and smiled, this time his hand lingered longer than usual.

⊹—⋇—⋇—⋇—⊹

Teague peered down at the strip of photos, remembering every tiny detail of that moment as though it had just happened. He sighed and pinched his eyes, wiping his tears away, then stared west at the blazing, orange orb descending on the horizon. The fiery curtain sank low, followed close by the icy blue of twilight. In the shadows, something metal screamed as it broke free and slammed to the ground, followed by the sound of scurrying footsteps.

He sat there, staring at the sky, until it was nearly black and littered with sparkling stars—both his mind and heart were numb. It was probably time to head back to the others, frankly, he was surprised they hadn't come searching for him yet. He rose to his feet and cracked his back. After a deep breath, he crunched and plodded the long way back to his friends who were camped out by the remains of the Big Easy Ferris wheel.

He passed the Sky Coaster to his left, followed by the Mega Zeph on his right. The structure, almost completely covered in vines, appeared to be something straight out of a post-apocalyptic landscape. As the Ferris wheel came into view, the faint glimmer of a fire flickered ahead.

"There you are!" shouted River, as soon as she noticed Teague. "I was about to suggest we go looking for you." She hooked her arm in his and coaxed him toward the others. "Cash made dinner." She giggled.

One of the best things to have happened was the coming together of Cash and River. Better late than never, in Teague's opinion. At least someone had a happy ending. He was glad it was them.

Cash placed a hot bowl in Teague's hands. "The specialty of the house, black beans and rice." He flashed a crooked grin and took a seat beside River.

Zac shoved a giant spoonful into his mouth. "It needs something," he said.

"Get out," replied Cash. He took a bite of his own. "It tastes perfect."

"I'm staying out of this one," added River.

"Well?" asked Zac, staring directly at Teague.

"Well, what?"

"What're your thoughts?"

Teague inhaled the savory aroma of the beans and rice. His mouth watered in anticipation. While the others watched, he scooped up a spoonful and shoved it into his mouth. "Mm," he said. "Zac's right, it's missin' somethin'." He climbed to his feet and strolled over to his pack. After rustling around for a bit, he pulled out a bottle of Cajun seasoning. He wiggled it in the air and smiled. "Gotta have some spices," he said, as he took his seat and added a small mountain of pepper spice to the stew.

Comfortable silence descended over the group as they dove into their dinner.

"I can't believe we never stopped here before," said Cash. "I mean, with all the times we've hit New Orleans, you'd think this would've been on the list."

"I agree," said River. "I like it here; it's got an eerie glow to it all."

Teague nodded. "Finn would love it—" And just like that, the mood darkened. What the hell was wrong with him? Why was he unable to go an hour without thinking about or talking about Finn? At this rate, he'd never get past this. He'd never move on. He wondered if Finn had moved on. Was he with someone else right now? Or was he blissfully alone somewhere in the mountains?

Dead silence from the others. To say it was uncomfortable would be an understatement.

The loud chirping of Cash's phone broke through the quiet. Relief washed over everyone when Cash pulled the device from his pocket. The cold glow of digital light illuminated his face as he stared down at the screen. "Hm," he said, "Something's up."

"Who is it?" asked Zac.

"It's Max," replied Cash.

"Yeah? What's he got to say?" asked River.

Cash moved his fingers across the smooth glass of his phone. "He said we need to get on the server right now."

"Anything else?" asked Teague, as he fished his phone from his pocket.

Cash shook his head.

River gasped.

Teague opened the app and scrolled down through the conversation.

One post from Ben stood out. "We got him!" he wrote in all caps.

A lump formed in Teague's throat, he tried to swallow but his mouth was too dry. His heart pounded against his rib cage; he could feel the blood rushing through his skull. Breathing was difficult. The message board was blowing up...


```
Bells: Finn?
   Ben: Yes.
   Gunner: Where are you?
   Ben: San Francisco
   Tripp: Holy shit!
   Bells: Woo-hoo!
   Bella: Is he okay?
   Max: After all this, he better be.
   Ben: He's breathing.
   Max: Hold up, lemme get Cash and the others on
here.
   Gunner: How bad was he when you found him?
```


Silence. Teague was sure that wasn't a good sign. San Francisco—Beth was right. Finn went where he knew nobody would look for him. How could he be so stupid?


```
Ben: Bad. Really bad.
   Gunner: You still in San Fran?
   Ben: Yes.
   Gunner: Stay put, we're just north of you. We
can be there by midmorning.
   Ben: Got it. We'll stay put.
   River: We're on our way too.
```


Teague wanted to say something, but no words formed. Finn is alive, but not doing so well. What the hell did he get into?

Across the fire, River cried tears of joy while Cash and Zac cheered. The overall mood was upbeat. Teague wanted to be happy, too. Why wasn't he happy? What the hell is wrong with him? Isn't this what he wanted? His mind reeled. What if Finn wanted nothing to do with them—with him? Did he want to find out?

Cash snapped his fingers. "Teague!" he shouted.

Teague shook his head and locked eyes with Cash.

"We got him," said Cash. "That's great news!"

Teague did his best to smile, it felt fake as though he were smiling with someone else's face.

"So, are we heading out first thing in the morning?" asked Zac.

"I don't know about you," said River. "But I ain't sleeping a wink. Not now." She glanced around at everyone, her eyes landing on Teague, pausing.

"I was hoping you would say that," replied Zac. "Cause I ain't gettin' any sleep either."

"So, should we just head out now?" asked Cash.

River and Zac agreed enthusiastically. There was a long pause as they all stared questioningly at Teague. He knew they were waiting on him to show some sort of elation or relief or something, but he simply didn't have it in him.

He looked around at everyone. "Oui," he said. "We should start out now."

Zac and River jumped to their feet and immediately went about packing while Cash got back on the message board to contact Porter.

Chapter Twenty-Three

FINN'S EYES FLUTTERED OPEN. His body was resting on something soft, too soft to be the ground of the alley. He pulled forth his last memory, the voices, the thoughts, the heartache, the needle. Hard as he tried, he couldn't recall how he got here. His head hurt like hell. He sat up and glanced around the room to find Ben seated in a chair nearby, staring at him with serious eyes.

"Good evening," said Ben. "Or good morning." He shrugged. "Whatever."

Silence. Finn wasn't sure whether he was dreaming or not. He struggled through the clouded haze in his mind to process what the hell was going on.

"I see you've gone completely feral," said Ben. "Now, we've all seen what you're capable of when you're raging." He paused, eyeing Finn up and down. "We're not gonna have any of that. Not now, not ever."

The mere reference to what he did was enough to send Finn into a spiral. The voices kicked in immediately.

Finn! What did you do?

Across the room, Ben continued to talk but the torrent of voices inside Finn's head drowned him out. Ben sat back in the chair and stared at him for a long while. He seemed to be waiting for some sort of response. But all Finn could hear were the voices shouting and screaming.

Stop! Finn! No! What did you do?

Ben stood up and walked over to the side of the bed, hovering ominously over him. "If you even so much as lift a finger against her or make her cry—" He moved close. "I will personally make sure it's the last thing you ever do in this life." He paused and stared. "Now, nod once if you understand my point."

The only thing Finn could do was a quick nod of his head. He wasn't entirely sure what he just agreed to.

"Good boy," said Ben.

The door burst open. Mara and Tanner entered the room, their arms laden with bags of food.

"You're awake!" exclaimed Mara happily. She opened a container of take out, grabbed a spoon and plunked down on the bed beside Finn. "It's cream of asparagus. It smells delicious. Open up," she ordered, then she shoved a spoonful into his mouth.

The soup was hot—too hot. It burned the inside of his mouth as it oozed down his throat like molten lava. As soon as he swallowed, Mara shoved yet another spoonful into his mouth. The urge to push her away was quickly squelched by Ben, hovering close. By the fourth mouthful, Finn's stomach could take no more. In a fit of rebellion against the first real food he had eaten in weeks, his stomach flipped and churned. With little thought for Ben's reaction, Finn shoved Mara's arm aside and made a run for the bathroom, barely making it in time before an explosion of cream of asparagus soup mixed with the chips he ate earlier that day erupted from his mouth. Hugging the toilet, he heaved and belched as his stomach purged everything.

Weak and covered in a cold sweat, Finn rested his head against the cool porcelain and breathed. The scent and taste of vomit made him want to throw up again. The room spun out around him, the lights went dim, then black.

He opened his eyes. Wherever he was, it was dark. Maybe he imagined the whole thing with Ben and Mara. He felt like death.

"Here," said a low voice, almost whispering. "Try to see if you can hold down some water." It was Tanner.

Finn's eyes adjusted to the dim light. The smell of food permeated the air, his stomach did a flip. Mara lay sleeping on the other bed, her head resting on Ben's lap as he sat there watching Finn with a keen eye.

Tanner shoved a bottle in Finn's hand. "Just try it," he prodded.

The cold of the bottle felt good against his skin. He pressed it against his forehead, trying to stop the swimming. His mouth watered —just one little sip. The chilly wetness slid past his lips and down his throat. As soon as the liquid hit his belly, it lurched in protest. Once again, Finn ran to the bathroom. The last thing he remembered was the sound of the voices in his head mixing with his own sobs and the feeling of the cold floor tile against his skin.

Snippets of conversations happening around him coupled with moments when soft hands brushed the sweat-soaked hair from his forehead were all that came through his fever dream. At one point he heard himself say he wanted to die, followed by a familiar gruff voice reply, "It's gonna be okay, son."

He awoke screaming. The warm sun peeped through the dingy curtains, the sheets surrounding him were soaked with sweat. His entire body ached in ways he never knew possible. He ran his fingers through his wet, knotted hair, instantly disgusted with himself.

Unfazed by his current condition, Gypsy jumped on him and licked his face, her tail wagging so furiously it made the entire bed jiggle. Her enthusiasm and unrestrained show of affection made Finn smile, a small laugh escaped his lips, shocking himself at how foreign it sounded to his own ears.

"Gypsy," ordered Gunner. "Give the man some room to breathe."

"It's okay," replied Finn, his voice shaky.

The little dog gave out a yap and threw herself on the mattress beside Finn, belly in the air, still wriggling. He glanced around the room at the solemn faces. Mara sat at the edge of the bed, with Ben standing sentinel right behind her. Over by the door stood Tanner. Nate and Gunner sat at the small round table. Everyone stared at him as though he were going to say something profound.

Gunner walked over and took a seat on the bed. He held out a bottle of water. "Think you can keep this down?"

Finn shook his head, he honestly didn't know. He took the bottle and slowly lifted it to his lips. He swallowed the tiniest of sips and waited. Nothing happened. He took a larger sip and waited. Again, nothing. Finn lifted the bottle one more time and guzzled half before Gunner pulled it away.

"Pace yourself," warned the bigger man. "You're dehydrated. Too much'll make you sick again. We want you to keep it down." He glanced down at Finn's arms.

Immediately self-conscious, Finn moved to hide or cover up the evidence of what he had been up to. Shame washed over him like a tidal wave. Gunner was the last person he ever could have wanted to see him this way. He had no intention of anyone he knew seeing him this way. All he wanted at that moment was to run away. To disappear and see none of the people in this room again.

He swung his legs over the side of the bed and tried to stand. Unfortunately for him, his legs were in no condition to do his bidding. At the first application of weight, his knees buckled, sending him careening toward the floor.

Gunner jumped up and caught him. Against the giant man, Finn felt like a small child.

"Where're we going?" asked Gunner. "The bathroom?"

Finn nodded, unable to muster enough energy to force out any words. Struggling with each step, Finn, with Gunner's help, made it into the bathroom.

Arms and legs trembling from the exertion, Finn held himself up at the sink and peered at his reflection in the mirror. The face that stared back at him was shocking. Sunken eyes, hollow cheekbones almost completely covered by a thick, wild, filthy beard. His hair was a cluster of ratted and tangled knots. His lips cracked and peeled.

Finn glanced down at his body, his collar bones protruding from an emaciated body that was covered in bruises, scrapes, and grime. He ran his fingers over the scar on his side, a welcome-to-the-neighborhood gift when he first came to San Francisco. A reminder for him to never get involved with anyone else's troubles again. His arms were veiny and rail thin, the only color was the tiny, red track marks all over. A dam broke inside, shattering like delicate glass. Tears sprang forth from his eyes, he leaned his head against the mirror and sobbed uncontrollably.

More than once, Finn nearly collapsed, but Gunner was there, holding him upright. As solid as a tree, unwavering, silent, and calm. It was a miracle this giant of a man didn't turn away from him in disgust, leaving him to rot in his own mess. He didn't deserve a friend like this. He was a monster who should be left to die.

Self-loathing and heartache mingled with all the dark thoughts and voices.

When he finally calmed, Gunner helped him back to the bed.

"Here baby," said Mara, with her soft voice. She handed a bowl to him along with a spoon.

Concern washed over Finn, remembering the last time he attempted to eat. Soup was the last thing he wanted to see.

"It's okay," said Mara. "It's miso soup this time." She smiled. "You'll be able to hold this down."

Warm vapor wafted up to his nostrils. Finn breathed deeply. The soup smelled amazing. He lifted the small bowl to his lips and took a long sip. It was pure heaven. He wasted no time downing the entire bowl.

This time, his body didn't reject the soup, much to his relief. He lay on the bed for a good long while, willing his body to keep the soup down, listening to the conversation going on all around him. For the first time all day, he was feeling whole again.

"Think you've got the strength to clean up a little?" asked Gunner. "I'd bet that'll make you feel more like yourself."

His own voice joined the chorus in his head. *I don't want to be myself.*

Once again, Gunner helped guide him into the bathroom. This time, he was able to stand steady on his own two feet. Gunner gave the room a good once-over. As he left, he made sure to leave the door open just a sliver. He didn't have to explain why, Finn knew. Standing alone in the bright light of the bathroom, he looked at his reflection one more time, noticing for the first time two silver rings dangling from the left corner of his bottom lip. Try as he may, he couldn't recall when those were done. Surely, he would have some memory of it. But there was none.

Finn raked his fingers through the thick, black beard that covered the lower half of his face, catching a flea under his nail. He squished the tiny bug and shuddered in disgust at his own condition. After making sure there were no other little critters hidden in his facial hair, he turned on the water and held his hands under the warm stream.

The smell of clean soap mingled with the faint scent of bleach surrounded him in the small, enclosed space. He stared down at his hands and watched as muddy water circled the drain, then disappeared. He wished his entire body could pour down that drain. A flood of memories rushed forth along with the voices. Finn pressed his forehead against the mirror and wept.

There was a gentle rap at the door followed by Gunner asking, "How's it going?" A faint hint of worry hung heavy in his voice.

Finn wiped his face. "It's fine," he replied.

When he emerged from the bathroom, the small room was different. Gone was the soiled bedding, in their place were crisp, white sheets. Fresh air rushed past the curtains, filling the room. The television was on, playing a sitcom. The others lounged about the tiny space, the overall mood was much more casual and relaxed than it was earlier. Even little Gypsy had a relaxed air about her as she lounged on the other bed alongside Nate as he watched the television, unconsciously scratching her fluffy head.

Mara rushed up to Finn. She wrapped her arms around him and hugged him tight.

He let himself relax against her soft touch, he breathed in the perfume of her hair and sighed. For the first time in months, he felt at ease.

"Teague is on his way," she whispered joyfully. "He and the others will be here soon." Mara pulled back and smiled.

Upon hearing that name, a rush of anxiety shot through Finn's body. His heart raced, he could feel the blood thumping in his skull. Unable to catch his breath, he shoved Mara backward, much harder than he intended. He rushed forward to stop her from falling.

A look of shock and fear spread across her face as she stumbled backward, nearly tumbling to the floor were it not for Tanner, who was standing close enough to catch her. "Ben! No!" she screamed.

In a flash, Ben flew across the room, cursing and flinging insults the entire way. He crashed into Finn with the fury of a locomotive. Fists flying, they toppled to the floor—Ben atop Finn landed one punch after another.

Finn did nothing to fight back, he merely covered his face and head in an attempt to shield himself from major damage.

Suddenly Ben was ripped away, mid-punch.

"Stand down!" boomed Gunner, as he shoved Ben back.

The room was silent. Finn remained on the floor, curled up, arms wrapped around his head.

"Ben, it's okay," said Mara. "He didn't mean to do that. Look at him."

Finn didn't look up, he didn't have to, he knew everyone was staring at him. Struggling to breathe, the voices in his head kicked into overdrive. A low buzz erupted deep in his skull, his head pounded. Darkness, bright light, darkness, bright light. The room swirled around him like a funhouse.

"Just breathe, son."

Finn! What did you do?

Finn! Stop! Please!

Daniel's maniacal laughter erupted. *You're a loser.*

"Leave me alone!" screamed Finn, rocking back and forth. "Please," he begged. "Just let me die." He thought his voice was in his head but the audible gasp from Mara told him it wasn't.

"It's gonna be okay, son," said Gunner.

"No!" screamed Finn. "It's not gonna be okay!" He grabbed two fists full of his own hair and pulled. "It's never gonna be okay!" he sobbed.

Gunner grabbed hold of him and pulled him close.

Finn wasn't sure how long they sat on the floor, by the time Gunner pulled away, he was completely cried out and exhausted. He had no more fight in him.

Shortly after, Gunner announced that he and Finn would head out alone. Nate was to take care of Gypsy. Gunner would contact him when things were settled, and Gypsy could be around. In a flurry of activity, Gunner assembled his gear, and it was time to leave.

At the door, Finn stopped in front of Mara. Ben stood; arms folded by her side. "I'm so sorry," he stammered, his voice cracking.

To his surprise, Mara jumped up and, once again, wrapped her arms tightly around him.

A scowl swept across Ben's face.

"It's okay, baby," she whispered in Finn's ear. "I love you." She stepped back and stared directly into his eyes. "I will always love you."

Tears he didn't know he had left, erupted from Finn's eyes.

Mara hugged him one more time, then kissed his cheek and stepped back.

Ben stepped forward, glaring. He shook his head. The scowl slowly melted into a sad smile. Holding out his hand, he said, "I'm sorry, brother."

Finn took the hand and shook. To his surprise, Ben pulled him in for a firm hug.

"You take care of yourself," said Ben, a hint of tears in his eyes. "This ain't the end."

Finn nodded, but he wasn't quite sure. A tiny part of him wanted to believe what Ben was saying was true, but a much larger part of him knew otherwise.

Ben stepped back and stared into Finn's eyes. "We'll see you soon."

Tanner stepped forward and hugged him. "Don't listen to your head, brother. I know what you're going through. Don't let the dark thoughts win." He stepped back and smiled. "We're all here when you're ready for us."

Don't listen to your head; Finn couldn't think of anything he would love to do more. If only it was that easy.

After a momentary stop to say goodbye to Nate and an ear scratch for Gypsy, Finn followed Gunner through the door, allowing it to close gently behind him. He didn't know where they were going, he was pretty sure Gunner didn't either. Finn didn't much care, as long as they were far away before the others arrived.

Chapter Twenty-Four

THE CALL OF THE TRAIN WHISTLE ECHOED OUT INTO THE NIGHT, signaling their arrival in San Francisco. This had to be the longest ride in Teague's life, and it wasn't over. They still had quite a distance to walk through the city until they reached the motel where Ben and the others took Finn. His nerves on end, he gnawed his nails down to the quick.

For the most part, the others were silent throughout the journey from New Orleans. The silence on the server didn't do much for Teague's anxiety. Every time he checked, there would be one or two posts from the others who were still out across the country. As for the group in San Francisco, it was nothing but radio silence, even Gunner went completely silent. Cash and River insisted this wasn't a big deal, that Gunner was busy traveling and Ben and the others were probably busy helping Finn. Teague wasn't buying it.

No, something didn't sit right. Teague was sure something was terribly wrong, that's what his gut was saying, and his gut was hardly ever wrong.

They hopped off the train and cleared the rail yard with no

issues. After Cash mapped their course, they set out on foot across the city.

Gunner's and Ben's words played on repeat in his head. How bad was he when you found him? Bad. Really bad. What did Ben mean by that? How bad was Finn? A deep fear of what he might find when finally face to face with Finn settled in his bones. Was he ready for that? Teague wasn't quite sure.

The city of San Francisco, like every city Teague had visited, had its own unique smell. This one was a mixture of dank sea water and a deep-set moldiness that could best be described as a wet dog, mixed with urine, vomit and alcohol. No matter the city, the last three were always present. He wrinkled his nose. Finn was right, the mountains are the best place to be. Clean air, wide-open spaces, and nature. Ah, Finn. What were you thinking? Why here? But Teague knew why. Beth was right, this was the last place anyone would have thought to find him. Everyone knew how much he loathed cities, especially if they were overcrowded. In hindsight, it only made sense that this would be where he ran to hide. Teague shook his head and berated himself for not seeing it as a possibility.

Thoughts churned in his head. Why hadn't he thought about this months ago? *How bad was he when you found him? Bad. Really bad.* Had he listened to Beth, they could have saved Finn way before he fell into whatever the hell he fell into.

"A couple more blocks up this street," called Cash, from up ahead.

Teague's anxiety intensified. What was he going to find when he got there? How bad is really bad? What exactly did Ben mean? Why the radio silence?

"I can't believe we're gonna see him," said River, barely able to contain the excitement in her voice. "Yes! Finally gonna have our boy back with us where he belongs." She turned around and walked back-ward. "Teague, are you ready to see our boy?"

Unwilling to expose his thoughts and unable to put his finger on why a deep sense of dread had settled into his bones, Teague merely nodded.

"And Zac," continued River, as she spun around to walk forward again. "Go light on our boy. You're not allowed to beat his ass. Understand?"

Zac grunted.

Teague studied Zac. He seemed to be feeling exactly what Teague was feeling, and, like Teague, Zac didn't want to verbalize it. Yeah, something was wrong—terribly wrong. A cold chill ran up his spine, he pulled his jacket tight around him for warmth, but the chill had already settled deep.

They rounded the corner and came to a stop in front of a small, outdated motel. The signage was new, but the outer walls said a different story.

"They're on the second floor," said Cash. "Room 215."

No one moved. They stood there, silently staring up the stairwell.

"Well, what are we waiting for?" prodded River. She ran toward the stairs. "Let's go!"

Zac followed slowly, leaving Cash and Teague to stand alone.

"You okay?" asked Cash.

"As okay as I'm gonna be, I suppose." Teague's body trembled, not from the cold, but from fear. This whole thing felt wrong.

Cash laid a gentle hand atop Teague's shoulder. "We're gonna get through whatever this is together, brother," he said his voice full of resolve.

Teague knew that Cash believed every word he said—too bad Teague didn't have the same faith.

"Come on," prodded Cash. "Let's go."

One by one, Teague climbed the steps. Each time his foot took on the weight of his body, every muscle trembled, threatening to collapse at any moment. Breathing was difficult, his heart raced. Thoughts in his head swirled, sending his emotions spiraling out of control.

The door swung open, and River disappeared inside the room with Zac and Cash close behind.

Silence. No shouts, cheers, or sounds of happiness—just cold, terrifying silence. Something was wrong.

At the top of the stairs, Teague paused to catch his breath. A deep sense of dread settled in his soul. This wouldn't be the happy ending they all wanted. He walked to the doorway and peered inside. The silence told him everything he needed to know. From the back of the room, little Gypsy barked and bounded toward him. Sensing his sadness, she stopped in front, barely wagging her tail, and whimpered. He dropped to his knees, allowing the little dog to leap into his arms, where she licked his face.

Before the door even closed behind him, Teague already knew Finn was no longer there.

The room stood frozen; the occupants hardly moved. Teague glanced around, noting all the somber faces. He wanted to turn around and walk away. He wanted to disappear forever.

"Teague, I'm—," began Ben.

"Where is he?" asked River, the tone in her voice exposing her fear.

"He ain't here," replied Teague, before any other others could. The looks on their faces confirmed his guess.

River spun around to be face-to-face with Nate. "Where's Gunner?"

"H—He's with Finn," replied Nate.

"And where the hell is that?" she demanded.

"Here," interjected Mara. "Come sit down." She moved to guide River to a chair.

"I'm not sitting the fuck down!" shouted River. "Now, someone's gonna tell me where the hell is Finn?" She glared around the room, locking eyes with everyone.

River's pain was almost too much for Teague to take. It mirrored his own, which just made his more difficult to contain. "Please, River, just sit down and be calm," he pleaded.

She stared at Teague, then without another word, sunk to the edge of the bed. Mara immediately sat down beside her.

"So, we all just gonna stand here staring at one another?" asked Zac. "Or is someone gonna step up and tell us what the hell is going on?"

"Teague's right," blurted Ben. "Finn's not here." He glanced down at his hands. "He was here, but now he's gone."

"Thank you, Captain Obvious," jeered Cash. "What the hell happened?"

"He started saying crazy shit," continued Ben, staring directly at Teague. "He was begging for it to end."

"For what to end?" demanded Zac.

"Everything," stated Teague.

"Yeah?" said Zac. "What the fuck does that mean, exactly?"

Teague said nothing, he stood silent, staring at Zac, waiting for him to realize what Ben was alluding to.

A flash of understanding ignited on Zac's face. He turned toward Ben. "And you let him leave? What the fuck is wrong with you?"

Ben shook his head. "It ain't like that."

"The hell it ain't," yelled Zac.

"Let's just," sighed Cash, standing in the middle of the room. "Everyone calm down." he glared at Zac, who stood firm albeit slightly less aggressively.

An uncomfortable silence descended upon the room. Teague found this far more upsetting than the arguing. He stared at Ben, painfully aware that his old friend couldn't maintain eye contact; scanning the room, Teague noticed that none of the others could either. How was it possible for things to go from horrible to worse?

"I'm gonna need you to start from the beginning," said Cash.

"Okay," replied Ben. "We found him in an alley." He stared at Teague. "High and out of his mind, covered in filth and unconscious."

Zac exhaled loudly and sat heavily on the edge of the bed.

"Tanner carried him back here," continued Ben. He looked at Cash. "That's when I messaged the group."

"We went out for some food while Ben stayed and watched him," added Mara. "When we got back, he was awake." She looked at River. "He couldn't keep anything down."

There were no words to describe how Teague was feeling at that moment. Finn had never done hard drugs. Teague understood their allure, but it never occurred to him that Finn would ever wander down that path. None of this was making any sense.

"It was Gunner's idea that they head out," said Ben. He looked down at the floor. "Alone."

Teague stared down at little Gypsy, her tail wagging ever so slightly whenever someone would make eye contact with her. "What aren't you telling us?" He glared at Ben.

"Nothing," he replied, staring down at his feet.

Teague wasn't a mind reader, but he knew when someone was lying to him. A tiny ember of anger ignited in his belly. "Bullshit!" he shouted. "Gunner would never go anywhere without Gypsy."

Ben stared, silent.

"Well?" demanded Teague. "Are you gonna tell us everything or what?"

Ben glanced over at Tanner, who nodded in encouragement. He turned to Mara, who looked as though she were about to cry. He sighed. "He flipped out." He swallowed and shot a glance at Teague. "When Mara mentioned your name, he lost his shit."

Teague's heart sank. The room swirled around him. He willed himself to remain calm and steady. He knew what Ben was trying to convey, but he needed to hear the words spoken aloud. "What do you mean, flipped out?"

Ben shook his head, unable to maintain eye contact. "Do you need me to say it out loud?"

Teague nodded his head slowly, steeling himself.

Ben raked his fingers through his hair. "When he heard your name, he had a breakdown." He stared at Teague, this time maintaining eye contact. "He doesn't want to see you."

He doesn't want to see you. Like a scratched record, the words played over and over in Teague's head. The world turned gray. His heart shattered into millions of tiny shards. The others were talking, but he could make no sense of what they said. All he could hear were the words, he doesn't want to see you.

Teague turned and walked out of the room, leaving the others in whatever conversation they were having. *He doesn't want to see you.* He inhaled the San Francisco night air, his senses immediately accosted by the stench of human waste mingled with garbage. Fitting, he thought, then chuckled lightly over the cruelty of life. Well, they found him—too bad he didn't want them to. Teague sat down, leaning against the wall, staring blindly at the neon sign of the strip club across the street. It was over. He was done chasing someone who didn't want him. He had to accept that whatever the future held, it didn't include Finn. Tears streamed down his face. He pulled the photo strip from his pocket and pinched the tears from his eyes. His heart ached to go back in time. But that was impossible; the past was behind him, and that was where it would always be.

Stunned, broken and alone, he ripped the photo into three pieces and tossed it over the railing, watching as the pieces floated on a current of air, to the ground below.

Cash sat softly beside him. "How are you doing?"

Teague sniffled and wiped his face. "Not too good."

Cash nodded. "I can't pretend to know how bad you're feeling right now," he whispered. "But, I'm here for you."

Teague didn't reply, he merely sat and stared out across the street at the patrons coming and going from the run-down bar. Slowly, everyone who was in the motel room wandered out to be near him. A lonely silence hung heavy in the air.

Ben took a knee in front of him. "I'm gonna tell you what I told Finn when he left. This ain't done. We're gonna see him again." He glanced up at the others. "This family has been through too much shit to break apart now." Ben turned to Teague once again. "Finn will be back, and this group will be whole."

Teague felt bad for Ben, he actually believed what he was saying.

All the same, he didn't want to depress anyone else. He climbed to his feet and wiped his hands off.

"What's the plan?" asked Zac.

Teague wiped his face and shook his head. "Let's get out of this city," he said. "I've had enough of this place."

Chapter Twenty-Five

THE SOUND OF CRICKETS CREATED A CHORUS OF WHITE NOISE, it was almost calming. Shane stared up at the midnight sky in awe over the sheer beauty of the Milky Way, shining brightly overhead. The new moon provided the perfect cover for the drop. The lack of light made it difficult to be spotted by law enforcement. It also allowed the full glory of the Milky Way to take up the sky. He wondered if Finn ever witnessed the sheer beauty of this.

"Radio check." Pillar's voice came through the handheld radio. "All clear. Over."

"Got ya," replied Manny.

Shane grinned, knowing that somewhere out there Pillar was cursing under his breath at Manny's nonchalant usage of the radio. "You should probably say, over or something."

"Oh yeah," said Manny. He keyed the handset. "Over." He turned to Shane. "It's been so long. You'd think our boy would've broken some of those habits."

Shane lit a cigarette and handed the pack over to Manny. He took a long drag, then turned his attention back to the stars, and exhaled.

In his pocket, his phone buzzed. Annoyed, he dug it out to see that Cat had sent a text message. She knew what they were doing tonight, that radio silence was absolutely imperative. It must be an emergency. Shane opened the message, dammit, she wrote a book. He didn't have time for this. Quickly, he perused the first line.

`Cat: My mom got a message from a priest.`

Irritation rose inside him. What the hell did he care about anyone getting a message from a priest. Especially the old woman, she talks to more priests than non-clergy. Shane scoffed and shoved the device back into his pocket.

"I think we got something," said Manny, peering through a pair of night vision binoculars.

Shane shifted to his belly and held his own set up to his eyes. Two, beat-up trucks plodded their way across the desert floor, heading directly for the drop point.

"Looks like these are our guys. Over," squawked Pillar through the radio.

Shane's phone buzzed again, this time it continued to vibrate, instead of leaving a text, she was trying to call. He didn't have time for this. He had no time for whatever Cat wanted to talk about, whatever it was, had to wait until he got home. He turned off his phone, then shoved it back into his pocket.

Shane brushed his annoyance aside, he'll deal with whatever was going on with Cat later, right now, he had bigger things to do. Through his binoculars, he watched as the lead truck came to a stop in front of their drop site, a large, muscular man hopped out of the passenger seat carrying two duffel bags. After an initial scan of the area, he plodded his way to the base of the sandstone hill where he moved the stone and tucked the bags inside the small cavern. One more scan, and he was on his way back to the truck. He paused and stared up at the ridge where Shane and Manny were perched.

Manny flashed his red signal light three times.

The big man nodded, then climbed into the truck. A moment later, both vehicles were wending their way back through the desert.

"Okay boss, looks like they're all clear. Over," reported Pillar.

Shane held the radio to his lips. "Let's give it another ten minutes, just to be safe, before you go in. Over."

"Roger. Over and out."

The sound of the nighttime desert took over once again. Shane and Manny sat silently, scanning the area through their binoculars.

Loud music erupted from Manny's phone, startling Shane.

The light of the screen cast an electronic glow over Manny's face.

Shane scowled. "I thought we agreed to have our phones on silent."

Manny shrugged and put his phone away. "Yo man, I can't help it if your wife is texting me."

"Cat?" said Shane. "That was Cat? Why the hell is she texting you right now?"

"I don't know, something about a priest."

Shane sighed and shook his head. The radio squawked.

"We're going in. Over," reported Pillar.

"We got you covered," replied Manny. "Oh," he muttered under his breath, then lifted the radio to his lips. "Over."

Shane glared, while Manny merely offered a sheepish shrug in response. Suddenly interrupted by loud music screaming from Manny's phone, once again.

"God dammit," cursed Shane.

This time, Manny turned his phone off and put it away. "Don't look at me, it's your wife," said Manny. "I tried to warn you." He shook his head.

Pillar's voice came over the radio. "Pick up's done. Over."

"Roger that," replied Shane. "We'll see you at the cabin. Over." He shot one more glance toward the night sky, then climbed to his feet and brushed off the dust. Without a word, the duo packed up and loaded themselves into Shane's old pickup truck. In absolute silence, they made their way through the dark hills to a small, rustic cabin. He pulled up and parked alongside Pillar's truck, and turned off the engine.

As he turned off the headlights, he glimpsed a coyote bolting through the beam of light in hot pursuit of a rabbit. In the darkness, a scuffle erupted, followed by cries and howls as the pack celebrated their kill.

Inside the cabin, the lighting was dim. To call this building a cabin was a stretch. A small, single-room structure with a rusted metal roof and four stone walls, each with its own window. The door was a rickety affair, pulled together with planks hanging precariously on rusted metal hinges. Outside, several yards away, was the only recent amenity the cabin offered, an outhouse. What the shack lacked in comfort; it made up for with privacy. There was nothing around for almost one hundred miles.

"Another successful drop," said Odie, smiling widely as Shane entered the room and closed the door behind him.

"Is it all there?" asked Manny.

Pillar sat in front of the table, the two bags open, exposing a pile of money and vials of medicine. While the others waited patiently, he counted the cash. "Four million," he said, looking up at the others. "It's all here."

"Alright," said Shane. "Let's wrap it up and get this back home so we can start the laundry." He smiled at Manny, Odie, and Pillar.

Manny and Shane took the lead while Pillar and Odie followed, keeping a safe distance as they weaved and bobbed over the gravel road on their way back to the highway.

"You should call your wife," suggested Manny. "That way she can get over being pissed between now and when we get home."

Shane chuckled. "Good point."

The phone rang four times, Shane was just about to give up when Catalina answered. "What?" she said coldly.

"Hey, Babe," replied Shane.

"Don't, hey babe, me!" she yelled. "You hung up on me."

Shane cleared his throat. "I didn't hang up on—"

"Bullshit!"

"Babe, I didn't hang up. I turned my phone off." He winced, realizing that was no better.

Catalina set off a string of curses in Spanish. Shane held the phone away from his ear and waited. When the cursing slowed, he put the phone against his ear just in time to catch the end of a sentence. "I could have been in an accident, bleeding out on the side of the road!"

"Were you?" interrupted Shane.

"No! But that's not the point!"

"Okay, then tell me what the point is exactly or I'm hanging up and we can yell over this when I get home."

"Fine!" blurted Catalina. "If you don't want to know where our son is, then you can just fuck off!"

Shane hit the brakes so hard, Manny slammed headfirst into the windshield. The truck skidded to a halt, kicking up a cloud of dust, forcing Pillar and Odie to swerve to avoid crashing into them.

"God damn!" shouted Manny, rubbing his head. "A little warning next time, eh?"

"Where's Finn?" asked Shane, his mouth suddenly dry.

"Maybe we should just wait till you get home—"

"No, no, Catalina—Cat," stammered Shane.

"Finn?" repeated Manny.

Pillar came up to the driver's side window and peered in. "What the hell?" he demanded.

"Cat has word on Finn," answered Manny.

"Woo-hoo!" shouted Pillar. "Yo, Odie, we found Finn."

"We don't know—" warned Manny.

Shane held his hand up to silence the conversation. "Please, Babe," he pleaded.

"Okay," sighed Catalina. "When you were in the Marines, did you know a priest?"

"Father Killoran," replied Shane with a nod. "Yeah. What about him?"

"He called my mom, looking for Manny first, but then he asked about you."

"I'm having a hard time following how this is important."

"I'm getting there," warned Cat. "He told my mom he wasn't calling for any specific reason, other than to catch up. Then left his number with her, for you to call when you had the time."

Irritation grew inside him. Shane pinched his eyes, waiting for his wife to get on with her story, knowing better than to prod her to move it along.

"I saw her this afternoon, and she gave me his number," continued Catalina.

God, he loved this woman with all his heart, but she had a thing for long stories. Holding back the urge to scream, Shane waited.

"Anyway, I called him about an hour ago. He's a nice man."

"Yes, yes, he has to be, he's a priest," replied Shane. "Catalina, please, I'm begging you, please get to the meat of this story."

"Apparently, you came to mind because he recently ran into a young man, new to his city," she paused. "With your eyes."

Shane's heart skipped a beat. He tried to say something but was unable.

"His name is Finn," continued Catalina. "You hear that? We found him."

"How long ago was this?" asked Shane, wary of getting his hope up.

"He first showed up a few weeks ago. Father Killoran said the last time he saw him was yesterday afternoon."

"Where?" asked Shane.

"San Francisco," replied Catalina. "If you hurry your ass, you can catch the next flight out. I can book the tickets for you right now."

Shane glanced down at the clock on the dash. "Do we have time to get there?"

"If you go straight to the airport, you'll just make it."

Shit! The drop! As if Pillar had read his mind, the larger man said, "Odie and I got it from here, you two go! Get our boy!" He clapped a hand on Shane's shoulder and nodded at Manny.

Shane didn't need a second offer. "Book the tickets. Manny and I will go meet with Father Killoran."

"Consider it done," replied Catalina. "Oh, and Babe."

"Yeah?"

"Please bring our boy back home."

Shane nodded. "I will. Love you."

"Love you back." She blew a kiss through the phone and hung up.

A few minutes later, halfway to the El Paso airport, Shane's phone lit up with the flight information.

The plane touched down on the tarmac in San Francisco, marking the end of the longest plane ride in Shane's life. Though only a couple of hours, it felt like days. Unable to relax, he ordered the two drinks the flight allowed, then had Manny hand over his two. Which he begrudgingly did.

At the gate, it took forever for the stupid passengers to disembark. Shane had all he could do to hold back his desire to run them all over on his way out. An opening in the crowd finally came into sight, he made a beeline for it, then he and Manny quickly made their way to the rental car desk.

The clerk at the desk was a little too chatty for Shane. "Just give me the keys and we'll find the car," he bellowed.

Startled, the clerk handed the keys over and pointed to the door leading to the parking garage. Without another word, Shane and Manny bolted through the door, and after several tense moments, they found the car, turned on the ignition, and sped out of the parking garage.

The city whizzed by, a blur of lights flashing one after the other.

The only people, as far as he could tell, were drunk or hopped up on one drug or another.

"Turn left up here," stated Manny, navigating Shane through the city. "The church rectory is a couple blocks up." He pointed.

Sweat seeped from his pores, the steering wheel felt clammy. Shane could hardly control his breathing. He pulled into a parking spot and stared at the tiny building, hidden behind the massive church, and sat there, paralyzed.

"You ready to go in?" asked Manny.

Shane lit a cigarette. "In a second."

Manny nodded and held his hand out for the cigarette. When Shane handed it to him, he took a long drag and exhaled while passing it back to Shane. "Think he's in there?"

"Father Killoran?"

Manny shook his head. "Finn."

Shane handed the smoke to Manny. "I don't think so," he replied, then shook his head. "Who knows?"

"Well, we're about to find out," said Manny. He took one last drag from the cigarette, snubbed it out, and climbed out of the car. He leaned back inside. "Come on, man, let's go see about my nephew."

Shane took the steps to the small door slowly. When he was two yards away, it swung open wide, revealing a familiar, though much older, face.

Father Killoran smiled. "You made it. That was quick." He stepped back. "Come on in."

Age had done little for changing the priest. A few more wrinkles, a lot of gray hair and a few more pounds, but the spark of life in his eyes was still there.

The priest stood before Shane. "Let me get a good look at you," he said. "I see a little of the young Marine I met years ago still in there." He chuckled. "We're both a little more gray though, aren't we?"

"It's great to see you again, Father," said Shane. He wasn't quite sure if he meant it or not. That whole period of his life was something he kept buried deep inside his soul. Until recently, he never ventured there.

The priest grunted and smiled, then turned to Manny. "Your mother is a special woman."

"She's got a mean streak, Father," replied Manny.

"I'm sure she does," chuckled Father Killoran. "Which is why I'm gonna tell you that having children is a blessing in this life." He smiled. "One of the greatest blessings one could receive."

"She got to you, didn't she?" asked Manny, shaking his head.

"I'm just trying to stay on her good side." The priest led them to the small table.

"Ah yes," replied Manny. "Just looking out for yourself here."

Father Killoran poured three shots of whiskey and handed them over to Shane and Manny. "I know when to follow orders. And your mom seems like the kind of woman one doesn't go against."

"You have no idea," muttered Manny.

"Slainte," said Father Killoran, holding his glass in the air.

They touched glasses, then downed their drinks.

"I should've known when I saw him," said the priest, staring at Shane.

"How would you?" replied Shane, pouring himself another shot. "Until a few months ago, we all thought he was dead."

A serious look spread across Father Killoran's face. "I remember. We mourned him." He stared down at his shot glass. "Someday, you'll have to tell me the story of how this all came to be."

Shane scoffed. "Yeah, someday. Still piecing it together myself."

"But in all seriousness," continued the priest. "Finn is a lot like you. How you were."

"Yeah? How's that?"

"He's angry. There's a coldness in his eyes." Father Killoran poured himself another shot, then downed it. "But you can see, hidden behind that is a very broken, confused and hurting young man." He stared at Shane. "He needs you. He needs a family and some strong guidance."

Shane glanced at Manny, then to Father Killoran. "How bad is he? What's he into here?"

"The usual," sighed the priest. "He's fallen into hard times."

"He's still breathing," interjected Manny. "So there's hope."

Shane nodded. Manny was right, as long as Finn was alive, there was hope. He slid his chair back and stood up. "Alright, Father, bring me to him."

Father Killoran guided them on a brief tour of the darkest corners of life in the San Francisco streets. Everywhere they turned, another poor soul was milling about like a member of the undead or passed out, lying in their own filth. It killed Shane to think that his son was among them. He knew, based on Father Killoran's information, that Finn was a mess and not much different from these poor souls.

"We're looking for Aidan," said the priest. "He's a young man about this tall." He held his hand about chest high. "Thin, medium brown short hair, rather feminine features, and narrow frame." He looked down an alley.

"Why?" asked Shane.

Father Killoran paused. "Aidan is sometimes my eyes on the street. He's a runaway, but he hasn't fallen down the rabbit hole like the rest of them. He stays in our shelter, which makes it easier for me to monitor him. His parents send him money once a month." The priest stepped off the curb to cross the street. "They call me every week to check on him."

"Why would a kid live like this when he has parents who love him?" asked Manny, sidestepping a pile of feces.

"Sadly, in this case, it's all a tremendous misunderstanding," replied Father Killoran. "A failure of communication that Aidan took great offense to."

Manny scoffed. "It sounds like he's a spoiled brat who needs his ass whooped."

Father Killoran chuckled. "I prefer to take a kinder approach."

Shane sighed. "You do you, I suppose," he said. "What does this kid have to do with Finn? Are they friends?"

"Kind of," replied the priest. "Aiden keeps tabs on Finn. I'm not so sure Finn reciprocates."

Shane cocked an eyebrow.

"He's obsessed with your son," stated the priest. "Looks up to him. Emulates him if you will. So much so—" He paused. "Well, you'll see."

They turned down an alley and came back out onto the street on the other end. A group of young adults were lounging on a stoop, clearly in their own world. Off to the side stood a thin character. Shane's first inclination was that it was the form of a young female.

"There he is," said Father Killoran. He dashed across the street. "Aidan!" he called out.

The young man turned and smiled at the priest. "Father K!" He smiled. "What are you doing out here?"

The priest gestured toward Shane and Manny. "These men are old friends of mine. They're looking for Finn."

Aidan's face fell. He stared suspiciously at Shane and Manny. "I don't know where he is." He shook his head.

Shane stepped forward. "Look, Aidan, I know you don't know us." Standing in front of this kid, it was striking just how small he was. Shane stared at his face. In the dim glow of the streetlight, he could see that Aidan was wearing two different contact lenses. He cleared his throat and tried not to appear taken aback. "We're not here to hurt Finn." Shane stepped back and removed the brown contact from his eye. He stepped forward into the light so Aidan could see clearly. "I'm Finn's father."

"He said his father was dead," argued Aidan.

"Did he tell you anything else?"

Aidan shook his head. "But the way he said it, he sounded glad you were dead."

Shane nodded. "I don't have the time or the patience for a full family history, son," he said. "I'm gonna need you to tell us where he is."

Once again, the skinny kid shook his head. Shane struggled to contain the urge to slap the kid into reality. He stared at Aidan, calculating what to do next.

"Look, Aidan," said Father Killoran. "I can vouch for these men. They're old friends of mine." He stepped closer to the kid. "Trust me when I tell you, they're good people, and they're here to help Finn."

More head shaking. Irritation swelled in Shane's gut.

"That's not an acceptable answer," interjected Manny, stepping ominously close to the kid.

Aidan held his hands out. "I—I don't—"

"You don't, what?" prodded Shane.

"I don't know where he went!" blurted Aidan.

The priest stepped in front of Aidan and placed his hands on the boy's shoulders. "What do you mean?"

"I mean." The kid licked his lips. "He's gone."

"Gone?" asked Shane, his pulse quickening.

Aidan nodded. "Two guys and a girl showed up yesterday. They showed me pictures of Finn with them." He glanced nervously between Father Killoran and Shane. "They called him their brother."

"Okay," coaxed the priest. "So, you brought them to Finn. What happened next?"

"Finn was high; he was passed out." He raked his fingers through his hair. "A tall one, covered in tattoos and missing some fingers, carried him away."

"Is that the last you saw of him?"

Aidan shook his head. "I followed them." He grinned nervously. "I wanted to make sure they were really friends."

"Go on," prodded the priest.

"They brought Finn to this motel. I stood outside and watched. The next morning a big guy, he looked like one of those guys you see in military movies or something, with another man, about Finn's size, but with blond hair, arrived." He licked his lips and swallowed. "They had a little dog with them. A few hours later, Finn left with the big guy."

"Did Finn appear distressed?" asked the priest.

Disappointment sunk heavily into Shane's heart, while anger rose from his belly.

"No," said Aidan. "He looked—" he shot a glance at Shane, then back at Father Killoran.

"He looked what?" demanded Shane.

"Broken," said the skinny teen. "He looked broken."

"Another fucking dead end!" boomed Shane. He turned and punched the brick wall, instantly regretting his action. He stepped back and held his now bloody hand. "God dammit!"

"There's more!" shouted Aidan.

"Then spit it the fuck out!" shouted Shane. He was all done playing games with this stupid kid.

Aidan winced and stared wide-eyed at him.

"Please Aidan," interjected Father Killoran. "Continue."

"The group at the hotel stayed put, so I stuck around and watched." He smiled proudly. "A few hours ago, another group showed up." He held up his fingers. "Three guys and a girl with long, blonde dreads.

"That's his crew," said Manny. "What happened next?"

Aidan shrugged. "I don't know what they said, but a few minutes after arriving, the blond guy came outside and sat alone. He looked real sad. He tore this up and tossed it." Aidan pulled a slip of paper from his pocket. "I picked up the pieces." He handed it to Father Killoran. "And taped it together."

The priest handed the slip to Shane. He stared down at the images. A young Finn, happy, smiling and obviously in love. He gently folded the photo and tucked it away inside his pocket.

"Hey, that's mine!" shouted Aidan.

Shane glared at the young kid.

Aidan immediately cowered.

"That's it?" asked the priest.

"Yes, Father." Aidan shrugged. "They left a little while after that." He stared up at Shane with watery eyes. "I followed them to the train yard." He licked his lips and swallowed. "They left."

Shane stepped off the curb and stalked away. Behind him, he could hear Father Killoran thank the kid. A moment later, both Manny and the priest were at Shane's side, keeping up with him stride by stride.

They said their goodbyes at the rectory. Shane paid little attention to any of it, in his mind, he was busy mulling over the fact that he missed Finn again. Jesus Christ! Could he ever get a break? He was thinking he may never find his son.

Chapter Twenty-Six

THE CLEAN, WHITE MARBLE FLOORS SPARKLED with the light of the crystal chandeliers that hung overhead. Zac dropped his pack with a loud thud echoing around the giant hotel lobby. The smell of floral air freshener mingled with a nightmare mixture of cologne, perfume and vapes. Each time a person walked past; he caught another whiff of synthetic flowers. It made him want to sneeze. He popped his back and stretched his arms overhead. The last ride was grueling, clinging to the porch frames of grainers all night. Every muscle in his body was stiff, a long soak in a hot tub was in order.

Zac took a seat against the shiny wall next to Teague. Since the night Finn went off the deep end, a strange transformation had taken place in him, Zac wasn't sure how he felt about it. It was subtle, easy to miss if one wasn't paying close attention. The Teague Zac had known for years was funny and thoughtful. Ever since the first morning after Finn's breakdown, a darkness had settled on him. As the weeks passed, Zac witnessed the old Teague melt away. A dark sharpness had settled in.

Back in San Francisco, something inside Teague shattered. In an instant, his countenance changed. The last vestiges of the person he used to be fell away, leaving behind a cold, calculating personage that Zac struggled with. He wanted the original Teague back, but he had no idea how to bring that about. He glanced over to River and Cash, holding hands, so truly in love, talking to Mara and Ben. A smile spread across his face. At least something was going right in his family.

Across the over-sized lobby, Tanner stood in line, waiting to check in. Awkwardly fidgeting from one leg to the other, he made eye contact with Zac and grinned.

Zac turned his attention back to Teague, who was staring off into oblivion; a typical thing for him to do these days.

"Whatcha starin' at?" asked Teague. He slowly turned his gaze to Zac.

"Nothin'," replied Zac.

Teague regarded him with an icy stare. "Got somethin' you want to say?"

Zac shook his head.

"Uh, huh," replied Teague. "Whatever." He turned away, his eyes following a group of young, college-age females walking across the lobby on their way to the gaming floor.

"Is everything okay?" blurted Zac.

An eerie smile spread across Teague's face. "It's all good, my brother."

"You haven't said much about—" The words became trapped in Zac's throat. He was afraid to say Finn's name aloud. He swallowed.

"Finn?" asked Teague. He shrugged. "There ain't nothing to say. Is there? He's made his choice."

There was a bitterness in Teague's tone that resonated with Zac's own feelings about the whole affair. "Nothin's permanent."

"It's over," stated Teague, anger rising in his voice. "You're right, nothing's permanent." He sneered. "Best to accept that and move on."

Zac could hardly argue with Teague, he didn't hold out much

hope that Finn would ever return. Admitting this, even in his silent thoughts, broke his heart.

"Aight dipshits," said Tanner, as he sauntered close. He dangled a key card in his hand. "Our room awaits."

"Room?" asked Mara. "As in singular? For all of us?"

Tanner grinned. "We got a two-bedroom suite."

"How the hell did you swing that?" asked Cash incredulous.

Tanner reached down to rub Gypsy's head, the little dog responded with a happy yap and furious tail wagging. "They were gonna charge us extra for the dog, anyway." He shrugged. "So, I just upgraded, spent a little more and got us a suite."

"Nice," stated Cash.

The elevator whooshed closed with a gush of cool, floral-scented air. The voice over the speaker called out the floors as they passed. "Fifth floor, sixth floor, seventh floor."

"What floor are we on?" asked Teague, watching the digital number change.

"Ten," replied Tanner.

"Tenth floor," said the odd female voice. The elevator stopped, then the doors slid open silently.

The sound of their chatter was oddly muffled as they walked down the hallway. Tanner stopped in front of a door and slid the key card into the lock, it released with an electronic click then he flung the door wide.

"Our accommodations for the next two nights," announced Tanner.

Mara rushed forward; River close behind. "This is amazing!"

Zac entered the large, central sitting area. Two sofas sat in the center opposite one another, across the room a vast wall of open windows peered out across the Las Vegas skyline.

"I figure the couples can each have a bedroom," grinned Tanner. "The rest of us plebs can spread out in here." He glanced around the room at everyone, as soon as his eyes landed on Teague, the smile melted, and he looked away.

Gypsy barked, running from room to room.

"Looks like she approves," chuckled Mara.

"You know," said Nate. "I think I'm gonna give her a bath." He scooped up the little dog and carried her into the bathroom.

River twirled and sauntered into one of the massive bedrooms. She plopped herself down atop the overstuffed comforter, legs swinging over the edge. "This is amazing, Tanner."

"I don't know about you," said Mara, from the other bedroom. She peeped out through the door. "But I'm gonna sleep well tonight."

"Brother, you've been holding out on us," teased Cash.

Tanner shrugged. "All courtesy of Uncle Sam." He flashed a mischievous grin. "All it cost me was a few fingers and a leg."

Teague had been silent the entire time, merely standing by the windows, peering down at the swimming pool below.

"Feeling like a swim?" asked Zac.

Teague shook his head. "Not right now. Maybe later, who knows?"

"How about we eat first," said Tanner, lifting the phone. "I'm thinking a little room service." He smiled widely as he wiggled the menu in his hand.

It was nearly midnight when they stepped off the elevator onto the cavernous casino floor. Flashing lights, electronic music, bells, and chimes mingled with the scent of perfume, aftershave, vapes, cigarettes and liquor. Zac was never quite sure how he felt about these places.

"You headin' to the card tables?" he asked Cash.

Cash raised an eyebrow. "You're not coming?"

Zac shook his head. "I'm gonna hang with Teague. Besides." He smiled. "You'll do a lot better without me there, holding you back. Go turn that fifty bucks into some real money."

"I'll do my best," responded Cash, with a crooked grin.

"Let's go bankrupt some fools," said Ben.

Zac stood alongside Teague and Nate as they watched Ben,

Tanner and Cash disappear into the crowd. He turned to River. "What do you two have in mind?"

"We're gonna wander around," she replied. "See what we find." She wrapped her arm around Teague's. "You wanna come along with us?" she asked.

"I think I'm gonna find me a drink," replied Teague, pulling his arm free.

"Sounds like a solid plan," added Zac. "You comin' with us? Or are you going with the girls?" he asked Nate.

"I feel kinda weird leaving Gypsy alone in the room," the younger man said.

"She's fine," replied Mara. "She's got a comfy sofa and lots of meat to nibble on."

Nate nodded in acceptance.

"Let's go!" shouted River. She locked arms with Mara and the two disappeared into the crowd, leaving behind Zac, Teague, and Nate.

A cocktail waitress sauntered past. She hovered in front of Teague, her eyes slowly taking him in from head to toe. "You want a drink, baby?" she asked, then held out her tray.

Teague took a shot glass of whiskey, downed the brown liquid, then swapped it for a second.

"Slow down, gorgeous," said the woman. "The night's young. You don't want to burn out before things get fun."

Teague smiled flirtatiously. "How much fun we talkin'?"

The waitress flashed a coy smile, moving so close you could barely fit a piece of paper between them. She leaned close, her lips brushing against Teague's ear, and whispered something.

"Don't make promises you can't keep," replied Teague.

With a smile on her face, the waitress turned around and sauntered away, glancing behind her provocatively.

"This is gonna be a good night," said Teague.

Chapter Twenty-Seven

T HE CRISP WHITE SHEETS WERE SOFT AGAINST HIS SKIN, he breathed in, wrinkling his nose at the subtle scent of bleach. Cash opened his eyes; the room was dark as night. Heavy drapes hung across the large windows, blocking out the early morning light. Confirmation was unnecessary, his body knew it was dawn.

Last night was a perfect night. Thanks to his prowess at the card table, their group now had a little over four hundred dollars, instead of the fifty he started with. While it was not necessarily a windfall, it was more than enough to sustain them for a while.

The sheets rustled softly beside him, followed by a warm sensation as River's body snuggled against his. She yawned and rested her head on his chest.

"Good morning," he said, gently kissing the top of her head.

"Mmm, morning," she replied sleepily.

Cash loved these quiet moments. Just the two of them, alone and silent, no words necessary. He ran his finger in tiny circles on her shoulder, relishing in the feel of her soft skin beneath his fingertips.

Outside the room, he heard the familiar sound of the others

moving around. He figured it was about time to get up, but he didn't want to abandon the moment of perfection. He pulled River close, her soft, warm body molding perfectly against his.

"We should get up," she sighed.

"We should stay right here."

River giggled. "But I'm starving."

The mere mention of food was enough to trigger his own hunger, he kissed her atop the head one more time, then lifted his arm. He sat up and slid a pair of jeans on while River slipped his t-shirt over her head. He stared at her for a moment, admiring her beauty. He loved her with all his heart.

At the door, River blew him a kiss, then flung it wide, stepping into the main room of the suite.

Zac and Tanner greeted them with smiles.

River lifted Teague's pack from the empty sofa. "Where's Teague?" she asked.

"Probably still asleep," replied Tanner, flashing a knowing glance at Cash and Zac.

"Asleep where?" Irritation rose in River's voice.

"In whatever hotel room he ended up in," replied Tanner.

River shook her head, then swirled around to face Cash. "What's he talking about?"

"Let's just say Teague got lucky," replied Cash, smirking.

"Lucky how?" She placed her hands on her hips, an obvious signal that her sense of humor was waning.

Cash cleared his throat. "He hooked up with a couple last night."

"A couple of what?" demanded River.

"A couple," he replied. "As in a guy and his girlfriend."

"And you let him go?" she asked. "Why would you let him do that?"

"Because we're not his mommy," replied Tanner, with a chuckle.

River's cold stare melted the smile off his face. "Let me get this straight," she said. "You let him go somewhere with someone we don't know that he also doesn't know, alone. And you're okay with that?"

"He knows them now," laughed Tanner, quickly glancing away to avoid River's gaze.

She reeled on Cash. "What is he talking about?"

"He's okay," replied Cash.

"How do you know that? You haven't seen him all night."

Tanner snickered, this only further enraged River. Cash did his best to hold a straight face.

The door to the suite whooshed open, Nate and Gypsy sauntered in. The little dog waddled up to River, tail wagging furiously, she leaned over and scratched the little dog behind the ears.

Cash hoped this would be the end of this whole conversation.

The door to the other bedroom whipped open. "Good morning!" shouted Mara in her customary bubbly way. She paused and looked around, noting River's angry stance. "What's going on?"

"Teague's not here," replied River.

"I'm still not following," replied Mara. "What's wrong with that?"

River scowled. "No one seems to think it might be a problem that no one knows where he is."

"Oh, we know," interjected Ben, with a smirk plastered on his face.

River grabbed hold of Cash's arm. "Explain. Now!"

"He's okay," replied Cash. Her grip was uncomfortably tight.

"How do you know that?"

"He's been sending photos." He shook his head. "You don't want to see them. But trust me when I say he's doing just fine."

River glanced around the room, pausing to lock eyes with each person as they nodded, then quickly looked away.

"I didn't get any texts from him."

"Neither did I," protested Mara, faking a pout.

"It's a guys-only chat," replied Cash. He pulled free from her vice-like grip then wrapped his arms around her waist. "Teague is fine. He's just burning off a little, excess steam."

A round of chuckles erupted from all the guys in the room.

River shook her head in disgust. "I don't even know which one is worse, the fact all y'all let him wander off with two strangers or the fact he texted y'all with photos of the whole thing."

More sheepish laughter.

Cash pulled her against his body. "I wouldn't say he sent photos of the whole thing."

She pulled away. "Do you even know where he is?"

"He's a few floors down. The couple he hooked up with have a room down there," replied Cash. "He's okay."

With that, the tension in River's body was released. She chuckled lightly. "I swear," she stated, shaking her head. "You boys are gonna be the death of me."

"And yet," sighed Cash, planting a kiss on her forehead. "You still love us and wouldn't know what to do without us around."

She slapped him playfully.

There was a gentle tap at the door. "Room service," called out a male voice.

"Yes!" exclaimed Mara. "I'm starving."

"Mara woke up hungry," explained Ben, as he opened the door and moved aside for the waiter to wheel in a cart of food. "So, we ordered a bunch of different things." He tipped the waiter and escorted him out of the room.

"The French toast is mine first!" shouted Mara.

The savory scent of cinnamon, coffee and chocolate wafted through the air, making Cash's mouth water. If he wasn't hungry before, smelling all that delicious food would have made him so.

Tanner dangled a piece of bacon in the air and whistled. "Here Gypsy."

The little dog sat upright, waiting patiently, tail wagging.

Cash made himself a plate of scrambled eggs, bacon and biscuits and gravy. He took a seat on the couch alongside Zac, who was already devouring a pile of food.

A strange sound, part squeal, part gurgle, erupted from Mara as she pushed her chair back, sprang up and made a run for the bedroom, all the while holding her mouth.

River leaped to her feet and followed close behind.

"What the?" asked Cash, glancing over at Ben.

The sound of Mara retching could be heard from the bedroom.

"Too much to drink last night?" asked Cash.

Ben shook his head. "She stopped drinking a couple of months ago." He shoved a piece of sausage into his mouth. "When she found out she's pregnant."

Zac choked and Nate stared in shock, both echoing Cash's feelings.

"Wh-what?" asked Cash.

"We were gonna wait another day or two," said Mara, wiping her face, as she entered the room.

River took a seat on the arm rest beside Cash.

"You knew about this?" he asked.

She winked and stole a piece of bacon from his plate. "Yup, she told me last night."

Mara poked the food around on her plate with a fork, the look on her face was one of disgust. She put the fork down. "It's the hormones," she said. "Nothing tastes right."

"You should still try to eat something," warned River.

Mara shook her head. "I just can't right now." She smiled. "It'll subside soon enough. If I'm right, I'm nearing the end of the first trimester. According to my momma and older sister, the first trimester is the worst. But, the more nauseous the first twelve weeks, the healthier the baby. It means all the hormones are working hard to make a perfect, little human." She rubbed her hand in circles over her belly. "Ain't that right?" she cooed to her tummy.

Cash glanced over at Ben, who was positively beaming at Mara. For a moment, he kind of envied them. He moved his gaze over to River.

"So, what does this mean?" asked Zac. "Y'all gonna settle down?"

Ben nodded. "Yeah, like Mara said, we were gonna tell y'all soon enough." He lifted Mara's hand to his lips and gave it a little peck.

"Wow!" said Nate. He ripped a piece of sausage off and fed it to Gypsy. "Does that mean you're going back to New York?"

"Hell, no!" stated Ben. "Not on your life. I would never raise my kid the way I was raised." He shook his head. "That lifestyle is soul-crushing poison."

"We're going back to Utah," said Mara. "Ben's gonna work for my uncle for a bit." She shrugged. "We'll figure it out after the baby arrives."

"Mara's parents are letting us stay in a small, in-law's apartment above their garage," added Ben.

Cash could hardly believe his ears; his emotions were conflicted. A part of him was happy for his friends, especially since they were both so happy about their future; another part of him was sad. A sense of melancholy swept over him—this was almost too much change for him.

"So, what?" said Cash. "You're gonna settle down and become suburbanites?"

Mara giggled. "Our plan is to stay with my parents' until the baby's born." She smiled at Ben. "After that, we'll decide what we want to do."

"Who knows," interjected Ben. "Maybe we'll build out a schoolie or something." He grinned. "Hit the road that way for a few years."

"Wow," said Cash. He turned to Tanner. "What're your plans? Are you staying with them?"

Tanner scoffed. "I ain't that joined to their hips," he replied. "I'm not in any hurry to be tied down with little rug rats. I'll see them settled, then I'm out." He clapped a hand on Nate's shoulder. "Nate and I discussed it and I'm gonna travel with him and Gypsy for a while."

Cash nodded. He honestly didn't know what to say. Judging by the look on Zac's face, neither did he.

"Which brings us to another thing," said Mara, cautiously. "Ben has Tanner." She flashed a coy smile. "River, would you be my maid of Honor?"

"Wait," interjected Cash. "There's gonna be a wedding too?"

Mara smiled. "Of course."

River squealed and jumped to her feet. "Oh my god, yes!" She ran over and hugged Mara. "When? Where?"

"We're gonna make the announcement to the group," replied Mara. "We want to have a little ceremony at Stoney's. I think I heard Spinner once say he was a licensed pastor."

"Of course he is," quipped Cash. "Why am I not surprised?"

River giggled. "This is gonna be so awesome!" She hugged Mara tight. "I'm so happy for you!"

"I wanted to wait 'till we found Finn," said Mara. "But that didn't work out exactly how I wanted." She looked around at everyone in the room. "Like any of us wanted."

Whenever Cash thought about Finn, he ranged between sadness and heartache to anger, with little in between. He'd give anything to have things return to the way they used to be. He couldn't help but wonder what the future of their little group would look like. Would they even be together in a year? He brushed aside the looming sadness, determined to enjoy the time they had together as long as possible.

Chapter Twenty-Eight

Mara and Ben's great news brightened the mood considerably. Though she would miss catching up with them in random cities, River knew that this, by no means, was goodbye. They promised they would make the trek down to Terlingua at least once a year to see everyone. Still, change was always difficult.

It was mid-afternoon when Teague finally wandered back into the hotel room. With hardly a word, he wrapped himself in a blanket and curled up on the sofa. River fought the urge to confront him about being away all night, after a long conversation with Cash, she realized it was probably best if Teague moved forward with his life. If he was happy, who was she to step in and ruin his fun?

Since no one wanted to keep Teague awake, the group decided to leave Gypsy in the room with him as he slept, while they spent the afternoon by the pool. Before they left, River wrote a quick note on a napkin and left it in a spot she was sure he would find it.

The desert sun felt warm against her skin. River lounged poolside for as long as she could, letting her body take in the sun's rays. Beside her, Mara chatted away enthusiastically about her pregnancy and impending motherhood. Her excitement was infectious. For the first time in her life, River found herself wondering what it would feel like to have a baby grow inside her belly. To be a mom. Startled by her own thoughts, River strolled over to the edge of the pool, and dove in, letting the clear, cold-water rush over her body.

It was close to dinnertime when they returned to the room. Much to River's dismay, Teague was already gone. He left a note on the table, informing them that he would see them down at the casino later. This bothered her. She didn't quite know why, but in her gut, something was off. It was almost as though he was doing his best to pull away. She didn't care for any of it.

"Do you really think he's okay?" she asked Cash.

He cocked an eyebrow. "Who? Teague?"

River nodded. "We haven't seen much of him since we got here."

"Based on the things he sent last night," added Ben, with a smirk. "He's doing just fine. Better than me, that's for sure." He quickly dodged a playful slap from her.

All joking aside, River knew something was off. It wasn't like Teague to stay away like this. Or was it? She realized that she never knew him without Finn. So how could she be sure this was unusual behavior? She turned to Zac. "What's your opinion?"

Zac shrugged, the look in his eyes told River all she wanted to know. He wasn't quite sure either, and it made him uneasy. That didn't bode well for her own feelings.

"Tell you what, Mama Bear," teased Cash. He grabbed her by the waist and pulled her close against his body. "Let's get cleaned up and head down to the casino. We'll track him down and you can see for yourself he's doing just fine." He leaned down, pressing his forehead against hers. "Sound good?"

River nodded her head, doing her best to push down her growing sense of unease.

The casino floor was a circus of activity. Lights, music, digital bells, chatter, laughter, and cheers with the odd call for drinks or cocktails created a party-like atmosphere. The sweet scent of candy-flavored vapes mixed with cigarette and cigar smoke permeated the air. Now and then, a slight skunky scent floated by.

Cash, Tanner, and Ben were eager to hit the poker tables again, but River insisted Cash stay with her and Zac as they searched for Teague. They wandered through row after row of electronic slot machines, past roulette wheels and craps tables—so far, nothing.

She was just about to lose hope when Mara gently tugged her arm. Her gaze followed where Mara pointed. Across the room, surrounded by people, sat Teague, playing blackjack.

A smile that never quite made it to his eyes spread across his face when he saw the group approaching. "Care to join?" he asked.

Cash took a seat to one side; Zac took the other. After some chatter with the dealer, they both put money on the table that the dealer exchanged for chips.

Teague took a drag from a cigarette.

That was something new. River tried to recall ever seeing him smoke anything other than weed but she couldn't. A blonde waitress sauntered up, tray in hand. She rubbed her body against Teague and smiled as she placed a fresh drink on the table. Anger welled up inside River, she knew it was irrational, but for her, seeing the woman hanging all over Teague felt—wrong. The waitress whispered something in his ear, then she sauntered off, disappearing into the crowd.

"You seem to be making friends," said River, her tone angrier than she meant to be.

He glanced up at her and smirked. "What can I say? I play well with others."

The dealer placed a card on the table in front of him. He tapped the table, and she placed a second and waited. He waved his hand to say he wanted no more cards, then the dealer moved on to Cash. Teague took a sip of his whiskey, then a drag from the cigarette.

"When did you start smoking?" asked River.

He exhaled in her direction. "Does it matter to you?" He took another drag. "There're a lot of things you don't know about me."

River didn't care much for his dismissive tone. Whatever his deal was, he needed to get over it fast.

The dealer flipped her cards, showing a total of seventeen. A round of cheers erupted around the table as the dealer stacked chips in front of everyone.

A tense cloud hung heavy between River and Teague. In an attempt to lighten the mood, she decided to change her tone. "You missed the good news," she said.

Teague grinned. "Really? Always up for good news," he said. "Fill me in."

The dealer dropped a card in front of Zac, he tapped the table, and she dropped a second for a total of nineteen. He waved his hand, and the dealer moved to Teague.

As soon as the dealer passed to Cash, River announced, "Ben and Mara are having a baby."

Teague peered up at Mara, then Ben. "That so?"

They both nodded.

"Is this good news?" asked Teague, looking at Ben. His tone was more cold than playful.

An irritated look spread across Ben's face. "Yes. Yes, it's great news," he replied.

"Well, then," said Teague, with a curt nod. "Congratulations." He let the conversation die right there, turning his focus to the cards on the table.

Mara took hold of River's arm. "Come on," she said. "Let's leave them to play."

River pulled away. She leaned closer to Teague. "We're leaving early tomorrow morning, so don't stay out too late," she warned.

"Going where?" asked Teague, taking another sip of his whiskey.

This time, Cash entered the conversation. "We're heading to Stoney's so Ben and Mara can get hitched."

"We put the word out on the server," added Ben. "Everyone's meeting there."

"Everyone, huh?" asked Teague. He lit another cigarette.

"Yes," stated River. "Everyone."

Teague tapped his smoke on the edge of an ashtray in front of him as he exhaled. Smoke billowed around his head. "About that," he said. He stared out across the casino floor. "I'm thinking I'm gonna stay here for a while."

"Come again?" asked Cash.

River could hardly believe her ears. She stood still, dumbfounded, staring.

"I'm not really feelin' the whole Nomad vibe anymore," said Teague dismissively. "I think I'm gonna stick around here and see what happens." He took another sip of his whiskey. "Maybe get a job slingin' cards." He winked at the dealer. "You know, do some more partying."

Zac jumped to his feet, knocking the chair over behind him. He tossed his chips atop the table, shook his head, and stormed away.

River knew she had to follow him, there was no telling what sort of trouble he could get into in his present state of mind. Even though she wanted to stay and hash this out with Teague, Zac needed her more. Before turning away, she leaned close. "You're an asshole. This ain't over," she said, as she shoved his shoulder, then took off after Zac.

"Zac," she called out, but the noise of the casino drowned out her voice. River picked up her pace, trying to catch up. In the corner of her eye, she could see security keeping pace, tracking Zac. She had to catch up with him before they did.

A short woman stepped in her path, River hopped to the side to avoid running over the woman, only to step on the foot of another lady sitting at a machine. "I'm so sorry," she offered, then bolted away. Lord, how was he getting faster? He didn't seem to be picking up his pace.

Zac broke free from the crowd, stepping into a small entry right as security caught up with him. He stopped when they told him to, shifting his weight from one leg to the other. River had seen this stance before, she understood all too well that at any moment, things could go south. She stepped between Zac and the guards.

"It's okay," she shouted, hands up in front of her. "We're going outside." She placed her hands against Zac's chest and could feel his heart pounding against his rib cage. She glanced back at the security guards. "We're just gonna get us some fresh air." She shoved Zac toward the set of glass doors. They whooshed open and a gush of warm, desert air hit her in the face, warming her entire body.

The artificial sounds of the casino vanished as the doors closed behind them. They stepped out into the night, Zac still maintaining an angry pace with his steps. River did the best she could to keep up, knowing that eventually, he would tire and stop long enough for her to catch her breath.

Traffic whizzed by on the street as they walked down the sidewalk, weaving through small groups of people, finally coming to a beautiful water fountain.

Bright lights illuminated sprays of water that exploded into the air, crashing down onto the smooth surface, creating ripples. Music played calmly in the background, creating a sense of serenity.

Zac finally stopped walking, he spun around, and for the first time, River could see his face. Tears streamed down his cheeks, his face was red and blotchy. He shook his head and raked his fingers through his hair, then slumped onto the ground, leaning against the fountain wall.

River rushed to his side and wrapped her arms around him, wanting to take his pain away. His face echoed her inner most feelings about what had just taken place with Teague, though she was too busy worrying about Zac to dwell on it.

His heavy body leaned against hers, jerking uncontrollably with each sob. She silently stroked his hair, waiting for him to calm down. If she had to sit there all night, she would. In all the years she had known Zac, she couldn't recall ever seeing him this distraught, though honestly, they had never experienced so much loss before. The past few months had been nothing but trauma. Thank goodness she had Cash. A pang of guilt stabbed her heart. Through everything, she had Cash to hold on to—to bring joy into her life. Zac had no one. He'd been suffering through all of it alone. From the first day he set out with Teague, to now, poor Zac had been holding everyone up, all the while struggling with his own emotions alone. Her heart broke.

His sobs subsided and a moment later, he sat up and rested his elbows on his knees. River hooked her arm around his, just to let him know she was there and she cared.

"I don't understand why," said Zac.

"Why what, honey?"

"Why does one person get to tear everything apart?" He turned to face her. "I honestly don't think I can do it no more." He shook his head, his face growing red again. "It feels like I'm pulling a trailer up this steep hill with everyone inside. Not only is no one helping, but they're all doing their best to drag the trailer backward."

A tear ran down his face. "I can't do it anymore, but I don't know what else to do."

River wiped the tear away. She smiled. "Baby, you don't have to do it alone anymore." Tears welled up in her eyes. "I'm here."

"For how long?" he wailed. "Everyone's leaving. My family's fallin' apart, and I can't do anything to hold it together anymore."

"You don't have to be the one holdin' things together," she shook her head. "Let me help."

She rested her head against his shoulder. "I ain't going nowhere." He kissed the top of her head.

After a long pause, he said, "It's bullshit, you know."

"What's that?"

"Why does Finn get to dictate whether we stick together or not, as a family?"

River sat up and wiped her face. "You're right. Why does he get to even have a say? He left."

"That's what I'm asking."

"I mean, fuck him," continued River. "If he doesn't want to be with us, then he can go fuck off and do whatever the hell he thinks is better."

A tiny chuckle escaped Zac. "Now you're sounding like the voice in my head."

"Well, sometimes you just gotta say the truth out loud," replied River. Her defiant mood shifted as she thought about Teague. "I feel bad for Teague though," she said.

Zac sighed. "I did too."

"Did? What do you mean, you did?"

Zac shook his head. "Something's changed in him. He ain't Teague anymore." He looked River in the eyes. "I mean, he's there, and it's his voice talkin' but—" He paused, struggling to find the right words. "His heart ain't there. It's like a major part of him is gone."

River thought about what Zac was saying. She poured through her memories of the past several weeks, quietly cursing herself for being so wrapped up in her own world. Combing through the images in her mind, every time she came close to seeing what Zac was referring to, an image of Cash, followed by a swell of happy emotions, changed her vision. She was so blind for so long. Maybe all of this was her fault. If she hadn't been so enthralled with Cash, she would have seen what Zac was seeing. She would have been able to intervene—to stop things from getting this far.

"Don't go beating yourself up for not noticing it," said Zac.

"You need to quit reading other people's minds."

He smiled. "Maybe you shouldn't be so easy to read."

She shoved him playfully. "I don't know what's gonna happen with Teague," said River. "But I promise you." She lifted his chin and stared into his eyes. "I promise you; Cash and I are here with you forever."

He smiled and pulled her in for a strong hug.

Cried out, and talked out, they sat by the fountain and watched the people as they passed by. The comfortable silence gave River the time she needed to come to terms with her own emotions.

It was nearly one in the morning when they entered the hotel room. Everyone was there, waiting for them. To River's surprise, Teague was there, too.

He waited until Zac took a seat, then pulled up a chair in front of him. Leaning against the backrest, he said, "I'm sorry."

Zac stared.

"I've been an ass," continued Teague. "I already apologized to everyone here. Now I need to say it to you." He smiled. "I've been an ass lately. I know. And you put up with it." He leaned back. "I'm surprised you've put up with me this long."

Zac said nothing. His face was red, tears welled up in his eyes. River wanted to run across the room and wrap her arms around him, but she knew it was best if she stayed out of this conversation. She took hold of Cash's hand and squeezed.

Teague leaned forward, holding his hand out to Zac who took hold of it and pulled him forward, chair and all, into a big hug.

They separated. Teague wiped a tear from his eye. "I guess I've been a real couillon."

"Yes, you have," agreed Zac. He flashed a small grin. "Try not to suck anymore. Please?"

Laughter erupted around the room.

Teague stood up and gently shoved Zac's head. He walked across the room and stood in front of River, allowing her to get a good look at him for the first time since the casino. She noted the small purple welt on the side of his cheek and a tiny split on the side of his lip, still a little red with a thin scab. "Frankly," he said. "I'm surprised you didn't kick my ass during all of this."

River glanced at Cash, then back at Teague, wondering what the hell happened after she left. Whatever went on, she was pretty sure Cash would fill her in later. She wrapped her arms around Teague. "You're lucky I had a distraction."

"I'm sorry, woman," said Teague. "Think you can forgive me?"

She kissed him on the cheek and hugged him hard. For the first time in a long time, a sense of real happiness had settled in. She had hope for the future. Things were beginning to feel right again.

Teague pulled away and strolled over to the table, where he poured several cups of juice. He walked around the room, handing one to each person. He stood in the middle of the room and lifted his glass. "To Ben, Mara and the little bean. May happiness and good health follow you." He winked at Mara. "And thank you for making this boy grow the fuck up."

Mara giggled.

He grinned. "Laissez les bon temps rouler. God help the world, they're about to be parents."

Cheers erupted around the room, followed by laughter and a sense of togetherness so strong, River was convinced the worst was finally behind them.

Chapter Twenty-Nine

CASH SLID BETWEEN THE COOL, CLEAN BEDSHEETS, a welcome end to a long day. River snuggled up beside him, her warm body generating an astonishing amount of heat.

He stared up at the ceiling, recalling the events that took place after River and Zac left the table. What a night.

When Zac stormed away, everyone stared at one another in shock. The fact that he was so upset he didn't even try to talk, was astonishing.

Cash could hardly recall an instance where his friend reacted in such a way. He watched as River disappeared into the crowd, chasing after Zac. He wanted to follow them, but he knew if he walked away now, he would lose the opportunity to hash this out with Teague. He turned and suggested perhaps they should follow. To his astonishment, Teague tapped the table to start another round as though nothing had happened.

"What the hell are you doing?" demanded Cash incredulous.

Teague studied his cards, then waved his hand. The dealer turned to Cash; he shook his head. "I'm done."

With a curt nod, the dealer proceeded with the other players around the table.

Cash was livid. He moved close to Teague. "Don't you think we should go see what's up with Zac?"

"What for?" Teague shrugged.

"Because he's our brother," stated Cash. "You telling me you don't care what he's upset about?"

"Mais la!" replied Teague dismissively. "I don't care. I'm done caring." He tapped his ear for emphasis. "Taton?" He stared into Cash's eyes. "I'm done giving a shit about anybody." He gazed forward. "I'm all done chasing after fools who wanna run away." He waved his hand. "People wanna go, let 'em go."

Electricity surged throughout Cash's body; his muscles twitched. Everyone around the table was staring, including a couple of big security guards who had materialized shortly after Zac took off. "Come on," said Cash, resting his hand on Teague's shoulder. "Let's take a walk."

Teague shrugged him off. "No," he said flatly, never even bothering to look at Cash.

That was it, something snapped. Cash grabbed hold of Teague by the shirt collar and dragged him off the table.

A scuffle ensued, ending when Teague shoved Cash away.

"Get your fucking hands off me!" boomed Teague.

A crowd gathered. Tanner, Nate, and Ben did their best to run interference with the guards.

"Please," begged Cash. "Let's just go outside and talk in private." He placed his hands on Teague's chest, trying to guide him toward the door, but Teague shoved him away. Cash stumbled backward, were it not for Tanner, he would have fallen to the floor. He lunged forward, landing a punch to the side of Teague's face.

Teague stumbled back, holding a hand to his cheek. He sneered and charged for Cash.

The next thing Cash knew, both were belly down on the floor. A knee pressed hard against his back while the guard wrenched his arms behind him, cuffing his hands. Security escorted them down into the bowels of the casino to a dank, windowless, concrete room. After cuffing them to opposite ends of the table, the guards walked out, leaving them to stare at one another.

Cash was far too angry to speak, he focused on the buzz of the fluorescent light overhead. The room smelled clean, like bleach, he couldn't help but wonder why. He glanced across the table and found Teague staring directly at him.

The instinctive reaction for Cash in tense situations was always sarcasm. He couldn't help it; it was how he was made. "I wanna thank you for helping me knock getting arrested in a Vegas casino off my bucket list," he quipped.

Teague shook his head. He smiled, then winced at the pain on the side of his mouth, a tiny trickle of blood appeared at the corner of his lips. "Fonchock," he muttered.

Cash snickered. "Admit it. You've always secretly wanted to see the underbelly of casino life." He glanced up at the ceiling. "With all the money this place makes, you'd think they could afford some better lights."

"And some better chairs," added Teague, with a grin.

"Right?" agreed Cash. "And some water." He turned to face the double-sided mirror across the room. "Hey, any chance of us getting some water in here?"

"Whiskey," chimed Teague. "I'd much rather have something with a little kick to it."

Cash nodded. "Excellent idea," he said. "On the rocks or straight up?"

"Oh, definitely straight up," replied Teague, grinning from ear to ear. "The ice only waters down the whiskey."

The door burst open and one of the giant goons who cuffed them entered the room, bringing with him the overpowering scent of cologne mixed with coffee. He sat at the table and stared back and forth at Cash and Teague.

"You, ah, gonna tell us why you dragged us down here to the

dungeon?" asked Cash. "Or are we just gonna sit here staring at one another?" He leaned back against the stiff metal chair. "I mean, if so, be warned." He smirked. "I always win staring contests."

"He's right, you know," interjected Teague. "I've seen it. The man has amazing staring capacity. His lack of brain mass comes in real handy sometimes."

Cash chuckled. "That sounded like a compliment all the way up 'til the end."

"That's what we call a chic, in my neck of the woods," replied Teague.

"Ah," replied Cash. "I thought it was canaille."

Teague shook his head. "No, no, no, that's what you call the person who's pulling a fast one."

Cash nodded. "Well, I learned something new today."

"Any day spent learnin' ain't a day lost," quipped Teague.

"Nice one," replied Cash. "That from your PawPaw?"

"I made it up just now."

"Ah, well, it's definitely one of your best," replied Cash. "You should write that down."

"I would," replied Teague. He lifted his hands as far as the cuffs would allow. "I'm a little indisposed at the moment."

"Enough!" boomed the giant guard. His voice reverberated off the concrete walls. He stared at both. "Care to explain why you came to my casino to cause your bullshit?"

"Well, I wouldn't say we came here to cause bullshit," said Teague. "I actually came here to win a few rounds of blackjack."

"And I, poker," added Cash.

"Maybe a little time by the pool," said Teague.

Cash nodded. "The bartender down there made these sweet cocktails."

"Really? I'm intrigued. What was it called?"

"Not sure. But it was good," replied Cash. "I wonder if he would share the recipe."

The guard scoffed. "You two are real jokers." He leaned back in his chair. "Do you realize how much trouble you could be in right now?"

"Sir, I promise you," said Teague. "Whatever trouble we're in for this, ain't nothin' when his girlfriend gets a hold of us."

Cash burst out laughing. "She is gonna kick our asses."

"That the blonde with the dreadlocks who ran after the big ol' boy?" asked the guard.

Both Teague and Cash nodded.

"She looks like a spitfire," said the guard. The big man's mood shifted. "Look," he said. "Your friends are outside waiting. The tall one, Tanner, explained a little about what was going on." He paused and stared. "He said you have a room upstairs. Now, I can't let you back out on the casino floor." The big man pointed a beefy finger at Cash, then Teague. "As of right now, you two are banned from playing in this casino indefinitely. You understand?"

They nodded.

"Good." The big man slid his chair back and stood up. "I'm gonna make you sit here while I do the paperwork. After that, you'll be escorted up to your room." He stared at them. "Which is where you'll stay the rest of the night. First thing in the morning, a couple of my men will escort you and your crew out of the building." He reached for the doorknob. "Bright and early fellas, so be ready." He stepped across the threshold, then paused and turned back. "And thank your buddy, Tanner. If he wasn't a brother, both of you would not be getting off so lightly."

The door closed, leaving Cash and Teague alone in the cold, dank room once again.

"He seemed like a cool dude," said Cash.

Teague nodded. A somber look took over his face. "I'm sorry."

"Forgiven," replied Cash.

"No, hear me out," blurted Teague. "I've been wrapped up in my own bullshit for so long, I forgot y'all were still around. I let myself fall into a hole."

"You've had your own stuff to work through. We all understood that."

Teague nodded.

"Look," said Cash. "No one's expecting you to get over it quickly. This whole mess has been hell on all of us. Most especially you." He sighed. "All any of us want is for you to let us in."

Teague smiled.

The chill of the room dissipated, even the buzz of the lights seemed to quiet.

"River's gonna beat our asses," said Teague.

"Yeah, she is."

"I've got some serious making up to do with Zac."

Cash nodded. "I'd say you do."

"I'll get on it as soon as Bubba cuts us loose." Teague leaned back in his chair. "Seriously though, you would think they could have some chairs that were a little more comfortable down here."

Not long after, another guard, every bit as beefy as the last, entered the tiny room, undid their cuffs, and escorted them through the bowels of the casino to a special elevator that was used only by staff. After delivering them to the room, the guard warned them not to leave.

In the quiet hotel room, Cash lay there in the dark, listening to the soft sound of River snoring. Yet another thing he adored about her. He smiled, feeling hope for the first time in a long time. Maybe this was the turning point. Maybe, just maybe, they could all get on with the business of living and enjoying life again.

Chapter Thirty

FINN HAD LITTLE RECOLLECTION OF THE DAYS FOLLOWING his run-in with Ben, Mara and Tanner, truth be told, he had little recollection of the past few months.

In stark contrast, he remembered the events of that horrible night all too well. They played over and over in his mind, like a horrific movie he couldn't turn off. An endless loop of nightmares he created with his own hands. The shouts, the screams, the sound of his fists pummeling Teague; the whimpers, the pleading. The metallic scent of blood, all of it, was permanently burned in his senses, no matter how hard he tried, he couldn't free himself of it. Every time he peered down at his hands, he saw blood stains that no amount of soap and water could wash clean.

The only reprieve from the horror came in the form of drugs. When he was high, the sounds, smells, and emotions slipped away. He was free, floating on a cloud of nothingness, and it felt good. His lucid states were few and far between, a montage of snippets of interactions with various people, many of whom were now faceless voices. Through the din, a scant few were vivid. Father Killoran was one of those. Finn wasn't quite sure why, but the old priest made an impression strong enough to embed their conversations deep into his psyche. A part of him liked Father K, but he had had enough of the pain and heartache that came when he allowed people to get close. That was enough to keep Finn from ever taking the old man up on his offers of help. He didn't want help; he wanted to be numb.

When he and Gunner left the others behind at the motel, Finn was still somewhat under the influence. Not quite enough to block out his thoughts entirely, but enough for him to remain calm and give him some sense of control over his own mind. As the hours ticked by, that control faded. The retching was constant. So much so, Finn wondered how on earth he could have anything left in his stomach to purge out. A deep, pounding headache throbbed mercilessly in his skull, the pain so intense, Finn was sure any moment his head would explode. At a certain point, the pain was so sharp; he wished it would happen, just to end his misery.

They trudged on. Sometimes Gunner carried him, other times he provided a solid form to lean upon. Vaguely aware they were walking, Finn continued to put one foot in front of the other, blindly following Gunner to wherever the hell they were going. Sidewalks gave way to country roads, which ultimately turned into hiking paths surrounded by tall trees. Up and down hills, through thick forests, all of civilization disappeared. In between bouts of vomiting and waves of dizziness, Finn spent his time staring down at his feet, willing his body to cooperate.

Off and on, when periods of lucidity settled upon him, Finn would attempt to run away. Gunner's only recourse during those times was to handcuff himself to Finn. The metal rings needed to be tight, to keep him from wriggling free. This didn't stop him from trying, he struggled so much, deep, dark purple rings formed around both wrists.

On the fourth night, Finn awoke to the sight of a bright fire burning. The familiar pop, crackle and sizzle sounds bounced off the wall of surrounding trees. His mind was clear—somewhat. He blinked, allowing his eyes to come into focus. A bottle of water floated in front of his face.

"Drink some," said Gunner with that deep, gravelly voice of his. "It'll make you feel better."

Finn took the bottle and stared down at it, afraid to drink for fear the retching would return.

"Go on," prodded Gunner. "Little sips."

The pounding in his head was a dull drone, every muscle in his body screamed for mercy. Finn lifted the bottle to his lips, said a silent prayer that this wouldn't trigger any more vomiting, then sipped. The cool water sloshed around his mouth and poured down his parched throat. It was amazing. He took one larger gulp, then Gunner pulled the bottle away.

"I said slow," admonished the older man, his tone calm. "Your body's been through the wringer."

He handed the bottle back to Finn, who clasped it tightly in his tired hands, holding it close to his chest like a prized possession.

The campfire crackled and popped, glowing embers erupted into the cool night air, escaping the hungry flames of the fire. He watched the bright, red flecks of fiery ash soar up, only to burn out and float to the ground.

Finn rubbed the purple bruises around his wrists, it would be at least another week before they went away completely.

With each sip, his body felt more and more like it belonged to him, the weakness was still there, but at least he was present. Unfortunately, that meant his mind was waking up. It started with the faint sound of a whimper, so vivid, Finn startled and searched around, positive he would find the person nearby who had made that sound. Nothing. He took another sip, reveling in the sensation of the cool water flowing down to his belly.

Finn stop!

He flinched. A cold chill ran down his spine.

You're a piece of shit!

He spun around, expecting to see Daniel whispering in his ear. Nothing.

Finn! What did you do?

He peered up through knotted, greasy hair to see Gunner watching him.

Don't even think he cares about you. Who could possibly care about you? You're a loser. A pathetic, shallow loser.

Finn shook his head. He tried to rake his fingers through his hair, but the knots proved too thick for any of that, instead, he pinched his fingers to his eyes. He opened them to a bowl of stew held before him. Steam rose, filling his nostrils with the savory aroma of beef and carrots. Finn's mouth watered. When was the last time he ate? He wrapped his filthy fingers around the warm bowl, fighting the urge to recoil at the sight of grime embedded around his overgrown and chipped nails.

"Take it slow," urged Gunner. "Like the water. We want you to keep this down."

Finn nodded or trembled, he wasn't quite sure which. His hand shook as he scooped a heaping spoonful of stew. Not entirely sure how this was going to go down, he held the spoon to his lips and sipped. The hairs from his overgrown mustache tickled his nose. He smoothed the hair away from his lips as best as possible. With this much facial hair, there was no way to be neat about things, so with no more fussing, he shoved the spoon into his mouth. A blast of flavors mingled on his taste buds. Savory meat and herbs, mixed with carrots and potato. He closed his eyes and chewed slowly, to prepare his stomach. Much to his surprise, it went down without an issue. He fought back the urge to swallow the rest of the bowl with one gulp, opting instead to take it one little bite at a time.

The voices continued to chatter, like ghostly companions of doom, they spewed a constant barrage of insults resting in a bed of steady, unrelenting reminders of all the atrocities he committed. In the sparse moments when the voices subsided, his heartache took over. Darkness and dread settled into his soul, there was no way out. He ruined everything he ever cared about. There was no going back. Even if the others could forgive him, which he was sure they wouldn't, he was incapable of forgiving himself. Daniel was right all along; he was a useless waste of flesh—a disease that would only destroy anything and anyone who dared get close. Why bother anymore? He was destined to live a life of solitude and loneliness, lest he become exactly what his father had. A cruel, hateful loser—that was his destiny.

Gunner climbed to his feet and brushed himself off. He stretched and peered down at Finn. "I'm gonna go take care of some business." He paused and stared. "Can I leave you alone for two seconds? Or do I have to take you with me?"

Finn shook his head. He had no plans to run—he had something else in mind. "You go," he replied. "I'm good."

"Hang tight," said Gunner. "I'll be right back." The bigger man walked into the tree line and disappeared.

Finn sat, listening to the crackle of the fire, straining to hear Gunner's footsteps falling softly on the forest floor, moving away, then he grabbed Gunner's pack and rifled through the pockets.

It was here somewhere. He could have sworn he saw Gunner put it away a couple of days ago. Not in either of the side pockets. He pulled open the main pouch and shoved his hand inside. His fingertips brushed against cold steel. Bingo! With a single sigh, Finn pulled the gun from the pack and held it out before him.

Now you're thinking right. Whispered the dark voice of Daniel. *What else have you got to live for? Do it!*

Finn faltered. His hand trembled. Tears streamed down his face, seeping into the mass of facial hair along his jaw. He sniffled. Why was he crying? What could he possibly be holding on for? There was nothing left for him, he made sure of that by his own deeds. The only thing he had to look forward to was a lifetime of heartache, anger, and pain.

A twig snapped by the tree line. Gunner stood, wide eyed, staring at him. "Son, put it down," he said, taking a step closer, his hands held up before him.

Finn shook his head.

Oh, for crying out loud, just fucking do it! shouted Daniel's voice.

Finn! What did you do!

Like father, like son!

The voices churned in his head, creating a din of noise so loud he could barely hear Gunner.

"This isn't the way, son," said Gunner, now a mere four feet away.

It was now or never. Finn raised the gun to his temple. Hand trembling, he sobbed as he closed his eyes and pulled the trigger.

A hollow click echoed around the clearing. Silence descended, the only sound that of the crackling fire. Finn opened his eyes. This can't be! He stared down at the gun in his hand. It was real. He raised the weapon once again and pulled the trigger. Nothing, just a hollow click. He pulled again, and again, and again. Nothing. Howling in anguish, he banged the useless piece of metal against his forehead until he finally dropped his hand on his lap, allowing the gun to topple to the ground.

Gunner was beside him in an instant. "It's okay, son," he cooed. He wrapped his giant arms around Finn, holding him tight while he sobbed.

Sometime after, exhausted and crushed, Finn fell asleep.

He awoke the next morning to the sound of birds chirping. He opened his eyes, squinting at the brightness of the morning sun, the trees swayed gently with the cool breeze.

"Good morning," said Gunner. He pulled a metal pot from the fire, poured some steaming hot water into a mug, then held it out.

Finn sat up and stretched, then rubbed his head, cringing momentarily at the greasy texture. He took hold of the hot mug, the warmth of the liquid within, felt good against his palms.

"Another beautiful day is cause to celebrate," said Gunner. He raised his mug as a salute, then took a sip.

Finn didn't repeat the gesture, he took a sip of the steaming coffee, feeling its warmth as it slid down his throat. "Is it?"

"Of course, it is," replied Gunner, his tone annoyingly upbeat.

Finn stared.

Gunner flashed a sympathetic smile. "One day, you'll understand that."

Finn took another sip from the hot coffee. He glanced down at his feet, taking note that the handgun was lying on the ground where he dropped it. Gunner didn't even try to put it away. Why would he? Without bullets, the thing was useless. Finn reached down and picked it up. He flipped it around, noting how it felt in his hand. Of course, now sober of mind, he could tell it was empty. He held it out for Gunner to take. "That was pretty smart of you, taking the rounds out."

Gunner took the gun and stuffed it into his pack. He shoved his beefy hand inside his pants pocket and pulled out several rounds. "Believe it or not, I've been in the same spot you are right now," he said, as he tucked the bullets away.

"Oh yeah?" replied Finn. "Who took the rounds away from you?"

"No one," replied Gunner. "An idiot from Boston stumbled into my camp, followed by his big ol' Alabama buddy." He chuckled. "They were lost in the woods, and just happened to see my fire."

A smile spread across Finn's face, remembering Cyrus and Craig.

Gunner grinned. "They were bickering."

"When were they not?"

"Yeah, those two were something else." Gunner shook his head. "The world is a darker place without them."

Finn nodded in agreement. He took a sip from his coffee and stared into the flames of the fire.

"Well, that's enough lounging about," said Gunner. "Let's finish our coffee." He pointed over his shoulder. "There's a creek over there that we can use to clean up a little."

Finn touched the mass of beard that covered his chin.

"After that, we could do some hunting," said Gunner. "You up for some strenuous activity?"

The thought of moving made Finn realize how stiff he was. He had to admit, rigorous, physical activity sounded good. The thought of fresh meat made his mouth water in anticipation. He downed the rest of his coffee, then helped Gunner prepare. An hour later, they were trekking through the woods toward an icy-cold creek.

When they returned to the campsite, the sun was setting in the sky. The day had been one of distractions and joy for Finn. Something about being in the wilderness, surviving with your own bare hands, made him feel alive. There was no talk about feelings or the past. Best of all, the voices were gone. He could sense them, waiting beneath the surface for an opportunity to leap out, but Finn was far too busy focusing on survival to give them a chance. Every hour that ticked by left him feeling more and more invigorated. Catching two rabbits with a makeshift sling shot was the icing on the cake.

Upon returning to the campsite, they wasted no time setting up a fire and preparing their hard-earned meal. The savory scent of fresh meat cooking over an open flame was intoxicating. Finn breathed in, relishing the moment. He could hardly wait to taste it. He glanced over and realized Gunner was smiling at him.

"What?"

Gunner shook his head. "Nothing."

"Why're you staring at me like an idiot, then?"

"Because I enjoy seeing the real Finn."

"The real Finn, huh? What might the real Finn be?"

Gunner sighed. "This." He waved his hand. "You're in your element out here. And it's a beautiful thing to behold."

"I think you're getting a little sentimental in your old age," replied Finn.

"Fuck you. Old age," scoffed Gunner. He gave Finn a gentle shove.

Finn smiled. "Thank you," he said.

"For what?"

"For hauling me away," replied Finn. "For carrying my ass all those miles. For nursing me to health." He sighed. "For taking the bullets out of that gun."

A warm smile spread across Gunner's face. "I meant what I said, one day you'll understand what a gift life is."

"I'll have to let you know about that."

"It'll get better, son."

Sorrow crept in, casting a shadow on Finn's mood. "I wish I had your optimism."

"Give it time," replied Gunner. "Learn to take things one day at a time. The rest will fall into place."

Finn shook his head. "I can't see how I can come back from what I've done." His voice cracked, as he choked out the words, "I deserted Cash when he needed me most. River, Zac." He swallowed. "Teague —" He couldn't bring himself to say anymore.

"Like I said, just give it time," said Gunner.

"How?" blurted Finn. "I can never see any of them again."

"Why not?"

"Because they can never forgive me," shouted Finn. "What I did —" He shook his head and stared into the flames.

"I'm gonna say that it's you who has the issue with forgiveness," stated Gunner. "The others show no sign of harboring anger toward you. They were actively searching for you this whole time. Everyone was."

Finn struggled to reconcile Gunner's words against his own thoughts. "I can't go back." He shook his head. "I can't look at T—" The name got stuck in his throat.

"They want to see you," said Gunner. "They miss you. Especially Teague."

Finn wiped his eyes.

He's lying. They don't want to see you.

He shook his head to clear his mind of the voices.

"How can you be so sure?" he asked.

"Because I've talked with them every day for the past few

months," replied Gunner. "I've seen the worry in their eyes. The heartache on Teague's face." He paused and stared. "I'm not gonna sugarcoat it, son. You fucked up. You went too far and caused real pain. And yes, there needs to be a reckoning for what you did. You've got a lot to make up for."

Finn winced.

"But I'll tell you this." Gunner stared until Finn looked up at him. "What you and Teague have is something most people can never even wish they had. It's special—it's worth fighting for."

"What if he doesn't feel that way? What if he can't forgive me?"

"Everything I know about you two says that's not gonna be the case."

"But you don't know for sure."

Gunner sighed. "Look, son, are there guarantees? No. Could I be wrong?" He shrugged. "It's possible, but highly unlikely. Of all the people I've ever known, I can say without a shadow of a doubt that you and Teague are meant to be together through this life and the hereafter."

Finn wanted to believe Gunner more than anything. A twinge of hope sparked in his chest. Maybe things could work out after all.

Don't fool yourself. He's lying. You don't deserve forgiveness.

"It starts with you forgiving yourself," said Gunner.

"What if he doesn't want me back?"

"Do you love him?"

Finn nodded. "More than anything."

"Then you fight," replied Gunner. "You fall on your knees and beg for forgiveness. If it's necessary, you grovel, you do whatever it takes to prove to him you're worthy."

Finn stared into the fire, rolling Gunner's words around in his mind.

"You know," said Gunner. He pulled his phone from his pocket and held it out. "It could start with a simple phone call."

Finn took the device and stared at it as though it were something he had never seen before.

Gunner climbed to his feet and stretched. "Now, I'm gonna take care of some business. You go ahead and use that phone." The big man turned around and, whistling, walked off into the forest.

Finn sat in front of the fire, turning the device over in his hand. Fear and hope battled in his heart. He touched the screen, opened the list of contacts, and scrolled down to Teague. Hands trembling, he inhaled deeply, then clicked the tiny phone icon and listened to it ring three times, then silence.

"Gunner?" said Teague.

Chapter Thirty-One

"H E DID IT AGAIN!" exclaimed Mara, her hand pressed against her belly. She grabbed Ben's hand. "Here, feel this."

"Holy shit!" shouted Ben, pulling his hand away. "I felt it that time." He put his hand back on her belly. "He's in there." A sublime smile spread across his face. He kissed Mara on her forehead, then leaned down and kissed her belly. "Hey there, little fella," he cooed.

Zac placed more logs inside the old fireplace, coaxing the flames to ignite. They were camped at the old shell house outside of Odessa. One more day and they'll be back in Terlingua. As far as he could tell, all the others were busy making their way down there to meet up. Everyone that is, except for Finn and Beth. Wherever they were, Zac hoped they were doing okay. He wasn't too worried about Finn since he had Gunner to rely on. Beth was another story. Hopefully she found a good group to fall in with. It was too bad she chose to leave; she would've enjoyed all the excitement. His lips curled up into a slight smile, Mara and Ben's sendoff was a big deal. That was one of the many things he loved about their eclectic collection of misfits and vagabonds. When something went down, be it good or bad, they gathered their resources and rallied. Not a second thought or moment's hesitation in the bunch.

"Come here, River, you have to feel this," exclaimed Mara.

Unsure about it all, River sat down and placed her hand against Mara's belly. She pulled it back as though the surface was hot. "Oh god!" She looked down at her hand. "That's so weird. But cool as hell." She turned to Cash. "Come on over here, you gotta feel this."

"Yeah buddy," taunted Zac. "You should go on over there and feel it." He smirked. "After all, you're next."

"Hur, dur, hur," replied Cash. He shoved Zac.

"Seriously, Cash, come on over," prodded River.

He shook his head. "I'm good."

Not being the type to take no for an answer, River walked over to Cash. She stood over him, holding her hand out. "Come on."

"You're gonna make me do this, aren't you?" he asked.

She smiled and nodded.

Cash sighed, took her hand, and allowed her to drag him over to Mara.

From his position by the fireplace, Zac watched Cash's face go from disinterested to sheer awe. If he had to guess, he would say that feeling that baby inside Mara's belly had a bigger effect on Cash than on River. He grinned and poked at the embers.

"You wanna feel it, Zac?" asked Mara.

"Nah, Ma'am," he replied. "Y'all go ahead and enjoy."

"You sure?" prodded Mara. "It's amazing to feel the baby moving." She paused, sorting her thoughts. "It's also kinda weird. I mean, this is a part of my body that isn't a part of my body."

"I remember being in awe when my momma was carrying Cole," replied Zac. "It's a beautiful thing for sure."

"How about you Teague?" asked Mara.

Teague shot a glance to Zac, grinned, then sat beside her.

Zac placed more debris atop the fire, the flames lit up bright orange-red as they devoured the leaves and dried grass. He watched

Teague, like the others, place his hand against Mara's belly, his expression changing from apprehension to awe.

There seemed to be a profound change in Teague since they left Vegas. Zac wasn't quite sure what was the true catalyst, but he was more than happy with the outcome. For the first time in months, the real Teague was back. No longer sullen and distant, he picked like he used to and laughed freely with the others. Even the sharpened features seemed to soften. However, his eyes remained cold. Zac hoped that in time, those too would go back to normal.

Amid the excited chatter, a tiny electronic sound erupted. Someone's phone was ringing. It took a moment for them to realize it was Teague's. He touched the screen, making it light up. "Gunner?" he said. Less than a heartbeat later, he hung up, stuffed the phone in his pants pocket and stared into the fire.

A lead ball materialized in Zac's belly as a sense of foreboding washed over him. The expression on Teague's face was painfully familiar. He, like all the others, sat holding his breath, waiting for Teague to explain.

Silence.

"Did Gunner get disconnected?" asked River, her tone apprehensive.

Teague shook his head.

"Then why did you just hang up on him?" prodded River. Her voice emitting a nervous, high pitch, punctuating Zac's own feelings.

Once again, Teague shook his head. "I didn't hang up on Gunner." He peered up at River. "That was Finn."

Improbable as it may have been, the air was sucked from the area. Dead silence descended upon the campsite. Time stood still, even the light breeze seemed to stop entirely.

"Wh-what do you mean?" stammered River. "Was that Finn on the other end?"

Teague nodded, staring into the fire.

"Why did you hang up on him?" she asked.

"Because," replied Teague. He stared directly into River's eyes. "He has nothing to say that I wanna hear."

"What the fuck?!" shouted River.

A commotion of chatter erupted around the campsite as everyone struggled to make sense of what just happened. For his part, Zac remained silent, studying Teague.

River stormed over, stopping with her hands on her hips. "Call him back," she stated. It was not a request; it was a direct order.

Teague stared back at her. He scoffed, then stood up and moved to walk away.

"Where the hell are you going?" demanded River, grabbing hold of his arm.

He wrenched it away from her grip. "Takin' a walk," he replied.

"The hell you are!" she shouted.

Zac could hardly recall ever seeing River quite this livid. She stepped forward, catching up with Teague, grabbed hold of him by the shoulders and spun him around to face her.

"Call him back."

Teague stood his ground. Halfway through a shake of his head, River shoved him.

"Call him back now."

"No."

Like a flash, River shoved him to the ground, then sat atop him and leaned down menacingly. She grabbed hold of his shirt collar. "You take out your phone and call him back right now," she ordered. When Teague didn't move, she continued, "You bull-headed asshat."

Zac struggled to hold back a snicker. Seeing River so angry was impressive. He leaned over to Cash and whispered, "Boy, you better take note. Your lady's fierce when she's angry. Don't piss her off."

Cash nodded. "It's kinda hot," he replied, grinning from ear to ear.

River shook Teague, his head banging on the ground. "You listen to me," she ordered. "When someone you love calls you to apologize for something they did wrong, you pick up the damn phone and listen."

"You give them a chance." She pulled his face close to hers. "Now, take out your goddamn phone and call him back right now."

Teague replied, but Zac couldn't quite hear what he said.

"Is your arm broken?" she demanded.

Teague shook his head. "No, but you're sittin' atop my pocket where the phone is," he replied, with a smirk.

River scoffed and shifted her weight just enough for him to fish the device from his pocket.

He held it in the air.

"Now, you call him back. Right now," commanded River. She leaned close one more time. "And I swear to god, if you hang up again, I am gonna shove that phone up your ass so far, you'll never get it out." She stared into his eyes. "Do you hear me?"

Teague nodded.

River gave out a sigh, then climbed to her feet and stood with her arms crossed.

Still holding the phone in the air, Teague stood up, straightened his clothes as best he could, then took several steps away. He made a big production of opening his phone, swiping the screen, and hitting a button then he spun around and with his back to everyone, he held the phone to his ear. A moment later, he walked into the woods.

Chapter Thirty-Two

Ｏ NE MINUTE TEAGUE WAS REVELING in the infectious
joy that Mara exuded, for the first time in months, he was
genuinely happy—it was wonderful to see people he
cared about so happy; the next moment, his entire world went dark
again. The sound of Finn's voice over the phone threw him for an
emotional loop. Anger, confusion, and deep heartache fused with a
sense of exhilaration at the mere sound of his voice. His pulse quickened like a schoolgirl whose crush called her for the first time. His
chest swelled with rage over his own reaction. Just when he felt as
though he finally climbed out of a deep, dark hole, Finn came along
and pried his fingers from the ledge, sending him careening back into
the abyss. Why does he have to do this? Why didn't he just stay
away?

Teague didn't want to talk to Finn—but he also wanted it more
than anything in the world. The seesaw nature of his gut reaction was
feeding his anger. He wasn't angry with Finn; he was angry with his
lack of emotional control.

Then suddenly River was on top of him. Her hands wrenching
his T-shirt, lifting him from the ground just enough to bang his head

against the dirt each time she shook him. A part of him wanted to laugh at the absurdity of it all. Her anger matched his own. They were both angry at the same person. Himself.

After banging his head into the dirt multiple times, she climbed to her feet and hovered over him, waiting for him to do as she ordered.

He sat up, shook the dust from his hair, then climbed to his feet and straightened his clothes while the others stared with comical looks on their faces. A lot of help they were. After making a performance out of placing the call, he turned his back to the group.

The phone rang once, barely a full ring, then silence, followed by Finn's shaky voice. "Teague?"

Words eluded him. Teague wanted to shout; to yell and curse. He wanted to reach through the phone and grab hold of Finn the same way River had done to him. His entire body trembled as he struggled to catch his breath. He glanced over his shoulder, the others stood watching him intently. He needed privacy for this, so Teague turned away and walked into the woods.

He held the phone to his ear and listened to the sound of ragged breathing coming from the other end. Finn was crying, he could hear it. In a strange, twisted way, he enjoyed hearing him suffer. After everything he'd done, Finn deserved to feel bad—to pay some price for all the pain and heartache. Teague's mood shifted suddenly, giving him emotional whiplash. His heart sank, he wanted to reach through the phone and comfort Finn. He shook his head and commanded himself to get a grip. To stop being such a fool.

"You gonna talk? Or are we gonna sit here listening to each other breathe all night?" demanded Teague, wincing at the harsh sound of his own words.

"H-How are you doing?" Finn's voice broke and trembled.

Teague's anger boiled over. "I ain't in the mood for small talk. Don't waste my time. If you got nothing to say worthwhile, I'm hanging up."

"W-wait!" shouted Finn, his voice high-pitched. "Don't hang up! Please."

"You have ten seconds. Start talking."

"I'm sorry."

Silence, not just over the phone, but all around him as well. Unable to see the others, Teague was positive they were listening.

"Is that it?" he asked.

A small squeak escaped Finn's throat, followed by the sound of him swallowing. "There's so much more," replied Finn nervously. "But I don't know where to start."

"Pick a spot," said Teague. "You can start with the way you ran."

"I don't know—"

"You don't know?" demanded Teague. "I'll tell you why. Because you're a fucking coward!" His voice echoed through the darkness, he cringed at his tone. "You should've stayed, but you didn't. You ran." Teague inhaled, struggling to calm his emotions. "You ran away from us." Tears welled up in his eyes. "From me." The painful sorrow in his voice mirrored Finn's. This brought on more anger.

"I know," interjected Finn.

"Fous toi!" boomed Teague. "You don't know anything! You know why you don't?" He paused, not for Finn's response, but to collect his own feelings. "Because you deserted us!"

"I get it!" shouted Finn. "I fucked up!"

The sound of Finn's anger ignited his own. "You know what?" He shook his head. "To hell with this! I'm tired of holding your hand —worrying about you. Putting your needs before anyone else's— before mine!" He sat heavily on the ground and crossed his legs. "I'm so tired of all of this."

"Please," whimpered Finn. "Give me one more chance." He swallowed and sighed. "Just one. I'm sorry. I can't take back what I did. If I could, I would erase it all."

Teague shoved his fingers into his hair. "You can't though."

"I know," replied Finn, defeated and broken.

Teague's anger melted away, leaving behind the love he felt for

Finn. The part of him that always picked up the slack was fighting to the surface. He wanted to reach through the phone, wrap his arms around him and tell him it was all gonna be okay. He moaned and rocked back and forth. Here he was, after everything, feeling more sorrow over Finn's pain than his own. When was he gonna learn?

When someone you love calls you to apologize for something they did wrong, you pick up the damn phone and listen. You give them a chance.

Teague inhaled, then exhaled. There was no sense in dragging this out. The heart wants what the heart wants. He knew without a doubt that he would walk barefoot through hell for Finn. His life was nothing without him. He wiped his face and sighed, resigned to the reality that, for better or worse, this was the man who held his heart in his hands. He cleared his throat. "We better work this out," he said, his tone softer, "River threatened my life if we don't."

A soft chuckle came through the phone, making Teague's heart soar.

"When she's done with me, you know she's gonna come for you." He cupped his hand over his mouth and whispered conspiratorially. "Between you and me, that woman's got a mean streak a mile wide. She's probably eavesdropping on us right now."

Loud laughter erupted in his ear. He smiled, listening to the most precious music Teague had ever heard.

Chapter Thirty-Three

R IVER STOOD AT THE EDGE OF THE CAMPSITE, as close as possible to the thicket Teague had just disappeared behind, straining her ears to listen.

Zac sidled up, tilting his head.

"What are you two doing?" asked Cash.

"Shh," replied River, with a finger to her lips.

Cash snickered. "Are you seriously eavesdropping?"

"Hush," ordered Zac. He turned to River. "Can you hear anything?"

She shook her head. It was impossible to hear anything with all this chatter. She could make out Teague's voice, but nothing of what he was saying. Frustrated, she leaned close to Zac. "What's he saying?" she mouthed.

Zac shook his head and shrugged.

River sighed and took a tentative step closer, trying to be as stealth as possible.

"Because you're a fucking coward!" shouted Teague, his voice booming out of the darkness.

The force behind Teague's voice startled River. She took a step back. This was bad. They weren't supposed to be fighting. The pain in his voice broke River's heart. She glanced over to Zac to find him red-faced, staring into the darkness.

"It's good for him to get it out," whispered Cash.

Both River and Zac turned and shushed him immediately.

Cash held his hands in the air. "Okay, okay," he said, as he backed away.

River brushed aside her annoyance and leaned in to listen again.

"Fous toi!" shouted Teague.

As she stood in the dark, leaning into the thorny, desert brush, River wondered if it was a good idea forcing them to talk. Judging by the words that Teague shouted, this little conversation was doing far more damage than good. What if this tears them apart? What if her meddling makes things worse? She shoved her doubts aside. How could things get worse than they already are? They weren't even talking. Hadn't talked in almost two months. At this point, any conversation was better than none. If nothing else, she knew now that Finn was alive, and he wanted to talk. That was a good place to start. She said a silent prayer that Teague would come to his senses.

River strained to hear more, but Teague's voice had dropped below anything she could hear above the stupid crickets and frogs. She cursed them for being so damn loud. She heard her name, or at least it sounded like her name. She turned to Zac. "Was that my name?" she asked.

He nodded. "I think so."

"So, what's going on?" whispered Ben, as he sidled up close. Behind him stood Tanner.

"Teague's been doing a lot of yelling," replied Zac.

"That's not good," said Ben.

Irritation overtook River's desire to hear what was going on. She turned to Ben. "If you don't shut up, we're never gonna hear anything."

Ben flinched and flashed a wide grin. "Yes ma'am, I'll be quiet from here on out."

She glared at him, then glanced around at the others. This was ridiculous. Not to mention hopeless. She had to let go, to trust that Teague and Finn can navigate their own relationship. Her hovering could only make things worse; she might have already done irreparable damage by prodding Teague to do something he wasn't ready to do. Her shoulders slumped as she sighed. "This is pointless," she said. "I'm gonna go back and sit down." She took hold of Zac's hand. "Let's go sit by the fire. This is gonna work out or it's not. Us standing here in the dark, trying to listen in, ain't doing anything for anyone."

Zac nodded and allowed himself to be led away.

River worried about Zac. His outburst in Vegas shed a great deal of light on the things he held dear. Since that night, she spent some time studying him. He always appeared so stoic. But the reality was much more complicated. Deep inside, he had weaknesses and fears. All he wanted was for his family to remain intact. She wanted that too; far more than she cared to admit.

They took their seats around the fireplace, everyone doing their best to pretend as though they weren't waiting on pins and needles over the conversation taking place just out of earshot. Mara did her best to keep the small talk going, but no one was in the mood.

Each time River caught herself straining to listen in, she would find one of the others doing the same. Teague was no longer yelling, which was a good thing—but his quiet tone made it impossible to hear what he said. She decided to accept the quiet conversation as a good sign.

Time ticked by at an annoyingly slow pace. How long have they been talking? It seemed like hours. Her eyes grew heavy. Zac let the fire die slowly until it was nothing but red glowing embers. River yawned. All around her, the others had settled down to sleep. Everyone but Teague, who was still in the woods.

The need for rest overcame her need to know what was going on.

She stretched and finally lay down beside Cash. He wrapped his arm around her and she snuggled in close.

"I think it's gonna be okay," he whispered.

River nodded. She certainly hoped so, it was out of her hands now.

Chapter Thirty-Four

THE EARLY MORNING SUN PEERED OVER THE TREETOPS, casting a bright, yellow glow as it burned away the morning dew. Finn lifted his chin toward the sky, letting the sun warm his body. Today felt different. For the first time in months, he had hope. Oddly enough, the voices weren't present. It was a new day.

He glanced up at the sky, noting the location of the sun, it must be around eight in the morning. Beside him, wrapped up in his fluffy sleeping bag, Gunner lay, snoring.

Finn decided to let the older man sleep, so, full of nervous energy, he went about building a fire. His mind replayed the conversation from the night before. The sound of Teague's voice, his anger, his laughter. Finn didn't care if all he ever heard again was Teague's angry voice, just so long as he heard him. How could he have been so stupid?

He set a pot of water on the fire, watching it come to a boil. As soon as it was ready, he added some instant coffee. The intoxicating aroma drifted to his nostrils. He inhaled and closed his eyes.

Gunner stirred. He rolled over, rubbing his eyes as they adjusted to the bright morning light. "What? No breakfast?" he asked.

"There's no more food," replied Finn. "Otherwise, I woulda had a whole spread made up for you."

"Well damn," replied Gunner. He sat up, scratched his head, and combed his fingers through the dirty, blond scruff that covered his jaw. "I suppose we're gonna have to set out today and head for civilization."

Finn smiled. He passed a freshly made mug of coffee to Gunner. "Then drink up, we've got a lot of walking to do."

"Calm down there," said Gunner. "Let an old man wake up before you start dragging him down the mountain." Gunner stared at him, smiling.

"Again with the starin'," said Finn.

"There's a light in you today that wasn't there yesterday."

Finn smirked. "I never took you for one of those spiritualists."

"I'm a lot of things," replied Gunner. "But spiritual isn't one of them."

"Come on, you don't believe there's a higher being out there, pulling all the strings?"

Gunner scoffed. "I've seen enough things in my life that I'd consider hard proof there's no such thing as a benevolent god in the sky, watching over us." He stared into the fire. "Or should I say there better not be?"

Finn cocked an eyebrow, waiting for an explanation.

"The endless parade of victims. A good man dying of cancer while some lying billionaire lives for decades. All the wars started by greedy profiteers, and the multitude of victims left behind from those. Flag-draped coffins filled with the remains of young, able-bodied men and women, while useless Generals collect medals for sending those young people to their death." Gunner shook his head. "I've seen no sign of a god in this world."

Finn mulled over Gunner's words. The more he considered it, the more he agreed, there was no sign that any benevolent being existed. After all, if he or she, or whatever, existed, surely, they wouldn't allow so much suffering. He thought about Father K. How could a man who spent so much time among the wreckage of human existence remain an ardent believer? How does someone witness pain and suffering in such large amounts every day of their life, yet still believe there's good in the world? What makes someone like Father Killoran get up and go out every day the way he does?

Morning coffee finished, Gunner packed their things while Finn made sure the fire was out and the campsite was clean. The hike to town was pleasant. Finn didn't recall the hike into the woods, so for him, the scenery was all new. Giant redwoods towered overhead, making it difficult to see the clear, blue sky overhead. The scent of cedar permeated the air. He inhaled deeply, savoring the scent.

They arrived in town by mid-afternoon. Quaint would have been the word River would use to describe it with its tiny buildings lining the main street. Shops that sold trinkets seemed to outnumber the ones that sold food. Finn's eyes fell upon a small diner at the end of the road. At the mere thought of food, his stomach grumbled.

"I'm starving," he said aloud.

Gunner paused, studying Finn up and down, then he turned around and looked at his own reflection in the glass window of a souvenir shop. He rubbed his head and ran his hand along his jawline. "There's a small motel up the road a bit," he said. We can get a room there, get cleaned up, then hit that diner for some food." He turned to look at Finn. "Sound good?"

Finn nodded enthusiastically. At this point, he'd do anything for a hot meal.

The small hotel room wasn't much, but it was clean. Finn sniffed the air, expecting to smell nicotine, but the only scent was the air freshener that hung on the wall. He plopped himself on a bed, recalling the last time he slept on a real bed like this. A wave of sadness washed over him. How could he let himself fall so far? What made him hang on as long as he did?

Because you're a coward. Said that negative voice.

He realized he hadn't heard it all day. The one thing he could count on over the past few months was that voice chipping away at his resolve. He shook his head. Not now.

Gunner walked out of the bathroom. "You can go first," he said, tossing his pack on the floor. After a long moment of digging around in the pockets, he pulled out an electric beard trimmer. He held it out to Finn. "Don't use these anywhere but your face," he ordered.

Finn flashed an impish grin and reached out to take the trimmer, only to have Gunner pull it back.

"I mean it." He stared at Finn. "Don't use these on any other body part."

"Got it," replied Finn with a smirk. "Don't use these on my balls." He took the clippers in hand, stepped toward the bathroom, and spun around. "Though, honestly, how would you know if I did?"

Gunner scowled and tossed a pillow across the room. Finn dodged and ducked into the bathroom, closing the door behind him.

He stared at his reflection in the mirror and once again, the ragged man looked back at him. He pulled off his shirt and flinched at the sight. Bruises, scrapes, and filth covered his torso. He could see every rib. Tiny, red scars dotted his arms. He rubbed them, hoping to make them go away. In time they would, but for now, they would remain—a constant reminder of how far he had fallen.

His lower face was covered in a grizzly, overgrown, black beard. The hair was so thick it surprised him. He looked so much older than his age.

He leaned close to the mirror and tried to run his fingers through his greasy hair. It was impossible, his natural oil had mingled with months' worth of grime, creating knots and dreads all over his head. He glanced down at his hand to find a tiny, black flea scurry across his finger. He cringed and shook it away.

Finn stepped back for one final look, to serve as a reminder to never allow himself to fall so far again. He turned on the trimmers, raised them high, then ran them straight down the center of his head. Clumps of oily, knotted hair fell into the sink. When he finished with his head, he turned them on his face, shearing the thick, wiry beard from his jaw.

When he was finally done, he stared at himself for a long while. Gone was the wild-looking mountain man, in his place stood a thin, pathetic young man who he barely recognized. He touched the two rings on his bottom lip, unable to recall when or where he got them. Should he take them out? Should he let them stay? In the end, he decided to leave them be, he could deal with it later if he wanted to. He reached into the shower and let the water run until it warmed.

Steam filled the air, mingling with the soft scent of soap. Finn peeled off his remaining clothes, leaving them to sit in a heap on the floor, and stepped beneath the warm shower stream. The water cascaded down his body, rinsing away the first layer of grime. He closed his eyes and let it wash over his head, reveling in its warmth.

After scrubbing himself three times, Finn was hard-pressed to put his old, dirty clothes back on. He didn't want to touch them at all. He wrapped a towel around his waist and stepped into the hotel room. A clean set of clothes sat on his bed. He lifted a pair of camo pants to his waist, they were gigantic against his narrow frame.

"That's all I had," apologized Gunner. "There's a belt there too. Maybe it'll help."

Finn held the t-shirt to his chest in awe over the sheer size difference between himself and Gunner.

"We'll do some laundry after we get back from dinner," said Gunner. He stepped to the threshold of the bathroom and looked down at the trash can filled with Finn's hair. "Holy shit! That's enough hair to make a whole dog." He grinned. "Anything in here gonna attack me?"

Finn chuckled. "I honestly can't say. I'd be cautious around the clothes myself."

Gunner snorted and used his foot to move the pile of dirty clothes out into the room, then closed the door.

Finn listened to the sound of the trimmers turning on, followed a moment later by the sound of water running. He slid the pants on and held out the waist, marveling at the size difference. He could probably fit two of himself in the pants. Thank goodness for the side-adjust drawstrings. He pulled them as tight as possible, still leaving far too much space in the waistband. Finn said a quiet thank you for the web belt Gunner put out for him. He felt like a young child wearing his father's clothes. The shirt wouldn't be much better.

Gunner didn't take nearly as long as he did to clean up, which was a good thing in Finn's eyes, he was starving. As soon as the bigger man was ready, they headed out to the little diner.

A single row of tables lined one wall, along the other stood a beverage stand, complete with coffee and tea. The kitchen was in the back, the sound of sizzling beef could be heard above the sound of country music that played over the tiny speakers suspended from the ceiling.

A pretty woman, Finn guessed to be in her mid-thirties, came up to their table. She held out her pad and clicked her pen.

"What's it gonna be?" she asked, staring at Gunner as though he were a grilled steak, and she hadn't eaten in weeks. Her name-tag read Colleen.

For his part, Gunner didn't seem to notice. Finn found this hilarious. How could Gunner be so blind to the way this woman was staring at him? She ignored Finn but took care to smile and giggle when she spoke to Gunner. As soon as she walked away, Finn leaned across the table.

"Do you seriously not realize she's flirting with you?" he asked.

Gunner glanced over at the waitress, who smiled back at him and winked. "I didn't until now," he replied. A warm, red glow appeared on his face.

Finn chuckled. He'd never seen this side of Gunner before, he liked it. It made him more human. This was too good to pass up.

Colleen came back to the table carrying two large drinks and placed them down on the wooden surface. She stood close to Gunner and peered down at him. "See anything you want?"

Gunner cleared his throat, visibly uneasy.

Finn dropped his fork loudly on the table, peering up at Colleen with an innocent face, he said, "I'm sorry, my hands are a little weak." He held them up, showing off the yellow and purple bruises around his wrists. "Those cuffs the other night were a little too tight." He flashed a sheepish grin. "Maybe you shouldn't be so rough next time."

Across the table, Gunner glared.

Finn stared up at Colleen with his best, doe-eyed gaze. "He gets a little rough some—" The word was cut short in his throat when Gunner kicked him. The table rattled and shook, causing the water from his glass to splatter, creating a puddle. With a ferocious grin, Finn blew him a kiss.

Colleen scoffed. "Do y'all know what you want? Or should I come back when you're ready?" she asked, her tone noticeably different this time.

Both Finn and Gunner placed their orders. When they finished, Colleen, stuffed her pen in her pocket and spun around to walk away, leaving them alone at the table.

Gunner seethed. "I'm glad to see you're feeling your old self again."

Finn flashed a wicked grin. "It was low-hanging fruit," he replied.

"Keep it up, little boy."

"You gonna cuff me tight again, daddy?" quipped Finn.

Another kick under the table, this time causing the flatware to clang against the water glasses.

"Enjoy it while you can," warned Gunner. "I'll get even."

Finn chuckled. He forgot how much fun it was to pick at people. He recalled all the times he and Teague would team up against the others. A cloud of sadness settled over him. He could hear the voices whispering. He shook his head. He had no intention of listening to them anymore.

Colleen sauntered up carrying several plates heaping with hot food. The savory aroma reminded Finn of his hunger. As soon as she put down the plates, he dug in.

Back at the little hotel room, Gunner lay atop his bed and

switched on the television. Finn had other plans. He and Teague agreed the night prior that they would talk more after their phones had charged.

Finn held up Gunner's phone. "You mind if I make a call?"

"Calling Teague?"

Finn nodded.

"Go ahead," replied Gunner. "Just be sure to plug it back in when you're done so we can use the map tomorrow. We got a long trip ahead of us if we're gonna make it back to Terlingua for the wedding."

Finn opened the door to the room and stepped outside into the fresh, night air.

"And don't stay up all night talking like two, teenage girls!" shouted Gunner. "I ain't carrying your ass no more." He grunted. "Especially after your little stunt in the diner."

Finn closed the door behind him and sat down with his back against the wall. He opened the phone and called Teague.

Chapter Thirty-Five

S HANE STOOD IN HIS GARAGE, COFFEE MUG IN ONE HAND, wrench in another, he stared down at the engine of his beloved, old truck. For as long as he cared to remember, working on his truck was the one thing that brought him clarity. No matter how crazy, loud or complicated things became, he could always walk outside, into his garage, and tinker away the hours until he achieved a state of calm. There was something empowering about being able to take something broken or worn out and, with your bare hands, bring it back to life.

This time, however, things felt markedly different. After the latest, wild-goose chase to San Francisco, a deep sense of failure had settled in. He now doubted he would ever find Finn. Every road led to another dead end.

Even the latest news from Derrick turned out to be a bust. He found Tricia, living in Florida under a new name, with a new husband. As soon as he heard the news, Shane paid Derrick to fly out to Florida and see what he could find. As fate would have it, Tricia had disappeared months prior. One day she was a happily married newlywed, the next a runaway bride. No one had seen or heard from her in months. That wasn't a surprise to Shane, especially since she disappeared shortly after Daniel was released from prison. It didn't take a genius to figure out she was the first order of business on the man's list. Shane was pretty sure the woman was fed to the gators a long time ago. While this bit of info brought him a moment of joy, it also angered him, as it was yet another dead end.

Shane placed the wrench and coffee mug down and pulled the picture strip of Finn and Teague from his pocket. "Where the hell are you?" he muttered. He was thinking it would have been better if he never found out that Finn was alive. At least that way, he could get on with the rest of his life. This constant state of limbo was driving him insane. It was driving a wedge through his relationships.

He set the photograph down and scratched his beard, then heaved the coffee mug across the garage. It struck the wall, shattering into dozens of pieces, splattering black coffee everywhere.

"If you didn't like the coffee, you could've just asked for a new cup," came a soft voice. Catalina leaned against the door frame, arms folded, a gentle smile on her face. She sauntered up beside Shane and glanced down at the photograph. "I see you're out here getting away from all the things that are bothering you," she said sarcastically.

Shane grunted.

"Babe," continued Catalina. "You have to put this into a place where it doesn't destroy you." She stared at him with her dark, brown eyes. "So, it doesn't destroy us."

"I don't know how to do that."

Catalina moved closer, pressing her body against his. She wrapped her arms around his neck and kissed him. "You start by taking it one step at a time." She kissed him again. "And slowly, but surely, you'll find it gets easier."

Shane pulled her arms away and stepped back. "Easy to forget, my son?" He shook his head. "I can't do that. I won't do that."

"No one is asking you to forget your son," replied Catalina, irritation rising in her voice. "We're asking you not to forget us."

"I'm not forgetting about you," he replied feeling defensive.

"Oh yeah? When was the last time you saw Gabby? Let alone talked to her for more than five minutes?" Catalina folded her arms.

The conversation was irritating Shane. He dug through the past few days to prove her wrong. The more he dug, the more he realized she had a point, he hadn't seen his youngest in days. Guilt descended like a storm-cloud. Here he was, so obsessed with one child, he was sacrificing another.

"Look, Babe," cooed Catalina. "I'm not asking you to stop searching for our boy. I want to find him as much as you do." Her brown eyes pierced his soul. "All I want is for you to learn how to share your time and attention between finding Finn and being with those of us who are here right now."

Shane sighed and pulled Cat close. He kissed her forehead. "I'm sorry," he whispered.

"No need for sorry," she replied, softly. "Just take baby steps."

Shane breathed in the soft floral scent of her perfume. He loved this woman more than he ever thought possible after Melody. He loved the girls and everything about the life they built. He needed to get it together. If he didn't stop hyper-fixating on Finn, he could end up ruining everything else he loved. It was time to accept that he might never find the boy.

"You're right," he sighed. "I've been an asshole."

Catalina peered up at him. "You love your children, and there's nothing you wouldn't do to keep them safe." She smiled and ran her fingers through his hair. "That's one of the things I've always loved about you. Don't try to change that." She kissed his cheek. "Just leave room for the rest of us."

He kissed her, letting the soft, warm sensation of her lips on his spread throughout his body. This woman was his anchor, it was time he started acting as though that were the case. Time to put the past behind him and embrace his present.

"Oh, ew!" said Mari. She stood at the doorway; arms folded. "Get a room."

Catalina pulled away, pausing long enough to plant one more peck on Shane's cheek. She winked at him, then spun around to face her daughter. "Besides spying on us, was there something you needed?"

Mari smirked. "Just wanted to pop in and let y'all know; I'm leaving for work." She pointed behind her. "Gabby's in the kitchen, making breakfast for everyone." She rubbed her belly. "Might I say her blueberry pancakes are amazing." Her face became serious. "So, you two need to get your butts inside and let that little girl make you some breakfast."

Shane wrapped his arms around Catalina's waist and pulled her into him. "Tell her we'll be right in," he replied, then kissed Cat's neck several times.

"Oh, ew," shouted Mari in mock disgust. "Whenever you two can stop acting like a couple of horny teenagers, your little girl will be waiting." She threw a kiss in the air at them, then spun around and strolled down the driveway. A moment later, the sound of her motorcycle erupted, followed by the sound of her peeling out along the long, gravel driveway.

Catalina shook her head. "That girl and her loud motorcycle."

"It scares most of the losers away," replied Shane.

"Are you feeling better?" she asked.

Shane nodded. "I think I am."

"Good." She wriggled out of his grasp. "We'll see you inside in a couple of minutes. Okay?"

He smiled. "Yes, be right there."

Catalina blew him a kiss and walked away.

Alone once again, Shane stared back at the house. He could see Gabby in the kitchen, now joined by Catalina, smiling and laughing. His heart soared. This was his life right now—this was what mattered most. He picked up the photograph of Finn and Teague and made a promise that he wouldn't stop searching, but going forward, he wouldn't allow the search to shadow the rest of his life. Other relationships were just as important. A sad smile spread across his face as he tucked the photo into his wallet. He glanced at the shattered remains of his favorite coffee mug scattered across the garage floor and decided that he could clean that up later, then he turned around and joined his family for some breakfast.

Chapter Thirty-Six

As THE MILES SCROLLED BY, Finn's mood and state of mind improved. He spoke openly with Gunner about the voices and intrusive thoughts. To his surprise, Gunner was not only understanding, but he also knew, firsthand, what it felt like to battle your own demons. How difficult it was to let go, and how destructive it was to continue fighting imaginary dragons.

At night, the hours were spent talking to Teague. As much as Finn enjoyed Gunner's insight, he looked forward to his chats with Teague most. For the first time in a long time, it was just the two of them. No drama and no interruptions. It was like the old days.

As for the rest of their family, Finn had yet to speak to any of them. Both Gunner and Teague assured him that everyone was looking forward to being reunited, but Finn still had anxiety over the whole affair. He was pretty sure Zac was going to inflict pain. While not necessarily something he looked forward to, it was also not something he feared. The real pain from Zac came from the knowledge that one of the most upright men Finn had ever known was disappointed in his behavior. That Finn had destroyed Zac's trust. How was he supposed to earn that back? Was it even possible?

River was another story. Did she think less of him? The mere consideration that River's opinion of him might have slipped into negative territory was almost too much to think about. What the hell was he gonna do about that? And Cash; what did his longtime friend think of him now? There was good news, according to Teague, River and Cash had finally figured themselves out. Finn looked forward to seeing what that looked like.

The train whistle blew as they rolled into El Paso, one more night, and they would be in Terlingua. Electricity surged throughout Finn's body, setting his nerves on edge. How was the reunion going to go? Was it possible to heal the wounds he created and get back to normal?

The train stopped on the edge of the rail yard, a perfect place to hop off. To their left, the city of El Paso spread out before them; to their right, the city of Ciudad Juárez sat just beyond the wall. Gunner and Finn gathered their belongings, hit the ground, and disappeared under the cover of the overpass.

Gunner tossed his pack on the ground and stretched. "Let's leave our things here and find some grub in town," he said. "I'm starving."

Finn's stomach was in knots, the thought of trying to eat something made it flip and churn. Due to the state of his insides, he hadn't eaten much all day. Weakness settled deep in his limbs, he needed to eat something. He didn't want to take the risk that he could stumble and injure himself—not when he was so close to home.

Gunner pulled out his phone, the bright, unnatural glow of the gadget created a circle of light all around him. "What the hell is this?" demanded Gunner, holding the device out so Finn could see the tiny image of himself standing seductively, chest bare, the top button of his pants undone.

A wicked grin spread across Finn's face. "It's your new wallpaper," he replied with a wink.

Gunner grunted. "Take it off."

"Come on." Finn leaned closer to the phone, checking out the image, nodding in approval. "That's a good-looking man right there."

"I don't want to be seeing your naked chest every time I open this phone," stated Gunner. "Take it off."

"It's not entirely naked," teased Finn. "If you look, you can see I'm wearing pants." He flashed a toothy grin.

Gunner glared. "I'm beginning to regret pulling your ass out of the fire." He stuffed the phone back in his pocket.

"You saved me because you love me," replied Finn, batting his eyes.

"I'm too hungry for this." Gunner shook his head. "When we get back, you're taking that off my phone."

Finn smirked, knowing full well he had no intention of doing anything of the sort.

The cool, desert air felt good against his skin. Overhead, a blanket of stars sparkled brightly in the cloudless, night sky. Finn's love of the desert ran deep, the dry air, the scent of sage and rock, the emptiness; he loved all of it.

They didn't have to walk long before they came upon a small, twenty-four-hour diner. Artificial light splashed over the desolate street corner. The savory aroma of burgers on the grill wafted through the air. Finn inhaled. Maybe his body would let him eat something after all. They took a seat at the nearly empty bar and waited for the server.

As soon as he placed his order, he made his way for the restroom, his hands were covered in silt.

The fluorescent light flickered, casting its lifeless glow across his hollow face. He sure looked like he had been through the wringer, no wonder the waitress looked startled when she first laid eyes on him. Finn pulled the black beanie off his head and rubbed the scrubby new growth of hair. It was gonna be a long time before he was used to the lack of wild, unruly hair on his head. He stared at his reflection in the mirror, saddened by what he saw. How had he allowed himself to fall so far? How did he not see it while it was happening? He washed his hands, then splashed cold water on his face. If nothing else, he was at least somewhat cleaner than when he entered the diner. He emerged from the restroom just in time for his food to arrive.

The greasy burger was positively massive, with a heap of french fries piled on the side. Finn leaned over and inhaled, reveling in the delicious scent.

"You gonna smell it or eat it?" asked Gunner.

Finn gathered a handful of warm, salty french fries, smothered in ketchup, and used them as a scoop for his strawberry shake. Grinning from ear to ear, he stuffed the dripping mess into his mouth.

"That's disgusting," said Gunner. "I don't know how you even put that into your mouth."

Finn swallowed. "I've eaten worse. Besides, it's just fries and a shake. You have that all the time."

"Not all at once. And not like that," responded Gunner. "That ketchup there adds a whole other level of disgusting."

Finn chuckled. "Don't knock what you haven't tried."

Gunner shook his head and reset his focus on his own plate.

Finn was a little worried about how his stomach would receive the fresh food. So far, it seemed to be taking it just fine, at least the shake and fries. He lifted the burger to his mouth and inhaled, taking in the savory scent of grilled beef covered in melted cheese mixed with the subtle scent of ketchup. His mouth watered and his stomach grumbled. He took a large bite.

Juicy beef and savory cheese danced on his taste buds. He reveled in each bite, pausing now and then long enough to shove a handful of fries, covered in the sweet flavor of artificial strawberry.

Two hours later, they were back at camp, building a fire. Finn wasn't quite sure if it was the heavy meal or the fact they were in the west Texas desert, but a sense of ease had come over his body. The intrusive thoughts were nowhere to be heard; even the voices had subsided.

The fire crackled and glowed. Finn stared into the orange flames, taking in the moment of calm, reveling in the sense of well-being that encompassed his body and mind. He truly felt as though things were going to be okay. He turned to Gunner.

"Thank you," he said sincerely.

"For what?" Gunner cocked an eyebrow.

"For putting up with my dumb ass. For hauling me out into the wilderness so I could clear my head." He stared at Gunner. "I owe you my life."

A warm smile spread across the big man's face. "I didn't do much of anything," he replied. "You did all the hard work." His face became serious. "It ain't gonna be easy, nothing worthwhile ever is. Those thoughts you had will come back sometime." He tapped the side of his head for emphasis. "You've got to be aware of them and be ready to fight them back. You're the only person who can fight that battle. For the sake of the people who love you, you need to be strong."

Finn mulled over Gunner's words and his warning. He dreaded the thought that the voices could return. That he could find himself, once again, standing on the ledge, staring down into darkness, and fall in love with its promise of quiet and solitude.

"Do you ever think about doing it again?" he asked.

The big man gave a curt nod. "You never quite get away from it. It'll hit you at odd times." Gunner smiled at Finn. "But you get better at fighting back against it."

"Why?" asked Finn. "Why can't you get past it? Why does it keep coming back?"

Gunner sighed. "I can only speak for myself." A mournful look spread across his face. "Believe me when I say, I've got a lot of red in the ledger."

"Is it mostly when you're alone?"

Gunner shook his head. "It's actually harder when you're in a group of people." He stared into the fire. "The worst times are when you're surrounded by people who love you—who you love. They're all happy and in your heart it's nothing but darkness and depression. You don't dare try to explain it, because you just know no one's gonna understand." He scoffed. "Hell, you don't even understand it yourself."

A couple of months ago, Finn wouldn't have been able to understand what Gunner was saying, now, however, he understood clearly. Fear welled up inside him. "What if I lose it again and I really do damage?" Holding back tears, he peered up at Gunner. "What if I—" He swallowed against the lump in his throat.

"You're the only person who can control your thoughts and reactions," stated Gunner. "You've gotta own up to that. No excuses. If you give yourself an excuse, the odds are higher that you could lose it again." He locked eyes with Finn. "You could very well kill someone you love. That's why you need to own it. Own what you did and what you're capable of. And be aware that you can either fall into that hole again or you can fight your way out of it."

Finn nodded.

"I mean it," said Gunner. "None of this victim bullshit. Yes, you had it shitty." He shook his head. "But that ain't no reason to allow yourself to be a shitty person. Don't see yourself as a victim, because when you do, you give yourself permission to do horrible things."

Gunner's words hung heavy in the air. The fire crackled as Finn placed another log on the flames, somewhere overhead an owl cried out. Finn mulled Gunner's warning over in his mind. He made a silent vow to never perceive himself as a victim.

Gunner's phone rang, startling them both. The big man pulled the device from his pocket, glanced over at Finn, then answered. "Yeah," he said aloud. "No, no, he can't talk until he fixes my phone."

"Is that Teague?" asked Finn, his heart skipping a beat.

Gunner nodded.

Finn reached for the device, but Gunner pulled it away.

"I mean it," said Gunner. "You aren't using this phone until you promise to get that shit off of it."

Teague said something through the phone, but Finn couldn't hear what he said.

"You ask him," Gunner replied to Teague. He turned to Finn. "Well?"

"Well, what?"

"If I give you this thing, you take your picture off my wallpaper. Got it?"

Finn smirked, nodded, and reached out.

Gunner jerked it away. "I mean it," he warned. "Don't make me beat your ass."

"I'll fix it," replied Finn, holding his hand in the air.

Gunner sighed and reluctantly handed the phone over.

"What's he talkin' about?" asked Teague.

"I gave him a gift, and he doesn't approve," replied Finn.

"What sort of gift?"

Finn smiled, climbed to his feet, and wandered away from the fire so he could talk to Teague in private.

Chapter Thirty-Seven

"Baby boy," sighed Bella, as she gently pulled Teague's hand away from his face. "Gnawing away your fingers isn't going to get them here any sooner." She flashed a warm smile and wrapped her arm around his shoulder. "Come on," she said, guiding him toward Stoney's porch. "Come, be with everyone else, take your mind off the wait."

Teague glanced down at his hands, frowning at the sight of his raw, red fingernails that he chewed to the quick. Yet another nervous habit he seemed to develop out of nowhere. This one he found particularly odd, since it was a pet peeve of his whenever Finn did it. Finn. The mere thought of him made the butterflies in Teague's belly go mad. A bevy of emotions surged throughout his body. One moment elated, the next anxious, and still the next terrified. This was the moment he wished for so many months ago. Why, then, was he such a mess about it?

"Here," said River, shoving a cold beer in his hand. "Drink this."

Teague stared at the dark, brown bottle as though it were a foreign object. "Isn't it a little early for alcohol?" he asked.

River scoffed. "On a day like today, there's no such thing as too early." She winked. "Besides, it's four o'clock. That's plenty late enough in the day."

Four o'clock? How could that be? He just looked at the clock a few minutes ago and it was ten in the morning. Where the hell did the day go? Masking his confusion, he downed the beer in one long drink, then grabbed a second and took a seat on the deck beside Zac and Nate, who was busy brushing Gypsy.

The little dog wriggled and snapped at the brush each time it came close. "Come on Gypsy, you wanna be all clean for dad, right?" Gypsy growled and snarled at the brush. "Zac," said Nate. "Can you hold her still while I get her belly done?"

"Hell no," replied Zac. "See them teeth right there?" He pointed at Gypsy. "They look small, but this whole time I've been sitting here, I can hear every time her jaw snaps shut." He shook his head. "No thank you, I ain't going nowhere near that. You're on your own."

Nate moved the brush closer to Gypsy, the little dog growled and lunged, snapping her jaw inches from his fingers.

"She really doesn't like that," said Teague.

"No shit," replied Nate, clearly at his wit's end. "I just want her to look good when Gunner sees her." He leaned toward the little dog. "Is that so much to ask?" The little dog wiggled her tail and licked his nose. "Is that permission?" He moved the brush closer.

Gypsy growled and lurched forward. With one strong snap of her jaw, she took hold of the brush, then bolted away toward the cabins.

Nate sighed and shook his head in defeat. "There goes another brush."

"She's gonna bury that one like the others, isn't she?" laughed Teague. He smiled at Nate. "Don't worry, I'm sure Gunner'll know how well you took care of his baby."

Teague took a sip from his second beer and took in the scene around him. Every single member of the Nomads was present, even Porter made it down and that was quite a feat. Tripp and Sam were busy playing a hand of cards with Cash, D.B., and Tanner. Little Spyder, the feral cat, a new, permanent fixture on D.B.'s shoulder, and not so feral anymore. Max was deep in conversation with Spinner. Whatever the topic of discussion, they were both very animated about it. Stoney sat nearby, chatting away with Porter like two brothers who hadn't seen one another in a long time. Bella and River were over by Mara; Ben, hovering protectively nearby. An unmistakable change had overcome Ben recently. Something about the prospect of becoming a father changed the man. It aged him. Subtle, yet unmistakable, the way he carried himself was vastly different from pre-pregnancy Ben. Far more serious, always physically close to Mara, doting on her every whim. If Mara complained of a stiff neck, Ben was right there, ready to massage away the discomfort. If she complained about the smell of something, Ben would move heaven and earth to eliminate whatever was upsetting her.

As for Mara, it was cliché, but she did indeed glow. A permanent look of contentedness had settled on her face, she had taken to randomly grabbing hold of the closest person, holding their hand against her belly as she excitedly announced, "Feel that?" Then she would forget all about the other person long enough to coo at the small baby growing inside her.

Bells plopped down beside Teague and handed him a slice of freshly baked bread. "If you're gonna start drinking now, better have something in your stomach." She popped a piece of bread in her mouth.

Teague grinned. "How come you're not over there hanging with the—"

Bells placed a narrow hand over Teague's mouth. "Shh," she warned. "Don't say it."

"Ladies," interjected Zac.

"You had to go there, didn't you?" quipped Bells. She balled up her fist and landed a playful punch on Zac's arm. "I'm excited for them." She nodded toward Ben and Mara. "I don't think I've ever seen anyone so happy."

"I agree," said Teague.

Bells grinned at him. "Our kids are growing up." She paused and stared at him with her serious dark brown eyes. "How about you?"

"How about me, what?"

"You ready to see your boy?"

Teague's stomach lurched; the butterflies were back. His mouth was suddenly dry. "I am," cracked his voice. He cleared his throat.

Bells chuckled. "It's good to see you nervous."

"Why's that?"

"It means you care," she replied. She turned her laser-like eyes on Zac. "How are you doing?"

Zac responded with a thumbs-up.

"You still planning on kicking his ass when you see him?" asked Bells, smirking.

"I can't," sighed Zac. He jerked a thumb at Teague. "He asked me not to."

"I only asked you not to punch him in the face," argued Teague.

Bells peered up at the sky. "It's a gorgeous day. Perfect for a reunion."

Teague followed her gaze. A fluffy, white cloud drifted aimlessly across the clear, blue sky. A warm, steady breeze carried the scents of the desert. It shouldn't be much longer. The last he heard from Finn; they were leaving Presidio. Stoney had offered to pick them up, but they both wanted to walk. He didn't say it aloud, but Teague was sure Finn was terribly nervous about seeing everyone. If he was to be totally honest, he too needed a little, extra time.

A faint, distant sound, like a short whistle, floated on the wind. Teague cocked an ear, straining to listen, convinced he was hearing things. A flurry of activity erupted between two cabins as Gypsy burst forth, barking furiously. She peeled off past everyone, leaving a tiny cloud of dust in her wake. Another whistle. There was no question about what was happening now. Teague jumped to his feet, his stomach in knots. Finn and Gunner had arrived.

He ran with the others and rounded the corner. Halfway up the long driveway stood the unmistakable silhouettes of Finn and Gunner. Gypsy had already made it to them and was busy saying hello, tail wagging furiously as she bounced up and down, all the while whimpering. Gunner was on his knees, petting and hugging the little dog while Finn stood nearby, shifting his weight from one foot to the other.

His nerves on end, Teague's entire body trembled. His breaths came at a short, rapid pace, his heart raced in his chest. He stood back behind the others.

Gunner lifted Gypsy in his arms and both he and Finn walked toward the waiting crowd. When they were a mere twenty feet away, River broke away from the group and ran forward, arms outstretched. She ran right past Gunner, landing heavily against Finn, causing him to stagger back a step or two. He wrapped his arms around River and hugged her tight.

River stepped back, allowing Cash to step in with a firm handshake. He grabbed hold of Finn and pulled him in for a hug. When they separated, both Cash and River stepped back, wiping their eyes.

Finn stood, red-faced, before Zac, his body tense. Zac smiled and pulled Finn in for a hug so strong it lifted Finn several inches from the ground. When they parted, tears streamed down both their faces.

One by one, the others said their greetings, while Teague hung back, taking it all in. Finn was so skinny it was almost shocking. Teague was aware he had shaved his hair off, but he was unprepared for how drastic a change that would be. It was as though he were looking at a completely different person.

Finn hugged and greeted everyone, finally coming to a stop before Teague.

They stood in silence, words had completely evaded Teague. His body didn't want to move. Every muscle in his limbs quaked. He tried to say something, but all words were trapped in his throat. Finn's eyes filled with tears, matching his own.

Teague reached out trembling and Finn fell forward into his arms with so much force, they both stumbled backward. A flood of emotions exploded inside Teague. Unable and unwilling to hold back his tears, he let them flow. Through his body, he could feel Finn tremble and shake with his own tears. Heads together, sobbing, they stood holding one another.

Chapter Thirty-Eight

RIVER PROMISED HERSELF that she would control her emotions, but when she laid eyes on Finn, she lost all control. She wrapped her arms around him and wept. The feeling of his emaciated frame against her body broke her heart.

"Please forgive me," cried Finn, his head buried in her shoulder. "I'm so sorry."

She pulled away and looked him in the eyes. "I already have," she said, shaking her head. "I'm never gonna turn away from you."

Tears streamed down his face.

River wiped them away. "Don't you ever do something like that again," she ordered.

He bowed his head and nodded.

Cash stepped close, reaching his hand out, but when Finn took it, Cash pulled him in for a hug. "I'm so glad to see you," said Cash, tears welling up in his eyes.

Finn wiped his face and sniffled. "Me too," he choked.

Zac stepped forward. He stood, arms folded across his chest, staring at Finn, his demeanor was calm. River wondered if Zac would go through with his threat of beating Finn's ass, her heart soared when Zac's face melted into the brightest smile. He pulled Finn toward him, and the two embraced. When they stepped apart, Zac stared directly into Finn's eyes, his face serious.

"I want you to know I promised Teague I wouldn't beat your ass," he said, with a small smirk.

"I'll thank him for that," replied Finn. He glanced over to Gunner, who was busy saying hello to a very excited Gypsy, then back to Zac. "Teague and I got a lot of talking and workin' things out to do."

"Glad to hear it," replied Zac. He wiped his face and stepped aside to make way for the parade of happy welcomers.

River stood by, beaming, as she watched everyone, in their own way, welcome Finn home. There was a moment of confusion when Porter stepped forward and wrapped his arms around him. Finn's face, was a mask of confusion, wondering who this stranger could be that seemed so familiar. As soon as he realized he was meeting Porter, face to face, Finn relaxed and flashed a huge smile.

There was only one person left. Teague stood alone behind the group; hands shoved in his pockets.

Finn stepped in front of him, his body fidgeting. River realized she was holding her breath. She glanced around, noting that everyone stood frozen in place, uttering not a word. Tension hung heavy in the air as time froze.

Cash took hold of River's hand, intertwining his fingers with hers. She peered up at him and smiled, then turned her focus back to Finn and Teague just in time to see them collapse into one another's arms.

Laughter erupted. The mood shifted from tense to utter joy. Cash wrapped his arm around River's shoulder and kissed the side of her head. The weight of the last several months had been lifted. She could breathe easily once more.

A silent agreement was made to leave Finn and Teague alone, so, with no fuss or fanfare, everyone slipped past the duo, who didn't seem to be aware of anyone else anyway, and made their way back to Stoney's porch.

"Looks like we survived this one," said Cash. "Think we can hold off on any other mishaps for a little while?" He flashed a perfect crooked smile.

"We better not have any more issues," replied River. "Not for a long time."

He kissed her cheek. "From your lips," he whispered.

Nervous energy coursed throughout River's body. It took every ounce of control she could muster to keep from sneaking around the corner to see what was going on. Thrilled that they were spending time alone, the wait was killing her. It felt as though hours had passed before Finn and Teague wandered around the building and joined the rest of the party. By that time, everyone had returned their focus to the next big thing, Ben and Mara's wedding.

It was to be a small, casual affair. Mara didn't want anything special, she only wanted to celebrate their vows with the people she considered her closest family. When she asked River to be her maid of Honor, of course, River agreed, but she had no idea what that meant.

The sun hung low on the horizon, soon the sky would turn a vibrant orange and red. It was time to prepare for the ceremony.

Beaming with joy, Mara took hold of both River and Bells' hands. "Come on," she giggled. "Let's go get dressed."

Get dressed? River wasn't entirely sure what Mara meant by that. She shot a glance at Bells, who shrugged back, then allowed herself to be dragged away.

Inside the cabin, Bella was already waiting for them, busily laying out what appeared to be two dresses and one pantsuit atop the bed.

"There you are," said Bella. She took Mara's hands and guided her to one side of the bed. "You said you wanted green, so I chose this for you." She picked up one of the dresses. "I hope spring green is good. It makes me think of new life—renewal." Bella smiled. "I thought it was rather fitting."

Mara squealed and held the dress against her body. She sauntered over to the mirror and gazed at her reflection.

The dress was a pretty, soft green. It reminded River of early spring in the mountains. Made of a soft, silky fabric, it flowed like water every time Mara moved.

"What do you think?" asked Mara.

"I think it's perfect," replied River. She turned to Bella. "You did well."

Bella nodded and smiled. "We're not done yet," she said, then nodded her head, suggesting River look down on the bed.

Mara giggled. "Go ahead, hold it up," she urged.

River was confused. She looked down at the bed, where a second dress of darker, emerald, green lay. "What's this?" she asked, but she was afraid she already knew.

"That's your dress, silly," replied Mara.

"Go on," said the older woman. "Don't be shy."

"Yeah," smirked Bells. "Don't be shy."

River stared down at the garment, afraid to touch it, let alone lift it up. She tried to recall the last time she wore a dress and couldn't come up with a single memory. The others watched her intently, she had no other choice than to hold the dress up. The fabric was soft in her hands, and light. Compared to her usual attire of jeans and t-shirts, this dress felt like air.

"Go on," prodded Mara gleefully. "Hold it up in the mirror."

River walked across the room and nervously held the dress against her body, peering at her reflection in the mirror. The dress was so unlike anything she had ever worn. The little girl in her was excited to wear such a pretty dress, the grown woman was nervous and scared. She looked down at her boots, then turned to Bella. "I don't have any shoes to wear with it."

Mara giggled. "Neither do I, silly." She twirled around. "Which is why I'm going barefoot."

"I figured you would, my dear," said Bella. She turned to River. "I imagined you'd need to have a dress you could wear something familiar with." She nodded down to River's feet. "So, I went with one that I think would look great with a pair of black boots." She smiled.

River stared at her reflection, wondering what she had gotten herself into. What were the others going to think? She would never hear the end of this, the teasing was gonna be relentless.

"I know you're not gonna make me wear one of those," said Bells, shaking her head, arms crossed.

"No dear," chuckled Bella. "I took everyone's taste in mind." She gestured to the suit resting atop the bed. "I knew you would prefer pants. Imagine my thrill when I saw a suit made of forest green."

A smile spread across Bells' face. "You had me worried there for a minute." She held the trousers against her body. "But I can totally do this," she said, nodding in approval.

"Come on, beautiful," cooed Bella. She placed her hand gently on Mara's shoulder. "It's time to get dressed."

As River worked to put Mara's hair up, she peered down at her friend, who was positively glowing. "You look amazing," she said.

Mara smiled and placed her hand on her belly. "What do you think?" she asked her small bump. She giggled and looked up at River. "He says he likes it." Her face grew serious. "Something old, something new," she said.

"Something borrowed, something blue," added Bella. "Don't worry, the dress came from a thrift shop, so that will be your something old."

"The baby can be something new," interjected Mara. She looked around the room. "We need something blue."

"Here," said Bells. On her wrist, she wore a silver bracelet. In the center, a blue stone sparkled. "Something blue." She pulled it off her wrist and placed it on Mara's. "It was a gift from an old girlfriend." She shrugged.

"And one more thing," added River. She reached up and unclasped her necklace. As she placed it around Mara's neck, she said, "Dawn gave me this for Christmas, the year before we left home." She closed the clasp and straightened it out. "It's probably pot metal, but it'll do for something borrowed." She smiled.

Mara sighed. "It's beautiful."

River stepped back, leaving Mara to study herself in the mirror.

"Alright, River," said Bella. "It's your turn."

Nervous yet excited, River went about dressing. The sensation of the soft fabric against her skin was odd, yet pleasurable. She studied her reflection in the mirror. The River staring back at her was somebody she had never seen before. She was beautiful.

"Wow!" said Bells. "You clean up nice, girl."

"You look amazing!" shouted Mara.

"Absolutely stunning," agreed Bella.

River had to force herself to take a breath. "I feel naked," she stated.

"You'll get used to it," said Mara. "I can't wait for Cash to see you." She smiled. "He's gonna lose it."

Oh god! Cash! A wave of nervousness washed over River. What was he going to think? Would he hate this? After all, he fell in love with the other River—the one who wore pants all the time. What if he didn't like her in a dress? Why did it matter so much what he thought?

"I think," said Bella, her arm around River's shoulder. "When Cash sees this gorgeous creature before us, he'll fall in love all over again." She nodded reassuringly.

"And get a total boner," added Bells, with a mischievous smirk.

"We'll be back for another wedding for sure," added Mara gleefully.

River shoved Bells, who feigned injury. "Alright smartass, your turn. Get those traveling clothes off your body."

"Oh boy!" declared Bells. "I thought you'd never ask."

Not long after, the trio stood before the mirror, Bella hovering in the background.

"Damn!" said Bells. "We're hot."

Butterflies fluttered in River's belly. Her heart raced in her chest. She wasn't supposed to be the nervous one. She wasn't the one getting married.

There was a gentle tap on the door and Bella rushed over. "Oh my word," she gasped. She glanced over her shoulder. "Okay girls, this is it. Mara, your escort is here." She stepped aside and let Stoney enter the room.

River could barely contain her surprise.

Bells whistled.

Freshly shaven, hair combed and wearing a pressed shirt with new jeans, Stoney stood at the door.

"Who are you?" teased Bells.

River chuckled.

"I'll have you know," said Stoney, holding out his arm for Mara. "I wouldn't shave for just anyone."

Mara giggled and took his arm. "I love it. You're one of the best, Stoney."

"Everyone ready?" asked Bella.

Fear and confusion washed over River. Her face was warm to the touch, her palms sweaty. She didn't know what she was supposed to do.

Bella smiled reassuringly. "Just follow my lead," she said. "I'll walk to the end of the aisle with you two girls, then take a seat. When the music starts, Bells walks down the aisle first. Once she's in place, River, you follow and take your place up front."

"What do I do if I trip?" asked River, suddenly self-conscious.

"What everyone else does," suggested Bells. "Skip once, and pretend you meant to do it."

"Come on. Stop worrying," said Bella. She flung open the door and gestured. "The ceremony begins."

Sunset had come with a fury. The sky was on fire with yellow and orange. A faint scent of sage wafted on the gentle breeze. Chairs had been arranged in two columns with an open lane in the middle. On either side, the others were seated—waiting. River's entire body trembled. She wanted to turn around and go back inside the room, but Bells was right there with her arm around her shoulder.

"Come on, woman," she urged. "If I can parade around like this, then you can too."

"Need I remind you that you're not the one wearing a dress," protested River.

"Trust me, the world would never recover if I wore a dress." Bells chuckled. "Besides, you're hot when you're all dressed up."

As River approached the gathering, she felt as though all eyes were on her. Every muscle in her body quaked, her knees were weak, each step she took, she feared she would fall or trip. Oh god! Just don't trip. She clenched her jaw so tight it was beginning to ache.

They paused at the end of the aisle. Never had she felt so self-conscious in her life. What had she gotten herself into? She willed herself not to fall.

"Check out your man," whispered Bells.

Down the aisle stood Cash, Zac on one side, Finn, and Teague on the other. His expression was one of the silliest River had ever seen. She couldn't tell if he was about to cry or pass out. She flashed a smile at him and winked.

Tanner appeared at her side, holding out his arm.

Thankful for the support, River wrapped her arm around his.

"You're trembling, girl," he said, with a smile.

River nodded. "Just help me make it down the aisle without tripping."

"That, I can do. Let's go."

With each step, River's confidence grew. The trembling ceased; her breathing became normal.

As they strolled by Cash, Tanner leaned over and said loudly, "Put your tongue back in your head, boy, you're embarrassing yourself."

A burst of laughter.

River took her place alongside Bells, leaving space for Mara. Ben and Tanner stood on the other side of Spinner. Notebook in hand, he gave a curt nod of his head, and Sam played his guitar.

All eyes turned to the end of the aisle where Mara stood, her arm in Stoney's. An audible gasp escaped Ben's lips.

Moving slowly, and keeping pace with the music, Mara and Stoney made their way to the front, coming to a stop before Spinner.

The ceremony was simple, short, and beautiful. By the time the bride and groom kissed, the sun had set. Dusk gave way to evening, the stars shined brightly, a blanket of billions of tiny flickering lights. As usual, Stoney outdid himself. Dinner was a banquet of smoked meat, fresh vegetables and fruit and several sweets he had a local friend make special for the occasion.

Laughter filled the air. A sense of family, love and belonging settled deep in River's soul. She breathed in the fresh, night air, savoring the scent of wood on the fire. Thinking back over the events of the night, she was surprised at how quickly she was able to relax in her new attire. Turns out, she rather enjoyed the way she felt all dressed up, though she would be hard-pressed to admit it publicly. She glanced over at Finn and Teague, happily chatting in their own little world. Across the fire, Ben and Mara smiled and kissed, both at different times, placing their hands on her belly. Even Gypsy was happy, laying across Gunner's lap, she refused to let him move without her.

A content smile spread across River's face.

"Now, that's a serene smile if I've ever seen one," said Cash.

She leaned back against him and sighed.

Chapter Thirty-Nine

FINN BOLTED UPRIGHT IN THE BED, his body trembling and covered in sweat. His eyes darted around the darkened room. It took him a moment to realize that he was safe, that he had awakened from a nightmare. He scrubbed his head and willed his breathing to stabilize. Beside him, Teague slept, the sound of his soft, steady breathing helped calm Finn's nerves. It was okay, everything was okay.

He knew it wouldn't be so easy, that the nightmares and voices were still there, lurking in the shadows, waiting for the right moment to resurface and remind him they had no intention of going anywhere. Even now, fully awake, safe in a darkened room, with Teague by his side, he could hear their faint whispers scratching at the edges of his mind. Finn ran his hands down his face, wiping away the sweat from his brow. He glanced over at Teague, watching his chest rise and fall with each sleeping breath. Should he awaken him? For what reason? To tell him about his nightmare? Why on earth would he do that? Finn could hardly bring himself to think about the nightmares, let alone verbalize them to anyone—even Teague. It was best to let him sleep. All Finn needed was some fresh air. He climbed out of bed, pulled on his pants, and padded over to the door.

Outside, the air was crisp and clear. The sound of the desert surrounded him. Overhead, a blanket of stars twinkled against the black, night sky. In the center of the compound, the fire still burned, fed patiently by Zac, sitting alone. Finn stepped off the small front porch and wandered over.

"What are you doin' up?" asked Zac.

Finn shrugged, unwilling to verbalize what had caused him to be awake. "I just need some fresh air, I suppose."

Zac grunted and placed another log on the fire. He took a swig from a bottle of whiskey and handed it over to Finn.

The door to another cabin swung open and both Cash and River stepped out into the night air. They sauntered over and took a seat near the fire.

"Can't sleep either?" asked Zac.

River smiled. "I woke up and saw you out here all alone, so I tried to sneak out." She nodded toward Cash. "He woke up and insisted on joining me." She glanced over at Finn. "Where's Teague?"

"Still sleeping," replied Finn, only to be interrupted by the sound of his cabin door opening and closing. Teague took a seat beside Finn and wrapped the blanket he was wearing around them both, kissing Finn on the side of his head.

Zac leaned back in his chair and grinned. "Looks like all is right with the world again," he stated, then took a sip of whiskey and passed the bottle.

Cash held the bottle in the air. "To family," he said.

"I gotta say," said Zac. "There were times I wasn't so sure we'd ever be sittin' here like this again." He stared at the fire.

"Yet, here we are," said River. "We made it. We survived the worst storm and came out together."

"I'm with Zac," said Teague. "I never would've thought we would all be back here, together." He sighed. "I'm ashamed to admit, I gave up. Zac was the one who hung on." He rested his chin on Finn's shoulder.

"Yeah," agreed Cash. "Zac was the one who never lost hope."

"He put up with all my shit," chuckled Teague.

Zac scoffed. "You were quite the pain in the ass, by the way." He shook his head and chuckled.

Finn thought about the past few months. He combed through the haze of drugs and nightmares, finally admitting to himself that all he ever wanted was to be back home. To be sitting by a warm fire, wrapped in a blanket with Teague, listening to the banter of his friends.

"Let me just say," said Zac, holding the whiskey bottle in his hand. He wiggled a finger at Finn and Teague. "You two aren't allowed to pull bullshit like this ever again." He took a swig and passed the bottle. "I don't ever wanna see either of you like that."

"Here, here," chimed River, as she held up the bottle and took a swig.

The bottle made its way to Finn. He took a swig and handed it to Teague. "I'm not planning on running anymore," he said, staring into the flames. He could feel Teague's arm wrap tightly around him.

"That's good," replied Zac. "Cause if you ever pull this shit again, I will—"

"Beat your ass," everyone interjected at once.

Laughter erupted.

"Go ahead, laugh," warned Zac. He shook his head. "I am a firm believer that every man needs his ass beat at least once in his life." He stared at Finn. "I am not afraid to do my part." He smiled.

"Looks like we gotta find somebody for Zac," said River.

"Sounds like a great idea," chimed Cash.

"Now don't go off playing matchmaker," warned Zac. "I have a very specific type of woman in mind." He grinned and leaned back. "I'll know her when I see her."

"Now, you know I'm not gonna let it drop like that," protested

River. "At least give me a small detail about her, so I know what to look for."

Zac smiled. "Well, she'll be hot."

"Of course," agreed Cash.

"And she'll be ridin' a big, old motorcycle."

"That's oddly specific," said River.

Zac shrugged. "What can I say, I got a thing for hot, biker women." He winked. "Bringing the conversation back on track." He looked at Finn. "Don't make me beat your ass for doing something stupid."

"You have my permission," replied Finn. "To beat my ass if I ever even fall down that hole again." He swallowed against the lump in his throat. He still didn't understand exactly what triggered his rage. If he didn't understand it, how was he going to prevent it? Fear grew inside.

"What is it?" asked Teague.

The air seemed to hold still, not a word was spoken as everyone waited for Finn to finish his thought. He swallowed again, only to find his mouth had gone dry. "I don't know," he croaked. "I don't know what happened to me." He peered around at the others. "How I could do the things I've done to all of you." He cleared his throat. "I think being violent is a part of my DNA or something." Tears swelled in his eyes. "What if I'm exactly like Daniel? What if that's who I really am?"

Silence.

"Oh Cher," sighed Teague. "You don't know."

"Know what?"

Teague rubbed his chin. "Well, it makes sense, you were so out of it, there's no way you could've heard what he said."

"What who said?" asked Finn.

"Daniel. That night when he attacked us. You remember?"

Finn nodded, not sure where this was going.

"He told me he wasn't your father," said Teague. He locked eyes with Finn. "Your bio dad is still out there somewhere and it ain't Daniel."

Finn gasped. Could it be true? He never wanted something to be so true in his entire life.

"Did you hear me?" asked Teague. "Daniel isn't your father. There's no DNA between you two." He smiled.

"Are you sure you heard it right?" asked Finn, more than a little scared it was all a misunderstanding.

Teague nodded. "Absolutely! He looked me straight in the eyes when he said it."

"But he's a natural liar. He could've been lying."

"He had no reason to," replied Teague.

Joy washed through Finn's entire body. He wanted to jump up and holler. His heart raced. "Did he say anything else?"

"Your eyes," replied Teague. "The only other thing he said was that you got your eyes from your bio dad. And that he was from a Podunk town in north Texas."

Tears erupted from Finn's eyes and streamed down his face. His thoughts swirled. He had so many questions, but most of all, he felt relief. A giant weight had been lifted from his shoulders. He wanted to know who this other man was. Where had he gone? How did Finn come to be with Daniel?

"That's great news," said River. "Don't you think?"

Finn nodded; words evaded him.

"So, what I wanna know," said Zac. "Is, are we gonna do some searching to find out who the mystery man is?"

"Only if you wanna," said Teague.

Silence descended, they were all staring at Finn, waiting on his response. Did he want to find out who his real father was?

"The only thing we got to go on are the eyes," offered Finn.

"And he's from north Texas," added Teague.

"I bet Porter could dig around and find something," interjected Cash.

Finn nodded. "I bet he could." He looked at Teague. "What do you think?"

Teague smiled. "I think we'll do whatever you wanna do."

"But is it a good idea?"

"I can't say," replied Teague. "It only comes down to what you want."

"We're in, no matter what," said River, followed by agreements from both Zac and Cash.

"Let's see what Porter can find," said Finn. His heart was lighter than it had been in months. "He might be dead, but I'd at least like to know who he was."

"That does it then," said Zac. "Tomorrow, we'll get with Porter, and we'll start our search for Finn's father."

A round of agreement followed.

"Um," said Finn, a little nervous. "Before we do that, Teague and I got something to do."

The faces around the fire became serious again.

"Finn and I are gonna take a trip alone," said Teague.

Zac stared. "Do you think that's a good idea?"

"I do," replied Teague. "We need this."

"I think it sounds like the right thing to do," offered Cash.

River agreed, though apprehension was written all over her face. "How long? A couple of weeks?"

Teague shrugged. "To be honest, we're not sure. It could be a month." He smiled at River. "We'll be in touch, the whole time, so you won't worry."

Zac nodded, never taking his eyes away from Finn. "If that's what y'all need to do, then do it." He shook his head slowly. "I can't believe y'all are leaving me alone with these two."

River tossed a pebble at him. "Shut up," she said playfully.

Finn leaned back against Teague, feeling the warmth envelope his body. He was home, surrounded by the most important people in his life.

"I've got a question," said River. "Why does Gunner have a collage of all y'all's bare chests on his phone?"

Laughter erupted.

"Seriously," she continued. "He spent the whole night asking anyone who would listen to help him get it off. Apparently, everyone he asked just added theirs to the wallpaper." She shook her head. "Y'all are a special kind of evil."

"So, did you fix it for him?" asked Cash.

"Psh." She waved her hand. "Hell no, it was too funny. I left it alone."

Chapter Forty

Beth

Newport Beach: Five months after leaving the Nomads

EIGHTY THOUSAND FOLLOWERS! Not only had she made back her follower count, she surpassed it. Beth could hardly believe it. Leaving the Nomads was the best thing she did since leaving home. She was more popular than ever! People all over the world followed her, commented on her posts, and publicly stated they wished they could be her. Yes, Beth was living her best life. Her videos were seen by millions and her posts were shared by the thousands. Why did it take her so long to do this? This was what she imagined it would be like when she left home.

Home—she hardly ever thought about that anymore, it was far too depressing. Just thinking about her parents, alone and probably worried, was enough to send her into depression. She knew any contact with them would only complicate things. They would beg her to return home and she'd feel guilty. It was best to leave all those thoughts behind. There was nothing in Denton for her, nothing her parents could do for her that would make her happier than she was now.

Beth looked out at the waves crashing along the shore. Newport Beach was such a busy place, which was one of the things she liked most about it. The constant parade of people provided plenty of opportunity to panhandle. The food vendors offered an array of choices whenever hunger set in. There was also a steady stream of riders passing through, this gave her plenty of options when it came time to leave. While she liked to wander around new places alone, Beth preferred to travel with others. Something about catching on and riding alone made her nervous. Also, she genuinely enjoyed meeting other riders. Apart from a small number, they enjoyed hearing about her internet fame.

Speaking of which, she hadn't posted for the day. She pulled out her phone and scrolled through her most recent photos, searching for something cool. She scanned the contents of her different albums, hoping to find inspiration in one of them. One contained photos of the gorgeous sunsets of all her travels. Another was nothing but photos of the cities she had stopped in so far. She scrolled to the one that contained images of all the other riders she met and clicked it open. So many interesting people. River's face appeared on her screen, she quickly swiped up only to settle on an image of Finn and Teague, she swiped that away, replacing it with an image of Zac. A rueful smile settled on her face. She had to admit; she had some fun times with the Nomads. She wondered what they were up to. Had they blown up yet, like she was sure they would? Did they miss her? What about Finn, did they ever find him? Was Teague still a mess? An embarrassingly large part of her wanted those two to suffer. She still harbored a great deal of anger in her heart toward them. They should have been the ones forced out of the group—not her.

Sometimes, when she was alone, she longed to be with the group again. What would it be like if she reached out right now and made contact? Would they even reply? Beth shook her head to clear away those thoughts. The past was the past; she had a different future ahead of her, and she was perfectly okay with that. They had all made their choices.

A soft, male voice disrupted her thoughts. "You coming with us?" asked Razor. Originally from Utah, Razor had become a regular in Beth's travels. Thin of frame, and taller than most people, he reminded Beth more of a sapling that grew too quickly and was waiting for the rest of its body to catch up—hence the nickname Razor, as in razor thin. For the most part, Beth liked it when she ran into him, though the last time he tried to hit on her, but she was able to turn him down with no drama, the poor guy was used to being turned down.

Beth smiled up at the tall, young man. "I think I'm gonna stick around here for the night, then head out in the morning," she replied.

Razor sighed and fumbled with the straps of his backpack. "Alright," he replied. "We'll catch ya next time." He waved goodbye and strolled off down the boardwalk with Ryan and Hawk, his two best friends.

Beth waved until they disappeared into the crowd of people. The only other riders left were Trace and his girlfriend, Kitty. Trace was okay in Beth's eyes; she wasn't quite sure how he came to be named Trace. He never offered to explain, and she never cared enough to ask. She found Kitty a little annoying. The girl was simply trying too hard to be cool. Her real name was Ashley, but she hated to be called that, so she decided on the name Kitty. She liked to pretend she was a cat woman, complete with dark makeup, fake, long nails, and hissing. Sometimes, she would even pretend as though she were cleaning herself.

As far as riders went, they were okay, in Beth's eyes. Not her first choice to catch on with, but just fine in a pinch. With any luck, another group would roll in tonight and Beth could leave with them, otherwise, she would head out with Trace and Kitty. Times like these were when she missed the Nomads most, she missed the easy camaraderie, the safety, and the lack of responsibility she had when being a part of a group. Maybe someday she would be able to cobble together her own found family, it worked for River—it can work for her.

"Hey, Beth," said Kitty. "We're gonna go get something to eat." She cocked her head toward the boardwalk. "You wanna come along?"

Beth did a quick inventory of the money she had on hand. She should have plenty for a sandwich. "Why not," she replied, and jumped to her feet.

The sun had set hours ago, but the boardwalk was lit up like Las Vegas. This was one of the many things Beth liked about this beach. She weaved her way through the waning crowd of people. It was getting late, in another hour or two, the people who had homes to go to would disappear, leaving behind the circus of homeless back-packers and riders that made this area their home. For the most part, it was easy for Beth to avoid the real problematic people, she kept a low profile and didn't interact with anyone she didn't discern as a rider. Luckily for her, they were easy to spot.

Beth followed Kitty and Trace to a burger stand. Wrinkling her nose, she glanced around to see if anything else might pique her interest. This was the last food stand that was open, if she didn't order soon, she'd have to wait till morning. With a resolute sigh, she placed her order and took a seat on a nearby bench with Trace and Kitty.

"So, Nomad Girl," said Kitty, staring down at her phone. "How's it feel to be internet famous?" She flashed a big smile.

Beth grinned.

"What's the follower count now?" inquired Trace.

"She's around seventy-five thousand," replied Kitty.

"Eighty thousand," corrected Beth.

Trace took a long puff of his vape. "How come you don't figure out a way to monetize that?" He exhaled a giant cloud.

Beth waved her hand to force the bubblegum-scented plume in another direction. "I guess I haven't thought about it." She shrugged.

"You should think about it," said Trace. "I mean, I would if I were you." He took another puff, then exhaled another sweet, scented cloud.

"He's right," added Kitty. "You should totally look into monetizing." She giggled. "You could sell T-shirts or copies of your photos."

"I can't imagine my stuff on coffee mugs," said Beth.

"I guess you're right," agreed Kitty.

Trace exhaled another cloud. "You could do a subscriber-only account. You know, where your paying subs get content, the others don't."

Beth was intrigued. She hadn't thought about subscriptions before. "Do you think anyone would pay?"

Trace and Kitty bobbed their heads up and down in unison.

"Absolutely," replied Trace enthusiastically.

Beth had to admit, the thought of monetizing her travels was appealing. If she could have a steady income, then she no longer had to worry about how much she spent on food or even where she slept at night. She could stay in hotels all the time. She could visit every major city and do it in style. She could go to Europe.

Another noxious plume of candy flavored vape wafted in Beth's face.

"Just imagine," said Trace. "If just two hundred of your followers paid five bucks a month, you'd have one thousand dollars a month." He winked at her. "That'd set you up real nice."

Beth nodded. She imagined what it would be like to make a living from her content. After all, she uploaded so much. And so many people loved her content, why wouldn't some of them pay for more? The more she mulled it over, the more she thought about how amazing it would be to not have to worry about money. "Just two hundred, huh?" she said aloud.

"I bet you could get way more too," added Trace.

"Think so?"

He grinned and nodded. "Absolutely." He shrugged. "Why not? Most of those people following you are living vicariously through your adventures, anyway."

The vendor called out their numbers, their food was ready. As she sat nibbling at her burger and fries, Beth mulled over the possibilities. In her mind, she fiddled with the math. If she played her cards right, she could be rich and famous.

Trace and Kitty continued the discussion, but Beth was deep inside her own head. Her calculations were far more interesting than any conversation. Had it not been for Kitty's tap on her shoulder, she wouldn't have known they were heading back to their campsite.

Sitting by the fire, Beth pulled her phone from her pocket. A red bubble told her she had accumulated several more followers. There were a few more comments than earlier, so she opened her app to read them. The typical fire emojis and thumbs up, nothing new. There was one comment from Max. A regular user of social media, he had found her new account shortly after she launched it. For the most part, he simply liked posts. Occasionally he would comment, but never did he reach out for a private chat. This bothered her. After all, wasn't she once family? Whatever his reason, Beth decided she didn't much care, so she never tried to reach out privately, either. However, every time she saw something from him, a tiny current of excitement would course through her body, followed immediately by a surge of melancholy.

"Glad to see you're livin' the life," he posted.

Beth liked his comment, then clicked on his avatar to see his profile. She was curious to see what he was up to. More specifically, she was curious to see if he posted anything about the others. Unfortunately, his page was void of anything interesting. His last post was made several months ago. She shook her head and went back to her own profile.

Kitty and Trace were laying out their sleeping bags. Beth glanced at the time on her phone, it was almost one in the morning. No wonder her eyelids felt heavy. All around her, the boardwalk had closed up for the night. The crowds of tourists and revelers had gone home, leaving behind only the locals. She yawned and put her phone away.

"Where are we heading tomorrow?" she asked, stretching her back.

"How about Phoenix?" asked Trace.

Beth scrunched her face. She hadn't been to Phoenix since that awful night. She shook her head, having no desire to revisit that place. "Let's go somewhere else," she suggested.

"There aren't a lot of places to go from here where we don't pass through Phoenix," replied Trace.

"Sure there are," said Beth. She visualized a map, hoping to come up with an alternative. "How about we go north and cross over toward Nevada?"

"I don't want to go to the mountains again," protested Kitty.

"So, we don't," blurted Beth, irritation welling up inside. "Come on," she said. "It can't be that hard to come up with a place to go that isn't Phoenix."

Kitty pushed out her bottom lip. "I like Phoenix," she whined.

"I know!" shouted Beth. "We can head east from here and stop in Vegas for a couple of days." She leaned toward Kitty. "That would be much more fun than Phoenix. Wouldn't it?"

Kitty nodded.

"I suppose Vegas would be cool," agreed Trace, rubbing his stubbly chin. He sat upright. "Let's do it."

Beth smiled. Crisis averted; thank goodness she didn't have to head out on her own again. She looked along the beach. Too bad no other riders came through. Oh well, at least she convinced them to go somewhere she would rather go. She spread her sleeping bag over the soft sand. Before crawling inside for the night, she would have to go visit the toilet. Beth glanced over at the collection of porta-potties sitting under the dim light from the streetlamps. She didn't want to walk over there alone, but Kitty and Trace were busy making out. Beth sighed and resolved herself to go it alone.

As she approached the units, one of the doors burst open, spilling out a ragged-looking beach dweller. He staggered past Beth, the stench of alcohol filling the air. Beth sidestepped to avoid getting too close. The tiny hairs on the back of her arms stood on end. She couldn't, for the life of her, figure out why she was feeling so creeped out. She had been on this beach for a week. Every night, she came to these same toilets. Nothing ever happened. She brushed aside her fears and ordered herself to get it together.

Beth slowly approached the door. Nothing happened. No one popped out, no one was even nearby. She shook her head, and silently scolded herself for being such a wimp, then she pulled open the door and stepped inside.

An internal battle ensued the entire time she was inside the porta-potty. Her senses on overdrive, she listened intently for any noise that might be out of the norm. She heard nothing. Her guts told her something was wrong, but her head told her she was being foolish. She decided to go with her head and brush aside all her concerns.

Out of nowhere, Zac's warning came to mind. "Always trust your gut; it'll never lie to you."

"Stop being so stupid, Beth," she mumbled. She pushed open the door, stepped outside, and breathed a sigh of relief. Nothing was different. Her fears were irrational. She was fine.

An arm snaked around her waist, just as a large hand covered her mouth. She tried to scream but her sounds were muffled as the stranger pulled her behind the porta-potties, into the shadows. The man leaned close enough for Beth to feel his hot breath against her neck. She struggled but couldn't free herself, he was simply too strong.

"Shhh," he whispered.

Beth struggled to control her breathing. She relaxed her body, hoping he would think she was surrendering and relax his grip.

He didn't. Instead, he chuckled.

Panic gripped her chest; she heard that chuckle before. Beth tried to wriggle free, but the more she struggled, the tighter his grip. Her heart raced; it was difficult to breathe. If she didn't get free soon, she might pass out. She bucked and heaved against his body, but he held her tight. Tears streamed from her eyes.

The stranger leaned close once again. "Now, now Beth," whispered a familiar, gravelly voice. "Is that any way to treat a long, lost friend?"

Once again, Beth tried to scream, but nothing came out of her constricted throat.

Daniel snickered in her ear. "You and I got some catching up to do," he said ominously.

THE END

Acknowledgements

I want to take a moment to call out a few folks for their undying support for the Nomads.

First, Vic Willette – this woman is a never-ending source of enthusiasm and emotional support for me. If y'all have a friend like her in your lives, you are truly blessed.

Samantha Dayton – Believe me when I say this woman has been there form the beginning. Her encouragement and feedback are things I honestly wouldn't be here without.

Brenna, Connor, Meagan, Shannon & Rory and the two significant others, aka my bonus sons, Cody and Logan. I spent two decades supporting and cheering them on to pursue their dreams and now these wonderful human beings are doing the same for me. From feedback, to shoutouts of support, to artwork and design help... seriously y'all, my kids rock.

And of course, we cannot forget, Robert McLaughlin, my partner —my rock—my best friend. He listens to my rants and ravings, all the while, offering input whenever he can. He is my road trip partner— my sounding board—my anchor. He will always be the love of my life.

Afterword

Number three down. And boy was this one a doozy. I know this one was hard, trust me when I say, this one almost did me in. What an emotion ride. If you're still here with me, thank you.

If you enjoyed the ride so far, please take a moment and leave a review or rating, it would be greatly appreciated. We Indie authors need reviews from people who had read and enjoyed our work. All reviews, ratings and feedback are greatly appreciated.

Want more Nomad stories? There are various origin stories of the characters available to read now FREE on my website. Scan the QR code below with your phone and it will take you right there. While you're there, be sure to sign up for my newsletter. That way, you'll know about upcoming releases and any free content as it comes available.

Or simply follow the link to my website below...
https://www.nancylmclaughlin.com/

As the third book in this series is released into the world, I am putting down the bones of book four – the final book in the American Nomads series. I hope to have that ready for release by the end of November of this year (2023)

I'm also working on several other projects. First up, Tricksters—A horror novel with my own gritty twist, based around a shapeshifting clan who hunt, live and thrive in the West Texas desert.

Second, Popular Monsters—Imagine the pied piper as a three-man, mask wearing, metalcore band, set on a mission to turn their fans into minions who do their evil bidding.

And finally, Feral—A female werewolf road tripping through the US, meets a young conman. The two fall in love, rob, wreak havoc and yes, murder as they rampage across the countryside. Think Bonnie & Clyde if Bonnie were a werewolf.

Suffice to say, it's busy in my head.

Okay, that's all I have to share for now. Thank you so much for giving my creations a chance. As always, feedback or input is always appreciated. If you want to keep up with what's going on, give me a follow on any of the Social Media platforms—I think I'm on all of them. You can find links on my website.

Zac

An American Nomads Origin Story

"I don't wanna go," said Cole, peering up at his older brother.

"It'll be fun. It's just the weekend. A sleepover," replied Zac, his throat tightened with each word.

Cole moaned. "Why can't you come along?"

"Because I've got a test to study for." Zac tousled the mass or auburn curls atop of Cole's head to appear playful. Inside, turmoil bubbled like hot, molten lava. He wanted to grab his little brother's hand and run as fast as their legs would take them.

A few feet away, their caseworker, Tonya Masters, shifted her weight from one foot to the other. She sighed audibly and checked her watch, a performance entirely for Zac to let him know her patience was wearing thin. "Okay, Cole, let's go; Mr. and Mrs. Parks are waiting for us." She extended her skeletal hand.

Cole wrapped his arms around his big brother's neck. Clinging tight, he whispered, "Got your back."

"Back at ya, buddy," responded Zac, fighting back tears, holding tight. He didn't want to let go.

"Alright, come on," Ms. Masters said, irritation radiated from her entire body. Out of Cole's sight, she glared at Zac.

Zac cleared his throat and pulled away, looking his little brother in the eyes. "You be good. And make sure you brush your teeth. Got it?"

Cole nodded.

Ms. Masters seized the young boy's arm with a claw-like hand, tugging him toward her black SUV.

Cole shouted over his shoulder, "See ya, Monday!"

Zac swallowed hard and tried to respond. His throat constricted, trapping the words he wished to say. In the end, all he could do was wave goodbye. Frozen in place, he watched the black SUV pull away from the curb and drive down the street. He glanced down at the license plate; IHLPKDS—I help kids. Of course, a person like her would believe they were helping. He closed his eyes and committed the letters to memory.

A soft hand touched his shoulder, startling him out of his thoughts.

"Why don't you come inside?" said Carla, his foster mother. She and her husband, Jorje, were the only two bright spots in their lives. A genuine, friendly couple who only wanted to help others, the Almeidas were a true rarity in Zac's world. After raising two kids of their own, the couple faced a choice; Do they downsize into a smaller home and embrace the empty nester lifestyle? Or do they make a difference in the lives of other young people? Luckily for the two brothers, the Almeidas chose the latter. The past four months in the Almeida home were a gift to the two boys. It was almost like being home... Almost.

"Come, have a seat in the kitchen," offered Carla. "I'll make some coffee and we can talk." Zac knew Carla only wanted to help him feel better. He simply wasn't up for it. He needed to be alone. After a brief apology, he made his way upstairs to the bedroom he and Cole shared.

A worn teddy bear sat silent against his pillow—a note lay atop its belly. Written in Cole's crooked handwriting with a dark blue marker, the message read—

. . .

Waffles is gonna stay and keep you company while I'm gone. I'll see you both on Monday.
Love, Cole

Tears flowed down his face. Cole didn't know he wasn't coming back. That the family he was spending the weekend with, a family they had both met multiple times before—were adopting him. Ms. Masters felt it was best not to say anything, especially since the family didn't want Zac.

"It's better if he doesn't know right away," she said in a hushed tone. "It could be traumatic for him and could disrupt the transition." She paused and waited for Zac's reaction. When none came, she continued, "You don't want him to end up in permanent foster care, do you?" She fiddled with the binder filled with all the information about the two brothers. Impatience emitted from her like a foul odor. "Don't forget, you're aging out in a few months. He can't come with you. You know that."

Zac stared. Silent. He studied her face. Her small, brown eyes reminded him of the rats that scurried around in the old barn. Her pinched face gave the impression she had just swallowed a lemon peel. He loathed her with every fiber of his being.

She leaned close, the noxious odor of sour coffee emanating from her breath. "Don't make this any more difficult than it has to be," she hissed. "We will do whatever we have to in order to make this adoption happen."

He understood the veiled threat loud and clear. Like everything else over the past few years, he was powerless to effect any change in the outcome. If he reacted to his feelings, he would make a bad situation worse than it already was. As much as he hated it, the severe woman was right. Any reaction would only traumatize Cole. Zac couldn't do that to the little guy. Cole had suffered too much already.

So, holding back the roiling firestorm of emotions, he played his part in the charade.

Zac lifted the ragged stuffed animal and sunk heavily on the bed as though the lead weight in his belly was pulling him down. Named after Cole's favorite food, the little bear was his most treasured possession. Whether in the backyard or bedtime—Waffles was always in Cole's arms. He even brought him along on his first day of kindergarten. The day the state came to take them away from their family home, Cole held Waffles firm against his chest with one arm while holding tight to Zac's hand with the other.

Matted fur covered the entire body, with small balding patches around the ears and face. A worn piece of black wool felt covered the hole where his left eye used to be. Zac ran his finger across the pilly surface, a sad smile on his face as he recalled the memory of that day. After an unfortunate accident involving a pair of scissors and a boy named Preston, their mom decided it was best to cover the hole with a patch. Worried over the plight of his fluffy friend, Cole paced nervously while their mom did her magic. Zac did his best to distract the little guy, playfully teasing. When their mom presented the newly repaired Waffles, Cole squealed with glee. What's better than a beloved teddy bear? Well, a pirate stuffed bear, of course. He ran around for days calling him "Waffles Black-Eye Flynn."

Zac sighed and pinched his eyes shut, breathing deep as a flood of memories washed through his mind like a tidal wave, bringing with them all the emotions he fought so hard to hold back over the past few years. He didn't want them—they hurt too much. There was nothing he could do; he stopped fighting and forced himself to concentrate on something happy.

Waffles. Zac remembered the first time he laid eyes on that bear. He saved up for months, taking on any chore his father would pay him for. The months flew by and his mom's belly grew. Zac searched every shop they visited for the right gift. It seemed an impossible task. He could never find the right item. The day Cole was born, his grandma brought Zac to the hospital to visit his new baby brother for the first time. Nervous and excited over the prospect of being an older brother, Zac insisted they stop by the gift shop before going upstairs.

It was now or never. His brother was here—he needed to find something now. His mind reeled as he wandered the aisles. *What if there's nothing here either?* He scanned the shop. Bright lights glinted off sterile glass shelves. In one corner, bright balloons brandishing messages like "Congratulations" or "Get Well" floated above bouquets of colorful flowers. Across the room, a shelf overflowing with stuffed animals beckoned him. His face lit up—finally, the perfect gift. The black bear popped out against a backdrop of grey stuffed elephants and pink bunnies. Face frozen in a permanent, though slightly crooked smile, arms outstretched as though he were reaching for Zac. This was it.

Though only nine years old at the time, he could vividly recall nearly every detail of the first time he met his little brother. The flickering buzz of fluorescent lights and the sterile scent of bleach as he walked down the long corridor leading from the nurse's station to the room where his mother stayed. His sneakers squeaking on the sparkling white floor tiles. The gentle smiles on everyone's faces as he passed by. His sweaty palms and the soft feeling of Waffle's fur against his fingers.

His Grandma pushed open the door. The first thing Zac saw was his mother sitting up in bed, her long red hair cascading over her shoulders. Her face turned down as she gazed lovingly at the tiny bundle in her arms. When he entered the room, she turned and beamed, one arm outstretched toward him, the other holding the new baby. Her smile was so beautiful and full of love. He ran forward and hopped up alongside her on the bed. She tussled his red hair and kissed his forehead. The baby writhed and let out a tiny, pathetic protest.

His mom gave him a quick hug, then introduced the two brothers.

"Zac, meet your new baby brother—Cole." She faced the baby. "Cole, this is your big brother, Zac. He's very excited to meet you."

"Hold up, hold up," said Zac's father. He got to his feet. "Come on over here, son. Sit down so you can hold him."

Zac hopped off the bed and climbed into the chair, his feet dangling inches away from the floor. He waited anxiously as his dad scooped the baby from his mother's arms and gently handed him to Zac.

"Be careful. Make sure you support the head," his father warned.

Zac nodded and stiffened his arm, making sure he was providing proper support. The baby was so tiny. Much smaller than he had imagined. Though, upon reflection, he realized he didn't know what to expect. The baby stretched and yawned, the most adorable yawn Zac had ever seen. How funny that he would think a yawn was cute. Around the room, the adults were busy talking. Zac heard nothing they were saying—he didn't care. At that moment, he and Cole were the only two people in the world.

"I got your back, little guy," he whispered.

The baby opened his eyes and stared up.

Zac kissed the top of his warm, fuzzy head, already showing signs of their signature auburn hair. After that, he lost track of time. It could have been minutes. It could have been an hour. The only thing he was aware of was the weight of the wee baby in his arms and the soft cooing sounds that emanated from the tiny being who had stolen his heart.

Alone in his room, the afternoon light flickered and waned as the sun moved across the sky. Staring up at the ceiling, Zac watched the orange-red light dim to a cool dusk blue. His sadness subsided, replaced by a deep, hollow emptiness. A black void where things like happiness and hope once lived. With Cole gone, his entire family was no more. Erased. The only proof they ever existed were the memories buried inside him. The memories that were too painful to recall. He wondered if there would ever come a day when he could think about the time before and not feel as though a red-hot poker was being shoved straight through his heart.

The hours passed. A gentle knock on the door from Carla interrupted his thoughts. A couple of hours later, it was Jorje. Zac didn't mind. He understood they wanted him to know they were there—in case he wanted to talk to someone. After a brief check-in, they left him alone to wallow in his misery.

It was nearly dawn when he finally rose and packed his belongings—he was leaving. One of the good things about being in foster care was the lack of personal belongings. Everything he owned fit in his pack with plenty of room left over.

There was no sense in waiting around for his birthday. The outcome would be the same either way. To their credit, months ago, the Almeidas told him he had a home with them as long as he wanted; regardless of his age. They let him know that he and his brother were welcome members of their family. With Cole gone, Zac couldn't imagine staying. Everywhere he looked, he saw his little brother.

He carefully folded Cole's note and stuffed it in a side pocket of his pack. *Now, what to do with you?* He stared down at the bear. Cole would be heartbroken if he never saw Waffles again. He needed to get the bear to his brother unnoticed. How was he going to find him?

IHLPKDS. That was it! He would find the government woman and get Cole's new address. He slid open the window and leaned his log outside, then scanned the room one last time—all set. As quiet as a shadow, he slid out the window.

The early dawn streets were empty—not a single person in sight. He was not in a hurry; both Carla and Jorje were asleep, as were all the occupants of the homes he strolled past. He was invisible—a ghost moving through the world of regular people. A world he hadn't felt a connection to for a long time. As the sky turned pale blue, birds chirped in their nests, hidden in the trees. He picked up his pace.

It was seven o'clock when he arrived at the front door of the library. His stomach growled, suddenly realizing he hadn't eaten a thing since yesterday morning. With two hours before the library opened, there was plenty of time to find some food. He pulled out his wallet and took stock of the money he had on hand—thirty-five dollars and some change. He cursed under his breath for not thinking ahead enough to pack some food before he left. Too hungry to worry about it, he shoved the wallet back into his pocket. Recalling the small, twenty-four-hour diner around the corner, he walked off in that direction.

A trio of strange teens sat on the curb across the street: one blond and two with dark brown hair. One of the dark-haired ones wore a pair of sunglasses—an odd choice for so early in the morning. Their disheveled clothes were not quite filthy, but not clean, either. As he passed along his side of the street, the teen wearing sunglasses studied him closely while the other two continued to banter back and forth. Zac nodded at him. No response. No wave or return nod. All he did was stare at Zac, smirking.

A little closer to the diner, a gray-haired, scruffy homeless man lay propped up beside the building's stone edifice, his black dog lay by his side. As Zac approached, the dog lifted its mangy head and wagged its tail.

The reek of sour alcohol, urine, and vomit wafted up like a noxious cloud, assaulting his senses. Zac recoiled and stepped aside, putting as much space between himself and duo as possible. The old man never looked up. The dog yawned and lay his head back down.

The old door to the diner slammed shut behind him with a loud thwack. Inside, the place was nearly empty. Fifties era rock and roll played quietly over the speaker. It was barely audible over the clanging and sizzling sounds emanating from the kitchen. The enticing scent of fried eggs and bacon permeated the air, making his mouth water. He took a seat in a tight corner booth at the far end.

The waitress, an older woman named Kim, kept calling Zac "honey" or "baby" as though she were his mother or an aunt. Not wanting to overspend, he kept his order straightforward and small, only to be met with a questioning, maternal stare.

"Is that all?" she asked. "One egg, one slice of bacon, and a piece of toast?"

He nodded. He wanted so much more, but he couldn't risk all his money on one meal.

Kim sighed, shook her head, and walked away.

Less than twenty minutes later, she returned with her arms full. One plate had three eggs with bacon, several slices of toast and hash browns. The other, a short stack of pancakes. This was not what he ordered. Nervous over the bill for so much food, he looked up at Kim and stammered, "There's a mistake. I-I didn't order this."

Kim shifted her body and smiled. "No, no, you didn't. I did. A growing boy like you needs more food than that."

Still worried about the bill, he struggled to form the words to explain that he couldn't afford such a meal. Kim was one step ahead of him.

"It's on me," she winked and smiled. "At least I know. No matter what else the day brings, I made sure at least one person was properly fed. Go on, eat up. It's getting' cold." She turned and walked away.

True to her word, Kim did not charge him for any of his food. Before leaving the diner, he tried to give her a tip, but she refused to accept. He thanked her. She didn't know how much he needed to meet someone like her at that moment in his life.

Back on the street, his steps were lighter than before. A feeling of hope had crept in. He could almost smile. Passing by the old man, the dog lifted his head again, wagging his tail. Zac was ready for him this time; he leaned over and pat the dog on his head. The animal responded with even more furious tail wags. The old man smiled. "She's a good old dog. Friendly—always friendly."

Zac pulled a napkin from his pocket. The meal really was too much food for him to eat alone, so when he had his fill, he tucked away a couple slices of bacon inside a napkin and put an egg between two pieces of toast. His intention was to pass the kindness along. He handed the food to the old man, who was full of gratitude.

Feeling buoyed by the two positive interactions, Zac headed back over to the library. As he passed the corner where he encountered the trio of teens, he noticed that only the one with sunglasses remained. The other two were nowhere in sight. Once again, Zac nodded. The teen nodded back.

As soon as the library lock clicked open, Zac pushed his way through the giant wooden doors. Without pause, he made his way over to the computers. He began his search, using the license plate to locate the home of the caseworker. A pang of guilt coursed through his body. His palms sweaty, heartbeat pulsating in his head like a drum. He scanned the area nervously, hoping that no one came close enough to see what he was doing. To his horror, the librarian came up behind him. *Where did she come from?* He didn't see her until she was right on top of him. To block her view of the computer screen, he leaned close. This only made him look suspicious, which caused the woman to move even closer.

Tsssss... crrrack... pop.

The distinct sound of someone opening a can of coke erupted behind the woman. She spun around on her heels, turning her attention to the sunglass teen who was standing in the middle of two bookshelves. He raised the can to his lips and took a large swallow, then let rip the loudest burp Zac had ever heard. The entire library stood still. All eyes were on the young man chugging soda. The sound of his gulps resounded throughout the building.

"Sir! You cannot drink that in here!" scolded the librarian as she rushed toward him.

Wearing a mischievous grin, the dark-haired teen allowed himself to be taken by the arm and guided out of the building. On his way past Zac, he gave a slight nod.

Taking advantage of the diversion, Zac found the address he was looking for and wrote the information down on a piece of paper. By the time the woman turned her attention back to him, his task was complete. He gathered his pack and left.

Outside, the teen was leaning against the corner of the building. He flashed a smile and waved two fingers in the air.

"Something tells me you did all of that on purpose," said Zac. "Thanks." He reached out his hand. "I'm Zac."

"Finn."

They shook hands.

"I appreciate the distraction."

Finn waved dismissively. "No worries. We wouldn't want her to interrupt your porn gazing."

"What? No!" Zac shook his head. "That's not what I was doing."

"Uh, huh."

"No, seriously." Zac scrambled to come up with a lie about what he was doing. His mind was blank.

"Hey, don't worry about it, I ain't judgin'," replied Finn.

"There's nothing to judge!"

"Aight, whatever you say, man. I don't care either way."

The other two teens rounded the corner, stopping abruptly alongside Finn.

"Don't care either way about what?" asked the blond-haired one.

"I don't care that he was watching porn on the library computer," replied Finn.

"Stop it!" shouted Zac. "Oh my god, I was not looking at porn! Are you always this thick?"

"Mais la!" laughed the blond. "Finn's got a real thick head." He tapped his head for punctuation. "Which is good cause he's always bangin' it up against something."

"This is true," agreed Finn, nodding.

Zac stood there, dumbfounded. Did he want to walk away? Did he want to stick around? He couldn't decide.

The blond one reached out a hand. "I'm Teague."

"This is Zac," replied Finn.

"Well, Zac," said Teague, "This is Cash. Unfortunately for you, you met Finn first."

Cash snickered.

"We're gonna go find somethin' to eat," said Teague. "Wanna come along?"

Zac wasn't hungry after his big breakfast earlier. It was still very early in the day, and he had several hours to burn before he could get close to the house without being seen. So, he decided he would spend some time with this new trio; to say he was curious would have been an understatement.

The afternoon sun peeped through the trees, casting tiny points of yellow light on the soft green grass. The air was warm, with a slight hint of honeysuckle. Zac couldn't recall the last time he was this comfortable around a group of people. They teased one another relentlessly and laughed wholeheartedly. Their presence made him feel better than he had in a long time.

"So, you hop freight trains to get around?" he asked.

Cash nodded.

"Where?"

"Anywhere we want," replied Cash. "Well, most places. Sometimes we have to hike a part of the way or catch a ride."

"What do you do in the winter?"

"Head south." Cash smiled. "Try to stay in the warmer climates where we can camp or find odd jobs to put us up for a couple weeks."

"You're welcome to come along," offered Teague. "I mean, it looks like you're on your own with not much else to do—"

Zac had to admit, the thought of taking off was intriguing. He really had nothing else to look forward to. Hell, he was already homeless. "Alright, I think I will," he responded. "But first, I have something I gotta do."

"Yeah?" asked Finn. "What's that?"

The mere thought of Cole caused a wave of sadness to wash over Zac. He inhaled. "I gotta bring my little brother's favorite bear to his new home. He'll be lost without it."

Silence. Long, uncomfortable silence.

"Where's this house at?" asked Teague.

"That's what I was doin' in the library. I got the license plate from the caseworker and looked her up on the state database." Zac glared at Finn. "I figure I can go to her home and maybe find the binder she had with our files in it. Maybe somewhere in there is the address where Cole's at."

Finn nodded. "Count us in." He sat up straight and popped the last bite of sandwich into his mouth. "Aight," he said. "Tell us where we're goin'."

Crouching low in the darkness among the bushes made everything all too real for Zac. *What the hell am I doing?* Across the street stood a neat, cozy white house. Inside, the caseworker paced back and forth. Cash and Finn snuck up for a closer look and returned to report she was getting ready to leave. That was good news. As they waited impatiently, Zac's mind reeled with thoughts about everything that could go wrong. Never did he imagine himself doing something like this. Adrenaline coursed through his body, his stomach in knots. The others seemed more at ease, a small benefit to having them along.

"How're we getting in?" asked Teague.

"There's a hidden key just off the back porch," replied Finn.

"Where?" asked Cash. "I didn't see a hidden key."

"That's cause it's hidden, dumbass," replied Finn. "It's under a rock. One of the big things in the prepper catalogs a few years back was these fake rocks. They're used for hiding extra keys. To the naked eye, they look like the real thing. There's a hidden compartment on the bottom for a spare key, cash, or whatever. She has one of those in the flower bed by a rosebush."

"And what if it's just a rock?" asked Cash.

"It ain't."

"How can you be so sure?"

"Because we had those same rocks. My old man had a bunch of them all over the yard. Some held money—others, spare keys to the cars, storage shed, sturdy boxes—"

A silver jeep pulled up in front of the house. A blonde-haired woman hopped out and ran up to the door. Shortly after, both women came out, laughing and chattering away as they climbed into the vehicle. A moment later, they drove away.

A bead of sweat trickled down the side of Zac's face. His hands were shaking. *Christ! What did I get into?* He wiped his palms on his thighs. Looking up, he realized the others were staring at him.

Teague placed a hand on his shoulder. "You okay?"

Zac nodded.

"Just hang back and follow our lead," said Teague. "We'll get us in there, then you can find that binder. It'll all be over quick."

They covered their faces with gaiters and bandanas, then crept out from the bushes and around to the back of the house. The black

SUV sat idle in the driveway. IHLPKDS—there were no words to describe how much Zac hated that license plate. They skirted around the vehicle. By the rose bush, Finn picked up a rock the size of an orange. To Zac, it really looked like the real thing. He would have never guessed it was manmade.

Finn opened the little compartment on the underside. Sure enough, there was a key. "Haha. What did I say, motherfucker?" he taunted. He crept up to the back door. "Fingers crossed." A moment later, they were walking into the kitchen.

The house wreaked of stale air and artificial room freshener. Zac could almost hear his Meemaw say, *"Open a damn window and get some fresh air in here."*

A barely audible beeping sound called out from somewhere. Zac strained to listen, only to realize the others were doing the same thing.

"You hear that?" asked Cash. He crept slowly—head tilted toward the sound, pausing in front of a door. He swung it open and peered inside. There on the back wall, a small keypad with flashing red lights called out one beep at a time. Cash turned back to the others. "We might have to do this a lot faster than we thought."

"Merde!" exclaimed Teague. "Alright, let's get this done. We probably got about fifteen minutes before cops arrive. Which means we need to be out of here in ten."

Zac's apprehension gave way to determination. He made his way through the living room, into a small office, where a table lamp cast a yellow glow across the top of an ornate wooden desk. A calendar, pencil holder, and an idle laptop sat neatly on the shiny surface. As he approached, he spied precisely what he came for—the black briefcase sitting on the brown office chair. A sense of joy spread through his body when he found the binder. He placed it down on the desk and flipped through the contents.

Finn's hand slid into his periphery as it swiped a sheet of paper. Until that moment, Zac had forgotten all about the others. He looked up to find them all standing around the opposite side of the desk. He set his focus back on the binder.

"Our boy here's got a temper," said Finn.

Zac didn't need to look up. He could hear the smirk in his voice. "Anything there about Cole?"

Finn shook his head. "Nah, this is all just about you and your anger management issues."

Zac reached for the paper, and Finn jerked it back only to have Teague yank it from Finn's hand. He shook his head and placed the sheet back on the desk.

"Let's not waste the little time we got," admonished Teague.

Zac flipped through the papers, scanning them as quickly as possible. He was about to give up when he came across a slip of paper with a photograph attached. It was the family who was adopting Cole. He lifted the photo and scanned the form. The address was there.

"Is that it?" asked Teague.

"Yeah, it is."

"Good," replied Teague. "Take a picture. Then put it all back exactly how you found it. We don't want to leave any sign that we were looking for that info."

Zac nodded. *Good idea.* He took extra care to put everything back. One last look around the office confirmed everything was in its place.

Outside, Finn placed the rock back under the rosebush, then picked up another large rock and threw it at a kitchen window. The sound of shattering glass filled the night.

"What did you do that for?" demanded Zac.

Finn turned to face him. "They already know someone tried to break in. I'm just givin' them a reason that ain't gonna lead them back to you. The cops will think someone tried to break in through the window, heard the alarm, and took off. Just a garden variety break-in."

As they passed the SUV, Finn stopped and pulled out his bowie knife. He turned the blade around and held it out to Zac. "You wanna do the honors?"

"What? You mean cut her tires?" Zac shook his head, "No, I don't. That's not who I am."

Finn flipped the knife, so the handle rested in his hand. "Well, it might not be who you are, but it is exactly who I am." He stabbed the blade deep into the rubber tire. Air hissed as he pulled the knife free.

On the other side of the vehicle, another hiss erupted. Teague stood holding his own knife. "Needing to replace four tires ain't that much of a price to pay for being an asshole, but at least it's something." He said as he punctured the other tire.

The vehicle sank.

Blocks away, the sound of sirens rang out. They took off through the neighborhood, not stopping until they were far away.

Across town, they pooled their money and got a motel room for the night. The air reeked of old cigarette smoke and mold, but the sheets were clean—at least they appeared to be.

Zac stood under the shower, letting the warm water envelop him from head to toe. He breathed in, letting the warm, steamy air fill his lungs. His mind reeled, trying to make sense of the last twenty-four hours. A week ago, he would have laughed if someone told him he would do any of the things he just did. What he found most surprising was the fact that he felt no guilt at all. In fact, he wished he would have taken the knife and stabbed a tire or two.

When he finally emerged from the bathroom, the room smelled of onions and ketchup. A cloud of steam billowed at his heels as he walked over to the worn-out table and reached for one of the greasy bags.

"I told you he'd come out when he smelled food," said Teague.

The smell was overpowering—Zac's mouth watered. He could hardly wait to dig in. As he raised the burger to his mouth, he shot a glance across the room at Finn and froze.

Sitting on the bed alongside Teague, Finn dunked a handful of greasy fries, covered in bright red ketchup, into what appeared to be a strawberry shake. Unceremoniously, he stuffed the entire dripping mess into his mouth. Cheeks puffing out like a hamster, pink ice cream, and red ketchup oozing out of the corners, he struggled to chew and then swallow. A moment later, barely stopping for a breath, Finn repeated the same action.

Unable to look away, Zac stared, his appetite temporarily suspended.

Cash's voice broke through his paralysis. "You won't ever get used to that." He flashed a crooked smirk. "It's best if you ignore it. Just don't look."

Over on the bed, Finn swallowed, then wiped his mouth with a napkin. "What?" he asked. "Y'all shouldn't be so worried about what I'm doing and worry about your own food."

No sunglasses. Zac realized he could see Finn's eyes for the first time since meeting him—he also realized why Finn hid them behind the dark lenses. His eyes were shocking—one blue, the other amber brown. Zac stared. He didn't want to; he just couldn't help himself. Finn fidgeted self-consciously. It was Teague who finally broke the uncomfortable silence by playfully shoving Finn's head.

His concentration broken, Zac set his focus on the warm, delicious smelling food in his hand and dug in.

2486 Amistad Circle. That was where the family who was adopting Cole lived—where Cole now lived.

Zac stood in the shadow of a copse of flowering trees and shrubs. Studying the house, his heart racing, his hands fidgeted anxiously with Waffles as he planned his next move. His mind blank. Truthfully, he didn't think he would get this far. He fully expected to be arrested while trying to break into the caseworker's home. *Okay, Zac, you've come this far—now what?* The mid-afternoon-sun sat high in the pale blue sky, not a single cloud in sight. A warm breeze rustled through the leaves, carrying with it the sweet scent of fresh flowers. He inhaled.

The house was impressive—gray brick with ornate mahogany trim. A large 3-car garage sat a little further down the driveway. A brand-new basketball hoop glistened in the sun above the center garage bay. In front, a perfect row of azaleas sat on either side of the narrow walkway that led to the giant front door. The house was more impressive than any Zac had ever seen.

"Nobody's home," said Finn. Fresh from a short recon around the property, he leaned close to the others to report back. "There's a dog door in the back of the house." He held his hands out to show the size. "It's big enough for a lab to get through, so you'll fit easily."

"What about the dog?" asked Teague.

Finn shook his head. "He's a big dopey, yellow lab. When he saw me, he came up waggin' his tail. He ain't gonna be a problem."

Teague nodded, then turned to Zac. "Cash'll stay out here and watch the street. Finn and I will keep the dog distracted while you go in and do your thing."

One more glance around the neighborhood, then the trio crept along the driveway and slipped quietly through the gate into the backyard. A giant yellow labrador loped toward them across the lush green lawn. Tail wagging so hard, his backside could barely keep up with his front.

"Come on, boy," called Finn. To entice the dog, he picked up a filthy tennis ball and tossed it in the air. It worked. The big dog set his focus on Finn and the ball, allowing Zac to skirt past and wriggle his way through the dog door.

The house was silent. The soft scent of lavender saturated the air.

Slowly, he made his way through the cavernous family room. Two sectionals sat facing a giant television hovering atop an impressive carved wood mantle and stone fireplace. Everything about this house was Texas-sized.

He peered down a high-ceilinged hallway. Sunlight poured in through the windows, casting a golden glow on ornate vessels filled with real flowers. At the end stood a large bedroom. From what he could glean, it was the master—nothing he needed there.

He took the stairs two at a time, halting at the top. The loft was a kid's paradise, complete with a pool table, comfy sofa, and another large television. He imagined Cole laughing and playing in this space. A sense of melancholy spread through his bones.

Keep your head in the game, man. Let's get this done. His left hand squeezed the little bear tight. Three bedrooms were visible from the loft. One door blank, another adorned with a colorful wooden name plaque "Tyler," it read. The last door had a similar plaque; only this one read "Cole."

Zac took a deep breath and entered.

The room was large. Much larger than any room they shared—even in the old farmhouse. Dark blue, Cole's favorite, was the predominant color. Toys littered the floor. Zac walked over to the bed, sat down, and stared at the single photograph atop the nightstand.

The faces of two smiling brothers stared up at him, their curly, deep auburn hair shining in the afternoon light. Running his finger over the surface, Zac recalled that day in vivid detail. It was his birthday, and they had just finished tossing the football around. He closed his eyes. Letting his mind wander, he could almost smell the savory scent of the smoker. His dad was great at bar-b-q. His mom's laughter echoed in his memory as she teased her two sons and snapped the picture. The world was full of promise. Their parents and grandma were still alive, and they lived in the old farmhouse in the country with the cows, cats, and the old rickety barn. A sharp pain stabbed at his heart. That time was long gone. *Best to move forward. Let it go.* He pinched his eyes to push back tears, then placed the picture back on the table. After a moment's pause, he gently placed Waffles against the pillows. From his back pocket, he pulled out a handwritten note.

Cole;

I realize you're probably too young to understand any of this, but I need you to know that I love you, and I will always have your back, little man. I have to leave for now. It's not what I wanted to do but, it is what it is.

Be good. We'll see each other again some-day. I promise. Until then, take care of Waffles.

With all my heart, I love you,
Zac

P.S. It's best you don't tell anyone about this. Keep it between us.

Zac folded the note and placed it down atop the bear.

He gave out a final deep sigh, and left the room. In the backyard he found Finn and Teague sitting under a magnolia tree. The giant lab lay on the grass between them, belly up, tongue lolling out the side of his mouth as they rubbed his belly. As soon as they saw him, they got to their feet.

"All set?" asked Teague as he wiped his hands off on his thighs.

Unable to say any words, Zac nodded.

Teague clasped a hand on Zac's shoulder and gave him a sympathetic smile. "You did good, big brother."

Zac's chin quivered. Tears welled up in his eyes. He struggled to hold them back.

"Aight, time to go," said Finn, shoving Zac toward the gate. "Enough of this heavy shit. We got a train to catch."

The End